SWE[image: barcode]

Brianna's lips parted in unconscious invitation as Lucas's breath mingled with hers. They came together in a kiss as natural as the rain in spring. Soft and warm, it enveloped them in a haze, blocking out everything else.

Brianna lifted her hand to his cheek in wonder.

"Lucas?" she whispered.

His answer was a groan as his lips swooped down on hers once more. This time there was as much passion as tenderness between them. Lucas pressed his body against hers, and the muscles in his back felt sleek and solid beneath her hands. Soon their hearts were beating as one, and Brianna gave in to the heady sensations overwhelming her.

Books by Carolyn Lampman

Murphy's Rainbow
Shadows in the Wind
Willow Creek
Meadowlark
A Window in Time

Available from HarperPaperbacks

A Window in Time

✦ CAROLYN LAMPMAN ✦

HarperPaperbacks
A Division of HarperCollins*Publishers*

This is a work of fiction. The characters, incidents, and dialogues are products of the author's imagination and are not to be construed as real. Any resemblance to actual events or persons, living or dead, is entirely coincidental.

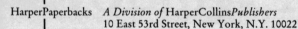

HarperPaperbacks   *A Division of* HarperCollins*Publishers*
10 East 53rd Street, New York, N.Y. 10022

Copyright © 1995 by Carolyn Brubaker

Cover illustration by Danilo Ducak

First printing: July 1995

Printed in the United States of America

HarperPaperbacks, HarperMonogram, and colophon are trademarks of HarperCollins*Publishers*

❖ 10 9 8 7 6 5 4 3 2 1

To Val, Dana, Kay, and Nancy, the sisters I never had. Our friendships have withstood the test of time.

And to Lynette, who gives an entirely different meaning to the words friendship and time.

I love you all.

Time is a point caged within a circle
To be released in the end by man;
Striking toward the future
Only to come 'round again.

—Louis R. Lampman
1995

Prologue

July 15, 1995

> *"All right, Chuck, let her go."*

"Oh, God," Brianna whispered as she closed her eyes and swallowed nervously. How in heaven's name had Linda talked her into going up in a hot air balloon?

"Heights bother you?" the balloonist asked with hint of amusement in his voice.

"No."

"Then open your eyes or you'll miss the best part."

"I'll wait until we're in the air."

"We already are."

"What?" Brianna cautiously opened one eye and peeked over the side of the basket. There had been no feeling of lift-off, but the crowd below on the soccer field already looked more doll-like than human.

"See, it isn't so bad, now is it?"

She gave a weak smile. "I-I guess not."

"Are you sure you're not afraid of heights?" the balloonist asked, raising an eyebrow.

"Not usually. In fact that's why I'm here. My friend Linda was supposed to be your passenger, but she got cold feet at the last minute." Brianna glanced uneasily at the ground again. "Actually my toes aren't feeling exactly toasty right now either."

He chuckled. "Then don't look down. The view is better in the sky now anyway."

Obediently, she lifted her gaze to the other balloons that had risen with them. "Oh!"

Bobbing along like so many magic bubbles, their jewel-like colors were bright against the early morning sky. Brianna's fear left as suddenly as it had come. The wind brushed her cheek in a caress as exhilarating as a lover's kiss, and she felt a peculiar rush of euphoria.

"Beautiful isn't it?"

"It's incredible," she said in an awestruck voice. She jumped in alarm a moment later as the propane burner roared to life right next to her and a huge flame shot upward into the balloon.

"Sorry," he said. "I forgot to warn you. This darn thing can scare the pants off of you if you aren't expecting it."

Brianna looked at the burner accusingly. "How often do you have to do that?"

"It depends. Don't worry, you'll get used to it."

"I wouldn't count on it."

He grinned and bent to adjust a gauge on one of the tanks on the floor. "I'm surprised your friend decided not to come along. She seemed really excited about the whole idea at the rally dinner last night."

"Oh, she was, right up until she thought about actually going up in a balloon. Her boss figured sponsoring a balloon and sending along one of his employees would be a great publicity stunt. When he offered to pay overtime for it, Linda volunteered, but the actual logistics of it didn't hit her until she tried to go to sleep last night."

Brianna paused and risked a glance over the edge of the basket. The soccer field was behind them, the crowd reduced to tiny ant-like creatures. "I never realized balloons moved so fast."

"When you're standing on the ground they don't. It's a matter of perspective, I think."

"I suppose." Brianna looked at the pilot curiously. Though the man was a total stranger he reminded her a little of her favorite cousin, with all that curly red hair. "You know, in all the excitement, I'm afraid I didn't catch your name."

"Thomas Shaffer, aeronaut extraordinaire at your service ma'am," he said, extending his hand. "My friends call me Tom."

She returned his smile as they shook hands. "Brianna Daniels."

The balloon gave a sudden jerk, then shot straight up and veered off to the left. Tom reached up to adjust the rigging, but the balloon continued on its wayward course. "Damn, we're caught in an updraft. I really thought I had a chance of winning today."

Brianna looked at the other balloons huddled together in the distance and suddenly felt very alone. "I thought you could steer this thing. Can't you adjust the flaps or something?"

"I have some control but we're pretty much at the mercy of the wind."

"I guess that's the whole idea isn't it?"

Though his disappointment was obvious, he didn't look angry. "Oh well, might as well try for distance then," he said cheerfully.

"Is it always this warm?" Brianna asked as she took off her windbreaker.

"That's just the hot air from the balloon. Relax and enjoy the flight. If we're lucky, it'll be a long one."

"I'm not sure I want it to be. What if we get lost?"

"Don't worry. My brother is on the chase crew. He'll follow us through a swamp if he has to. See, there they are."

He pointed to a bright yellow pickup driving along the highway beneath them. "He loves the challenge of the chase. Hey, is that a road block up ahead?"

"Must be," Brianna said. "Look at all those fire trucks. I wonder what happened."

"I don't know but they seem to be headed toward that odd looking building over there. Do you know what it is?" A veritable army of men and trucks swarmed around the metal structure.

"It has to do with crude oil," Brianna said. "I think it might be a sour gas plant but I'm not sure."

As they drew closer, Tom pulled a pair of binoculars out of his backpack on the floor. "Uh oh," he said training them on the building below. "Everyone down there is wearing air packs and face masks."

"Maybe there's a leak somewhere. I don't know exactly what sour gas is, but I do know it's poisonous."

"I'm not taking any chances. Let's see if we can gain some altitude."

For the first time Brianna was glad when the propane burner roared to life. As they lifted higher into the air, the wind caught the balloon and carried it south at an even faster rate. "Do we have enough propane to keep us going?" she asked nervously.

"Sure hope so. I always carry two tanks just in case I have a chance to go for the distance record."

"How far can we go?"

"Today, probably not much more than forty miles, but you never can tell. One day last winter we flew almost two hundred. Good Lord," he said gazing off into the distance. "Am I seeing things? Those cliffs must be seven hundred feet high."

"That's Beaver Rim." Brianna looked at the familiar

landform with new eyes. It stretched for miles in either direction and looked incredibly high. "A-are we going over it or should we just land?"

Tom picked up the binoculars again and looked back toward the gas plant. "I don't know. It doesn't look like the chase crew is going to get around that road block. Is there another road somewhere?"

"Well . . . they could go around through Riverton and Lander then backtrack to us from Sweetwater Station."

"How long will that take?"

"An hour and a half or so."

"Where does this other road come in at?"

"Over there." She pointed toward a ribbon of highway snaking down off the rim to the west.

Tom turned his binoculars that way. "Uh oh. Looks like there's a road block there, too." He scanned the cliffs ahead. "Wow, I'll bet the thermals are wild this time of year. Anybody ever do any hang gliding off of it?"

"I used to have a friend who did," Brianna said. "He said it was one of the best places he'd ever been. Are we going over?"

"Don't see we have much choice." Tom reached up and fired the propane burner. "Chuck can't get to us if we set down here. We'll have to land on top somewhere."

"Do you think it's safe?"

"We'll be fine. The air currents off the face of those cliffs will probably lift us up and over without any help from me. Better put on one of these just in case." Tom handed her a crash helmet.

To Brianna's anxious mind, they were moving toward Beaver Rim frighteningly fast. Though it was actually almost ten minutes, it seemed like much less before the cliffs loomed menacingly above them.

Suddenly the balloon jerked and danced crazily for

several seconds. When it righted itself, the wind seemed to double in velocity and they headed up at an alarming rate of speed.

"Hang on!" Tom yelled.

Brianna felt like she was on a wild carnival ride as they zoomed upward. Her stomach turned cartwheels and a sensation of vertigo made her light-headed. Tom's whoop of exultation was a good indication that she was alone in her distress.

Their speed diminished almost immediately as they popped over the top of the rim a few seconds later. Brianna spared a glance for her companion and was unsurprised to see his eyes sparkling with excitement.

"Wow!" he said. "That was great."

"If you say so."

A wide grin split his face. "Do I detect a note of disagreement there?"

"Let's just say I didn't inherit my great-grandfather's love for balloons."

"Your great-grandfather?"

Brianna nodded. "Great-great actually. He was a balloonist during the Civil War. That's really why I let Linda talk me into this. I wanted to see what ballooning was like." She looked back at the edge of Beaver Rim ruefully. "I don't think there's much of my Grandfather Daniels in me."

"Not Lucas Daniels!"

"Yes, as a matter of fact. You've heard of him?"

"Heard of him! He's from my hometown in Missouri. The library had a copy of his journal and I've read it so many times I practically have it memorized. I named this balloon Dream Chaser after his."

"You're kidding."

"Nope. He wrote mostly about his spy missions for the Union army. It was uncanny the way he seemed to know how a battle was going to turn out before it was even fought. I used to want to grow up and be just like him. I already had the hair," he said with a grin as he ran his fingers through his coppery locks.

"He was a redhead?"

"According to his journal he was. Seemed to think it was important for some reason."

"I should have known. In my family we call red hair the Daniels' curse." She touched the blonde French braid that hung down beyond the bottom of the helmet. "In the right light you can even see red in mine. Have you ever seen a picture of Lucas?"

"No, do you have one?"

Brianna shook her head. "Not yet but a distant cousin of my father's and I have been trading genealogy information. She's sending me his wedding picture. If you'll leave your address with me I'll mail you a copy."

"Hey, that'd be great. Thanks. Have you ever read his journal?"

Brianna shook her head. "I never even knew he had one."

"The only place I've ever seen it is the library at home. He donated the money to have the place built and set up a trust to keep it going. His only stipulation was that people be allowed to read his journal. They've made copies now so they can preserve the original."

"Really? I'd love to read it sometime."

"Maybe I can get you a copy." Tom grinned. "I just can't believe you're actually his descendant."

"It's quite a coincidence isn't it? I was even named after his wife Brianna."

"Lucas called her Anna," Tom said with a faraway look. "He loved her, you know. It was obvious even to a kid like me who was more interested in spies and balloons than girls."

Brianna smiled as she touched the antique locket at her throat. "This was hers. I wore it today for luck."

"Seems to have worked. This is the best flight I've had in a long time." Tom glanced around as he reached up and fired the burner. "Do you have any idea where we are?"

"That's Split Rock over there," Brianna said, pointing to a granite mountain to the south. A v-shaped notch in the top was obvious even from this distance. "Are we going to land?"

"No reason to yet. We have a great tail wind and plenty of altitude. I'd like to stay in the air as long as possible so Chuck can find us. Where's the highway?"

Brianna pointed to the west. "Somewhere over there I think."

"Hmm." Tom pulled a map out of his backpack and studied it intently. "That puts us about here then." He looked at the instruments in front of him. "If this wind keeps up we should intersect with the highway just about the time we run out of fuel."

"How convenient."

He flashed her an impudent grin. "Of course. I planned it that way. Want a granola bar?"

"Sure." Brianna watched as he once again delved into the backpack near her feet at the bottom of the gondola. "What else do you have in that thing?"

"A little of everything. You never know what you'll run into on . . . now that's weird. The barometer is going wacko." All at once the balloon shuddered and took off at an alarming rate of speed. "What the hell?" Tom reached up and pulled on a rope. It seemed to have little effect.

"Wh-what's happening?" Brianna couldn't help the quaver of uncertainty in her voice.

"I don't know. I've never seen anything like this befo . . . Jesus, what's that?"

Brianna gasped in horror. A huge black cloud roiled

in the distance. As she watched a giant vortex appeared in the center and a nightmarish shrieking filled the air. They were inexorably pulled toward the ghastly thing. A hysterical bubble of laughter rose in her throat. Linda's boss was going to have to pay her double overtime and a half for this.

"Hang on tight!" Tom yelled, pulling on the rigging attached to the main valve. "I'm going to try to drop below that thing."

Brianna grabbed the support with one hand and the edge of the gondola with the other. The hiss of escaping air was lost in the horrible screeching like a thousand tormented souls. The balloon swayed sickeningly as Tom tried to wrench it free of the mighty force that drew them relentlessly forward.

The bright silk balloon abruptly disappeared into an odd blue mist, and a scream of pure terror burst from Brianna's mouth. A sudden bolt of brilliant white light surrounded them and the world became a crackling eternity of burning pain. She tried to back away but her feet became tangled in something and she felt herself falling backward. Spots of vermillion swam before her eyes as she slipped into blessed darkness.

1

July 15, 1860

"Ohhhh . . . " Brianna felt as if she'd been run over by an entire football team and left on the field for dead. Every part of her hurt. A cursory check revealed all her body parts still attached and her feet tangled in the straps of Tom's backpack. How stupid. Now that she thought of it, she remembered tripping. She felt the ground beneath her hands. Good Lord, had she fallen out of the gondola?

She sat up. Her head swam alarmingly for a moment then settled down to a dull ache as she looked around in bewilderment. Where in the world was she?

An old-fashioned freight wagon lay on its side behind her, one back wheel hanging at a crazy angle and its contents scattered across the prairie. She frantically scanned the surrounding landscape for her companion, but here was no sign of Tom Shaffer or his balloon. "Tom . . . Tom, where are you?" she yelled as panic threatened to overwhelm her.

A groan on the other side of the wagon brought her head around with a jerk. Tom must be lying behind the wagon. She scrambled to her feet, her head reeling with nausea. Closing her eyes for a moment, she concentrated on staying upright. Gradually the spinning stopped and she opened her eyes. Cautiously she made her way around the wagon.

At a glance she saw that the man pinned beneath the wagon was a total stranger. At least he was alive; corpses didn't groan. When Brianna knelt next to him to check his pulse, she was relieved to see there was a space of several inches above his legs. Thank heavens the side of the wagon was resting on a boulder instead of his body.

Brianna could see a deep gash across his ribcage beneath his torn shirt. The wound was beyond her reach and bleeding heavily. She knew it needed to be stopped immediately but she'd have to pull him out from under the wagon to do it. She bit her lip. If only there were some way to tell if he had a neck or back injury. Maybe if she'd taken that first-aid class in college, she'd know what to do.

She was still trying to decide what to do when she heard a horse galloping up the road. With a surge of relief, she stood up and peered over the top of the wagon.

Bent low over the horse's neck, the rider looked as if he was competing in the Kentucky Derby as his mount thundered down the dirt road sending a cloud of dust into the air in his wake.

"Hey!" Brianna yelled, waving her arms to get his attention.

The rider waved back but didn't even slow as he approached the wreck.

"Wait a minute," she called, running around the end of the wagon. "There's an injured man here."

Still the horse came on, his speed undiminished. With a flash of anger Brianna ran out into the road and planted herself firmly in the middle of it. "Stop, damn it. There's been an accident."

For a moment she thought the horse was going to run right over the top of her, but the rider pulled the animal back at the last minute. Brianna ducked as the flailing hooves pawed the air above her.

"Get out of the way!" the man yelled fighting to control his horse.

"No. There's an injured man over there, and I'm not budging until you help him."

"Whoa, Archimedes," he said as the horse stopped rearing and started dancing sideways on the road. When the young man finally looked her way, Brianna was surprised. He didn't look much more than sixteen. "I can't take the time to help," he said.

"Why not?"

"It's against company policy to stop for any reason."

"What company?"

"The Central Overland and Pike's Peak Express Company."

"Never heard of them," Brianna said, shaking her head.

He rolled his eyes. "The Pony Express."

"The Pony . . . oh, I get it." Suddenly the old fashioned wagon made sense, too. People were always trying to relive the Old West along the Oregon Trail. "You're doing a reenactment."

He looked confused. "No, I'm doing my usual run to Split Rock Station, and I can't stop."

"Oh, come on. That's carrying realism a little too far, don't you think? What if that man over there bleeds to death?"

"Look, Mrs. Daniels," he said as he guided his horse around her, "I'd like to help, but I can't right now."

"How do you know my name?"

He gave her an odd look. "We met at Platte River Bridge day before yesterday. Don't you remember?"

"I've never seen you before in my life."

"Maybe you better change your hat," he said. "That might be the fashion back East, but out here it's dangerous. Too much sun can affect your thinking."

"It's not a hat, it's a crash helmet."

"Ugly, too," he muttered. "I'll be back as soon as I pass the mail on to Billy. In the meantime, you might want to put on a dress if you want to impress Lucas."

"I don't want to impress anyone. I need help. That man over there is far more important than the reenactment you're doing."

"The first thing you're going to have to learn as the wife of a station master is that nothing is more important than getting the mail through." He kicked his horse.

"You're just going to leave us here?"

"I'll be back in an hour or so," he called back over his shoulder as Archimedes broke into a gallop.

"At least call 911 and have them send the Flight for Life helicopter!" Brianna yelled after him. He gave no indication that he'd heard and she turned away in disgust.

"Talk about getting too much sun. That guy's brain is totally fried." Irritated, she walked back to the injured man. A glance under the wagon showed his condition hadn't improved. If anything, the wound looked worse than before.

"Well, mister, I guess you're stuck with my feeble skills. I hope Tom Shaffer has a first-aid kit in that backpack of his."

It didn't take long to locate the familiar red, white, and blue box. Brianna wasn't surprised to find it well stocked. Now all she had to do was get the patient out from under the wagon, stop the bleeding somehow, and bandage him up. A piece of cake, she thought sardonically to herself. About as easy as flying to the moon under her own power.

First things first, Brianna thought as she removed her helmet. None of this made any sense. The hard plastic of the helmet was unscathed. How could she have fallen that far and survived with only a few minor aches and pains?

She scanned the blue sky overhead. Surely Tom had landed the balloon by now. As soon as the chase crew found him, they'd come looking for her. She refused to even consider the possibility that the balloon had crashed.

"Uhhh . . . " The pain filled moan brought her attention back to the man under the wagon. There was no way she could wait until the crazy teenager brought back help, if he ever did.

With a sigh, she bent down, grasped the man beneath his arms and pulled. At first nothing happened; he felt as if he weighed a ton. Then slowly, the limp body began to move. It took several tries, but Brianna finally managed to get him far enough out that she could reach his wound.

She looked around for something to wash the blood away and almost immediately located a water barrel lying on its side. Most of the water had spilled but there was little left in a puddle on the side. That was where her good fortune ended, for she could find nothing to use for a rag. She was about to tear a sleeve off her T-shirt when she noticed the trunk laying among the wreckage near the wagon. Maybe she'd get lucky and find something she could use inside.

Expecting an empty prop or a cleverly disguised beer cooler, Brianna gasped in shock as she opened the lid. It was filled with women's clothes. With a weird feeling, she pulled out a long dress and stared at it. The darn thing looked real. In fact, it appeared about half worn out. Whoever set up this reenactment was a stickler for detail.

Shaking her head in amazement, Brianna set the dress aside and dug down into the trunk looking for something to clean her patient's wound with. She had just located a plain white handkerchief when a small book caught her eye. A journal. Brianna flipped it open and smiled at the first entry on the page. Though the book looked new, it was dated April 27, 1860. To start a journal dated to match the time period was a nice touch of realism, Brianna thought to herself. So was the charming little fabrication the writer had begun.

> *It is fitting that I begin a new journal today for I am also starting a new life. Aunt Grace's incessant harping and cruelties finally drove me to answer Mr. Smyth's advertisement for mail-order brides. This morning I was married by proxy to a man I have never met, and am going to join him in the Wild West. I know very little about him, only that he is a station master along the Pony Express route. The letter Mr. Smyth gave me seemed more concerned with finding a cook than a companion. No matter. He's bound to be better than Aunt Grace. We leave tomorrow for St. Joseph, Missouri . . .*

It was difficult to resist the temptation to read further, but Brianna put the little book back. The man under the wagon needed attention.

With a sigh, she filled a tin cup with water, returned to the injured man and prepared to dress his wound. As she unbuttoned his flannel shirt, she nearly gagged at the overwhelming stench of body odor and stale whiskey that rose from the man. "Must have something against soap," she muttered as his shirt fell open to reveal a dingy gray undershirt beneath.

The scissors from the first-aid kit made short work of the garment and she soon had most of the blood sponged away. Though the cut was nearly six inches long and half an inch wide, it didn't appear to be very deep.

The first-aid kit contained iodine, hydrogen peroxide, and an antibiotic ointment. Unsure as to which would work the best, Brianna decided to use all three. When she poured iodine in the open wound, the man's hand suddenly rose from the ground and grabbed her wrist.

"Christ almighty," he said trying to focus his eyes. "What the hell are you doing?"

"Cleaning your wound. There's been an accident and you were injured. I'm sorry about the iodine, but I wanted to make sure it was disinfected."

"You don't need to torture me. I told you I didn't know who you was when I tried to kiss you. There ain't no way I'm going to tangle with that husband of yours."

"But I'm not marr . . . "

"If I'd a known you belonged to Lucas Daniels I wouldn't have laid a finger on you."

Brianna stared at him in shock. "D-did you say Lucas Daniels?"

"Man has a damned nasty temper if you cross him," he murmured as his grip on her arm started to slacken. "Never meant to insult his wife. Didn't even know he had one. . . . " His hand fell to the ground as he drifted back into unconsciousness.

Brianna stared down at the man in opened-mouth shock. The crazy teenager had also mentioned Lucas. How could they possibly know about her great-great-grandfather?

A dream. That's all this was. She was probably lying unconscious at the bottom of Tom Schaffer's gondola while her mind invented this incredibly real illusion.

That rationalization didn't do much to calm her as she placed two sterile cotton pads over the wound and secured them with adhesive tape. Never in her life had she experienced such a life-like dream.

The book in the trunk drew her like a magnet. Maybe it would help make sense of this somehow. She retrieved it and settled down in the shade of a large rock to read. The back of Brianna's neck prickled as she scanned the first page.

The diary wasn't a clever prop created by an overly active imagination. It belonged to Anna Daniels, her own great-great-grandmother.

2

"I decided not to wear my crinolines today. They are just too impractical on the trail. My skirts are a little too long without them, but a least I don't have to worry about showing an unseemly amount of ankle if a good strong wind comes along. I plan to put them on again before I meet Lucas for the first time. I wouldn't want him to think me dowdy."

Brianna smiled. Crinolines, for heaven's sake. She was totally caught up in the other woman's hopes and dreams before she'd read five pages. This was not some romantic fantasy woven by a frustrated fiction writer, but a day by day account of a young woman's trek west. It was impossible to not feel compassion for Anna as she struggled with the difficult conditions of the trip and wondered about the man who waited at the end of it.

Underlying every entry was the desperate hope that they'd come to love each other. Brianna suspected that Anna had known little love in her life. The few references to Aunt Grace were always disparaging. Near the end of the journal, her brows drew together for Anne's cheerful optimism suddenly disappeared.

We reached Platte River Bridge today. After the usual spurt of curiosity, everyone pretty much ignored me until I came out of the Suttlers store. Without any warning, a man stepped out from between two buildings and tried to kiss me. He had obviously been drinking heavily. It was horrible. Who knows what would have happened if a brave young man hadn't come by right then and saved me. A few well-aimed punches and my attacker was unconscious on the ground.

By strange coincidence, Seth, my savior, is a Pony Express rider assigned to Lucas's station. He knew so much about me, I realized Lucas must have shared the contents of my letters. Perhaps my new husband is as anxious as I for this to be a happy marriage.

Seth was on an errand and couldn't stop to talk but promised to visit with me this evening after supper. I was surprised when he suggested it for he seems strangely nervous around me, but perhaps he has a message from Lucas. I also discovered the driver who is to take me north to Lucas is none other than the disgusting creature who accosted me. I can't imagine traveling so far alone with such a vile man.

Brianna spared a glance for the man stretched out next to the wagon. From what little experience she'd had with him, vile and disgusting seemed a pretty apt description. As she turned back to the journal, Brianna couldn't help wondering how Anna had managed to instill the fear of God, or more truthfully, the fear of Lucas Daniels in him.

> *I feel like such a fool! All this time I've been comforted by the thought that Lucas Daniels wanted a wife and a companion. Now I find none of that is true. Lucas didn't send for a wife, Seth did. More precisely, Seth and the other rider named Billy decided Lucas needed a wife and answered Mr. Smyth's advertisement on his behalf. Lucas doesn't even know I'm coming!*
>
> *Seth admitted it all tonight. I was furious with him. I've traveled all this way for nothing. I can't bear the thought of going back, or what Aunt Grace will say. Seth says he will reach Split Rock station before I do and will have time to prepare Lucas for my arrival. I can't imagine how he's going to break the news to Lucas. I certainly didn't take it very well. In fact, I lost my temper with him and was quite scathing.*
>
> *After I calmed down a bit, Seth explained he and Billy didn't mean me any harm, they just hadn't really thought the scheme through. They did it because they can't stand Lucas's cooking, of all things. As stationmaster it is his responsibility to cook for everyone who is assigned there. It seems Lucas is an inventor and often gets distracted when he's supposed to be fixing a meal. If the food isn't burned, it's half raw.*
>
> *According to Seth, Lucas is devoted to his tinkering and his horses. Since he doesn't appear to care overly much for the domestic side of life, perhaps I can make myself useful and convince him to let me stay if not as his wife then as a cook.*

*At least Seth has promised to speak to Bart
Kelly, the driver who attacked me. He seems to
think the knowledge that I'm married to Lucas
Daniels will be enough to keep him on his best
behavior. What sort of man is Lucas Daniels
anyway?*

The journal continued on for several more pages in a
similar vein. Brianna felt like crying as Anna's hopes
and dreams crumbled. Finally she closed the book and
gazed off across the prairie.

The air was sweltering, and the ground beneath her
uncomfortably rocky. If this was a dream, it was the
most intense of her life, but the only other explanation,
that she'd traveled through time, was too bizarre to
even consider. And yet she couldn't dismiss the notion.
The cloud that had pulled them in and the azure mist
that swallowed the balloon were like nothing she had
ever even heard of. A time portal of some sort? It was
probably too little oxygen.

The entire hallucination must be the result of Tom's
revelations about Lucas and Anna Daniels, nothing
more. Still, if it were all her imagination, why wasn't
Lucas Daniels a balloonist instead of an inventor? He
sounded like some kind of nineteenth century computer nerd.

A groan from Bart Kelly brought Brianna from her
musings.

"Water . . . " he croaked.

"There isn't much," she said, rising to her feet and
walking to the overturned water barrel. She scooped
up half a cup and returned to the wounded man.

"Better drink it slowly," she cautioned. "You could
be in shock from your wound."

He slurped the water then collapsed back on the
ground. "Funny looking togs yer wearin' there."

Brianna glanced down at her Balloon Rally T-shirt, sneakers, and blue jeans. "Where I come from everybody dresses this way."

"Reckon I'd like a place where the women folk run around in their underwear."

Underwear! Well, maybe to a man who was used to seeing women covered from neck to ankle it did look that way. "I was just getting ready to change clothes when you called me."

He looked disappointed. "You was?"

"Yes, and now that you've had your drink I'll go finish the job."

Brianna walked around the wagon to the trunk and opened the lid. Anna's mirror lay facedown near the top, and Brianna picked it up, almost afraid to look. It was a relief to see the same face she stared at every morning when she brushed her teeth.

Why didn't Bart Kelly realize she was a different person? Maybe because she wasn't. If this was a dream . . . Brianna sagged in relief. Of course it was.

Brianna touched the dress that lay at the top of the trunk. Then why did it all feel so incredibly real? Was she hovering near death in an intensive care ward somewhere? Maybe she was already dead. Accounts of people who had died on the operating table then were brought back always mentioned incredibly realistic dreams. A shiver ran down her spine. Suddenly, time travel didn't seem quite so bad. If she really had gone back in time somehow, what had happened to Anna? Was she in 1995? The way back to their own times, if one existed, was from here. Her first priority had better be to convince Lucas Daniels to let her stay. With a sigh, Brianna pulled out the long dress. It was bound to be hot and uncomfortable.

After casting a quick glance to make sure Bart Kelly couldn't see her, Brianna stripped down to her underwear then slipped the dress over her head. The skirt was a good inch off the ground and baggy on her. Though she and Anna obviously were not built the same, they were fairly close to the same size. She had just finished buttoning the long row of buttons up the front of the dress when she heard someone call her name, or at least Anna's name.

"Mrs. Daniels, where are you?"

A lone rider was coming toward them leading a team of horses that appeared to be pulling some sort of two wheeled vehicle. As he drew nearer Brianna recognized the Pony Express rider that had passed them earlier. Brianna took a deep breath. This was where her masquerade would begin.

"I see you made it back, Seth."

"Yup." He pulled to a stop and glanced down. "Bart Kelly isn't dead is he?"

"No, and I don't think he's in much danger of dying either. His wound looks far worse than it is."

"Then it didn't matter that I couldn't stop earlier. I felt bad but that's part of my job. Billy was champing at the bit as it was."

"What if Bart Kelly had bled to death?"

Seth shrugged as he swung down from his horse. "We'd have buried him, I guess. Aren't you curious where I found the horses?"

"A little." Frankly, she couldn't care less. Until he'd ridden up, she hadn't even thought about them being gone.

"They were down by the Sweetwater, hung up on a big old boulder. The wagon tongue got caught in a crack."

Wagon tongue? Brianna focused on the team for the first time and blinked in surprise. What she'd thought a small vehicle was really the front wheels and tongue of Bart Kelly's freight wagon. "How in the world did they manage to tear the wheels off the wagon?"

"I was hoping you'd tell me."

"I don't remember any of it," she said truthfully.

"Mr. Kelly can probably explain when he wakes up again. Can you fix the wagon?"

"I think so. The wheels and axle are fine and it doesn't look like anything else was broken. I guess the first thing is to unhitch the horses."

Brianna watched Seth for several long minutes. There was something very appealing about his tousled blond hair and ready smile. He was much smaller than she had first realized, about the same height she was. It didn't take long to realize he was hiding something. He hadn't looked directly at her once. "Did you tell Lucas?"

"Not exactly."

"What do you mean not exactly?"

"He was busy. It's not a good idea to bother him when he's involved." Seth's full attention seemed to be fixed on the work he was doing as he continued to avoid looking at her.

"Wonderful. What now?"

"Well, he'll have to let you stay at the station until somebody came through going to Fort Laramie. He can't send you back till then."

Brianna sighed. Small comfort when there was no place to go back to. "When will that be?"

"Might be any day. You never know when somebody might come along. If nothing else Bart Kelly will be back through in a week." He glanced up at her. "You'll have to convince Lucas to let you stay before then."

"How am I supposed to do that?"

"I don't know. He's been out here a long time," Seth said. "He's probably lonely, and you are legally married."

Brianna stared at him. Seduce her own great-great-grandfather? Not likely. "I don't think . . . "

"That you, Seth?" Bart Kelly asked trying to focus his bleary eyes on the other man.

"Sure is."

"Would you fetch my bottle? I'm feelin' right poorly."

"The last thing you need with that wound is more whiskey," Brianna said wondering if alcohol rather than pain might be the reason he kept drifting off.

Bart groaned and closed his eyes as if in great pain. "She's a hard woman, Seth. A man could die of thirst with her around."

"It wouldn't hurt you to sober up some," Seth said. "What happened here anyway? Mrs. Daniels says she doesn't remember any of it."

Bart opened his eyes again and looked at her in surprise. "That so? I ain't gonna forgit as long as I live. Damnedest thing I ever saw. All of a sudden this big ugly cloud showed up. Sounded like somebody was twisting a mountain lion's tail. . . . "

Gooseflesh raised along Brianna's arms as she listened to Bart Kelly describe the same experience she and Tom had gone through right down to the weird mist. It was becoming harder and harder to convince herself it was all a dream.

"Mrs. Daniels is right, you don't need any more whiskey," Seth said shaking his head. "That's the craziest story I ever heard."

Only because I haven't told him mine, Brianna though to herself. *It makes Bart Kelly's sound sane.*

"I'm going to need some help putting this wagon back together," Seth was saying. "You up to it, Bart?"

"Well . . . I reckon I can try," he said. Then suddenly broke into a fit of feigned coughing.

Brianna eyed him with disgust. "It looks like you're stuck with me, Seth. Just tell me what you want me to do and I'll . . . " she trailed off as she realized both men were staring at her as though she had suddenly grown an extra head. "What's the matter?"

"It's men's work," Bart Kelly said repressively. "Ain't likely a woman like you could handle it."

Seth nodded his head. "He's right, Mrs. Daniels. We'll take care of it. Why don't you wait over there in the shade until we're done?"

Brianna looked back and forth between the two men. They honestly thought they'd do better without her in spite of Bart Kelly's injury. "Oh, for pity's sake," she said at last. "Do it yourselves then. See if I care." With a toss of her head, she retrieved Tom Shaffer's backpack and went over to a shady spot beside the rock.

She ignored them as they struggled to right the wagon and reattach the wheels. It was time to take stock of what she had. Besides the first-aid kit, she knew there were over-the-counter drugs for just about every malady known to man but she hadn't really looked at what else the nylon bag contained.

Even Bart Kelly's curses, some of which she'd never heard before, failed to distract her as she dug through Tom's survival kit. A waterproof packet of matches, a huge bag of high energy trail mix, a box of sugar cubes, some granola bars, several packages of dried food, and a bottle of hot sauce to make it edible, a space blanket, a camera complete with a strobe and a couple of rolls of film, a notebook, several pens and pencils, even a calculator, and some cash had been stowed inside.

Brianna smiled as she reached the bottom. In a plastic sack with his toothbrush, toothpaste, and soap she found a bottle of sunscreen. Leave it to a redhead she thought gratefully as she rubbed the lotion into her skin.

Underneath a towel and washcloth she found a package of balloons and a small bottle of helium wrapped in a magazine. What in the world? Flipping through the pages of the magazine, she raised an eyebrow at the scantily clad models standing next to gorgeous sports cars. Tom had indeed been prepared for every emergency, even boredom. God only knew what the helium and balloons were for though.

By the time Brianna had hidden the backpack at the bottom of Anna's trunk, the wagon was once again sitting solidly on its front wheels. It took the better part of an hour to reload all the supplies and rehitch the horses.

At last they were ready to go and Brianna helped Bart get settled in a makeshift bed in the back of the wagon. He was feeling very sorry for himself, but she suspected it was as much from the case of smashed whiskey bottles they'd found as from his wound.

Brianna had a moment of consternation when she realized she didn't have the faintest idea how to climb up to the wagon seat. She was still trying to decide exactly how it was done when Seth grasped her around the waist and gave her a boost.

"How far from Split Rock Station are we?" she asked when he joined her on the wagon seat.

"A couple of miles. It won't take us very long."

"Good, I'll be glad to get there. I feel like I've been traveling forever."

"It's a long trip."

Brianna couldn't help noticing how he kept glancing at her from the corner of his eye as he drove down the road. "Is something wrong?" she asked finally.

"Your face."

Brianna raised her eyebrows in surprise. "Excuse me?"

"No, I didn't mean it that way," Seth said turning bright red. "It's just that you look different."

"Different how?"

He studied her intently for a few seconds then shook his head. "I don't know quite what it is, but you've changed in the last couple of days."

Brianna forced herself to laugh as though the idea were ridiculous. "Maybe you just forgot."

"Maybe." But he continued to watch her uncertainly for the rest of the trip.

Brianna was still wondering what Anna Daniels looked like as Split Rock Station came into view. Except for a pole corral full of horses, the place might have been deserted. Even when they drove into the yard, there was no sign of life.

"Lucas must be working," Seth said uneasily as he climbed down from the wagon and helped her alight. "He was right in the middle of something when I left. I better go see if I can find him."

"And we certainly wouldn't want to disturb him would we?" Brianna muttered to herself as Seth disappeared into the cabin.

"Not if you have a lick of sense," Bart Kelly said from the back of the wagon.

"Why, what will he do? Bite my head off?"

"It's a distinct possibility," said a deep voice behind her.

Startled, Brianna turned and nearly crashed into the man behind her. Where the devil had he come from?

"L-Lucas?" she asked uncertainly wondering if he could hear how hard her heart was pounding.

His gaze raked her from head to toe. "You have the advantage of me I'm afraid, Miss . . . "

"Daniels, Brianna Daniels."

One black eyebrow rose. "Daniels? Are we supposed to be related?"

"Hold on just a cotton-pickin' minute," Bart Kelly said from the back of the wagon. "I thought you two was married."

"What?"

Brianna winced as the single explosive word hung in the air between them.

"Lucas . . . " Seth called, hurrying out to join them. "I can explain."

"Explain what?" Lucas glanced at Brianna then back at Seth with a look of dawning comprehension. "Oh, Lord. What have you and Billy done this time?"

"I-I think I better tell you in private."

Lucas closed his eyes for a moment then gave a resigned sigh before walking to the corral with Seth.

As the two men talked, Brianna studied Lucas Daniels. He wasn't at all what she expected. The combination of coal-black hair and light-gray eyes was stunning even from this distance, but where was the red hair he was so proud of? Nor was he tall and slender like the other men in her family. Though he wasn't short, he was an inch or so shy of six foot and on the stocky side. In fact, if she hadn't known better she'd think he spent hours in a gym pumping iron.

There was no way her imagination had created this version of Lucas Daniels. She'd never seen anyone who looked less like a computer nerd in her life. Come to think of it, he didn't look much like a grandfather either.

3

July 15, 1995

"What the . . . ?" Tom Shaffer watched in horror as his passenger began to glow with weird blue light. At first he thought it was electrical energy of some sort, balloons often attracted lightning. Suddenly, Brianna gave a terrified scream and started to waver before his eyes. For an instant he stood frozen as the smell of burnt electrical wiring and a high-frequency screech filled the air. Right in front of his incredulous gaze she became translucent and began to fade from sight.

"Brianna!" Tom grabbed for her, but his hands seemed to pass right through her as the balloon lurched and he was thrown to the floor of the gondola. A bright light burst in his head and a sudden weight pressed down on him as he lost consciousness.

Tom could feel her breath rasping uneasily across his face as he came to. "Brianna, are you all right?" There was no response. "Damn," he said trying to twist around to look at her.

It was nearly impossible to move in the cramped

confines of the gondola especially with her weight on top of him. After a full minute of concentrated effort, he managed to struggle into a more or less upright position and transfer her into his arms.

"Ohhhh . . . "

She opened her eyes and Tom's own widened in shock. Her eyes had changed from blue to brown. He'd heard concussions sometime caused eye color to change but he'd never actually seen it before. It made her whole face look different. Her hair even looked a slightly darker shade of blond. "Are you all right?" he asked trying to keep his voice steady.

"I hurt all over." She blinked up at him. "Who are you?"

"Tom Shaffer, don't you remember?"

"Where's Mr. Kelly?"

"Who?"

"Mr. Kelly, the driver."

Tom's eyebrows came together. "Do you feel okay, Brianna?"

"How do you know my name?"

"You told me. Brianna Daniels."

"I said that?" She was clearly startled. "But I've never told anyone . . . Good heavens, what's that?"

Tom peered up at the bright blue and pink nylon stretched above them. "Just my balloon."

"B-balloon?" Anna closed her eyes. She was dead and this was her punishment. Aunt Grace always said she'd come to a bad end. The man, Tom, must be her guide to whatever came after. That's why he knew her real name. Right now he was staring down at her as if he didn't quite believe his eyes.

"I still don't know what hap . . . " the rest of his statement was lost as the balloon suddenly lurched and he struggled to his feet. They were going down fast even though Tom fought to control their descent.

Anna stared over the side. Surely if they were on their way to heaven they'd be going up.

"If I don't put her down pretty quick we could be in serious trouble. Grab the extra helm . . . Good grief, what are you wearing?"

"My best dress. Why?"

As Tom looked from the long dress to her oddly different face it suddenly all came together in his mind. "You're not Brianna," he uttered in a shocked voice.

"W-well, I usually go by Anna."

"But how did you get into my balloon and where's Brianna?"

She looked up at him, with tearful brown eyes. "I don't have any idea," she whispered.

None of it made sense, but Tom couldn't spare the time to figure it out now. He pulled his extra helmet out from behind the propane tank. "Here put this on. It isn't much to look at, but we may have a pretty rough landing."

Anna took the battered helmet with a look of dismay but after a glance at the one Tom wore, donned it without complaint.

"Hang on," he said opening the parachute valve at the top of the balloon to control their descent. As they came down Tom scanned the surrounding area searching for his brother's familiar yellow pickup on the distant ribbon of highway. There was no sign of the chase crew, just empty miles of pavement stretching across the prairie. The only indication of life was a ranch house a couple of miles to the north.

In spite of his fears, their landing was relatively smooth. The minute the gondola touched down, Anna gave a heartfelt sigh of relief and started to clamber over the side of the basket.

"No, stay here," Tom said grabbing her arm. "Our weight holds the basket stationary. Without it the balloon will drag the gondola all over the prairie."

"Oh. I-I didn't know." Reluctantly she settled back and watched the huge balloon drift gracefully toward earth.

Tom realized she was several inches shorter than Brianna and a bit more rounded. The difference only served to emphasize the incredible likeness between the two women. Suddenly his eyes focused on the locket around her throat. It was identical to Brianna's. Who was this woman? More importantly where had she come from and where was Brianna Daniels? This couldn't be happening.

"Where are we?" she asked.

"In the middle of Wyoming somewhere north of highway 287 I think," Tom said as the balloon collapsed in on itself and settled to the ground in a pool of brightly colored nylon.

She gave him a bewildered look as he vaulted over the side with the ease of long practice. "Is that close to Split Rock Station?"

"I understand that's Split Rock over there." Tom said pointing to the landmark before lifting Anna out of the basket.

"I wonder if Mr. Kelly went there without me."

"Is that where you were headed?"

She nodded. "My . . . husband is there."

"Are you sure? I didn't see any signs of life when we flew over."

"He's the stationmaster."

"Of what? All I saw was a place for tourists to stop and take pictures."

"Lucas runs the Pony Express station there."

"Oh." Tom removed his helmet and replaced it with a green baseball cap. A gas station/convenience store situated out in the middle of nowhere with a name like Pony Express was bound to be pretty good size. He wondered uneasily how he'd managed to miss it. Of course it wasn't nearly as unsettling as misplacing his passenger. "Is that where you came from?"

"Not exactly. Mr. Kelly and I were on our way there when the storm came. It was horrible!"

"I agree. I've never seen anything like it in all my years of flying." He picked up the parachute line and squatted down to tie off the mouth of the balloon. "Did you happen to see that bolt of lightning that hit us?"

"I'm not sure. It all happened so fast. The noise spooked the horses so bad Mr. Kelly couldn't get them stopped and then th-they just disappeared into a blue mist. I think we hit something because I heard a loud crunch and the wagon started to tip. The last thing I remember was falling and a flash of bright light. Do you suppose that was the lightning?"

Tom stopped in the process of wrapping the cord to stare at her. "You were in a horse-drawn wagon?"

"The stage wasn't due through for another couple of days." She blushed and looked down at her hands. "I-I didn't want to wait any longer."

"Stage as in stagecoach?" As Anna nodded, Tom swallowed hard. It was obvious his question had taken her completely by surprise. "What's today's date?" he asked suddenly.

"July fifteenth."

"What year?"

"1860."

"Where did you get your necklace?"

"I-it was my mother's. I never take it off."

"What did you say your name was?"

She looked at him as though he'd lost his mind. "Anna Daniels. Why are you asking me all these questions?"

"Just checking for oxygen deprivation." Tom hid his dismay by turning his attention to the deflated balloon. Lord, he should have known the instant he saw the long dress. Insanity. It was the only explanation. The truly frightening thing was that he really wasn't sure which of them was crazy. Either Brianna thought she was her own great-great-grandmother, or he was having one hell of a hallucination.

"Is there anything I can do to help you?" she asked shyly as she removed her helmet and he started to work.

"Yeah, grab my backpack would you? That's where my marker balloons are. We'll inflate some so my brother can find us. "

"Backpack?"

He glanced over his shoulder at her. If she was faking that look of confusion, she was the best darn actress he'd ever seen. "It's a bag about this big," he said showing her with his hands. "Should be in the bottom of the gondola somewhere."

"All right."

Tom walked along the deflated balloon folding the edges over until it lay in a long straight line. Within a short time he was finished and returned to Anna.

"I couldn't find your pack," she said apologetically as she held out Brianna's windbreaker for his inspection. "This is all that was in there that wasn't tied down."

"My backpack's gone?" A quick glance at the interior of the basket showed it empty except for the propane tanks and flight instruments. "That's really strange," he said scratching his head. But then he couldn't account for much of anything that had happened since take-off. Even the distance they'd come was unbelievable for summertime. "Well without the marker balloons I guess our only other choice is to head for that house I saw and call Chuck."

"Does he live there?"

"No. He has a mobile phone in his pickup. This isn't the first time we've lost each other during a flight."

"I see." But it was obvious she didn't.

"This shouldn't take too long. You can stay here and

sit in the shade of those rocks over there. I'll leave you the canteen."

"I'm coming with you."

"It's too hot. You could get heat stroke."

"So could you."

"I'm not wearing a long dress."

"No, but then I'm used to it." She untied the sunbonnet that was hanging down her back and put it on her head. "Besides, I-I don't want to stay here by myself."

The stubborn tilt of her chin couldn't disguise the quaver in her voice and Tom's resistance melted like ice cream on a barbecue. "All right then, let's go."

The sun beat down unmercifully as they walked through the sagebrush, skirting cactus and knee-high anthills as they went. In spite of it all, Anna remained determinedly cheerful though Tom had a sneaking suspicion she was badly frightened by all that had happened.

The further they traveled, the more convinced he became that he had lost his mind. Though he hadn't been around Brianna Daniels long, she was very different from the shy soft-spoken woman who walked beside him now. Too different.

No one could change that much.

Anna was just as he had always fancied her during the hours he had spent pouring over Lucas Daniels's journal. He knew she was a figment of his imagination, and yet she appeared so genuine. A slightly crooked front tooth where Brianna's were beautifully straight, and a skirt that was a little too long, added to the illusion of reality.

But the most damning evidence of his instability was the way he felt toward her. He had been mildly attracted to Brianna, but Anna was something else. From the moment she confessed she didn't want to stay behind, the need to protect her became a driving force within him. It was all he could do not to put his arm around her shoulders and guide her steps.

They hadn't gone much more than half a mile when Tom suddenly realized why he was having such a bizarre hallucination. Lucas Daniels had loved his wife deeply and had described her in the most glowing terms. Tom had grown up thinking she was the epitome of what a woman should be and had been waiting for someone just like Anna all his adult life. If the truth were known, he was probably halfway in love with her already. The lightning or whatever hit them in that balloon had scrambled his brain and created the illusion. Thank God he and Brianna hadn't been talking about a sci-fi horror movie or something.

The walk across the prairie was long and uncomfortable, but they arrived at the ranch house far too soon for Tom. He knew it was only a matter of time before Anna disappeared back into his imagination and Brianna took her place.

As he reached up to knock on the door, Anna grabbed his arm and he glanced down at her questioningly.

"Are you sure this is a good idea?" she whispered. "Everything here looks so strange."

Tom looked around in surprise. It was a typical ranch headquarters with a battered old pickup and variety of farm machinery surrounding the huge trapezoid-shaped shop across the barnyard. Corrals were visible behind the shop and fields green with alfalfa stretched clear to the base of a large hill beyond. Though the fence around the yard needed a coat of paint and the lawn was overdue for a mowing, the house itself was good-sized and well-kept. There was absolutely nothing out of the ordinary. "What do you mean?"

Before Anna could answer, the door opened and Tom turned his attention to the boy who stood in the doorway.

"Hello," he said with a smile. "Is your mom or dad here?"

"Nope, they went to Riverton and probably won't be back till after the rodeo tonight. The boy looked over Tom's shoulder and raised his eyebrows. "Did your car break down?"

"No, as a matter of fact we came by balloon. We got caught in a crosswind and lost our chase crew. I need to make a phone call to tell them how to find us."

The boy's face brightened. "You're from the balloon rally?"

"That's right."

"Wow! You're a long way from Riverton."

"I know. It was quite a ride. Could I use your phone?"

"Oh, sure," he said stepping aside. Then a shadow crossed his face. "Well, I think so anyway."

"If you'd rather I didn't come in, I can give you the number . . . "

"No, it's not that. I'm not sure the phone's working. My experiment blew every circuit in the house." He crossed the living room, put the phone to his ear and sighed in relief. "It's all right," he said handing it to Tom. "Good thing, too. My dad is going to be mad enough."

Tom wasn't surprised that the boy didn't give Anna's long dress a second glance. The delusion was his alone. It only took a few moments to dial the number, but Anna edged so close she nearly knocked him off balance. When he looked down she was staring at the TV in undisguised horror. Tom glanced at the screen and grinned. "That's got to be the worst sitcom they ever came up with. My sister-in-law won't even let her kids watch it," he said just as his brother answered the phone. "Hello, Chuck. I think we might have broken the record this time . . . "

Anna's only answer was to step even closer. Unable to resist, Tom put his arm around her with a comforting squeeze as he repeated the boy's directions for finding them.

"He'll be out there in forty-five minutes or so," Tom said as he hung up the phone. "That will give us enough time to get back to the balloon so he can find us."

"I'll give you a ride," the boy offered eagerly. "We'll have plenty of time to get there if we take the pickup."

"If it wouldn't be too much trouble," Tom said with a smile. "It must be a hundred degrees outside."

"No problem. My name's Scott Martin by the way."

"Tom Shaffer," Tom said sticking out his hand, "and this is Brianna Daniels."

"Hi." Scott shook hands with Tom and smiled at Anna. "Nice dress. Did you make it?"

Anna blushed a bright red. "Y-yes."

"My sister would turn green if she could see it. She spent three days sewing her dress for the parade this afternoon and it isn't half as nice as yours." He missed both Tom's startled expression and Anna's look of consternation as he turned and walked away. "I have to finish fixing the fuse box, but it won't take long. I only have a few more wires to replace."

"Shouldn't you get a licensed electrician to do that?"

"Nah, I know how. My dad said if I was going to keep blowing the wiring I had to learn to fix it myself. Can't wait to see your balloon. This will be even better than going to the rally. I was supposed to go but Dad made me stay home."

"You must be disappointed," Tom murmured as he gave Anna a shrug then followed Scott through the kitchen into the laundry room.

"Yeah, but I guess I sorta deserved it. I accidentally deleted all the ranch records last night because I needed more memory on the computer. He said I couldn't go anywhere until I had them all back on the hard drive." Scott sighed. "He's going to go ballistic when he sees this."

"Good Lord, what happened?" Tom stared in disbelief at the cinder block wall above the fuse box. It was blackened all the way to the ceiling and the stench of burnt wiring filled the room.

"I overloaded the circuits." Scott picked up a pair of needle nose pliers and reached into the fuse box to twist two wires together. "I thought if I boosted them with aluminum foil it would give me the extra amps I needed, but it didn't work out quite the way I planned."

"No, it doesn't look like it. What in the world were you doing?"

"Just working on a theory of mine." Scott pulled out a chunk of melted metal and studied it closely. After a moment he sighed and threw it onto the washing machine with the burnt wires and fried fuses. "I just hope my surge protector saved the computer. If I wiped out those records again, I'll be grounded for the rest of my life!"

Tom watched in amazement as the boy rewired the fuse box. His skill was nothing short of miraculous. "What's this theory you're working on?" he asked.

Scott didn't even look up from his work. "You'd just laugh at me like everybody else does."

"No, I wouldn't."

Scott stopped and studied Tom intently for a moment. "Promise?"

"Promise."

"All right, but remember you can't laugh. I think I've figured out how to twist the time-space continuum into a Möbius strip."

Tom felt as though the air suddenly became too thin to breathe. "What-what exactly does that mean?"

"Well, not much yet, but some day I hope to be able to travel through time."

"Scott," Tom said in a strangled voice as he reached down and grasped Anna's hand. "I think that day has arrived."

4

July 1860

"If you and Lucas is married, how come he don't know nothing about it?"

Bart Kelly's voice grated along Brianna's nerves like sandpaper on cardboard. She resisted telling him it was none of his business. At this point she couldn't risk alienating anyone, even the disgusting man in the back of wagon. "Lucas has quite a sense of humor."

"Not that I ever noticed. What the hell is going on anyway?"

"Maybe you should ask him."

Bart looked nonplussed for a moment then shook his head. "Don't reckon I need to know that bad. Lucas don't like folks prying into his business."

It didn't appear that he was particularly fond of people who came to visit without an invitation either. His glowering expression didn't change as he listened to Seth nor did he so much as glance in Brianna's direction. It didn't look promising. With Seth's inept handling,

Lucas would probably stick her on a horse and send her straight back to Platte River Bridge today.

Before her better sense could intrude, Brianna decided to take matters into her own hands. The look Lucas gave her as she walked toward the two men was far from welcoming, but she pretended not to notice. "I think you and I need to talk," she said meeting his enigmatic stare squarely.

Lucas's jaw hardened. "There is nothing to discuss."

"I . . . ah . . . I'll be in the barn if you want me," Seth mumbled backing away from the two of them. "I need to go check the horses."

Lucas's lips thinned. "What you need is a damned good thrashing," he said as the younger man hurried away.

"I know you didn't ask for this," Brianna went on, "but neither did I. I'm as much a victim as you are."

"I didn't come west looking for a husband."

"No, but then I had no way of knowing you hadn't really sent for me."

"If you hadn't been so desperate to catch a man, you wouldn't have been fooled."

"Look, Lucas, we can stand here all day blaming each other, and it won't change a thing. On the other hand, with a little effort I think we can find a solution that will benefit both of us."

"I doubt that. I have no need of a wife."

"Maybe not, but you do need a cook."

"I've survived this long without one."

"On the contrary, it seems to me your cooking is what landed you in this predicament in the first place."

"It's not my cooking, it's picky eaters. Nobody could please those two."

"Cut me some slack, Lucas. I know darn well you don't like to cook."

The look he gave her was distinctly unfriendly.

"There isn't any slack to cut. Even if there were, I doubt if you could get Seth to eat it."

Brianna almost smiled and then thought better of it. "As long as I'm here anyway, why don't you let me try. If you decide you don't like my cooking, you can always go back to doing it yourself. The way I see it you've got nothing to lose."

Lucas crossed his arms and regarded her suspiciously. "And what do you get out of this?"

"A place to stay, room and board."

"Why don't you just go back home?"

Brianna thought of Anna's disparaging remarks about the home she'd left behind. "There's nothing to go back to."

"Is that why you married yourself off to a total stranger?"

She shrugged. "It seemed like a good idea at the time."

"Well, if it's a husband you want, I'm sure you can find someone willing to marry you either at Fort Laramie or Fort Bridger."

"According to the contract in my trunk, I already have one. Legally I'm not sure I can marry anyone else until the first marriage is undone."

"It's not worth the paper it's written on," he growled. "I didn't sign it."

"I know and I have no desire to hold you to it, but I need time to reconsider what to do with my life. Apparently getting married wasn't such a good idea."

As far as Brianna could see she hadn't thawed him one bit. Too bad she'd never perfected the art of feminine tears.

"All right," he said suddenly. "You can cook, but just until Bart Kelly leaves."

Brianna suppressed a sigh of relief. It wouldn't do to let him see how much it meant to her. "Thank you."

"Supper's at sundown," he said turning away.

"Hey, wait a minute. I can't just . . . "

He looked back over his shoulder. "Change your mind already?"

"No, but . . . "

"Well, then cook. I'm right in the middle of an important experiment, and I've wasted enough time already." With that he walked away and left Brianna standing there with her mouth open.

"Of all the . . . " Brianna watched him disappear into a long log building that she assumed was the barn. He wasn't going to give an inch and he fully expected her to fail. A slow grin crossed her face. Lucas Daniels was in for a big surprise. She hadn't done much cooking lately, but she happened to be quite good at it.

She turned and went into the cabin. After the bright sunlight, the interior was dark and oppressive. She crossed the dirt floor to the single window and threw open the shutters. There was no glass in the opening, but the fresh air was as welcome as the light.

Brianna glanced around the tiny cabin in dismay. A roomy fireplace dominated the far end of room with a collection of blackened pans hanging next to it on one side and a small cupboard on the other. Two bunks were built into the walls on opposite sides of the room. Both were rumpled and unmade as though the occupants had just risen. A heavy table and four chairs were the only movable furniture in the room aside from a flat topped chest at the foot of one of the bunks. Brianna eyed the odd collection of wire, glass and unfamiliar pieces of metal littering it.

What a mess. The whole place looked and smelled as if it hadn't been cleaned in a long time. Lucas would probably expect her to do that too once she convinced him to let her stay. Right now the first order of business was supper.

Brianna grinned to herself as she rolled up her

sleeves and headed toward the fireplace. Lucas thought she'd be daunted by the fact that there was no stove to cook on.

In reality she was far more at home with the fireplace than a wood stove. Her family had gone on countless weekend camping trips during her youth and she could cook over a campfire almost as well as she could in her ultramodern kitchen at home.

In no time at all she had the fire going and began digging through the cupboard to the left of the fireplace. That's when her good humor began to fade. There was nothing to cook, other than a tin of dried beans, a few cups of weevily flour, and a smidgeon of cornmeal. That rat Lucas knew it, too.

Well, she'd show him. Brianna was famous for her three bean chili. There wasn't any hamburger, but chili didn't have to have meat in it. Of course she'd always used canned beans but if she soaked them first this should work just a well. She dumped some into a pot and searched around for the water bucket. It was next to the door and nearly empty but there was enough to cover the beans.

Now for the flavoring. Brianna dug back into the cupboard. She found salt and pepper, but that was about it. There were no tomatoes, or tomato sauce or even onions. She unearthed a bottle of molasses and hesitated only a moment before pouring a bit into the pot. Molasses went into baked beans, after all.

Clear at the back of the cupboard, a half full bottle of whiskey lay on its side. Brianna pulled it out with a big smile on her face. Her secret ingredient. Maybe there was hope after all. She poured a generous amount into her beans, looked at the bottle for a moment then added some more for good measure. At least it would have some flavor. What she wouldn't give for a bottle of ketchup right now.

"Mrs. Daniels?"

Brianna looked over her shoulder and saw Seth standing uncertainly in the doorway. "Better call me Brianna," she said turning back to her beans. "Lucas isn't very happy with either one of us right now."

"I know. Would you like me to bring your trunk in?"

Brianna suddenly remembered the bottle of hot sauce in Tom Shaffer's backpack. It might mean the difference between boring and tasty. "If you wouldn't mind." She stirred the beans then picked up the water bucket. "I used the last of the water. Where do I refill this?"

Seth paused in the process of pulling clothing off the pegs over one of the bunks and looked at her in surprise. "Down at the river. Don't you want me to do that for you?"

"No, I could use the exercise. What are you doing anyway?"

"Lucas said to get Billy and me moved out to the barn so you can have the other bunk."

"As pleased as Lucas is to have me here I'm surprised I'm not the one sleeping in the barn."

Seth gave her a horrified look. "But you're a woman."

"No kidding." When he continued to stare at her, Brianna gave a disgusted sigh and headed for the door. "Just think, only a hundred years till women's lib."

The walk down to the river wasn't particularly pleasant. The afternoon sun beat down on her unmercifully and mosquitoes swarmed around her in a cloud. Thank goodness for the long sleeves of her dress. By the time she reached the river, Brianna was hot and grouchy.

The river meandered slowly across the flat plain forming a deep pool at the bend nearest the Pony Express Station. Its crystal clear depths sent out a silent invitation to Brianna as she stood on the bank, hot, itchy and more than a little grubby.

Lord she was tempted. A quick glance over her shoulder ended any thought she had of going swimming. Bart Kelly was standing by the back of the wagon watching her with his little pig eyes. Even hidden behind the screen of willows that grew along the shore on either side of the trail, she wouldn't be safe.

With a deep sigh, Brianna filled the water bucket and started back up the well-worn path. It wasn't long before she wished she had let Seth get it for her. The wooden bucket itself was heavy. Filled with water it seemed to weigh a ton. Every few feet Brianna had to stop and transfer the load from one hand to the other.

At first she thought Bart Kelly might to come to her rescue, but the minute he saw her struggling, he disappeared into one of the outbuildings. Honestly, the man was almost too obnoxious to be real. By the time Brianna finally reached the station, her arms and shoulders were aching from the strain and the bucket was less than three-quarters full. Water conservation suddenly took on a whole new meaning as she wondered how many times a day she was going to have to make the trip. For all she knew hauling water from the river to the cabin was the reason Lucas Daniels was so muscular.

The cabin was deserted, but Seth had brought in her trunk as he'd promised. Brianna retrieved the backpack, and dug out the hot sauce. Though the bottle was nearly full, she used it sparingly. If she were here very long she might be very glad to have it.

Brianna looked at the beans in the pot critically as she gave them another stir. She really didn't know how long beans had to soak but surely they'd been in the water long enough. Besides, sunset couldn't be more than a few hours away. With a shrug, she put the beans on to cook.

As she straightened up, a small cracked bowl on the

mantle caught her eye. She peeked beneath the cover and made a face when she saw the thick gooey dough inside. One whiff of the sour mixture was enough. The rest of the cleaning could wait until tomorrow, but this was too nasty to ignore. Brianna carried it outside and scraped it out onto the dirt behind the cabin.

After scrubbing out the bowl with a dab of her precious water, Brianna put it in the cupboard and turned her attention to Anna's trunk. She felt less like an intruder this time, though she still wasn't very comfortable going through the other woman's possessions.

There was very little in the way of clothing. A faded brown dress that had been patched repeatedly, a waistless dress of green calico that looked like a granny gown from the sixties, a black wool skirt, and a full-sleeved white blouse apparently made up the rest of Anna's wardrobe.

Brianna thought longingly of her closet full of clothes as she pulled out an odd wire contraption covered with a tightly woven fabric of some kind. What in the world? When it unfolded into a large bell-shape she realized it was meant to wear under a dress. A crinoline maybe? Brianna shook her head. The things women did to be in fashion. All she needed now was a corset. But that particular item was curiously missing. Nor was there much in the way of underwear; only one long slip-like garment and a single pair of knee length pantaloons.

As Brianna held up the last item her eyes widened in shock. They were split all the way to the waistband and had obviously been made that way. Anna didn't seem like the type to go in for scandalous underwear. One thing for sure, Brianna would wear her own.

As she folded the clothes and put them back in the trunk, she suddenly realized where the corset was. Anna was wearing it, of course. That must be where the shoes were, too. Brianna wondered where Anna was and how she was faring.

What would happen when they changed back? Would Anna be able to handle the volatile Lucas? Perhaps, but only if she had some idea of what had gone on in her absence. Brianna's gaze fell on the book in the top compartment of the trunk, Anna's journal. That was the perfect solution. She'd write everything down the way Anna had.

Immensely pleased with herself, Brianna got a ball-point pen from Tom's backpack, and sat down on the bed to write.

Dear Anna,

I am writing this hoping you will have the chance to read it someday. Assuming we have switched places you'll need to know what has gone on while I was here. I'm not sure what happened to us, but surely the process can be reversed and we will be returned to our own time. I'm finding it difficult to cope with your world and can't even imagine how much harder it must be for you in mine.

Lucas is not what I expected. . . . Here Brianna stopped and nibbled the end of her pen thoughtfully. How did one describe Lucas? The words pig-headed and irritating came to mind. So did chauvinistic, unfair, and suspicious. Then an image of beautiful gray eyes and a body that wouldn't quit popped into her mind. Whatever else he might be, Lucas was definitely easy on the eye.

Brianna pushed the unwelcome thought away in disgust. She was in enough trouble already without a case of raging hormones complicating matters. . . . *I find it very difficult to remember he is my great-great-grandfather.*

5

Lucas glanced at the darkening sky as he headed toward the cabin. He'd been so involved in his experiment that he hadn't realized how late it was. It was nice not to have to worry about supper for once, but even that wasn't going to change his mind about sending the woman on her way. The last thing he needed around here was a female, especially a pretty one.

He eyed the freight wagon as he walked by. The horses had been unhitched, but the supplies hadn't been touched. He felt a spark of annoyance with himself for not telling Seth to take care of it. On the other hand, without supplies, there was no way *she* could fix a meal. Good, he'd won the first round without even trying.

But when he stepped through the door, an enticing smell assailed his nose. What in the world had she found to cook? As his eyes adjusted to the dim light he saw her sound asleep on her bunk with a small book open across her chest. A flicker of compassion ran through him. It was impossible not to notice how pathetically thin she was. Her clothes didn't even fit. Lucas found himself wondering about the desperate circumstances that led her to travel so far and marry a man she'd never met.

It wasn't any concern of his, though, and he wasn't stupid enough to play into her hands. Irritated with himself for even wondering, Lucas cleared his throat loudly.

"Oh!" Brianna jerked awake and blinked up at him as though she didn't know who he was. After a moment of confusion her expression cleared and she sat up. "I must have fallen asleep. What time is it?"

"Sundown. Is supper ready?"

"I think so." She glanced down at her hand then, with a guilty start, hid something under the edge of her skirt. "Where is everybody?"

"They'll be along soon." Lucas couldn't help wondering what she had in her hand as he put some water in the wash bowl and went outside to wash up. Not that her deceit surprised him. She was a woman, after all.

Seth came up the path whistling cheerfully until he saw Lucas. Looking properly contrite he joined the older man at the wash bowl. "How did your experiment go?"

"Fine. Why didn't you unload the supplies?"

"I wasn't sure which were ours, and Bart was sleeping off his drunk."

"See that it gets done right after supper."

"I will." Seth sniffed appreciatively. "Something sure smells good."

Lucas didn't even bother to answer.

By the time they finished washing, Brianna had the table set. Bart Kelly arrived just as Seth finished filling his plate with beans and passed the pot on to Lucas.

"Reckon I'll be leaving tomorrow," Bart said sliding into the empty chair.

Brianna gave him a skeptical look. "Are you sure that's wise?"

"Ain't no sense sticking around here."

"But what about your wound?"

"He's more concerned about the lack of whiskey," Lucas said sardonically as he lifted a fork full of beans to his mouth. "What the hell?"

His look of surprise was echoed around the table as each man started to eat. Puzzled, Brianna took a bite. The flavor wasn't bad but the beans were hard as rocks. "Didn't you soak them?" Lucas asked accusingly.

"Of course I did." She looked at her plate uncertainly. "I guess it wasn't long enough."

"That's pretty obvious." With a scornful glance Lucas rose from the table and went to the chest at the foot of his bed. After rummaging around for a moment, he came back with a small leather pouch and tossed it onto the table. "Here, have some jerky."

"Mighty tasty beans, Mrs. Daniels," Bart Kelly said apparently oblivious to the conversation going on around him. "Best I ever ate."

"Probably my secret ingredient," Brianna muttered as she pushed the inedible beans around her plate. Her stomach growled uncomfortably, but there was no way she was going to eat Lucas's jerky. So much for impressing him with her cooking.

She watched Seth manfully trying to choke down the beans, and pretended to ignore Lucas's self-satisfied smirk. It was all she could do not to dump the rest of the beans on his head.

By the time the meal was over, it was dark outside. Bart retired to the barn for the night, as Lucas and Seth unloaded the supplies. Brianna kicked herself a dozen times for not thinking of the food in the wagon. Lucas was probably laughing at her stupidity. She'd had one chance to prove herself and she'd blown it.

Worse yet, she'd nearly been caught with the ballpoint pen. Things were touchy enough without having to explain something that wouldn't be invented for a hundred years or so.

With a sigh, she rolled up her sleeves and started the dishes. It wasn't an easy task since she had to use a bar of lye soap and had nothing to rinse them in. She vowed to never take her dishwasher for granted again.

As soon as the supplies were inside, Lucas went back outside. Brianna could hear him talking to Seth. There was a deep chuckle and more low voices. At least they seemed to have patched up their differences. Maybe Lucas wasn't the type to hold a grudge.

When Brianna took the dishpan outside to empty it, Lucas was alone by the door watching the stars as he puffed contentedly on his pipe.

"Where do you want me to dump the water?"

"Over there," he said gesturing toward the side of the cabin.

Brianna gave him a surreptitious glance as she emptied the dishpan. She was going to have to do some fast talking if Bart Kelly was to leave in the morning without her. Lucas appeared more interested in the night sky than what she was doing. In fact Brianna wouldn't have been surprised if he had forgotten she was there.

"Nice night," she said coming to stand beside him and gazing up at the sky. "I always like to watch the stars during the summer. They look like you could reach out and touch them."

"Mmmm."

"Are you interested in astronomy?"

Lucas gave a noncommittal shrug and she tried again. "My favorite is the Big Dipper. It's always so easy to find."

"It's over there," he said taking his pipe out of his mouth and pointing over her left shoulder with the stem.

Startled, Brianna turned around. Sure enough there was the familiar constellation. "Oh, of course. During all that time on the trail, I got turned around."

"The Oregon trail runs pretty much east and west. Shouldn't have been much change in the stars at all."

Brianna resisted the urge to kick him. "I never was very good with directions. I get lost in parking lots all the time."

"In what?"

Her stomach lurched as she realized her mistake. "Ah . . . it's a place close to where I grew up."

"Well, you better be careful around here. Getting lost out on the prairie could be deadly."

Silence fell between them as Brianna desperately searched for the right words to convince him to let her stay. "I don't want to leave with Bart Kelly tomorrow morning," she finally blurted out.

"We had an agreement."

"You agreed to let me try. One meal isn't enough to base a decision on. Besides it was nice not to have to cook it yourself, wasn't it?"

"Maybe so, but it hardly seems worth starving to death."

"Oh, for pity's sake, Lucas, you couldn't have done any better than I did, and you know it. Give me a another chance."

He stared up at her for a long moment. "We'll see," he said sticking his pipe back in his mouth. "I'll be done out here in about ten minutes."

"So?"

"So you've got ten minutes to get ready for bed."

Brianna bristled. "What if I'm not ready to go to bed?"

"Suit yourself. I just thought you'd like some privacy."

She glared at him for a full minute before turning on her heel and flouncing into the cabin. It wasn't until she'd undressed and put on Anna's voluminous night-gown that she realized his words might have been an ultimatum. Brianna glanced uneasily toward Lucas's bunk. Surely he hadn't meant . . . no, of course not. They had high morals in the 1800's . . . didn't they?

Her mind flashed back to Seth's assurance that she had only to sleep with Lucas to win him over. She herself had told Lucas she considered their marriage legal. Outside the door she heard him clear his throat and she practically dove under the covers of her bunk. Brianna hardly noticed the lumpy mattress and scratchy wool blanket as he spoke from outside.

"All right if I come in now?"

"Y-yes." She huddled under the covers as though it were the dead of winter.

Lucas walked in and set his pipe down on the chest at the foot of his bunk. "You can bake bread can't you?"

"Bread?"

"It's made out of flour and you eat it at meals," he said sarcastically as he blew out the lantern.

"I-yes, I know how to make bread."

"Good, because we're out." He shrugged his suspenders down off his shoulders and started to unbutton his shirt. "I suppose you'll be wanting to get up early to bake while it's still cool. The sourdough starter is on the mantle. "

Brianna's breath caught in her throat. "In the little bowl?"

"Right. You already saw it then?"

"I think so. Don't you have any yeast?"

He grunted slightly as he pulled off his boots. "Nope. It doesn't keep worth spit out here. Sourdough makes a lot more sense. The more sour it gets the better it works and as long as you keep a little around you'll never run out. Do you want me to shut the window?"

"Wh-what?"

"The window. I usually sleep with it open, but I'll close it if you're cold."

"I'm fine." Was he crazy? It must be ninety degrees in the cabin.

"Good," Lucas said removing his pants. "The way you're wrapped up in that blanket, I thought you might be chilly."

"No."

"Well, good night then."

"Good night." Brianna turned toward the wall. How was she supposed to know the nasty stuff was important? Sourdough starter, without it there would be no bread and there was no way to get more. Lord, Lucas would never forgive her for this. She felt sick when she thought of what his reaction would be.

As she lay there wondering how she was going to get out of this one, Brianna gradually became aware of how uncomfortable she was. The lumps and bumps in the mattress didn't conform to her body, but the wool blanket did, every itchy, smelly, inch of it. She needed a bath, her muscles hurt, and she was miserably hot.

Worst of all, she'd failed. Once Lucas sent her away tomorrow neither she nor Anna would ever get back where they belonged. She was doomed to spend the rest of her life in the past. In fact, there was probably no future to go back to. Because of her, the whole Daniels family didn't even exist in her time. None of them would ever be born. Sudden tears trickled down her cheeks, and she was powerless to stop them.

Lucas listened to the muted sounds coming from the other bunk and felt a stab of remorse. She was crying and didn't want him to know it. If she had begged or cried earlier it would have hardened his heart against her. He knew firsthand how little tears meant coming from a woman. As it was, he'd felt a reluctant flicker of admiration every time she stood there challenging him with that blue-eyed gaze of hers.

Though he wanted her to give up and go back where she came from, he might have pushed her a little far with the sourdough starter. It seemed like the perfect opportunity when he'd noticed it missing, but now he felt vindictive and small. She had come a thousand miles expecting a husband who would welcome her with open arms. Instead, he'd made her cry and he didn't think she was one who cried easily.

A pitiful little sniff nearly wrenched a groan from him. Unable to stand it any more, Lucas put on his pants and crossed the room. She seemed unaware of him until he sat on the edge of her bunk. Her head came up with a jerk as the mattress dipped beneath his weight.

"L-Lucas." She stared up at him in wide-eyed consternation.

"Miss . . . er . . . Brianna. I might have been a little hasty this afternoon . . . "

"Oh, no," she broke in, "you were perfectly right."

"I was?"

"Seth admitted he forged your name. You can't be held accountable for something you didn't actually sign."

"That's not what . . . "

"And it wouldn't matter even if it really was your signature." She scrambled away from him until the wall was at her back. "A legal contract doesn't become binding until it's put into effect."

"It doesn't?" Lucas wondered if she had any idea what she was talking about. He certainly didn't.

"Don't you see?" she said clutching the blanket to her chest like a shield. "Even if it is legal, we can get the marriage annulled as long as we don't . . . you know."

"As long a . . . ah, yes of course." Suddenly Lucas

understood what she thought he wanted and it wasn't the proposition he'd been about to offer her. "What exactly are you trying to tell me?"

"To be perfectly honest with you, Lucas, I'm not any more anxious to be married than you are. But it's imperative that I stay here."

"How so?"

She made a face. "It's difficult to explain." Difficult? How about impossible? "I think we can make a deal that will be mutually beneficial."

"What are you suggesting?"

"If you'll just let me stay, I'll do the cooking, cleaning, laundry, and whatever else needs to be done."

"Seems to me that's the same agreement we had before."

"No, I'll stay out of your way. You'll hardly know I'm around. All I'm asking is that you be patient with me when I make mistakes and . . . " she trailed off as though she didn't know quite what to say.

"And?" he prompted.

"And no hanky-panky," she said meeting his gaze squarely.

"Can't say I've ever heard it called that," he said sardonically, "but I assume that means I'm supposed to ignore any lustful impulses you might inspire in me."

"That's right."

"As a mail-order bride, I thought you planned on being my wife in every way."

"I changed my mind."

For some reason that irritated him almost as much as the way she avoided looking at his bare chest. "Don't worry. I have no intention of taking you to my bed."

She sighed with relief. "Thank you. I'll make sure you don't regret this."

"I already do," he muttered rising to his feet and stomping back to his bunk. This time after he removed his pants, he took off his underwear as well. To hell with her maidenly sensibilities he thought as he slipped into his bunk naked. It was too damn hot to wear anything to bed. If she wanted him to act like she wasn't here, then she'd just have to get used to his sleeping habits.

Lucas told himself he was glad she didn't find him attractive and he'd be glad when she finally admitted defeat and left. The difficult frontier life would send her hotfooting it back home quicker than a cat could lick its ear. Things were going exactly the way he wanted them to without him having to lift a finger.

So why did the word "bully" keep popping into his mind?

6

"Time to get up," Lucas said, shaking Brianna's shoulder.

Brianna opened one eye and peered up at him. "Are you crazy? It's the middle of the night!"

"It'll be full daylight soon." Lucas thought about pulling the blanket off Brianna as he would Seth or Billy but decided against it. He felt guilty enough about all the tossing and turning he'd heard from her bunk during the night. "I set out everything for mush. We'll be back in for breakfast in about forty-five minutes."

"Goody for you," Brianna mumbled turning her back to him and snuggling down under the covers. Idiot. There was no way she was getting up until her alarm clock went off at six-thirty. Who did he think he was anyway?

Brianna slept peacefully for a full five minutes before her eyes suddenly popped open in dismay. Lucas Daniels! How could she have forgotten? With her heart racing, she threw back the blanket and jumped out of bed. The half-light of dawn filtered in through the open window. How long had she slept? Stupid, stupid, stupid! With the sourdough starter a thing of the past, she was in enough trouble already without making him any madder.

Scrambling into her clothes, Brianna cursed the many buttons up the front of her dress. It seemed to take forever to fasten them all with her fingers shaking in the chilly morning air. She glanced toward the fireplace. In order to fix breakfast she'd need to light the fire but a visit to the outhouse came before anything else.

Brianna hurried to the tiny shack out back. Indoor plumbing was another thing she'd never fully appreciated. As she hassled with the yards and yards of material in her skirt she suddenly wondered if Anna's underwear was split to the waistband for convenience. It would bear thinking about . . . when she had time which was definitely not now.

On her way back to the cabin Seth waved cheerfully from the corral where he and Lucas were feeding the horses. As Brianna returned his greeting, she tried to be glad Lucas was ignoring her again. He'd agreed to her terms last night, but he might reconsider in the light of day.

The fire rekindled easily, and Brianna was soon digging through the cupboard. Midway through the interminable night she'd realized there were other kinds of bread she could make. It was, at best, a temporary solution, Lucas couldn't be put off with biscuits and cornbread forever. Still, it should buy her a little time.

With a crow of delight, she unearthed the baking powder. The biscuits were as good as done!

By the time she buried the Dutch oven under the coals some fifteen minutes later, Brianna was immensely pleased with herself. Just wait until Lucas sank his teeth into one of her biscuits. He'd forget all about the sourdough bread she was supposed to be baking. Brianna eyed the bag of cornmeal and pan Lucas had set on the table. Great, she didn't have the foggiest notion how to make the mush he wanted. Then again, he did say he was leaving everything out for her. She opened the bag and looked inside thoughtfully. Other than being somewhat coarser it looked just like the cornmeal she was used to.

Maybe mush was like cooked cereal. From what she'd read of the stuff it must have a similar consistency. What the heck. It was worth a try. Too bad nobody thought to put the directions on the outside of the cornmeal bag the way they did hot cereal. By adding a little at a time to a pan of boiling water, she soon had a pot of something that looked like a cross between cooked cereal and grits.

Brianna had just finished dishing it up when she heard the men coming up the path. She hurriedly dug the Dutch oven out of the coals and sighed in relief. The biscuits were done to perfection.

"Morning, Brianna," Seth said, coming through the door with his usual jaunty smile.

"Good morning, Seth."

"Sumpthin' smells mighty fine." Bart Kelly was right behind him, just as repulsive sober as he'd been drunk. His words were pleasant, but the look in his eyes made Brianna distinctly uncomfortable.

Bart and Seth were instantly forgotten when she saw Lucas looking at the table in surprise. Ha, so much for his superior atti . . .

"Where's the gravy?"

"Gravy?"

"How are we supposed to eat biscuits and mush without gravy?"

Brianna stared at the table in consternation. She hadn't even thought about there being no butter for the biscuits or milk for the cereal. She cleared her throat nervously. "I . . . ah . . . never thought of gravy. What do you usually make it from?"

"What do you . . . Good Lord, and you call yourself a cook?" Lucas didn't even bother to hide his scorn.

"I'm sure if you told me . . . "

"I don't have time to teach you how to cook."

"Oh, for pity's sake, Lucas, just tell me what it's made from. Gravy isn't all that tough to make."

"Salt pork," Seth said promptly.

Brianna gave him a confused look. "I don't know if we have any . . . "

Lucas rolled his eyes. "Bacon."

"Oh right." She pulled the slab out of the cupboard and gingerly unwrapped it. She hadn't considered bacon for breakfast because there were no eggs to go with it. Now she saw it was mostly fat with very little of the pink lean she was used to. "You make gravy from the grease?"

"That's the general idea."

"It shouldn't take me long to fix it then," Brianna said deciding to ignore his sarcasm. "Why don't you sit down and have a cup of coffee while you wait."

"I'm surprised you knew how to make that," Lucas said pulling out a chair and sitting down. It was obvious he fully expected her to serve them.

Brianna gritted her teeth and reminded herself how much depended on keeping Lucas happy. "I'll get your coffee as soon as I slice the bacon," she said sweetly.

Seth jumped to his feet. "I'll cut it for you." He pulled a wicked looking hunting knife out of the sheath at his waist and began carving the slab of salt pork into thick slices.

Brianna gratefully went to get the coffee. By the time she'd poured four cups there was a pile of bacon on the table ready to fry. She threw it into a pan on the fire, then wiped her hands on her apron thoroughly disgusted by the heavy fat. No wonder these people didn't live much past fifty.

Watching the bacon fry took little effort and her mind wandered to the sweat that was already starting to form on her brow. It was barely light and already the tiny cabin was stifling. Suddenly her full attention focused on the conversation around the table.

"Talk around the fort was the Republicans done nominated that rail splitter from Illinois," Bart was saying.

"Probably not a bad choice. Lincoln's about the most conservative candidate they have." Lucas sighed. "But I don't know if the South will accept him. We need a strong president that everybody wants if we're going to hold this country together. I'm afraid he's too anti-slavery."

"Lincoln ain't no abolitionist."

"No, but he doesn't think slavery should spread west either. The South will support Lincoln before Douglas, but they'll probably come in pretty strong for Breckenridge."

Brianna was fascinated. They were talking about Abraham Lincoln and Stephen Douglas! For the first time in her life she wished she'd paid more attention in her history classes. "Who's Breckenridge?"

All three men turned to look at her in surprise. "The Vice President," Lucas said after a moment. "The Southern Democrats nominated him for president."

"Oh, right." Brianna winced. They must think she was pretty stupid. Of course, they obviously thought all women were. "So he supports slavery?"

Lucas nodded. "And state's rights. He feels the Southern states should be able to secede if they want to."

"Oh my God," she said. "The Civil War."

"It's a distinct possibility unless people realize how stupid it is."

Seth straightened indignantly. "You think it's stupid to fight for your principles?"

"There are very few things in this life worth dying for, Seth. Politics isn't one of them."

"But if the South is allowed to secede . . . "

"It will become a separate country and in a few years will resume normal relations with its neighbors." Lucas said. "Unfortunate, but far better than the alternative."

"Brother against brother," Brianna murmured.

Lucas nodded. "Exactly."

Seth was outraged. "You're a secessionist."

"No, and I'm not an abolitionist either. I came out here because I want no part of any of it. Think of it, Seth, what if you and Billy suddenly found yourselves on opposite sides in a battle? Would you be able to kill him?" Lucas asked.

"That couldn't happen."

"Are you so sure? Have you ever discussed it in those little notes you leave each other?"

"Well, no."

"Then you really don't know how he feels. If it comes to civil war it won't matter who wins. Both sides will be devastated and the entire country torn apart."

A long moment of silence filled the room until Lucas glanced over his shoulder at Brianna. "The bacon's burning."

"Oh!" Startled, Brianna turned back to her work. There was a great deal to think about as she dished up the bacon and made gravy out of the drippings. She knew Lucas Daniels had been a spy for the Union army during the Civil War. Yet he was filled with total antipathy toward the whole idea. What could have happened to change his mind so much in such a short time? Had Anna influenced him somehow?

The conversation around the table turned to other things as the men dug into their meal. Brianna hadn't eaten since breakfast the morning before and was famished. Even the thought of the bacon grease didn't stop her from spooning gravy over her food. Maybe she'd jog down to the river later to work off the extra calories.

Lucas tried not to feel anything as he watched her wolf her food down, but it was impossible. The poor thing must be half starved. He couldn't remember ever seeing a woman so pitifully thin.

He took a bite of his third biscuit. Doing without the amenities of civilization had never particularly bothered him before, but he sure wished he had some butter and jam this morning. The biscuits were not only a surprise they were delicious. He hated to admit it, but Brianna was one heck of a cook even if she didn't always seem to know exactly what she was doing.

"Reckon I'd best be goin' soon as breakfast is over," Bart Kelly said around a mouthful of mush. "Don't suppose you'd be willin' to give me a hand with my team seein' as how I'm all stove up."

Lucas glanced at him. "Are you sure you're strong enough to drive? Maybe you better stay a day or two longer."

"No, no," Bart said hastily. "I ain't in that bad a shape. 'Sides, they'll be expectin' me at Green River. Them fellas depend on ol' Bart Kelly, they do."

"I'm sure they do, especially if they have more whiskey around than they need," Lucas murmured.

Bart either didn't hear or chose to ignore him as he turned his full attention to Brianna. "Can you take a look at my wound before I leave, Miz Daniels? That bandage ain't like nuthin' I ever seen before."

"Oh, right . . . ah . . . it's something new they're trying in the East. I suppose I should change it." She glanced uncertainly at Lucas. "Do you have something I could use for a fresh bandage?"

"There's a pile of clean rags in the cupboard." A new

kind of bandage? Lucas wondered what could be done to improve a bandage. Maybe he'd just stick around and see what Brianna had used to patch Bart up.

When they finished eating, Brianna cleared the table and set the water on the fire for dishes. She wondered why Lucas didn't leave as she busied herself around the cabin. There was no way she was going to let him see that bandage. Bart Kelly might be fooled by her glib story but Lucas certainly wouldn't be. Adhesive tape and gauze would be impossible to explain away. "Did you want something else, Lucas?"

"I might have another cup of coffee."

"There isn't any left."

"Too bad." Silence fell and the seconds ticked by with nerve-wracking slowness. Finally, when Brianna was ready to scream, Lucas stretched lazily and stood up. "Well, guess I'd better get to work. Have a good trip, Bart. I suppose we'll see you in a couple of weeks?"

"I reckon so."

Brianna gave a sigh of relief as he sauntered out the door. Now to get Bart tended to and on his way before Lucas changed his mind about letting her stay. "If you'll lay down on that bunk over there and pull up your shirt, Mr. Kelly, this shouldn't take long."

She was careful to stand between Bart and her trunk so he couldn't see Tom's backpack. In spite of her dislike for the man, she didn't want to take a chance on his wound getting infected. Using the hydrogen peroxide was out. If it foamed on the cut, even Bart would be suspicious. With the iodine clutched in her hand, she closed the trunk, grabbed some rags, and turned back to her patient.

"You don't have to stay here with Lucas, you know," Bart said as she approached the bunk. "I'd be right happy to escort you on over to Fort Bridger."

"Thank you, but I'm quite happy right here."

"You don't have to pretend with me, Miz Daniels. I can see you and Lucas ain't exactly thrilled with each other."

Brianna set the iodine down and rolled up her sleeves. "Actually, I think he'll make a wonderful husband," she lied as she studied the bandage. One piece of adhesive tape was stuck to his chest hair, and the skin was puckered around the rest. It was going to hurt like the devil when she took it off.

"Lucas ain't no lady's man."

Brianna tried to pry up one corner of the tape with the edge of her fingernail. "Then I won't have to worry about him being unfaithful."

"Reckon you'll get mighty lonely out here with Lucas spendin' all his time at his tinkerin'."

"I'm not too worried about it. Seth seems nice enough, and I'm sure Lucas will thaw." Brianna bit her lip. The tape wasn't coming loose.

"A woman needs more'n friends." Bart shifted slightly so his hand fell against her thigh. "Reckon you and I could be real close."

Brianna took a step back. "I seriously doubt that."

"Think about it," he continued as his hand wandered up her hip to her waist. "All them nights together before we get to Fort Bridger . . . "

"I have no intention of going anywhere with you, Mr. Kelly. Now, get your hands off me."

With amazingly quick reflexes, he reached up and grabbed her wrist. "I know you came west to find a man," he said pulling her closer. "Reckon I'm as good a man as Lucas Daniels, you just don't realize it."

"What the hell is going on here?" Lucas's voice thundered through the room just as Bart's fingers made contact with her breast.

Equally startled by both, Brianna suddenly realized how she could hide the bandage from Lucas and get rid of Bart's unwanted attentions at the same time. In the blink of an eye, she grabbed the edge of the gauze and gave a sharp jerk upward.

Bart's agonized scream stopped Lucas in his tracks. He looked from Bart to Brianna and back again in utter astonishment.

"That's the problem with this new bandage," Brianna said calmly rolling it up and tossing it into the fire before Lucas could get a closer look. "It stings a bit when you take it off."

7

"When is Billy supposed to get here?" Brianna asked as she watched Seth saddle his horse.

"No way of knowing. I get ready first thing in the morning and wait."

That suited Brianna just fine. It sounded like Seth and Lucas would be busy here for a while. She'd been waiting ever since Bart Kelly left for a time when she could sneak down to the river and take a much needed bath. "How long does it take you and Billy to switch?"

"According to company rules we have two minutes," he said. "We're working on being able to pass the mochila while both horses are running."

"The mochila?"

"The mail pouch. It's a piece of leather cut to fit right over the saddle. There're four pockets called cantinas for the mail, two in the front and two in the back."

"Like saddlebags?"

"Well . . . not really. They're only about this big," he

said tracing a rectangle about the size of a business envelope in the air.

"You're kidding. How do you fit all the mail in there?"

Seth shook his head. "I don't. It's already in the mochila before I get it."

"What about the new letters you pick up?"

"New letters?"

"You know the ones people mail at Fort Laramie or even here."

"St. Jo and Sacramento are the only places mail goes into the pouch and pretty much the only places it comes out, too."

"Pretty much?"

"The three locked cantinas can be opened at the forts, but I've never actually had that happen."

"They're locked? What for?"

"I don't know." Seth rubbed his upper lip. "Military secrets maybe. Only the highest officer at the forts has the key."

"Well, then what's in the one that isn't locked?"

"Business letters."

"What, no private mail?"

He shrugged. "Who can afford five dollars an ounce?"

Brianna was disappointed. "No love letters then?"

"Nope."

"Or urgent messages summoning a wayward son to his father's deathbed?"

"I doubt it."

"I don't suppose you ever carried medicine that saved a whole town either."

Seth grinned. "Definitely not. Where did you get such crazy ideas anyway?"

"Stories I heard here and there," Brianna said vaguely. All her romantic illusions of the Pony Express had been stripped away in a few short minutes! She should have known better that to believe anything she saw on TV.

"I suppose the next thing you're going to tell me is that it isn't all that dangerous either."

"No, it's dangerous enough. Most threats we can outrun, though. The Pony Express has the fastest horses in the country."

"What if you were ambushed?"

He patted the leather sheath at his side. "That's why I carry my bowie knife."

Brianna eyed it skeptically. "How is that going to help you on horseback?"

Seth's hand was almost a blur as he whipped the knife out of the sheath and sent it flying through the air. It hit a post on the side of the corral with a solid *thwok* and stuck there quivering slightly in the bright morning sunlight.

"Oh," she said faintly.

"Some riders carry pistols, but my knife is faster."

"How did you learn that?"

"Practice. Not much else to do around here between rides."

"Do you think you could teach me?"

"I don't know. I guess so. Why?"

"A woman never knows when she's going to need protection out here. Look at Bart Kelly."

Seth chuckled. "I don't know what you did, but I doubt he'll ever bother you again. He lit out here like he had a pack of wolves on his tail."

"Maybe not, but I'd like to be ready just in case he forgets. Besides I have a feeling there are a lot more like him around."

"That's true enough. Do you want to start now?"

"No, we'll have plenty of time when you come back on the next trip. I have something else I have to do this morning. If I don't see you again before you leave, have a safe trip."

"Thanks." He flashed her a smile. "But don't worry

about me. I'm riding Lucas's fastest horse. Nothing can catch DaVinci."

"Funny, last I heard he was a turtle," Brianna murmured.

"What?"

"Never mind. Just remember what you promised to bring me."

"Don't worry. I won't forget."

"If you do, I'm going to tell Lucas it was all your fault!" Brianna said with a smile as she headed back to the cabin.

Collecting what she needed for her bath only took a few minutes. Deciding how to carry it took much longer. She'd rather neither Lucas or Seth knew was where she was going. Bathing in the open was a little daunting anyway without worrying about unwelcome company. Besides, she didn't want either of the men to see the plastic soap dish, shampoo bottle or tube of toothpaste. They might be a trifle difficult to explain.

As she looked around the room, her eyes suddenly focused on the empty cornmeal sack. The perfect solution! It took less than a minute to stow her bathing supplies and hairbrush inside. As an added precaution, she dropped the bag into the wooden water bucket. Neither Lucas or Seth would give her a second glance if she walked by with it. Heaven knows she made the trip down to the river for water often enough.

Brianna was filled with anticipation. The thought of being clean again was nearly intoxicating. One more item to add to the growing list of things she wouldn't take for granted if she ever got home again.

Seth paused in his whittling to wave when she walked by. Lucas didn't even look up as she passed the door of his workshop on the backside of the barn. Brianna felt a tiny sting of irritation. The only time he noticed her at all was when he found something to criticize.

If only she felt the same about him. Unfortunately she was all too aware of the man. He was what her friend Linda would term a hunk. She might not enjoy his irascible personality, but he was definitely easy on the eye. Much as she hated to admit it, Brianna enjoyed looking at him. He seemed oblivious of his attractiveness. So far his lack of conceit was about his only redeeming quality.

At least he hadn't talked any more about her leaving. Of course Bart Kelly would have refused to take her with him. Brianna tried to feel some remorse for the pain she'd caused him but couldn't quite manage it. At least his cut had looked clean and healthy.

Brianna dismissed Bart from her mind as she reached the river. Several large clumps of willows grew along the bank effectively screening her movement from the station. She set her bucket down near the thickest of these and checked to make sure no one could see her. Satisfied the seven-foot-high barrier was adequate, she unbraided her hair before taking off her clothes and hanging them over a bush. A bend in the river formed a natural pool, its crystalline depths so clear Brianna could practically count the pebbles on the sandy bottom.

As a kid, she'd learned there was only one way to do this, fast. Taking a deep breath she plunged into the stream and came up gasping for air. Lord but the water was cold! Well, either her teeth would start chattering or she'd get used to it. At this point she wasn't sure which.

Determined to get clean no matter what, she grabbed her shampoo off the bank. By the time she'd washed her hair Brianna had adjusted to the water and found it quite pleasant. She loved to swim and the urge to indulge herself was irresistible. Though it was her first time skinny-dipping, and she wasn't used to such cold water or a current, paddling about the small pool was rather fun.

It was on the third time around doing the back-stroke that she thought she saw a small cloud of blue mist out of the corner of her eye. But when she jerked herself upright, there was no sign of it. Could it have been something to do with whatever force had brought her here? Brianna treaded water for several minutes as she gazed hopefully toward the spot where the apparition had appeared. There was nothing to see.

With a surge of disappointment, she swam to the shore and climbed out. Drat her overactive imagination anyway. For a few blissful moments she'd forgotten the mess she was in. Now, all the joy was gone from her swim.

As she dressed, Brianna couldn't help pondering the possibility that the blue mist hadn't been her imagination, after all. If Tom Shaffer had survived whatever had happened to her, he'd surely realize a switch had been made . . . wouldn't he? His brain wouldn't be clouded by alcohol fumes like Bart Kelly's. If nothing else, Anna's clothes would tip him off, not to mention Anna herself.

Of course, there probably wasn't much Tom could do unless he could figure out what had happened to them. The chances of that were pretty slim. No, the mist had been wishful thinking on her part.

With a sigh, Brianna finished buttoning her blouse and sat down to put on her shoes. No one had said anything about her sneakers, but she'd seen Lucas eye them on more than one occasion. Not that she could do much about it anyway.

Even if Anna hadn't been wearing her only pair of shoes, they probably wouldn't have fit. Unlike the drawers, which had turned out to be surprisingly comfortable and very convenient, nineteenth century shoes were bound to be more constricting than their later counterparts. All in all Brianna was glad Anna had taken her shoes and corset with her.

By the time Brianna had secured her hair in a French

braid and filled the bucket with water, the morning was well advanced. Tucking the top of the cornmeal sack into the waistband of her skirt, she set out for the cabin. The heavy bucket of water hadn't become any lighter over the last three days, but she was starting to get used to it.

She was about halfway there when she heard Seth yell, "Rider coming in!"

Sure enough, a fast-moving speck was approaching from the West. With a surge of excitement, Brianna hurried up the hill. Imagine, she was about to actually see the famous Pony Express in action!

Even from this distance, she could sense Seth's anticipation as he paced back and forth across the yard leading his horse. His slight body seemed to vibrate with suppressed energy as he watched the rider coming down the road in a cloud of dust. Prancing about with his head high and his ears forward, DaVinci seemed just as impatient to be off. Seth was right, the horse was a magnificent animal.

"Stay out of the way."

Brianna jumped as Lucas strode past her. She hadn't even seen him come out of the barn. She frowned in irritation. How like him to assume she wouldn't know enough to stay back. One of these days she was going to stuff that superior attitude of his right down his throat.

Brianna's annoyance was forgotten a moment later. The sound of pounding hooves filled the air as rider and horse thundered into the yard. In the blink of an eye, Billy was out of the saddle and jerking the leather mochila off the back of his horse before the animal even stopped.

DaVinci was already moving when Seth threw the mailbag over his own mount and vaulted into the saddle. The horse took off at a high lope with Seth leaning out over his neck like a jockey.

Brianna watched them disappear down the road with a satisfied smile. In spite of her earlier disillusionment, the Pony Express clearly deserved the mystique that surrounded it in her time. Not even television could do justice the incredible scene she had just witnessed.

Her faith in the legend fully restored, she turned to Lucas and Billy with her eyes shining. "That was wonderful."

Neither man paid any attention to her as Lucas snapped his watch shut and slipped it back into his pocket. "A little slow today. Took almost a minute and a half."

"I know. I'm afraid Copernicus is going lame," Billy said. "The last mile or so he's been favoring his left front leg." Billy's voice was an interesting combination of Southern drawl and Western twang.

"Let's have a look." Lucas knelt down and ran his hands down the slender foreleg. Then he picked up the hoof and closely examined the bottom of it. "Looks like he bruised the frog," Lucas said studying the soft center part of the foot. "Better get him cooled down before we worry about it though." He took the reins from Billy and led the animal around until its sides stopped heaving with each labored breath and the lather disappeared from its hide. "How was your trip?"

"Not bad. Saw a Sioux hunting party between South Pass and Rock Creek, but they were pretty easy to outrun."

Brianna waited patiently, thinking Lucas would eventually get around to introducing her to Billy. It wasn't until he took Copernicus into the barn for a rub-down, and Billy disappeared into the cabin that she realized he wasn't going to.

Ohhhh, that man was aggravating. Hefting the bucket of water again, she followed Billy into the cabin. He was small like Seth but dark-haired and stocky rather than slender and blond. Right now he was staring around in apparent amazement. Good, it was about time someone noticed all the house cleaning she'd done. "Hello," she said. "I'm Brianna Daniels."

"That's what I figured. Where's all my gear?"

"Lucas moved it out to the barn."

He gave her an unfriendly look. "What for?"

"Well . . . er . . . I think it had something to do with me being here. He wasn't too pleased."

"I didn't expect him to be, but you've had three days to change his mind."

"How am I supposed to do that?"

"That's your problem."

"Seth didn't seem to think so," she snapped.

"Probably not, but then Seth is a sucker for a pretty face."

"Was that supposed to be a compliment?"

Billy shrugged. "If you want to take it as one. Lucas hasn't sent you on your way so I suppose you can cook."

"He hasn't complained." *Well, not much anyway,* she added to herself.

"Good. Getting you here cost me nearly a month's pay."

"I'll do my best to make sure you aren't disappointed," Brianna said sarcastically.

"I hope so." He turned and stalked out the door. "I hate to throw money away."

Brianna glared after him. What a jerk! He was asking for a swift kick in the backside, and if the little pipsqueak wasn't careful she'd give it to him.

Shaking her head with disgust, she put the cornmeal sack in her trunk and turned her attention to fixing lunch. One thing for sure, compared to Billy, Lucas was a peach!

8

July 15, 1995

"I still can't believe I actually brought you forward in time!" Scott said with a chortle as the pickup bounced along the rutted dirt road.

Anna gripped the seat nervously. "I have a little trouble accepting it myself."

"Let's just hope you can figure out how to send her back. There's the balloon over there." Tom pointed to the south. "You can just see the gondola."

"Oh, yeah, I see it. Hang on."

Anna gasped and grabbed Tom's arm as Scott guided the pick-up out across the sagebrush. Tom covered her hand with his and gave her a reassuring smile. Everything must be terrifyingly strange. There wasn't much he could do about it except stay with her until she got back where she belonged. He owed her that much at least.

"DNA!" Scott said suddenly as he pulled up next to the deflated balloon and stopped the pickup.

"What?"

"Anna and Brianna, their DNA has to be nearly the same."

"They do look a lot alike," Tom said doubtfully.

"Genetically they must be almost identical, you know like twins. That's how they got caught in the time warp. It formed a magnetic field on both sides and they were pulled in like two halves of the same person. I'm not real sure why they switched places, but the power surge when they passed through each other is what blew all the circuitry."

"They passed through each other?"

"Well, I think so, anyway." Scott glanced at Anna. "You do have all your own parts don't you?"

She looked down at her hands. "I-I guess so."

"If there was a piece of you that belonged to someone else I'm sure you'd have known immediately," Tom said comfortingly. "Scott, do you have any idea where Brianna Daniels is?"

"Only that she's somewhere in 1860. Even if I knew where they were when they switched, she would have moved by now."

"So we have no way of locating her?"

"I know where she is," Anna said suddenly. "She's at Split Rock Station. There's no place else for her to go."

Tom nodded. "That's true. In 1860 this was probably pretty much all wilderness. Anyway she'd probably stick around pretty close hoping to find a way back."

"If I could get some of her DNA, I could program the computer to find her," Scott said thoughtfully. "In fact, it might help focus the time warp."

"Brianna's windbreaker is in the gondola. Could you get enough off of that?"

"We probably could if we took it to the state crime lab in Cheyenne. They've got all kinds of specialized equipment."

Tom sighed. "If we could get anybody to believe us, which I doubt, the whole investigation would be so tied up in red tape we'd die of old age before anything happened."

"Yeah, I guess we're on our own."

"Have you decided what you're going to do about your parents?"

"No sweat. The whole family is supposed to leave in the morning for a week-long pack trip in the mountains." Scott flashed them a grin as he opened the door and jumped out of the pickup. "After I get done with the ranch records, my dad will not only leave me home, he'll probably ground me for six months. Hey, there's a scorch mark on the side of your basket. I must have dipped into the infrared spectrum when I created the time warp."

Anna gave Tom a bewildered look as Scott slammed the door and went to inspect the gondola. "Do you know what he's talking about?"

"Not always," Tom said ruefully as he opened his door. "But I suspect he's used to that. I don't imagine many people are smart enough to understand him."

"Do you think he can really get me back where I belong?"

Tom stepped out of the pickup and reached in to help her. "I don't know, but he's the only chance we've got."

Half an hour later, the balloon was nearly ready to load, and Scott and Tom had solidified their plans. The discovery of keys in Brianna's windbreaker gave Tom the idea of going to her home to look for something that would give Scott the DNA he needed. Anna stood silently staring at the picture on Brianna's driver's license.

"Something wrong?" Tom asked.

"Not really. It's just that she looks so much like me." Anna looked up at Tom. "Scott's right. Brianna could be my twin."

"She's taller and has a touch of red in her hair."

Scott leaned on the gondola. "Probably got better nutrition when she was growing up. On the whole people are bigger now."

"There's my brother," Tom said as he spotted the yellow pickup coming down the road. "Looks like they brought two vehicles so the chase crew wouldn't have to ride in the back."

Anna watched the approaching cloud of dust uncertainly. "What are you going to tell your brother?"

"I don't know yet. I'm not sure he'll understand. Chuck doesn't have much imagination."

"Oh." Anna wasn't quite sure what that had to do with it, but then she was confused about everything else, too.

Though Chuck Shaffer was short and stocky where his younger brother was tall and slender, he had the same curly red hair and easy smile. Anna liked him on sight.

The feeling seemed to be mutual for he tried to include her in the conversation as the chase crew loaded the balloon. It was nearly impossible with Scott's incessant questions and Tom's technical answers. At last Chuck gave her an apologetic wink and admitted she was seeing firsthand why his wife refused to come with them.

At last the balloon was loaded, and the members of the chase crew split between the two pickups. As Chuck started the yellow pickup, Scott waved cheerfully.

"Good-bye. See you tomorrow, Tom. Remember, don't come until after one-thirty or so."

"I will. And I'll find the information you need by then."

"Tomorrow?" Chuck draped his wrist over the steering wheel and looked at his brother in surprise. "Tom, we're scheduled to be in Spearfish by eight-thirty tonight."

"I'm not going to South Dakota with you."

"What? You're supposed to fly tomorrow."

"Pat can do it."

Chuck stared at him. "I don't get it. You moved mountains so we could spend this summer hitting all the balloon rallies and suddenly Pat can do it?"

"Something's come up."

"Something's come . . . Christ, Tom, ever since you were a kid all you've talked about was flying balloons. While the rest of us were chasing girls and playing computer games on TV, you had your nose stuck in Lucas Daniel's diary." Suddenly his eyes widened as he's gaze dropped to the woman between them. "Brianna Daniels. That's it isn't it?" He shook his head as he threw the pickup into gear and headed down the road. "I suppose she's related to him."

"His great-great-granddaughter."

"It figures."

Tom squeezed Anna's hand. "I can't explain, Chuck, at least not yet."

"No, I don't suppose you can," Chuck muttered sarcastically. "I've never known you to think with your gonads before."

"That was uncalled for." There was a thread of steel in Tom's quiet voice.

Chuck glanced at Anna. "Yeah I guess it was. I'm sorry, Brianna. It has nothing to do with you."

The tension between the two brothers eased somewhat during the long drive back to Riverton, but it was obvious Chuck didn't approve when he dropped them off at the college parking lot. "We'll be back in one week," Chuck said as Tom pulled his duffel bag from the back of the pickup. "You damn well better have this resolved by then."

"I'm sorry your brother's mad," Anna whispered as Chuck drove away.

"He'll get over it. Anyway, he's the least of our worries right now. Let's hope that's Brianna's car over there."

"How will you know?" Anna asked as they approached the only vehicle in the parking lot.

"The keys will fit . . . just like that," he said with a grin as the lock clicked open. "Now to find her house."

Anna said nothing as they climbed into the car and Tom reached over to fastened her seat belt. It wasn't until he finished studying the city map he'd pulled from his duffel bag that she spoke.

"How do you know about Lucas?"

"I read his journal when I was a kid." Tom smiled as he reached down and started the engine. "He was one of my heroes."

It took less than fifteen minutes to locate Brianna's house from the address listed on her driver's license. "This is it," he said as they pulled up in front of an odd metal structure on the edge of town.

"This is a house?" Anna asked skeptically. Only the beds of flowers that bloomed in profusion amid the short thick grass were even remotely familiar.

"A trailer actually. Good thing she lives alone. We'd have a tough time explaining any of this to a roommate."

Anna thought it looked more like a railroad car than a house. Brianna's home was as foreign as everything else in this crazy world. Even Tom's words made no sense. Suddenly it was all too much. She bit her lip to keep it from trembling.

"Hey," Tom said softly as he reached over and ran a finger gently down her cheek. "It'll be all right."

She turned tearful eyes to him. "Are you sure of that?"

"Positive. Look, you're hungry, tired, and completely disoriented. What you need is a nice hot bath, followed by a good meal, and a long nap." He smiled. "Trust me."

It was impossible not to respond to that warm, friendly smile. "All right. I-I'm sorry to be such a coward."

"In your position I'd probably be scared out of my

head." He gave her hand a squeeze. "Let's go inside and see what we can find to eat."

Tom went through three keys before he found one that unlocked the door, and they stepped inside.

Anna looked around in amazement. In spite of its odd appearance outside it was surprisingly luxurious with thick carpets on the floor and wood paneling on the walls. "Is Brianna rich?"

Tom dropped his duffel bag and headed forward into the kitchen. "Not if she lives in a trailer, though I'll have to admit this is a pretty nice one. Darn, wouldn't you know it?" he said peering into the refrigerator in disgust. "Nothing but skim milk, yogurt, and fruit. Which would you rather have a banana or a nectarine?"

"I-I don't know."

Tom glanced over his shoulder. "Oh, yeah, I guess you wouldn't. Here, have one of each." He thrust the fruit into her hand then grabbed a nectarine for himself. "Tell you what. I'll get you started on your bath, then go out and get us some real food."

"You're leaving?"

"Not for very long. Come on, I'll bet the bathroom's in the back."

Tom's guess proved correct, and Anna soon discovered something fully as astounding as vehicles that moved at incredible speeds, Brianna's bathroom. She thought lights that clicked on and off with the touch of a finger was the most exciting thing she'd ever seen until Tom showed her the faucets that produced hot and cold water instantly. "You mean everybody has this whenever they want?"

"Pretty much, though some people prefer showers." He added some bubble bath to the water running into the bathtub. "There, that should make up for the fact that it's such a small tub."

Anna refrained from telling him she had no idea

what the bubbles were for nor that she'd never bathed in such a big tub.

"Brianna's bedroom is right through there," he said pointing to a door on the other side of the bathroom. "You can find clothes in there."

Anna hesitated. "A-are you sure she won't mind?"

"I don't see that you've got much choice. Besides, she's probably using yours."

"I suppose."

"Go ahead and take your bath. I should be back fairly soon."

Anna fought the urge to run screaming after him when he left and concentrated instead on how long it had been since she'd had a real bath. Almost a hundred and fifty years she thought with wry smile, and darned if she couldn't feel every grubby second of it.

She luxuriated in her bubble bath until her skin started to wrinkle. When she heard Tom return, she dried off and went into Brianna's room. The sheer quantity of clothes astounded her. Anna, who had never had more than three or four dresses at one time, suddenly had an entire closet full of choices. It didn't take long to discover most of them were too tight even with her corset.

At last she found a brightly colored full skirt with some sort of expandable waistline and a simple white blouse. It didn't quite reach her ankles but wasn't nearly as scandalous as some of the clothing she'd seen women wearing in town.

Anna's own underwear was obviously inappropriate, but Brianna's was as confusing as everything else had been all day. Though the style was bizarre, she knew what to do with the legless drawers. The other garment she found baffled her completely. From the shape it was obviously meant to fit over her breasts somehow but she couldn't get all the straps and hooks figured out, at least not so it fit properly. After several minutes of frustration, she gave up and donned her own shift in disgust.

Anna had just done up the last blouse button and picked up Brianna's hairbrush when she heard the front door open.

"Bree?" came an unfamiliar feminine voice. "I stopped to see how your balloon ride went. "Oh . . . "

Anna winced when she heard the surprise in the woman's tone. She'd obviously seen Tom. Heaven only knew what she'd do about a strange man in her friend's house.

"Well," the woman said after a long moment. "Obviously it went just fine. Er . . . where's Brianna."

"Taking a bath. Linda isn't it?"

"Right and you're Tom. We met last night." There was an uncomfortable silence, then, "I'm sorry, I didn't intend to intrude. It didn't occur to me Brianna might . . . I mean she never . . . er . . . Look, just tell Brianna I stopped by will you?"

"Sure."

"She knows I'll be out of town till next week. I'll give her a call when I get back."

"Ok."

Oh . . . and Tom?

"Yes?"

"Tell her she owes me one."

"I think we both do."

There was a feminine laugh and the sound of a door closing before Tom's muttered, "And wherever Brianna is, I'm sure she agrees wholeheartedly."

"Who was that?" Anna asked stepping into the hallway.

"Brianna's friend Linda. Indirectly, she's the cause of all this. If she hadn't convinced Brianna to trade places . . . " His voice trailed off, and he stared at Anna as though he'd never seen her before.

"Wh-what's the matter? Do I have something on wrong?"

Tom felt as though a giant fist had hit him square in the chest. "No, I just wasn't expecting . . . You look very nice." Nice didn't even begin to describe how she looked. Breathtaking was closer to it. Even with damp hair hanging around her like a curtain, she was beautiful. Suddenly the object in her hand came into sharp focus. Brianna's hairbrush.

"Anna, have you used that brush?"

"Not yet, why."

"Because I think we just found the DNA Scott wanted."

Anna stared at the brush blankly. "We did?"

"He can get what he needs from the hair in her brush." He smiled at Anna's skeptical look. "Never mind. We'll take this out to Scott tomorrow. In the meantime, you can use my brush."

"All right."

The look she gave him made Tom feel like he'd just handed her the world on a silver platter. "Let's eat," he said gruffly.

Anna wasn't particularly impressed with the hamburgers Tom had brought back, but the milkshake was an instant hit. The afternoon and evening passed quickly for both of them. In spite of the strange circumstances that had brought them together, there was no constraint between them. They shared the memories of their pasts, and their dreams for the future. By unspoken agreement, they avoided any mention of the man that stood between them.

At ten o'clock Tom reluctantly decreed it was time for bed. After settling Anna in Brianna's bedroom, he retrieved a sheet and blanket from the linen closet and made a bed for himself on the couch. Sleep overcame him quickly and he fell asleep with a smile on his face.

Anna's screams brought him awake instantly two hours later. With his heart pounding, he slid into his pants, and raced back to the bedroom. "Anna what is it?"

"Tom?" her voice quavered through the darkness.

Three strides took him to the bed. "I'm here, Anna," he said switching on the bedside lamp.

"Oh, Tom, it was awful." She shuddered and covered her face. "The blue mist, and Bart Kelly and the balloon. . . . "

"Shh." Tom sat on the edge of the bed and pulled her into his arms. "It was a dream."

"If only it were," she sobbed. "You don't know how bad I wanted to wake up in my bedroll under the wagon. Instead, the first thing I saw when I opened my eyes was that." She pointed to the lighted dial of Brianna's digital alarm. "This is worse than my nightmare because it's real. Tom, I'm scared."

He hugged her tighter. "I know, but it will work out."

"How can you be so sure?"

"I've read your husband's diary. You have a long, full life ahead of you."

"I'd forgotten that," Anna said putting her arms around his waist and pressing her face against his naked chest as though she was afraid he'd leave. "Tom?" she asked after a moment. "Wh-what did Lucas say about his marriage?"

Tom was surprised by the flash of jealousy that knifed through him. Anna and Lucas Daniels had loved each other deeply, he reminded himself. It was only natural that she'd wonder. "You probably know the answer to that better than I do."

"I've never even met Lucas."

"What?"

"It's all so embarrassing."

A feeling of unreality settled over Tom as he listened to Anna's story. She was an unwanted mail-order bride uncertain of her reception by a man who didn't even know she was coming. If she stayed in 1995, Lucas Daniels would never know the difference. Tom pushed the tempting thought away as soon as it occurred.

"Lucas may not have sent for you, but he loved you once you got there. That I'm sure of. Don't worry, we'll get you back somehow."

"Don't leave me."

"No, I won't," Tom said lying down next to her and cushioning her face against his shoulder. "I'll be here as long as you need me."

He lay there with her nestled against him all through the interminable night. He knew it was wrong, but no woman had ever felt so right in his arms before. It was ironic, he'd spent years looking for a someone who affected him this way. Now he was in danger of losing his heart to a woman who belonged to a man she'd never met, a man Tom would never betray.

9

July 1860

"You didn't stay at the station very long," Lucas said as Billy came into the barn. There had barely been time to finish doctoring the injured hoof.

"No. How's Copernicus?"

"I pulled this out of his foot." He held up a long sharp cactus spine. "Must have been on the road somewhere. I may have to put a poultice on it, but he should be all right in a couple of days."

"Good."

"Your gear's over there." Lucas nodded toward the back of the barn as he picked up the currycomb and started brushing the horse. "Seth moved it into the tack room."

"Is that where he slept?"

"Yes."

"Jesus. Looks like Bart Kelly was right."

"Oh? Where did you see him?"

"He got to Green River last night. All he could talk about was the devil-woman you married."

The shadow of a smile crossed Lucas's face. "Somehow I don't think that would bother her much."

"He said she tried to kill him."

"Wouldn't blame her if she had. I was about to give him a good thrashing myself."

"Why?"

"I didn't appreciate what he was trying to do." Lucas grinned suddenly. "I'm still not sure what she did, but Brianna took care of the problem without the least assistance from me or anyone else. She's not a woman to trifle with."

Billy sounded surprised. "You like her?"

"Like her?" The rhythmic movement of the currycomb slowed as Lucas considered this. He admired her spunk, and loved her biscuits, but Brianna herself was like a burr under the saddle. He was constantly aware of her, and it irritated the hell out of him. "I don't know as I'd go that far."

"She sure took over in a hurry," Billy grumbled. "Can't believe I have to sleep in the barn!"

"You're the one who decided I needed a wife."

"What's that got to do with it?"

Lucas raised a brow. "It didn't occur to you that my *wife* and I might want some privacy at night?"

Billy stared at him blankly for several seconds then his face reddened slightly. "Oh. I hadn't thought of that."

"You hadn't thou . . . What did you expect me to do with a wife, for God's sake?"

"You don't have to be so mad. I mean it's not like she's ugly or anything."

"I don't give a damn what she looks like, I don't want a wife. It wasn't very pleasant to suddenly find myself married to a complete stranger."

"Seth was the one who wrote the letters and set it all up," Billy said.

"He said it was your idea."

Billy had the grace to look embarrassed. "I was just joking. He thought we needed to buy you a cookbook, and I said we'd be better off getting you a wife who could do the cooking for you. The next thing I knew, he'd sent off for a mail-order bride."

"You paid half the money."

"Well, sure but Seth is the one who answered her letters. He convinced her to come, not me."

The currycomb came to a complete stop. "Letters? She wrote to you?"

"Er . . . sort of. She thought she was writing to you. Anyway, Seth decided she sounded like just the sort of wife you should have."

"Oh? I'm almost afraid to ask what you thought qualified her to be my wife."

"Mostly cause she said she could cook, but she sounded real sweet tempered and amiable, too. We both figured you'd like that bein' as how you don't want nobody bothering you when you're working." Billy looked pensive. "Her letters made her sound kind of shy. I thought she'd be, I don't know, easy going, I guess."

"Either you two did a poor job of interpreting what she said, or she lied outright," Lucas said sardonically. "I've never met a less peaceful female in my life."

"I know. The first thing she did was throw Seth and me out of the station!"

"Actually, I did that."

"What for?"

"I wasn't too pleased with the two of you. If I'd known you'd been writing to her in my name, I'd probably have dumped your gear in the river." He glared at Billy and shook his head. "I always thought you were good at reading character. Easy going. Lord, you couldn't have been more wrong if you tried."

"Well, read her letters and see what you think!"

For a moment, Lucas was tempted, but then his better sense intruded. He knew Brianna Daniels as well as he wanted to. He was already spending too much of his valuable time thinking about her, wondering where she was or what she was doing. The last thing he needed was to see into her soul. "There's no point in it. She won't be staying long."

"I thought . . . "

"I know what you and Seth thought, but I'm not falling in with your plans. I won't be manipulated by a couple of striplings barely old enough to shave."

"But where will she go?"

"Back home probably. I really don't give a damn."

"Lucas, it took her almost two months to get here!"

"You should have thought of that before you sent for her."

"But you can't make her go back home just like that. None of this was her fault."

The expression on Billy's face surprised Lucas almost as much his words. Billy, the tough, hard-bitten cynic who didn't need anybody or anything looked . . . stricken. What the hell was in those letters?

"I'm not sending her anywhere," Lucas said gruffly. "But it's obvious she doesn't belong on the frontier. Everything is a struggle for her. She's like a fish in the desert here, helpless. You should have seen her getting water the first day." He shook his head as he went back to currying the horse. "It won't be long before she packs up her trunk and leaves on her own." Lucas wondered why the thought didn't bring him any joy.

Brianna set the table for lunch and waited. No one came in. It was very unusual. The men were always there ready to eat before she even got the meal on the table.

Where were they? After fifteen minutes she decided to go looking.

Billy was nowhere to be seen but she found Lucas in his workshop at the back of the barn. Brianna entered cautiously. Seth had told her more than once Lucas didn't like to be disturbed when he was in the middle of something. As her eyes adjusted to the dim light she saw he was seated on a high stool bent over a workbench. Suddenly there was a small flare and a puff of smoke.

"Damn!" Lucas muttered.

Curious, Brianna stepped closer and peered at the work bench. The surface appeared to be cluttered with a variety of materials. She only caught a glimpse before Lucas turned and pinned her with an irritated glare.

"What?"

"I-it's lunchtime," she said backing away hastily. "I can bring you a plate if you're busy."

Lucas looked at his workbench and sighed. "No, I'm not getting anywhere here." He stood up and stretched. "I didn't realize it was so late."

"Do you know where Billy is?"

"No. Last I saw of him he was headed to the tack room to read Seth's letter."

"Seth left him a letter?"

"That's how they communicate." Lucas flipped a couple of switches and started pulling wires out. "Seth started it right at the beginning when he decided he wanted to know Billy better. It's the only way since they're never here at the same time."

"I hadn't thought of that. They're not much alike are they?"

"Nope. In fact they're almost complete opposites." Apparently satisfied his work area was secured, Lucas headed out the door.

"Billy's from the South?"

"Virginia. I can't tell you anything else about him other than his last name is Fry and he's an orphan."

"Is that why he's so . . . difficult?"

"I don't know for sure. He's always suspicious of anything new. I take it the two of you didn't exactly hit it off."

"About as well as you and I did."

Startled by her frank answer, he gave her a sidelong glance as she fell into step beside him. "I guess that proves you can't judge by first impressions. Look how well we get along now."

"Do we? I hadn't noticed."

Lucas grinned in spite of himself. "What happened to the woman who promised to make my life easier without me ever knowing she was around?"

"Still keeping her end of the bargain."

"Somehow I don't see how sarcastic remarks are supposed to make me comfortable."

Brianna gave him an innocent look. "You don't? But I thought you'd enjoy conversing in your own language."

He laughed and shook his head. "I suppose you think you can beat me at it, too."

"It's a distinct possibility." Brianna smiled as he laughed again. The deep rich sound gave her an unexpected warm feeling inside. This was a side of Lucas Daniels she'd never seen before, but one she found she liked very much.

"Well, well," he murmured after his chuckles subsided. "It appears you made more of an impression than you realized."

Brianna followed the line of his gaze and blinked in surprise. Billy was coming up the trail from the river with two brimming buckets in his hands. "Where did he get that extra bucket?"

"From the barn. We have a lot of equipment stored there."

"I don't suppose there's a barrel by any chance?"

"Yes, three in fact."

Brianna rolled her eyes. "It never occurred to any of you to use one for water?"

"We never needed it."

"Don't you find it kind of inconvenient to never have more than one bucket of water at a time?"

"No, but then none of us uses as much as you do either."

"I don't doubt that," Brianna said a little stung. "But then I don't think cleaning was ever much a priority around here either."

"That's true enough. I suppose you'll want me to set up a water barrel for you."

"Heaven's no! I wouldn't want you to put yourself out," she said sarcastically.

"Good, I see you're developing the right attitude after all."

Brianna glanced up at him in irritation and saw his lips twitch. He was teasing her! A reluctant smile tugged at the corner of her mouth. "That's one point for you," she conceded.

"Then we're even."

They grinned at each other. In that one unguarded moment their eyes met and something unexpected flared between them. It was warm, wonderful, and completely unwelcome. Brianna was the first to pull her gaze away. "I'll go dish up lunch," she murmured hurrying into the cabin.

Shaken, Brianna leaned against the wall just inside the door. What was the matter with her? Lucas Daniels was her great-great-grandfather for God's sake. It was unthinkable to let him affect her this way. Yet when she tried to dismiss the attraction, somehow all she could think of were those gorgeous gray eyes of his. She simply had to find some way to remind herself who he was.

By the time Billy and Lucas came in several minutes later, she had herself well in hand. She thanked Billy for the water and was surprised when he blushed. He didn't seem the type to be embarrassed by female attention.

"I brought you a newspaper, Lucas" he said, handing it to him. "It's from last summer but I thought you might like to see it anyway." Though he was nonchalant, Brianna had the distinct impression that it was a peace offering of some sort, just like the water had been.

Lucas set it in the middle of the table and sat down to eat.

"I'll take a look at it later. What's the news from Green River?"

It wasn't long before Brianna had finished eating and was totally bored, so she picked up the newspaper. Anything was better than hearing about people she didn't know, even news that was a hundred and thirty years old. She didn't realize it would be like stepping into history. In a surprisingly short time she was so engrossed she didn't notice the odd looks she was receiving from her companions.

"I'd have thought you'd find that news a little stale," Lucas said finally, breaking through her concentration. "That paper came out long before you left home."

You'd flip if you knew how long before, Brianna thought to herself. "It's got some pretty interesting articles in it."

"For instance?"

"Well, there's a story about a transcontinental railroad for one thing."

"They've been talking about that for years."

"They have? Er . . . I mean I know they have but it's an exciting thought."

"Maybe, but it would be next to impossible to build."

Brianna felt herself on shaky ground as she flipped through the paper. On the one hand she knew too much. On the other she didn't know nearly enough. Suddenly an article caught her attention. "Here's one that will interest you, Lucas."

"Oh?"

"John Wise, world-famous balloonist, flew his balloon from St. Louis to Lake Ontario in nineteen hours and 50 minutes," she read. "Though a gale forced Mr. Wise to land before reaching his original destination, his twelve hundred mile trip proves once and for all that long distance balloon flight is possible."

"Damn fool," Lucas muttered.

Brianna looked up in surprise. "What?"

"I said the man's a damn fool. Only an idiot would go up in one of those death-traps."

"You can't be serious."

"Of course I am. They're too unpredictable to be practical."

"Haven't you ever considered how exciting it would be to pilot one?"

"I wouldn't go up in a balloon if you paid me a thousand dollars," Lucas said adamantly as he scooted his chair back and stood up. "Now if you'll excuse me, I have work to do."

Staring after him in open-mouthed shock, Brianna watched him stomp angrily out the door. "What's the matter with him?"

Billy grinned. "Reckon you hit his sore spot."

"I did?"

"Yup, he doesn't like to be reminded of his weakness."

"What weakness?"

"He's scared to death of heights. There ain't a man anywhere less likely to fly a balloon than Lucas Daniels."

10

"*Thank you, Billy.*" *Brianna* watched him set a full bucket of water down next to the new water barrel.

"Uh huh."

Brianna sighed as he walked away. Thank goodness Seth would be back tomorrow. Three days with Billy were plenty. She couldn't figure him out. He was surly and uncommunicative, but she hadn't had to carry one bucket of water since he'd been here.

She pushed her hair back from her face and gazed toward the corral where Lucas was working with the horses. What was going to happen to him during the next few years? She'd been mulling it over almost constantly for the last two days and was no closer to the answer than before. Was it possible Lucas would overcome his phobia of heights and pilot a balloon over enemy lines during a war he thought senseless? Not likely. But then, nothing else fit either.

All the evidence pointed to the probability that Lucas Daniels, at least *this* Lucas Daniels, was not her great-great-grandfather. Brianna wondered for the dozenth time how there could be another one and where that left her. If only she knew more about Anna and her married life. None of it made any sense.

As she watched Lucas lead four horses through the gate, she felt the familiar tightening in her stomach. Why did he have to be so damned attractive? Not for the first time she wondered if the idea that there was no blood relationship between them might be based more on wishful thinking than cold hard facts. It was quite possible that something might happen in the next year or two that would change his political views. It was even conceivable that he'd lied about his hair color in his journal for some reason.

Her thoughts suddenly focused on the present as Lucas brought the horses up to the station and tied them to the hitching rack. "What are you doing?" she asked in surprise.

"What does it look like?"

"Like you're leaving the horses right next to the house."

"Smart lady," he said sarcastically as he finished tying them up.

"They're just outside the window, Lucas."

He glanced at the open shutters. "So?"

"Think of all the flies that'll come inside."

"Lord, woman, you do worry about the damnedest things," he muttered walking away.

"But it's so unsanitary."

Lucas just shook his head and continued back to the barn leaving Brianna to stare at the horses in bewilderment. She had never seen a wagon on the premises yet all four horses had collars around their necks and heavy straps down their backs. What was he doing?

In a few minutes Lucas was back with the rest of the harness straps slung over his shoulders and arms.

The last thing Brianna wanted to do was ask a stupid question about something she should know but her curiosity was overwhelming. "I didn't know you had a wagon," she said cautiously.

"I don't. These are for the stagecoach."

"What stagecoach?"

"The one that's coming down the road."

Startled, Brianna looked over her shoulder and saw a cloud of dust approaching from the southeast. "The stage stops here?"

"Just long enough to change horses."

"Can I watch?"

He shrugged the heavy load of straps off his shoulder. "Suit yourself. Just make sure you . . . "

" . . . stay out of the way," she said mimicking his deep voice. "Don't worry, Lucas. I wouldn't think of doing anything stupid. If the driver is like the rest of the men around here he'd probably just as soon run over me as not."

The corner of Lucas's mouth twitched, but he said nothing as he turned his full attention to the horses. By the time the stage rumbled into the yard, he had everything hooked up and ready to go.

"Ten minute stop," the driver called out as he brought the horses to a standstill. "Howdy, Lucas."

"Morning, Jack. Any deliveries for me today."

"As a matter of fact there is." He tied the reins to the brake lever then turned around and pulled a wooden crate from the roof of the stage. "Pittsburgh glass-works," he read. "Reckon this is what you've been waiting for."

Lucas's eyes lit up and his face broke into a smile as he reached up to take the box. "Finally!"

Brianna blinked in surprise. It was the first time she'd seen him truly happy, and the difference was astonishing. He looked almost boyish in his enthusiasm.

What in heaven's name could he be getting from a glass-works that would affect him so?

"Only ten minutes?" The feminine voice brought Brianna's head around with a jerk.

An army officer was just stepping down from the stage. "That's what the driver said, ma'am," he said turning back to help the woman alight.

"Oh, dear."

Brianna could hardly believe her eyes. The woman looked like she had just walked off a movie set. The skirt of her dress stood out from her impossibly tiny waist like a bell. In spite of the heat she wore long sleeves, white gloves, and a stylish bonnet covered with artificial flowers. When she saw Brianna, her eyes widened slightly, then she hurried over.

For the first time since her arrival, Brianna was uncomfortably aware of how badly her clothes fit, and how odd she must appear. It was funny how having another woman around made one fashion conscious.

"Where is your convenience?" the woman whispered.

"Convenience?" Brianna looked at her blankly. It was quite obvious the lady was in some distress. Then, suddenly she understood. "It's over there," Brianna said nodding toward the privy.

"Thank you." The huge bell-shaped skirt made it appear the woman was floating over the ground as she hurried up the path to the outhouse. Brianna watched in amazement, wondering how all of it fit into the stagecoach and still left room for the other passengers.

"Is there a dipper for the water?"

"What?" Brianna tore her gaze away from the retreating figure. The three male passengers were standing near the bucket of water. "Oh, I . . . sure. I'll get it for you."

When she returned, she set all four of Lucas's cups on the bench and handed the dipper to the first man.

To her utter surprise and complete revulsion they all ignored the cups and drank from the dipper, one after another.

As soon as the woman rejoined them, the men tipped their hats. Then one-by-one, unobtrusively disappeared up the path to the outhouse while the two women pretended not to notice.

"Would you like some water?" Brianna asked politely.

"Yes, thank you." The other woman took the proffered cup and sipped the water delicately. "I haven't seen many women out here."

"Neither have I," Brianna said truthfully. "In fact you're the first."

"It must be horribly lonely."

"Well, it has taken some getting used to."

"I suppose being with your husband is worth it though."

"I guess so."

"I'm going to join my husband at Fort Bridger." She took another sip of water. "We'd only been married a short time before he was sent West. I was excited to come, but I had no idea it would be like this."

Brianna felt a flash of sympathy. "There are more people at the fort. I expect you'll get settled in soon enough. Besides, think how wonderful it will be to see your husband again."

"My husband isn't like yours," she said wistfully looking at Lucas over the rim of her cup.

"Nobody's husband is like Lucas. He's one of a kind."

"I don't blame you braving the trip for him."

"I didn't have much choice."

"Everybody back on the stage," the driver yelled as he climbed back onto the box.

"Oh, dear. Time to go already?" The woman set the cup down on the bench with a sigh. "It seems like we just stopped."

"At least you haven't much farther to go."

"That's true. Thank you for the drink."

"You're welcome." On an impulse, Brianna put her hand on the other woman's arm. "And good luck," she said softly.

"I . . . thank you." With a fleeting smile, she climbed back onto the stage.

Brianna watched it lumber out of the yard with an odd feeling of sadness. Life was tough out here, especially for women. As she bent over to pick up the cups the clink of metal drew her attention. There were several coins in the bottom of one. "Well for heaven's sake!"

"What's the matter?" Lucas asked.

"They left money in the cup."

"Probably thought they had to pay for the water. Most stage stops charge for food and drink."

"Food? Were they expecting something to eat, too?"

Lucas shrugged. "I have no idea. I wouldn't worry about it if I were you."

"How often does the stage come?"

"Twice a week. The Westbound stage comes through on Wednesday and the Eastbound on Thursday."

"So there'll be another one tomorrow?"

"That's right."

Brianna smiled and rattled the coins in the cup. "Good, I'll be ready for it." With that she turned and walked into the cabin completely oblivious to the look on Lucas's face.

She's leaving tomorrow on the stage. Lucas thought and wondered why it didn't give him any satisfaction. He'd been waiting for her to leave since the day she arrived. Yet now that the time had come, he had a strangely hollow feeling.

It was just the thought of losing his cook that bothered him, he told himself as he led the horses into the barn. So what if it was nice having another adult around to talk to? He'd survived with only Billy and Seth before.

Irritated with himself, Lucas removed the harnesses and hung them on the wall. He knew the pennies in Brianna's cup wouldn't even come close to paying for her ticket home, but if she was ready to go he'd gladly loan her the rest. Hell, he'd even give her the ticket just to get her out of his hair once and for all. He was looking forward to the peace and quiet her absence would bring.

He wouldn't think about eyes the color of the summer sky or a lilting laugh that made him feel warm inside. He'd forget the exchange two days ago that had turned the blood hot in his veins and brought forbidden images to his mind. She was a woman like all others, deceitful, conniving, and completely untrustworthy. Don't waste precious time wondering where she'd go or what she'd do. She wasn't worth it.

Determined to put her from his mind completely, Lucas turned his thoughts to his long awaited shipment from the Pittsburgh glassworks. He was anxious to see if his idea was going to work. There would be time to unpack the crate and maybe even set up an experiment as soon as he finished with the horses.

Lucas successfully distracted himself right up until he walked into the tack room where Billy and Seth now slept. His head was so filled with plans of what he was going to do that he hardly noticed the papers he moved out of the way to get the currycomb. He gave them only a cursory glance until his name written at the top suddenly came into sharp focus.

It took him about half a second to realize they were the letters Brianna had written him. If he were smart he'd turn around and walk out. There was nothing there he needed to know. They'd be full of her thoughts, her feelings, her dreams, all the things he least wanted to learn. The dumbest thing he could do was read those letters.

He reached out and picked up the first one.

Fifteen minutes later he folded the last page, picked up the currycomb and walked back out to the horses. Billy was right. There was little resemblance between the Brianna he knew and the woman who had written the letters. Her words gave the impression of a quiet, demure little mouse who had sought marriage to a stranger as the only way to stop her aunt's autocratic running of her life. Somehow, Lucas couldn't imagine Brianna bowing down to anybody.

Lucas was pensive as he began brushing the horses. At least he finally understood why Billy was so protective of her. Brianna Daniels had been through hell and back. Orphaned at an early age, she'd grown up under the thumb of her vindictive spinster aunt. At fifteen she'd been married against her will to a man old enough to be her grandfather, and widowed a month later.

She didn't ask for sympathy, only patience and understanding. From her apologetic explanation of why she had no dowry to her sincere assurances that she would do her best to make him happy, her words were enough to make any man see himself as the brave hero who would rescue her.

Lucas dismissed the sentimental claptrap with disgust. How could Brianna have written something so foreign to her nature? Even the handwriting didn't seem right. The beautiful flowing copperplate didn't match her vibrant personality at all.

Too bad he hadn't read the letters before she burst into his life irritating the devil out him, making him act like a cantankerous old bear. It would have saved them both a lot of trouble, because the sweetly giving woman who wrote those letters wouldn't have interested him at all.

11

"*What were you planning* to do after lunch, Billy," Lucas asked looking over the rim of his cup.

"Go hunting. Why?"

"Could you lend me a hand exercising the horses? Some of them haven't been out for several days."

Billy sighed. "I guess so."

"Don't worry. It won't take more than an hour or so."

Brianna looked up from her lunch. "I can help, Lucas."

"Help what?"

"Exercise the horses."

"Thanks but we can manage." Lucas's tone was even more condescending than usual. "We don't have a saddle for you."

"That's a bare-faced lie," Brianna said indignantly. "There are at least four in the barn. If you'll adjust the stirrups I can ride any of them."

"Astride?"

"Of course astride."

"Now that should be interesting to watch."

"Look, darn it, I can ride better than most men."

Billy chuckled. "Most peg-legged sailors maybe."

"I'll have you know I went to college on a rodeo scholarship in barrel-racing!"

"You're welcome to race any of the barrels," Lucas said with a grin, "but you'd better leave the horses alone. These animals were chosen for their speed and endurance. Most of them are high-spirited, and some down-right mean-tempered."

"I can ride any horse in your corral," Brianna said recklessly.

The men exchanged glances. "What do you think, Billy? Shall we let her try Franklin?"

"She did say any horse."

Brianna tossed her head. "You get him saddled and I'll meet you at the corral." She stood up and stomped over to her trunk. "If you'll excuse me gentlemen, I need to change clothes."

Her flare of anger lasted clear through Billy's and Lucas's snickering departure, right up until she slipped into her jeans and T-shirt. She was thinking rationally by the time she went through the familiar motion of tucking in her shirt into her pants and felt the first tremor of foreboding. Franklin? Was it more than a coincidence the horse was named after the man who liked to play around with lightning? He was probably the worst horse out there. She should have never let Lucas goad her into this. Of course to be truthful, all he'd really done was ignore her since the stage came in this morning. He was paying attention now, but she wondered uneasily if it was worth the price she was going to pay.

She ran a mental inventory of all the horses in the corral. The vast majority were the epitome of the Pony Express. Fleet-footed and strong, they were the kind of fast, dependable mounts it took to carry a rider past any threat in all kinds of weather. Nothing to worry about. They were used to being ridden and wouldn't give her any trouble.

Tom Shaffer's backpack caught her eye as she started to repack the trunk. Maybe there was a way to hedge her bet. Brianna pulled out the food pouch and found what she was looking for right away. With a grin curving her lips, she tucked her insurance into her pocket and headed outside.

Her worst fears were realized when she saw the horse Lucas and Billy expected her to ride. No, she corrected herself, they didn't think she'd ride Franklin at all. In fact it was obvious they thought she'd turn tail and run the minute she saw the huge sorrel gelding. She might have a problem. Franklin was obviously one of the big raw-boned animals used to pull the stage. Did they break carriage horses to the saddle, she wondered, or was she going to be climbing onto the back of what was essentially an untried bronc?

The two men stood leaning against the fence laughing, probably at her expense. She squared her shoulders and marched down to join them. "I didn't realize this was the horse you were talking about," she said as she reached them. "I've had my eye on him since the first day I saw him."

"I'll bet."

Brianna ignored Lucas's snide remark and walked over to the horse. "Hello, Franklin," she said in a soothing voice as she held out her hand. When he nudged her palm with his soft muzzle, Brianna resisted the urge to sigh with relief. It meant he accepted her, though he still might not let her on his back. "My, you are a beauty aren't you? Billy," she said without changing her tone of voice, "can I borrow your boots?"

"What?" Billy jumped guiltily as he tore his gaze away from the jeans that hugged her legs from hip to ankle. "My boots?"

"I can't ride in these. There's no heel to keep me from sticking my foot clear through the stirrup. I have no desire to get dragged to death if I should get bucked off."

He looked at her sneakers uncertainly. "I have an old pair in the tack room. I guess you could use those."

She smiled. "Thanks."

"Er . . . do you want me to get them for you?"

"If you wouldn't mind."

Brianna continued stroking Franklin's neck and talking soothingly as Billy went to the barn.

Lucas leaned back against the fence and crossed his arms over his chest. A slight smile played about his mouth. "Interesting outfit."

"Makes more sense than riding in a dress."

"True." Privately, Lucas liked the way she looked in the pants, but it wouldn't do to admit it. "I doubt if the style will catch on though."

"You might be surprised."

"Here's the boots," Billy said coming out of the barn.

"Great." She gave Franklin another pat, then took the boots from Billy's hand and sat down to put them on.

Lucas's smile deepened. What an actress she was. Too bad he was onto her tricks and knew it was all a clever ruse to make him back down. It would be interesting to see just how far she'd go.

"A little big but not too bad." Brianna stood up and took a couple of experimental steps. "I wouldn't want to walk very far in them, but they'll do."

Billy gave her a worried frown. "Are you sure you want to do this?"

"Of course."

Billy looked almost panic stricken. "Lucas . . . ?"

"I can't stop her."

"But Franklin's . . . "

"She knows what she's doing," Lucas said with a shrug.

Brianna took advantage of the momentary distraction to unobtrusively reach into her pocket, get her secret weapon, and move between Lucas and the horse. "Thanks for your vote of confidence." She put her hand up to Franklin's muzzle again and smiled when he moved his mouth across her palm to accept her offering. "Well, it's now or never," she said untying the reins from the fence and giving the gelding's neck one last pat.

Before Lucas had time to react she'd stepped into the stirrup and swung up into the saddle. The smile disappeared from his face in an instant. "What the hell are you doing?"

"What does it look like?"

"All right," he said stepping toward her. "This has gone far enough."

"You think so?" Brianna held the reins tightly as Franklin pranced around. It was like sitting on a keg of dynamite with the fuse lit. If she didn't do something he was going to blow sky-high. She'd better get him defused and fast. "Come on, Franklin," Brianna said, kicking his ribs. "Let's go for a ride."

Franklin took off like a streak of lightning straight down the road toward Platte River Bridge. For several breathless seconds Brianna wasn't sure which of them was in control. An experimental tug of the reins slowed him a trifle and Brianna relaxed. He just wanted a good run. "All right, sweetheart, let's find out what you're made of."

As if he understood her words, the horse lengthened his stride to a gallop that made the landscape pass in a blur. It was like riding the crest of a giant wave, fast and exhilarating. Franklin wasn't the smoothest horse Brianna had ever ridden, but he was one of the most powerful. She could feel his strength beneath her as they raced along the road and she felt like shouting with pure joy.

Brianna could have gone on and on but her better sense intruded. Cautiously, she pulled back on the reins. Franklin gave a snort of displeasure and tried to resist. After several minutes of constant pressure, he eventually stopped, but it was obvious he didn't want to.

His agitated prancing was a warning, and Brianna heeded it without hesitation. She didn't take a chance on losing control as they turned and headed back toward Split Rock Station at an easy canter.

Less than five minutes passed between the time Brianna and Franklin left and when they returned, but it was enough to throw Lucas into a pelter. He'd caught a horse, bridled it, and had headed out after her without taking the time to throw on a saddle.

Brianna smiled at the sight of him loping down the road bareback. He moved with a smooth, easy grace that made him appear a natural extension of the horse. Poetry in motion, she thought appreciatively. He was going to be furious when she rode right by him, but trying to stop Franklin again would be foolhardy. Lucas's temper was survivable, but Franklin's might not be.

She had a brief impression of Lucas's anxious frown changing into an expression of shocked surprise as they swept by him in a cloud of dust. There was no doubt in Brianna's mind that it would be white-lipped anger by the time they reached the corral.

Billy was waiting by the fence as Franklin thundered into the yard. He grabbed the reins the minute the huge horse came to a stop, and Brianna slid to the ground gratefully.

"Damn, you can ride," Billy said.

"I practically grew up in the saddle." She patted the horse's neck. "Besides, Franklin is a sweetheart." Never mind she'd almost lost him a dozen times and wouldn't get back on him for a year's salary.

"What the hell do you think you're doing, woman?" Lucas shouted as his mount slid to a halt a few feet from her and he jumped off.

"You're repeating yourself, Lucas," Brianna said calmly. "I told you before I was going for a ride, and that's exactly what I did."

"That horse is barely broken to the saddle."

"You picked him, not me. Anyway, I think I proved my point. Now will you let me help exercise the horses?"

"No," he said flatly.

"No! Why not?"

"Because it's company policy. Nobody but employees of the Central Overland and Pike's Peak Express Company ride these horses." Lucas tossed his reins to Billy. "You don't qualify."

"You made that up," she yelled as he stomped off to the barn. "Darn it, Lucas, come back here . . . Oooo that man!"

"He didn't exactly make it up," Billy said. "The company put Lucas in charge of the horses. He decides who rides what."

"That figures."

"How did you manage it?"

"What, making Lucas mad?" Brianna glared at the barn. "I don't know. It just seems to come naturally to me."

"No, I mean how did you control Franklin?"

"Oh, that. I charmed him, of course. He's not unreasonable like some people I know."

Billy laughed. "Maybe you could charm Lucas the same way."

"I doubt it. The secret is letting the horse get used to you. The more I'm around Lucas the more we irritate each other."

"Aw come on, Brianna," Billy said with a grin. "Petting Franklin might have gotten you on his back, but that's not what kept you there."

Brianna glanced at him in surprise. Billy had never called her by name before. For that matter it was the first time they'd carried on a decent conversation. "Actually it wasn't so much a matter of controlling him as figuring out what he wanted to do," she admitted. "He's trained to run, so I let him."

"And?"

"That's it."

"Not quite. I saw you give him something."

"Oh, you mean the sugar lump."

"Sugar?"

Brianna nodded and reached into her pocket for the last lump. "Horses love it. I've never seen one yet that didn't have a sweet tooth."

"Well, I'll be."

"Don't tell Lucas," she said as Franklin accepted the sugar eagerly. "He'd probably say I cheated."

Billy grinned. "Don't guess it will hurt to keep him guessing a bit. I'll put Franklin away if you want."

"Why thank you, Billy, and thanks for letting me borrow your boots."

"Happy to. It was a pure pleasure to see you get the best of that ornery old cuss."

Brianna wondered if he was referring to Franklin or Lucas. Not that it mattered, she thought with a wry smile. It was an apt description for both.

In spite of her altercation with Lucas, Brianna was fairly pleased with herself as she turned toward the cabin. She might not have accomplished what she set out to do, but it looked as though she'd finally broken the ice with Billy. Her theory was proven correct when Billy returned from his hunting trip several hours later. With eager pride, he handed Brianna the skinned, gutted carcasses of two jackrabbits. Somehow she managed to hide her instinctive recoil and accepted them as the valuable gift they were meant to be.

Cut up, liberally coated with flour, and fried like chicken, the fresh meat was a welcome change at supper. Though Brianna was a bit skeptical, she was pleasantly surprised by the taste, and was soon eating as enthusiastically as the men. As far as food went it was a very successful meal.

Billy was so completely different, it was like meeting a new person. Though he didn't exactly chatter, Brianna found him surprisingly good company. It was just as well, for Lucas didn't utter a word during the entire meal. Every time Brianna looked his way he was glowering at his plate. He ignored her so pointedly that Brianna had to fight the urge to hit him. By the end of the meal she was ready to give him a piece of her mind in no uncertain terms.

As usual, Lucas didn't cooperate. The minute supper was over, he stalked outside and stayed there until long after Brianna put out the light and went to bed. Usually she was asleep minutes after she slipped beneath the blankets, but tonight was different. The hot muggy weather coupled with her irritation at Lucas kept her wide awake. Even the bright fullness of the moon worked against her. It was like having a streetlight shining in the window.

Brianna was still wide awake when Lucas came in at last. She feigned sleep, watching him beneath lowered lashes as he moved around the small cabin. When he paused in front of the open window and glanced her way, she closed her eyes, afraid he'd see she wasn't really asleep. As she lay there listening to his movements, she realized his hair had been gleaming unnaturally in the moonlight almost as though it were wet. Wet? Of course, he'd been swimming!

Suddenly she felt twice as hot and sticky as she'd been before. The thought of visiting the river immediately took possession of her mind, and she could almost feel the cool water caressing her body. With the stage and Seth both coming in she'd probably miss her chance tomorrow. That would mean she'd have to wait until Billy came again. Six days without a bath? Brianna couldn't bear the thought.

If Lucas could do it at night, why couldn't she? With a full moon shining outside, it was almost as bright as daylight. The sounds across the room ceased and Brianna cautiously opened her eyes. Expecting to find Lucas safely tucked into bed, she nearly choked on her surprise. He was standing there, stark naked, gazing out the window at something that had drawn his attention.

Moonbeams bathed his body in silver, the cool light blurring lines, softening curves and hiding nothing. He looked like Michelangelo's statue of David, every inch of him superbly muscled and beautifully male. If there was a speck of softness or a hint of flab Brianna couldn't see it.

She had no idea how long she lay there staring at him in unabashed admiration, only that she couldn't have torn her eyes away if she wanted to. Suddenly, almost as if he sensed Brianna's gaze upon him, Lucas turned his head and looked straight at her.

Brianna slammed her eyes shut in mortified embarrassment. Had he seen her spying on him clear across the room or was the moonlight too dim for him to tell? Minutes ticked by, absolute silence filled the cabin. Brianna could feel the heat in her face. Though she knew it was ridiculous, she couldn't shake the feeling that she was glowing in the dark.

Hoping to fool him into thinking she'd been asleep the whole time, Brianna shifted slightly and mumbled a few unintelligible syllables. A long moment passed, then she heard the quiet rustle of blankets and a deep sigh. She cautiously peeked through her lashes and found him settling comfortably into bed.

Hardly daring to breathe, Brianna lay there until the sound of soft snores finally came from the other bed. She waited another half an hour just to make sure he was asleep before quietly gathering her things and creeping silently out of the cabin.

The cold water of the river was just as refreshing as she had anticipated. Unfortunately, it did nothing to cool the heat that filled her with restless energy. No matter how many times she swam across the pool and back, she couldn't erase the image of Lucas in the moonlight or deny the effect it had on her.

Brianna didn't know which was worse, the memory of that gorgeous body and the knowledge that every night he slept less than ten feet from her, gloriously naked beneath his blankets, or the realization that he disliked her more with every day that passed.

12

"Are you finished?" Brianna asked Billy as he sopped up the last of his gravy with part of a biscuit.

He looked up from his breakfast in surprise. "I guess so."

"Then let me get that out of your way." She whisked his plate off the table leaving him with a half-eaten biscuit in his hand and an astonished expression on his face. Brianna didn't seem to notice as she started washing the dishes.

"Is something wrong?" Billy asked.

"No, I just need to get some things done this morning."

Like pack to leave, Lucas thought with a strange tightening in his chest. "Are you going to be ready by the time the stage gets here?"

Brianna gave him a startled glance. "Er . . . well . . . I hope to be. How did you know what I was planning?"

"It wasn't too hard to figure out."

"And you don't mind?"

"None of my business what you do," he said scooting his chair back. "I'll be in the barn."

Billy watched Lucas stomp out the door then glanced at Brianna curiously. "What's going on?"

"How in heaven's name should I know? That man thrives on confusing me. What are you grinning about."

"I was just thinking, he said almost the same thing about you."

"Oh he did, did he? Well I'm sure I couldn't care less what Lucas Daniels says."

Billy's grin widened. "He said that, too."

"Hmph. Don't you have to go write to Seth or something?"

"As a matter of fact I do," he said with a chuckle as he polished off his biscuit and headed out the door.

"Men!" she muttered to herself plunging her hands back into her dishwater. At least Lucas had approved her plan. She'd been a little worried about how he'd react after he refused to let her ride any of the horses. The supplies did belong to the company after all.

As soon as the dishes were done, she set to work with a vengeance. For the dozenth time she wished she had some eggs and milk. It seemed like every recipe she wanted to use called for one or both. Even Anna's cookbook depended heavily on them. Well, one thing she'd learned to do since she'd been here was to improvise. Cinnamon rolls were beyond her, but with a little ingenuity and some sugar, her biscuits should serve her purpose just as well.

Brianna was just putting the finishing touches on a plate full of biscuits when she heard the telltale rumble of the stage. She smoothed her apron over her skirt and patted her hair to make sure it was still tucked securely into the french braid. Then she picked up her biscuits and stepped outside to greet the passengers.

This time the stage carried only men. They acted pleasantly surprised to see her and her sugar-topped biscuits. It wasn't long before Brianna's cup was satisfyingly heavy and the plate nearly empty. On a whim, she picked up a biscuit, poured a cup of water, and intercepted the stage driver on his way back from the outhouse.

"You look like you could use a bite to eat," she said with a smile.

"Why, thank you, ma'am." He accepted the food with a pleased grin. "Mighty kind of you."

"Don't mention it."

"Is your trunk ready to load?"

"What?"

"Lucas said you'd be taking a trunk."

"Taking it where?" she asked in bewilderment.

"Why, to St. Joe, of course," he said, taking a bite of his biscuit. "At least that's where he bought your ticket for."

"He bought me a ticket?"

"Yup. This is awful good, Mrs. Daniels."

"Hmm?" She gave him a distracted glance. "Oh . . . thank you. Would you excuse me? I need to have a word with Lucas."

"Sure thing. We'll be leaving in about five minutes."

Brianna barely heard him as she stalked over to where Lucas was changing the teams. "You don't waste any time getting even do you?"

"Getting even?"

"Don't play stupid with me, Lucas. You couldn't stand the thought of me being right could you? I proved you wrong and suddenly the deal we made means nothing."

"What are you talking about?"

"In spite of what you think, you don't own me. I'll go where I want, when I want, and it just so happens I don't want to go to St. Joseph."

"That's just the end of the line. You can get a stage anywhere you want from there. I paid extra so you can transfer."

"You don't get it, do you? Open your ears, Lucas. I'm staying! I don't care if this is 1860, your chauvinistic attitude is straight out of the dark ages and I'm sick to death of it. We had a deal and you're sticking with it if I have to shove it down your throat. I'm not leaving just because I proved you wrong by riding that damn horse yesterday."

"What's that got to with you leaving?"

"You tell me. You're the one that's sending me away."

"What gave you that idea?"

"Oh, I don't know," she said sarcastically. "Maybe because you bought me a ticket on the stage. Damn it, Lucas, you didn't even have the decency to tell me yourself. Y-you left it up to the d-driver!" To Brianna's horror her voice quavered and her eyes filled with tears.

"Brianna . . . " Lucas took an involuntary step toward her. "I bought you a ticket because I thought you wanted to leave."

She swiped angrily at her eyes with the back of her hand. "Well, I don't."

"Then why were you so anxious to get rid of us after breakfast?"

"So I could get my biscuits baked before the stage got here."

"Biscuits?" He glanced over at the group near the cabin.

"Yes, and they went over just like I hoped they would. I haven't counted the money yet, but I'm sure there's enough to pay you for supplies and still have some profit left."

"That's what this is all about?"

"Of course, what did you think?"

"That you had finally had enough and decided to leave."

"Wishful thinking on your part," she said with a toss of her head. "Don't worry, if I decide to leave you'll be the first to know."

Watching her flounce off toward the group near the cabin, Lucas had the absurd desire to laugh. He was right back where he started. Brianna was still an unwanted burden, one he wasn't likely to get rid of any time soon. The black mood he'd been in all morning suddenly lifted, and he turned back to the horses with a smile.

Brianna was still fuming when the stage pulled out. The nerve of that man. Trying to get rid of her that way and then acting as if he'd misunderstood her intentions, it was enough to make anybody see red. She slammed around the cabin straightening up, doing her best to hang on to her anger. It was difficult when she kept remembering the expression on his face when she'd almost burst into tears. He'd looked as upset as she felt.

Of course, Lucas had been overly touchy all day. He'd left the breakfast table in such a hurry he'd forgotten to put on his vest. As she picked the garment off the back of his chair an image of his body covered with nothing but moonlight invaded her thoughts. Irritated with herself, she pushed the enticing picture away and dropped the vest on his bunk.

It slid from the bed and hit the floor with a clunk. At the unexpected sound, Brianna looked back in surprise. As she bent to pick the vest up the glint of metal caught her eye. His watch fob, of course. How silly.

Afraid the watch might have been damaged when it hit the floor, Brianna reached into the pocket and pulled it out. For a long moment she stared at it in shock. She'd seen that intricately carved horse head more times than she could count.

The gold watch in her hand was her Uncle Todd's most prized possession; he'd carried it as long as Brianna could remember. As a youngster he'd found it in the bottom of an old trunk his grandmother had stored in her attic.

Brianna released the catch with her thumbnail. If there had been a shadow of doubt in her mind, it disappeared the second she saw the familiar inscription inside the cover. *"To Lucas, my one and only love. Marie."*

Brianna felt sick to her stomach. Lucas *was* her great-great-grandfather. Until that moment she hadn't realized how badly she wanted it not to be true.

"Ah, you found it." Lucas's voice startled her as he walked up beside her. "I couldn't remember where I took my vest off this morning."

"Y-you left it on the back of your chair."

"It's so blamed hot I didn't even notice I wasn't wearing it."

Brianna snapped the cover shut and slipped the watch back into the pocket before handing the vest to him. "Who's Marie?" she asked telling herself it was curiosity not jealousy that prompted the question. After all, her entire family had speculated about it as long as she could remember. The muscles in his jaw flexed as he slipped the vest on. "Someone I used to know."

"No kidding," Brianna said sarcastically then sighed. "It's none of my business, right?"

He didn't answer, just pulled the watch out of his pocket, flicked it open, and stared down at the inscription silently.

"Look, I'm sorry I asked."

"She was my betrothed," he said heavily. "I carry this watch to remember her."

"Oh, Lord, Lucas. I'm sorry."

"Me, too."

"How did she die?" Brianna asked softly.

"She didn't. Marie married my cousin Charles two weeks after my grandfather finally took my advice and made Charles his heir instead of me. Poor Charles never knew it was Grandad's fortune and the family business she was after." Lucas closed the watch and slid it into the watch pocket of his vest. "As long as I look at this watch a dozen times a day, I'm in no danger of forgetting what deceitful creatures women really are."

"Not all of us."

"Oh, no?" He met her eyes squarely. "Can you swear to me you've been completely honest with me?"

"I-I . . ."

Lucas gave her a scathing look. "Don't bother. I read your letters, or should I say your sad little tales of woe?"

"L-letters?"

"Did you think I was so stupid I wouldn't know the difference?"

"Rider coming in," Billy called from outside.

"Be right there," Lucas yelled back. Then he pinned Brianna with an accusing stare. "I've never met a woman yet I could trust," he said heading toward the door. "Lying comes so naturally to your sex, you don't even realize you're doing it."

Stunned by his revelations, Brianna followed more slowly. No wonder Lucas was so difficult. He'd obviously loved Marie, it wasn't surprising her perfidy had soured him on women. But to think all of them were the same?

Seth was just coming into the yard as Brianna stepped through the door. Passing the mail from one rider to the other was just as exciting to watch the second time and Brianna wondered if it would ever lose its thrill for her.

"A minute and fourteen seconds," Lucas said putting his watch away. "How was your ride?"

"Not bad other than I ran into a dust storm between here and Independence Rock. It slowed me down some." Seth slid off his exhausted horse. He didn't look a whole lot better himself but he gave Brianna a jaunty grin as he reached inside his shirt. "I didn't forget," he said in an low voice as he handed her a small bottle. "Here's the sourdough starter you asked for."

"Oh, thank you, Seth. Now I can bake . . . " Her voice trailed off as she tipped the bottle back and forth. The substance inside didn't move. "How do you get it out?"

Seth looked surprised. "That's strange. The station-master at Platte River Bridge gave me some of his. It was runny when I put it in the bottle."

"It must have set up."

Lucas looked at them curiously. "What's going on?"

"Er . . . nothing." Brianna started to hide the bottle behind her back, but Lucas's expression of disbelief stopped her in her tracks. He fully expected her to lie. " . . . nothing you need to concern yourself about."

"Everything around here is my concern."

"Maybe so, but this is a surprise."

"I don't like surprises so you might just as well tell me about it now."

"I'd rather wait at least until tomorrow."

"Why? It doesn't make a bit of difference whether I find out now or later."

"That's right and that's why I'd just as soon wait." She clutched the bottle nervously. "I'm not all that sure I can make it work."

Lucas stared at her for a long moment and then shrugged. "It obviously doesn't matter what I say. You'll keep your little secret anyway."

"Just until tomorrow," she said as he led the horse away toward the barn.

"Oh, by the way." He glanced back over his shoulder. "All you have to do is find something to scrape it out of the bottle with. You can get a new batch of sourdough going with even a little bit of the old."

There was a moment of stunned silence as his words sank in. He was nearly to the barn when Brianna found her voice. "You just wait, Lucas Daniels. I'll get you for that!" She thought she heard a deep chuckle as he disappeared into the dark interior of the barn.

It took some ingenuity but by using part of one of Tom Shaffer's ballpoint pens, Brianna was able to get enough sourdough out of the bottle to start a new batch. Following the recipe in Anna's cookbook, she soon had a smooth mixture that smelled a bit like the concoction she had thrown away the first day. Satisfied that she was on the right track, she covered the bowl with a cloth and headed down to the river to get water.

As Brianna filled her bucket, she couldn't help but think of Billy. She'd never figured out why he made sure she always had water. Even after Lucas brought the big barrel up to the cabin, Billy had kept it filled with water. She certainly appreciated it.

With a sigh, Brianna started back up the trail. She hadn't gone more than twenty yards when she came to an abrupt halt. A swirling blue mist formed on the trail in front of her. Before her eyes, it grew until it was nearly eight feet tall. Slowly, the mist began revolving, gathering near the middle. Toward the center, Brianna could see vague outlines that resembled people.

Then, quickly as it had appeared, the apparition was gone. Unable to move, Brianna stood there wide-eyed with shock staring at the place it had been. Either she was losing her mind or she'd just seen the way home.

13

July 16, 1995

Tom jerked awake as the phone next to the
bed rang. Though he was disoriented at first, everything came back into sharp focus as Anna shifted in his
arms. He had intended only to comfort her after her
nightmare, not fall asleep in bed with her. Of course
now, he was far too comfortable to even consider going
back to the couch.

The phone rang again. Tom snuggled closer into
Anna's warmth and ignored it.

Click. "Hello, you've reached Brianna's phone clone.
If you want to talk to the real thing, leave your name
and number and she'll get back to you"

Tom opened a bleary eye and peered at the clock.
Four-fifteen! Only an idiot would call at this time of
night. Answering machines ought to be outlawed, especially ones with supposedly clever sayings on them.

Beep. "Tom, if you're there answer the phone."

Tom groaned as he rolled over and picked up the

receiver next to the bed. "Christ, Chuck, do you know what time it is?"

"Yup. We're getting ready to leave for the balloon rally. I see you didn't have enough sense to get a motel room for the night."

"Did you call me long distance to give me a lecture on morals?"

"Would it do any good?"

"No."

"Didn't figure it would. Actually, I promised Sandy I'd call."

"You think your wife's disapproval will have any more effect on me than yours?"

"She doesn't disapprove. In fact, she said it was about time some woman grabbed your interest. She'd given up hope."

"So you woke me up at four in the morning to tell me your wife approves of my amorous adventures?"

"No, I called to apologize. Sandy reminded me how important this must be for you to turn your back on your dream. I don't know what's going on, and I'm not particularly comfortable with it. But you're one of the most level-headed men I know, and I trust your judgement."

There was a moment of silence as Tom digested the unexpected compliment. "I . . . thanks."

"Tom?" Chuck's voice was suddenly hesitant. "This is more than just a torrid love affair isn't it?"

"Yeah."

"You aren't in any trouble are you?"

Tom closed his eyes and pinched the bridge of his nose between his thumb and forefinger. The urge to unburden himself to his older brother was strong. "No, Chuck, it's nothing for you to worry about."

"I just hope you have this all worked out by the time we come back through next week."

"So do I."

"In the meantime you have our itinerary. Don't hesitate to call if you need me."

"I won't . . . thanks."

"Don't thank me. It was Sandy who read me the riot act."

Tom smiled in the darkness. "You have a damn smart wife."

"Yeah, yeah, I know. And she's the best thing I ever did for the family. Just get yourself together by next week or you'll have her on your back, too," Chuck said gruffly. "We love you, you know."

Surprise held Tom's tongue for a long moment. "Y-yeah, I love you, too." His voice tripped over the unfamiliar words. "I'll see you next week."

"Right. Good-bye."

Tom hung up the phone thoughtfully.

"Where is she?" Anna asked.

Tom turned his head to look at her. "That wasn't a she at all. It was my brother, Chuck."

"No, I mean the woman who woke us up?"

"Oh, that was Brianna or actually a recording of her voice."

"What?"

"Look, I'll show you. It's a machine that answers her phone." He rolled over, pushed a button and waited as the sound of Brianna's message once again filled the room.

"Brianna has a phone to talk to Chuck?"

"She doesn't even know Chuck."

"Then why does she have a phone?"

"So she can talk to everybody else who has a phone, which is nearly everyone."

"Everybody has one," she said in awe. "How does it work?"

"Beats me. It goes through a wire so it must be electrical."

"Like a telegraph?"

"Sort of, I guess."

"And you're so used having a phone that you take it for granted just like running water and touch lights."

"Touch lights?"

"Whenever you walk into a room, you touch the wall and the lights come on."

Tom propped himself on an elbow and grinned down at her in the moonlight filtering in through the window. "You're right, we do take things for granted."

"I want to see all the wonderful inventions you don't even notice any more. Will you show me?"

If she'd asked for three bars of pure gold right then he'd have promised to get them for her. "We'll spend the morning exploring before we go out to Scott's."

"Is it time to get up?"

He glanced at the clock. "No, we've still got a couple of hours." He resisted the urge to trace the line of her jaw with his fingers. "Go back to sleep."

She smiled and curled against his body with a sigh. Tom told himself it meant nothing as he put his arms around her again, that he was merely giving comfort. But he couldn't deny the intense satisfaction he felt that she'd come willingly back into his embrace.

They woke up again at six. Her shy smile of greeting was nearly Tom's undoing. He'd never wanted to kiss anybody so badly in his life. This beautiful, demure woman was everything he'd ever wished for.

Half an hour later he discovered she had a stubborn streak that wasn't quite so endearing. By the time he finally convinced her to trade in her high button shoes for a pair of Brianna's sandals he was revising his opinion of her sweet, easygoing nature.

They had to wait fifteen minutes to get a table at the restaurant. Their order was eventually taken by a harried waitress who barely had time to smile before she hurried on to her next table. It didn't matter that they had a long wait for their food. Sitting together in the busy restaurant sipping their morning coffee was a pleasure neither wanted to end too soon.

Everything was so new to Anna. She was equally fascinated by the ice cubes in her water, the plastic flowers in the centerpiece, and the revolving ceiling fan.

After breakfast, Tom took her to a huge discount store and shared her wonder as they wandered the aisles looking at the vast array of items for sale. It was an adventure to see his world through her eyes. He told her about jets, space shuttles, and computers. But she was just as impressed with traffic lights, fire engines, and air-conditioning.

Tom parked at the bank and they went in to get some cash from the automatic teller machine. Anna watched in amazement as the machine rolled out four crisp twenty dollar bills. From there they walked down the street to an ice cream shop. On the way Anna exclaimed over the wide cement sidewalks, was scandalized by the women she saw in shorts, and practically knocked Tom off the sidewalk when a man in a bubble-faced helmet rode by on a motorcycle.

The hot caramel and fudge sundae Tom bought her at the ice cream shop was pure inspiration on his part. With the first bite Anna closed her eyes. "This is so good it has to be sinful."

Tom grinned. "Only if you're counting calories."

"I didn't expect to experience anything so wonderful this side of heaven."

"Neither did I," Tom said softly. Watching her enjoy the treat, he felt something tighten in his chest. He knew he'd never meet another woman like her, and their time together was so limited. If Scott was right she could well be out of his life by tonight. The sound of the spoon clattering into the empty dish was like a death knell to his heart. He was missing her already, and she wasn't even gone.

Anna looked up with a satisfied sigh. Her smile faded when she saw the expression on his face. "Tom, what is it?"

"Nothing really. It's just been such a good morning, I hate for it to end," he said, regretfully glancing at his watch. "If we're going to get to Scott's by one-thirty we better get moving. We need to stop at Brianna's again then be on our way. Are you ready?"

"I think so."

"You know," Tom said a few minutes later when they stopped in front of Brianna's house, "it might be a good idea to grab a few extra clothes for you just in case."

"Most of Brianna's are too small."

"That figures. From the looks of her refrigerator, she probably starves herself to stay thin. Never mind, there's bound to be something we can use."

"I don't know, most of her dresses are down right indecent and I refuse to wear trousers . . . what's that noise?"

Anna asked as they stepped into the bedroom.

"It's the answering machine." Tom switched off the automatic beeper and pushed the message button. "Maybe Chuck called again."

Beep. "Brianna, this is Sadie Johnson, Lucas and Anna Daniel's granddaughter." Tom and Anna's eyes met in shocked surprise as the woman's elderly voice continued. "When my daughter Betsy told me about you and your family research, I suddenly remembered a sapphire ring my Grandma Anna gave me when I was a little girl just before she died. I was to give it to the first grandchild with the name Brianna Marie Daniels. That's you, my dear. My daughter is sending it with the picture of Lucas and Anna. Betsy doesn't approve, but she'll do as I wish. I hope you'll write to me when you get a chance. I would love to share my memories of Anna Daniels with you."

The machine switched off while Anna and Tom continued to stare at each other. "What do you suppose that means?" Anna asked in a whisper.

"I don't know."

"My granddaughter. Oh, Tom, sh-she was so old." Anna's eyes filled with tears. "And I d-died when she was just a little girl."

Tom put his arms around her. "That was another lifetime, Anna."

"No, Tom, it wasn't another lifetime. I-it was mine. I'm n-not su-pposed to be here."

"Anna," he said pulling her closer into his embrace. "You're a young woman with your life ahead of you. Somehow we'll get you back where you belong and you'll live out your destiny."

"And what if I can't get back? What if I'm stuck here forever?"

Pillowing her face against his shoulder, he stroked the back of her head. Unbidden an image of what could be arose in his mind. "Would that really be so bad?"

"You can't be serious!" She pulled back and looked at him. "I don't have the faintest idea how to live here." She gestured toward the closet. "I can't even dress myself."

"You'd learn."

"How?"

He tenderly brushed the hair back from her face. "I'd be here to teach you."

"Oh, Tom." She reached up and touched his cheek. "But we mustn't even think of it."

"Why not? You and Lucas haven't met yet. We wouldn't be hurting him."

"If it were just the three of us . . . but it's not. All

this time I've been feeling sorry for myself and haven't even considered how much worse it must be for Brianna. Not only is she having to get along without all this," Anna said gesturing to the room, "she can't even tell anyone what's happened to her."

"No, I guess not. They'd think she'd lost her mind."

"And if I'm not there to be her grandmother, that sweet little old lady we just heard on the phone will probably never be born."

Tom sighed. "I know, Anna, and I promise I'll do everything I can to get you back where you belong." But he couldn't do anything about the traitorous corner of his heart that hoped they would fail.

14

August 1860

"Stage is comin' in, Brianna," Seth said sticking his head in the door. "Want me to help you carry the grub out?"

"If you wouldn't mind. You get the cookies and the coffee and I'll grab the sandwiches."

"Those sandwiches are about the best idea you've had yet."

"I hope so. Lucas thinks I cooked way too much of the antelope Billy shot yesterday, but I figured I could sell what we don't eat before it spoils."

Seth grinned. "We ate half of it for supper last night."

"It seemed a shame to turn it all into jerky when everybody enjoys fresh meat so much. I hope he's wrong about how much will go to waste."

"Lucas was just surprised. I don't think he was expecting such a huge roast."

"I did get a little carried away," Brianna conceded.

And I sort of forgot we don't have a refrigerator, she added to herself. Oh how she hated to admit that Lucas might be right. The sandwiches had been an inspiration to save face.

"Well, quite a feast you have set out today," Lucas commented as he joined them.

"Now you see why I fixed such a big roast last night," Brianna said defiantly. "Those poor stage passengers haven't had a meal since Fort Bridger. By the time they get here, they're half starved."

Lucas raised an eyebrow. "Funny, you've been doing this for five weeks now and you've never worried about anybody starving before."

"This is the first time Billy has shot anything big enough to share."

"That's because Billy doesn't like to waste meat. He wouldn't have shot the antelope if it hadn't been injured." Lucas grabbed a cookie and returned to the horses as the stage rumbled into the yard. "I just hope the stage is full and everyone's hungry," he called over his shoulder.

"Sure, you do," Brianna muttered under her breath.

"Don't worry, Brianna," Seth said. "Once it gets cold Billy and me will keep you well supplied with fresh meat."

"What I'd really like is a couple of chickens and a good milking cow. "

" 'Fraid I can't help you there." With a wave and a grin, Seth headed for the barn as the passengers began to get off the stage.

"Make sure you save some of that for me, Mrs. Daniels," the driver called out. "Got a whole stage full today. Reckon they'll eat it all before Lucas and I finish changing the horses."

"It'll be waiting for you when you're ready, Silas."

The first passengers arrived at her makeshift lunch counter and Brianna turned on her charm. She had decided early on that payment would be voluntary. For one thing she didn't have the faintest idea what to charge and refused to show her ignorance by asking Lucas. It didn't take her long to realize that western men, starved for female attention, were likely to pay more than she asked anyway. There was an occasional customer who left nothing, but for the most part they were very generous.

"Hello again," said a soft melodious voice.

Brianna looked up and was surprised to see the young woman who had stopped the first day on her way to Fort Bridger. "Well, hello. I didn't expect to see you again so soon."

"I didn't think I'd be back either. My husband has been transferred back East."

"You sound pleased," Brianna said with a smile.

"Oh, I am." The woman was joined by her husband, a middle-aged officer with a pair of impressive sideburns.

"This is my husband Lieutenant Jeremy Jones. Jeremy, this is the woman I told you about."

"P-p-pleased to m-m-eet you," he stammered. "S-S-Sally said sh-sh-she wasn't s-s-sure she'd made the r-r-right choice unt-til she met y-y-you."

"All I did was give her a cup of water."

"No, you reminded me of why I came out." Sally smiled up at her husband adoringly.

"And I'm glad you did, my love. It's been the best month of my life," he said softly, and dropped a kiss on her forehead. Then he smiled at Brianna. "I'll l-l-leave you l-l-ladies to your t-t-talk. I-i-it was nice to m-m-meet you."

Brianna hid her astonishment at the way his stutter came and went. "You, too, and good luck on your new assignment, Lieutenant Jones."

"Th-th-thanks."

"Isn't it amazing?" Sally said as he walked away. "When he's with me his stutter is almost cured, and we owe it all to you."

"Me?"

"All the way to the fort I kept thinking about you and your husband. I wanted that same magic with Jeremy."

"What magic?"

"Oh you know that special glow you two have. Even the short time I was here I could see how much you loved each other."

"You could?"

"Oh, yes, the way he looked at you when you weren't watching, and that soft little smile you got when you talked about him, it's all so beautiful." Sally gave a dramatic sigh. "Anyway I decided to start over with Jeremy. From the moment I arrived, I acted the way I imagined you do when you're alone with your husband. His response was most gratifying." She blushed. "Thanks to you I've fallen in love with my own husband."

"I-I hardly know what to say."

"You don't have to say anything, just accept my gift."

"Gift? Oh, no, I couldn't take anything."

"Nonsense," she said handing Brianna a brown paper parcel. "You're taller, of course, but other than that we're about the same size. Without hoops it should fit nicely." She sighed. "You can't wear hoops in this incessant wind anyway."

"You're giving me a dress?"

"I didn't have anything else. I hope you aren't offended."

"Goodness no! A new dress to wear will be sheer heaven. I'm so tired of what I have. Thank you."

"I also wanted to give you this." Sally fished a pretty little jar covered with hand-painted flowers out of her reticule. "It's a special cream my mother gave me to

keep my skin white. I couldn't help but notice your . . .
um . . . the sun out here is so . . . er . . . well, I thought
you might like to have it," she finished lamely.

"How thoughtful." Brianna said biting back a grin.
How ironic was more like it. For once in her life her
fair skin had a decent tan and the only other woman
around felt sorry for her instead of envious. "Won't
you need it?"

"Oh, no. I'll get some more when I get home. Jeremy's
being sent to Fort Sumter. It's close to my parent's
home."

Brianna's smile froze on her face. *Oh Lord, wasn't
Fort Sumter where the Civil War had begun?* "How
nice for you," Brianna murmured feeling sick. It was
highly likely that Sally would soon be a widow. For the
hundredth time, Brianna wondered exactly when the
war started. Why hadn't she paid closer attention in
her history classes? Impulsively she reached out and
grasped the other woman's hands. "Can I give you a little piece of advice?"

"Of course."

"If you want to have a happy marriage live every day
as though it's the last one you'll ever spend together.
Never miss an opportunity to show him how much you
love him."

"Then you think I should stay with him, too! Jeremy
wants me to go live with my parents because he's afraid
it will be too dangerous at the fort, but I know my
place is with him."

"Well I . . . "

"And that's why you're way out here in the middle
of nowhere isn't it?" Sally was awestruck. "You stayed
with your man no matter what."

"That's not exactly . . . "

"Oh, here comes your husband now. You two are
such an inspiration." She squeezed Brianna's hands

and touched her cheek with her own. "I'll remember your advice. Good-bye."

"But . . . "

"Here she is," Lucas said walking up beside her.

Brianna hardly noticed as she watched Sally hurry away and join her husband by the stagecoach.

"Brianna, there's someone I'd like you to meet."

"Huh?" Her head swiveled toward him. There was distinct warning note in his voice that she'd never heard before.

"This is James Bromley." He stood next to a well-dressed gentleman who was smiling at her expectantly. "James, I'd like you to meet my . . . wife."

"How do you do, Mr. Bromley?" Brianna said offering her hand.

Instead of shaking it, he surprised her by kissing the back. "Ah, Mrs. Daniels it's good to meet you at last. I've heard so much about you."

"You have?"

"Certainly. The customers have been talking about this stop for the last month."

"Customers?"

"The stage passengers." Lucas explained. "Mr. Bromley is a superintendent for the Central Overland and Pike's Express Company. He supervises the stretch from Fort Laramie to Salt Lake City."

"I see." No wonder Lucas seemed uncomfortable. This was his boss. Maybe there was a rule about having wives.

"Lucas says the idea to serve food and drink was yours?"

"W-well, yes it was." And Lucas hadn't hesitated to throw her to the wolves. Brianna wondered why that hurt. She shouldn't have been surprised. It was no secret he didn't want her here. "I really didn't plan to go into business. It just kind of happened."

Bromley beamed at her. "Pure inspiration."

"It is?"

"Certainly. Since this station is halfway between Platte River Bridge and Green River, it looks like we're doing everything we can to make our customers happy. You don't even charge them."

Brianna glanced at her half full change cup and Bromley smiled. "At least it appears you don't charge them."

"Then you don't mind?"

Bromley looked surprised. "Far from it. In fact I'm planning to tell Bart Kelly to bring in supplies for you. If there's anything you need, feel free to order it through him."

"B-Bart Kelly?"

"Surely you know him. He's the company freighter."

"Well, I . . . "

"Oh, she knows him all right," Lucas said with a wicked grin. "The problem is, he knows her, too."

Brianna gave Lucas a quelling glance. "Mr. Kelly and I don't exactly get along."

"The truth is, Bart Kelly stays as far away from Brianna as he can. He hasn't been inside the cabin or stayed overnight here since she arrived."

"Why not?"

"I think he's afraid of her. You ought to see the contortions he goes through so that he doesn't have any contact with her. It's about the only entertainment we get around here." Lucas chuckled. "Anyway, I can give him her order."

"Bart Kelly has always been a bit odd." Bromley gave Brianna an uncertain look. "Well, the driver seems to be ready to leave. MacTavish should be here early tomorrow."

"Good, we'll be looking for him. Have a good trip."

"Thanks. I'll see you on the way back through. It was nice meeting you, Mrs. Daniels."

Brianna smiled. "You, too, Mr. Bromley."

Sally leaned out the window and waved to Brianna as the stage pulled out of the yard. Brianna felt a pang as she waved back. What if her "advice" put Sally in the wrong place when the war broke out? She'd never really thought about the possibility of changing the future by what she did here. Would her thoughtlessness wipe out future generations of some family?

"Looks like luck was with you." Lucas's sardonic amusement broke through her musings. "They ate every scrap."

"It wasn't luck. I planned it."

"Sure you did."

"Face it. You were wrong, and I was right, as usual." Brianna rattled her money cup and smiled sweetly up at him. "See you at lunch, Lucas."

He couldn't quite keep the grin off his face as she sashayed into the cabin with an exaggerated swing to her hips. With a shake of his head, he went to take care of the horses.

Brianna was thankful she had kept a little of the roast in reserve. Otherwise it would have been impossible to put lunch on the table at noon. As it was, Seth and Lucas were waiting like a couple of starving vultures long before she was ready to serve the meal.

"Why was Bromley on the stage?" Seth asked watching Brianna dish up lunch.

"Business at Fort Laramie. He also wanted to tell me he finally found another man for the station."

Brianna looked up in surprise. "Another man! What for?"

"We've been one short here since Fredricks died."

"Who?"

"Jake Fredricks, the stock tender. He took an arrow in the chest about two weeks before you got here."

"I-Indians?"

"Well it wasn't the army."

Brianna's eyes widened. "I never thought about the Indians. Are they a big problem in Wyoming now?"

"Wyoming?" Lucas looked at her oddly. "Not as far as I know but then I never spent much time in Pennsylvania."

"Pennsylvania?"

"Isn't that where the Wyoming Valley is?"

"No, I mean here, in Wyoming Territory."

"I think you took a wrong turn somewhere on your trip out here. This was Nebraska Territory last I heard."

Brianna raised an eyebrow. Nebraska? When had it become Wyoming? "What about the Indians?"

"The worst of it has been to the West with the Paiutes," Seth said. "Just a few weeks ago Egan's station in Utah was attacked by about eighty of them savages. The Indians didn't have any guns but there were so many Mike Holton, the stationmaster and a rider named Wilson were pretty easily overwhelmed."

"The Indians killed them?" Brianna asked fearfully.

"No. They demanded bread and then kept Holton and Wilson baking more until the flour ran out."

Brianna sighed in relief. "And then the Indians let them go."

"Nope. The filthy savages took them outside and tied them to a wagon tongue that had been stuck in the ground. Planned on burning them at the stake I guess."

"What happened?"

"A rider named Dennis was on his way in from the West. When he saw what was going on he turned around and headed back. He ran into a Lieutenant and his troops about five miles back. The army surprised the Indians and managed to save Holton and Wilson before they were roasted alive."

"Oh, God," Brianna whispered in a horrified tone. "I never thought . . . "

Lucas gave Seth a warning look. "We haven't had much trouble here. So far Fredricks is our only causality, but we keep our eyes open."

"Billy goes out hunting all the time," Brianna pointed out, her throat tightening.

"True but he never gets out of sight of the station. That's the advantage of this location. You can see for miles in three directions."

"Then we're safe here?"

"Well . . ."

"Tell me the truth, Lucas."

He sighed. "The truth is, no. In fact the stretch from Fort Laramie to Salt Lake City is considered the most dangerous on the whole route."

"Because of the Indians?"

"Partially, but this part of the trail is also the roughest, has the worst weather and the least protection."

"But Seth and Billy . . ."

"They knew the risks when they took the job. We all did."

"That's right," Seth said. "They pay Billy and me a hundred dollars a month to take those risks."

"A hundred dollars a month?" Brianna was aghast that they lay their young lives on the line for so little.

"Yup. Pretty amazing ain't it? I was making twelve dollars a month working for a farmer over near Salt Lake City and thought I was dang lucky to get it."

"How old are you, Seth?"

"Seventeen next birthday," he said proudly. "Only a year younger than Billy."

With a lump in her throat Brianna wondered if either of them would ever see twenty. For the second time that day the Civil War loomed menacingly on the horizon and she wanted to cry.

"Don't look so frightened, Brianna," Lucas said softly. "We're very careful."

Not trusting herself to speak, she merely nodded, and let the topic of conversation change. The dark unhappiness brought on by the discussion hung over her through the meal and on into the afternoon. She was so distracted by it that supper was bubbling away over the fire before she remembered Sally's gift.

Just thinking of it lightened her mood and she sat down on her bunk to open the package. She pushed the paper aside and gasped in surprise. From what little she'd seen of Sally she'd halfway expected the dress to be something totally inappropriate, a magical creation of silk, satin, and lace. This was anything but. It was made of blue cotton, eminently practical, and elegantly simple. A slight frothing of lace around the neckline and cuffs kept it from being too plain.

Brianna held it up in delight. It was actually something she could wear. A quick look outside convinced her neither Lucas or Seth was likely to intrude. She closed the door, stripped down to her underwear, and donned the dress.

It was a bit snug at the waist, and a little too full in the bosom, but Brianna suspected that was because the dress had been made to wear with a corset. On a whim, she fished Anna's crinoline out of the trunk and put it on underneath the full skirt. It was a struggle but when she finally finished she was pleased with the result. She felt like a fairy princess. If only she had a full-length mirror.

What would Lucas think? The thought flashed into her mind so suddenly it surprised her. The man irritated the devil out of her. Why should she care what he thought?

Quick on its heels came the memory of what Sally believed was between them. Had the other woman imagined it or was there a grain of truth there somewhere? Confusion swirled through Brianna's mind. Did

Lucas really watch her when she didn't know it? Did she want him to?

As though he'd read her thoughts, Brianna heard him ride up to the front of the cabin. Suddenly she had an impulse to surprise him in her new finery just to see what his reaction might be. Maybe it would give her some insight. Before she could loose her courage she crossed the room and threw open the door.

"Supper isn't for another hour . . . " her voice trailed off in embarrassment as she looked up into the startled face of a complete stranger.

"Well, hello. I wasn't expecting such a beautiful welcoming committee," the man said swinging his lanky frame down out of the saddle. There was a twinkle in his sky-blue eyes as he turned to face her. "Somehow I doubt that you're Lucas Daniels."

"I-I'm Brianna Daniels."

"Ian MacTavish at your service." He swept the hat from his head and grinned down at her. "Is your husband around?"

Brianna hardly heard him. All she could do was stare at the bright red hair that had been hidden under his hat. This was the man she'd expected to find at the Split Rock Station. Tall, slender, and red-haired, Ian MacTavish was the spitting image of the Lucas Daniels she had always imagined, the patriarch of the entire Daniels clan.

15

   "Brianna, did you . . . oh, hello." Lucas's deep voice snapped Brianna out of her shocked immobility and her face flooded with color. Ian MacTavish must think her a total fool to stand there staring at him that way.

   "This is my husband, Mr. MacTavish," she said, her tone sounding breathy and shaken even to herself. "Lucas, this is the man Mr. Bromley told us about."

   MacTavish didn't seem to notice as he greeted Lucas with a big smile and a friendly handshake. "Ian MacTavish," he said. "Ian to my friends."

   "Lucas Daniels. We weren't expecting you until tomorrow but we're sure glad to see you. Been a bit shorthanded around here."

   "Mr. Bromley told me to get here as fast as I could. I rode almost straight through."

   "Are you hungry?" Brianna asked.

   "A little."

   "Then how about something to eat? Lucas needs to

fill you in on the operation anyway. You might as well relax while he does it."

"I wouldn't want to put you to any trouble."

"No problem. I have some leftovers from lunch."

"Some what?"

"She means food we didn't eat," Lucas explained. "Brianna has her own words for things.

"Oh, well I'd be pleased to eat a bite then. I need to see to my horse first, though."

"I'll give you a quick tour of the barn," Lucas offered. "We'll be back in about ten minutes, Brianna."

"Bromley didn't tell me you were married." Ian glanced back over his shoulder as they walked to the corral. "The last thing I expected out here in the middle of the prairie was a woman. I thought I was seeing things when she popped out of that door."

"Brianna's full of surprises," Lucas said dryly.

"Like the way she talks?"

"Among other things." Lucas looked at his companion curiously. What was there about this man that had Brianna so disconcerted? When Lucas came around the corner of the house she'd been white as a ghost. Maybe he reminded Brianna of someone, a brother perhaps or an uncle. With those cornflower-blue eyes he could easily pass for a relative of hers. Watching while the younger man went about the business of putting his horse away, Lucas was favorably impressed. Clearly, Ian MacTavish had a way with horses, and Lucas suspected, with people. It was impossible not to respond to his open friendly manner.

"Where are you from?" Lucas asked him.

"No place special. My mother lives in Salt Lake City."

Lucas raised his eyebrows. "You're a Mormon?"

"No. Ma married one a few years back, but I didn't cotton to the lifestyle. I stop to visit her once in awhile." MacTavish grinned engagingly. "I'd been there about a week when my stepfather introduced me to James Bromley probably hoping I'd get a job and move on again. He doesn't like me associating with my stepsisters."

Lucas wasn't surprised. MacTavish was a handsome devil if you were attracted to the lean lanky sort, not someone a man would want hanging around his impressionable young daughters. *Or a beautiful young wife.* The thought came out of nowhere and Lucas pushed it away in irritation. He should be so lucky. If Brianna and MacTavish did fall in love, the other man was sure to take her off Lucas's hands and he'd be rid of her once and for all. It would be the perfect solution.

"When do I start my new duties?" Ian asked eagerly.

"No hurry. The mail isn't due for a couple of days and the stage won't be through until next week."

"Doesn't matter. I hate to sit around doing nothing."

"Don't worry, there's plenty to do," Lucas said with a smile. "That corral is full of horses that need to be ridden and ridden hard every day. We've only been getting them out about half often enough."

"I've heard some of them have run themselves to death on the route."

"That's true. It takes a lot out of a horse, even one in top condition, to lope for ten miles. So far we haven't lost any from here, but I'm afraid we will if they don't get enough exercise on the days they don't carry the mail."

Ian leaned on the fence and watched the horses for a few minutes. "Pretty impressive herd."

"The best money can buy. It's our job to see they stay that way."

"I think I'm going to like this job. It isn't everybody who can get paid for riding horses like these."

Lucas smiled. "It does have its benefits."

"And one of them is home cooking. I hadn't expected that. In fact I'd heard the food was pretty bad at most of the stations."

"The company doesn't consider that a priority like they do feed for the horses. Brianna can do pretty amazing things with the supplies we do get."

"You're lucky your wife came with you."

"She didn't exactly come with me."

"No?"

Lucas sighed. "It's a long story." There was a long moment of silence while Ian waited for Lucas to explain.

"When will I get to meet the riders?" Ian finally asked, tactfully changing the subject as they entered the station.

"Seth will probably join us at supper. He just got in this morning and they usually sleep most of the day after a ride. Fifty miles at a dead run tends to wear a man out."

Ian shook his head admiringly. "I really wanted to be one you know."

"One what?" Brianna asked looking up curiously.

"A Pony Express rider." He smiled ruefully. "I don't even come close to the size requirement."

"What size requirement?"

"The one that says a rider can't weigh more than a hundred and twenty-five pounds," Lucas told her. "The ride is grueling enough for the horses without carrying a lot of extra weight."

"Ohhh," she said as though someone had just explained a great mystery to her. "That's why Billy and Seth are both so small."

"I wouldn't recommend you let either of them hear you say that," Lucas advised as he pulled out a chair and sat down. "They won't appreciate it. Have a seat, Ian."

"Yes, do," Brianna said eagerly as she set a plate of food on the table in front of him. "I'll get you some coffee, Lucas."

Half an hour later Brianna and MacTavish were acting

as if they'd known each other all their lives. Lucas tried not to view the blossoming friendship with a jealous eye as he pulled his pipe out of his pocket and filled it with tobacco.

He liked the young man himself; why wouldn't Brianna? So what if she seemed to respond readily to his charm?

Lucas told himself he was pleased as he lit his pipe and relaxed against the back of his chair. Let someone else listen to her inexhaustible supply of chatter. He had far more important things to think about . . . like how beautiful she looked and wondering if she'd dressed to please Ian MacTavish.

"What's the occasion?" Lucas asked a few minutes later as she rose to refill the coffee cups. His voice sounded sharp even to his own ears.

Brianna looked at him in surprise. "What do you mean?"

"You're all dressed up."

She smiled and twirled around. "Do you like it?"

Like it? When the color made her eyes so incredibly blue he felt like he could drown in them and all he could think of was pulling her into his arms and kissing her? How could he like a dress that swept away his better sense? Lucas shrugged as he puffed on his pipe. "I don't remember you ever wearing it before. That's all."

"Oh." Her shoulders drooped slightly. "No, I haven't worn it before. The lady on the stage gave it to me today. I was trying it on when Ian arrived and haven't had a chance to change back."

Her disappointment was obvious as she turned to the fireplace and Lucas felt his heart clench painfully. Damn, he hadn't meant to hurt her feelings. "It's very pretty."

"Thank you," she said but her smile didn't reach her eyes as she returned to the table to pour the coffee.

"I've had enough," Ian said smiling up at her. "I should be getting my gear stowed. If you could tell me where I'm supposed to sleep . . . " His voice trailed off and he looked at Lucas expectantly.

Lucas hadn't given any thought to that. Seth and Billy shared the bunk Fredricks had slept in. He'd wanted to be near the horses and had traded bunks with them right at the beginning. Brianna slept in the bunk that by rights belonged to MacTavish. Lucas chewed on his pipe stem as he considered the dilemma.

"I-I guess that one is probably yours," Brianna said looking at her bed uncertainly before Lucas could think of an answer.

Ian glanced back and forth between the two bunks. "Er . . . I'd really rather sleep in the barn if you don't mind."

"There's only one bunk out there," Brianna said reluctantly. "Billy and Seth sleep in it."

"Doesn't matter. I can bed down in a pile of hay just as easy as not." He stood and picked up his hat. "Thanks for the meal, Mrs. Daniels."

"Brianna," she corrected him. "I'll send Lucas to get you at supper time."

"Another meal?" Ian grinned as he put on his hat and walked to the door. "I think I'm going to like it here."

Silence fell inside the cabin broken only by the sound of Ian's cheerful whistle as he covered the distance to the barn.

"Guess he thought it was pretty strange we don't sleep in the same bed," Brianna ventured at last as she began clearing the table.

"I doubt if he realized it." Lucas took his pipe out of his mouth and peered down into the bowl. "No way to tell if that other bunk is used or not the way you keep this place so neat and clean."

Brianna frowned. "I never really thought about why there was an extra bunk. I feel guilty about using Ian's bed. Isn't room and board part of the job?"

"Yes."

"There you see, and I'm keeping it from him."

"If it bothers you that much, we can give it to him."

"W-what?"

"I said we can give him your bed." Lucas didn't look up as he calmly tapped the dead ashes out of his pipe. "We'll rig some sort of a curtain between the two bunks, and you can sleep with me."

"A curtain?"

"MacTavish probably didn't like the idea of sharing his sleeping quarters with a married couple."

"So what difference would a curtain make?"

"This cabin wasn't exactly built with privacy in mind. A curtain would take care of that."

"What are you talking about? It wouldn't do a thing to stop sound. He could hear everything that went on!"

Lucas had to struggle to keep a straight face as he stared at her in apparent shock. "Why, Brianna, whatever were you planning on doing?"

She blushed to the roots of her hair. "I wasn't . . . I thought . . . I . . . "

Lucas laughed outright. He hadn't expected her to take him seriously.

Brianna's eyes narrowed as she realized she'd been duped. "You think you're pretty funny don't you, Lucas? Well, just remember, paybacks are hell and you'll get yours." Brianna threw her dish towel at him as she stalked out the door. "It would serve you right if I called your bluff and crawled into your bunk with you tonight!"

The image of Brianna snuggled up against him in the narrow confines of the bunk hit Lucas with the force of a mule kick. In his mind's eye he could see his sun-darkened fingers against the white of her skin as he slowly slid the demure cotton nightdress down her shoulder and followed its path with his lips. He could almost feel her hands against his naked back, stroking, caressing, driving him to the brink.

The laughter died in his throat as the blood surged hot and heavy through his veins and his body responded to the erotic pictures his imagination created. Lucas closed his eyes and swallowed hard, trying to force his thoughts into less dangerous channels. Whether she knew it or not, Brianna was already getting her revenge.

16

"*I'll be outside if anybody* needs me," Lucas announced pushing his chair back from the supper table.

Ian looked up. "What's the plan for tomorrow?"

"Billy should be in sometime and we'll send Seth out on Copernicus. Other than that it's up to you."

"Just the usual routine then?"

"As far as I'm concerned." Lucas glanced a Brianna but she was busy clearing the table and paid no attention. Wondering why that bothered him, he went outside to smoke his pipe.

It had taken two days of hard work for Lucas to drive away the lustful images his imagination had created around Brianna's taunt. The problem was he'd had too little time to devote to his scientific studies. Now that MacTavish was here to take over Fredrick's duties, Lucas could spend more time in his lab and wouldn't have time to think. With any luck, MacTavish and Brianna would fall in love and take care of the problem once and for all. They certainly seemed to like each other.

Of course, everyone liked MacTavish, including Lucas himself. It was obvious from the moment Seth and Ian met at the supper table that they were destined to be friends. To Seth, Ian's twenty-three years seemed a great age, and his tales of trailing cattle from Texas, riding shotgun for the Butterfield Stage and scouting for the army fascinating. On the other hand, Ian was highly impressed that Seth's equestrian skills were good enough he'd been chosen to ride for the Pony Express.

They happily exchanged stories all evening, every evening with Brianna hanging on their words, obviously enjoying the conversation as much as either of them. Tonight she hardly seemed to notice when Lucas went outside to smoke his pipe. He told himself he didn't care; that he was pleased Brianna was so attracted to MacTavish. But he found himself straining to hear the conversation inside.

"It's called the Pony Express mount," Seth was saying.

Ian's tone was skeptical. "I can't believe a horse would let you run up behind him, put your hands on its rump, and vault into the saddle."

"Well we haven't exactly trained very many of them yet, but Billy and I are close. From what I hear, other riders along the route are working on it, too."

"It's possible," Brianna said. "I've seen stunt men do it on . . . well, I've seen it done."

"Stunt men?"

"They're . . . um . . . people who teach horses to do all kinds of tricks."

"Is that where you learned the trick you used with Franklin?" Seth asked eagerly.

"N-not exactly . . . Hey, wait a minute how did you know about that? You weren't even here."

"Billy told me. You should have seen it, Ian . . . "

"Well I'll be damned," Lucas muttered to himself as he listened to Seth's enthusiastic tale. Sugar! He'd wondered how she'd managed to charm the brute. He smiled reluctantly. That woman never ceased to amaze him.

"No wonder Lucas managed so well for so long. You helped exercise the horses!"

Brianna gave an unladylike snort. "Not hardly. He won't let me within ten feet of one of his precious horses."

Ian was incredulous. "Why not?"

"You tell me. I gave up trying to figure him out long ago."

"Maybe he's afraid you'll get hurt."

"He knows better. He saw me ride." She sighed. "I don't know, maybe it really is a company rule. Lucas says only employees of the Overland Trail Pony Express Stage Company can ride these horses."

"Central Overland and Pikes Peak Express," Seth corrected with a chuckle.

"Whatever. Anyway, I guess I can understand his attitude if that's the case, but I sure wish he'd change his mind."

"You can ride my horse," Ian said.

There was a moment of surprised silence. "I can?"

"Sure, why not. You'd be doing me a favor. With as many horses as there are to exercise here I don't have time to ride Taffy."

"I hardly know what to say."

"I'm sure we'll even the score soon enough," Ian said cheerfully.

Brianna's voice was warm. "I'll do my best to think of a way."

Lucas's jaw began to ache suddenly, and he forced himself to stop gritting his teeth. Now what caused that? Events were progressing exactly the way he wanted them to, he told himself. He was even able to smile benignly and say good night when Ian and Seth left half an hour later.

What he couldn't do was go to sleep after he finally put out his pipe and went to bed. Lucas rarely suffered from sleeplessness, but tonight he lay in his bunk and stared at the ceiling. He turned on his side and stared at the wall. He flopped to his other side, closed his eyes and tried to force himself to sleep. Nothing worked.

After forty-five minutes a slight sound came from the other bunk and he opened his eyes a crack to see what was going on. Brianna was sitting on the edge of her bunk peering at him intently.

Apparently satisfied that he was asleep, she stood up, tip-toed to her trunk, and lifted the lid. The hinge squeaked slightly and she froze in place. The glance she threw over her shoulder at him could only be described as furtive. Lucas didn't stir and after a moment she turned back to the trunk.

By the time she had retrieved what she was looking for, Lucas's suspicion was thoroughly roused. He didn't have the faintest idea what she was up to, but it sure wasn't a midnight trip to the outhouse.

As she slipped out the door and closed it quietly behind her, Lucas remembered the conversation he'd heard between Brianna and Ian that evening.

"I'm sure we'll even the score soon enough," he'd said.

"I'll do my best to think of a way."

Suddenly Brianna's words took on a new meaning and Lucas frowned in the darkness. She was going to MacTavish. Was it the first time or had she been there before? Something painful tightened in his chest as he thought of how pleased she'd been when the three men had built Ian a bunk in the tack room yesterday. He'd thought it was just her natural generosity showing through. Ha! She'd had plans for that bunk.

It shouldn't surprise him, all women were deceitful especially the pretty ones. Brianna was just more adept at hiding it. Lucas wondered how long it would be before Brianna convinced Ian to run away with her. Probably not long. Women controlled men with sex. Poor MacTavish wouldn't stand a chance. Meanwhile, all Lucas had to do was stay where he was and let nature run its course. He hated to lose Ian, he was a good hand, but it would be worth it to be rid of Brianna.

With that settled in his mind, Lucas was out of bed and dressed in a flash. He was still buttoning his shirt as he crept out the door into the night. To his surprise, Brianna was already past the barn and moving purposefully down the path to the river. Of course, she and MacTavish couldn't very well meet in the barn with Seth there. They must have set up a rendezvous.

A darker shadow slipped from the barn and headed down the path after her. Lucas did a double take as he recognized the short, wiry stature and familiar rolling gait. Seth? Good Lord, how long had this been going on? Seth was hardly more than a boy! If the truth were known Brianna probably wasn't much older. Still . . .

Knowing he should go back to the cabin, go back to bed, and leave the other two to their tryst, Lucas followed a discrete distance behind Seth. When they reached the river Lucas suffered another shock. Instead of Seth joining Brianna at the river's edge, he snuck quietly into the bushes and sat down where he could watch her.

Brianna didn't even seem to know Seth was there as she unbraided her hair and shook it free. A moment later Lucas forgot all about Seth. Sublimely unaware of her audience, Brianna unbuttoned her nightgown and shrugged it off her shoulders. Her slender body gleamed white in the moonlight as she turned to hang the garment on a nearby bush.

Lucas nearly choked. God, she was beautiful! He couldn't have been more surprised if he'd discovered she had green skin. If he'd thought about it at all, he would have expected her skinny body to be boney and unattractive. It wasn't. She was still thin, but the weeks of decent food had filled out the hollows and added some much needed weight. Now she was softly rounded in all the right places. Gone was the emaciated waif; there wasn't a sharp angle or boney protrusion in sight.

Lucas's heart hammered in his chest and his ears began to buzz as she turned toward the river once more. With a start, he realized he was holding his breath and released it with a whoosh. It relieved the discomfort in his ears but did nothing to slow the pounding of his heart.

He couldn't tear his eyes away as she gingerly waded out into the river. It wasn't until she took a deep breath and dove beneath the surface that Lucas remembered he wasn't the only one watching. Filled with righteous indignation, Lucas headed toward the bushes. He never would have pegged Seth for a peeping Tom.

Lucas had barely entered the thicket when a twig snapped behind him. Before he could turn, his arms were locked behind him in a vise and he could feel the cold metal of a knife against his throat.

"Don't move if you want to see sunrise," a voice whispered menacingly in his ear. "I'd feel real bad if I accidentally slipped." The razor-sharp edge of the knife pressed warningly against his neck.

"Not near as bad as I'd feel."

He was released as suddenly as he'd been captured. "Lucas! What are you doing here?"

"Funny, I was coming to ask you the same thing," Lucas said rubbing his throat.

"What do you think I'm doing? I'm guarding Brianna while she takes her bath."

"And just how did you know she'd be taking a bath?"

"She does almost every night."

"She does?"

"Yup. The only time she misses is during a new moon or when you come instead."

"How long has this been going on?"

"Almost as long as she's been here. Billy followed her one night to see what she was up to."

"Billy's in on this, too?"

"He's the one who decided we needed to protect her. She doesn't have any idea the kind of danger she could be in out here alone."

Lucas glanced toward the river. Brianna was busily washing her hair, completely oblivious to them. The fact that Seth was right didn't make Lucas feel any better. "How do you think she'd react if she knew you were spying on her?"

"Aw heck, Lucas, we don't watch her get undressed or anything. Well, not much anyway," he added when Lucas gave him a disbelieving look. "Billy knew if we said anything you'd tell her not to come, and she'd probably do it anyway just to defy you. We figured this was the best way."

"Don't you think I should be the one to protect her?"

"No, why?"

"She *is* my wife."

"Not really, you don't even like her. Besides this is one way Billy and I can make it up to her for bringing her all the way out here for nothing."

He didn't like her? Is that the way it seemed to Seth and Billy? To Brianna? Suddenly the way he'd been going about things seemed unfair. He hadn't really thought about it from Brianna's point of view. She'd pinned all her hopes on this marriage, so much so that she'd stayed even when it was obvious he didn't want her to. Seth, Billy and now MacTavish had made her welcome. Only he had remained aloof and distant. Lucas looked back toward the river and found her swimming back and forth across the pool with long sure strokes, obviously enjoying herself.

"She does that every night," Seth said admiringly. "sometimes for half an hour or more. I've never seen anybody that could swim like she can."

"Better go get some sleep. You have to ride tomorrow. I'll stay here and protect Brianna."

"But . . . "

"Don't worry, she's safe with me."

"Well, I don't know . . . "

"Seth, we sleep in the same room every night. If I were going to do something, I'd have done it long ago."

"Yes, I guess you would have." Seth looked back toward the river. "She loves it, you know. I think it's about all the fun she has."

Lucas winced. Seth obviously thought he'd try to take this away from her, perhaps with reason. Lucas exactly hadn't been nice to her. "I won't tell her to stop. As you already pointed out, it wouldn't do much good anyway."

"Do you want my knife?"

"I suppose, though I don't know how much good it would do me if I got into trouble."

"You should have brought your rifle," Seth said accusingly as he handed Lucas his knife.

"I didn't know I was going to do guard duty."

"You're sure you don't want me to stay instead?"

"Good night, Seth. I'll see you in the morning."

"Right." He looked toward the river one last time. "Good night, Lucas."

After Seth left, Lucas sat down to watch. The younger man had been right. Brianna was enjoying herself. Not content with simple swimming, she floated on her back, dove, and even did somersaults. As she cavorted through the water, he was reminded of a family of otters he'd seen playing. Gradually the notion that it would be fun to join her took hold of his mind.

Come to think of it, this might be a good way to show her how dangerous coming down here alone could be. Before he had time to think better of the idea, he'd shed his clothes and slipped quietly into the water.

Brianna floated on her back staring up at the stars. She was pleasantly tired, peaceful. The water felt even better than usual tonight, but she knew it wasn't going to last much longer. It was already the middle of August. By the end of September the river would be uncomfortably cold. She'd definitely have to come up with something. A winter of no baths was unthinkable.

Suddenly the water right next to her erupted as a huge animal of some sort came up from the bottom of the pool. Brianna screamed and tried to get away but it grabbed her around the waist. As it pulled her closer, she realized it wasn't an animal, it was a man.

Brianna fought with every ounce of strength she had, screaming, kicking, clawing, trying to twist away, but the band of steel around her middle tightened relentlessly drawing her backward against him.

"You shouldn't come swimming in the middle of the night by yourself," a familiar deep voice said in her ear.

"Lucas?" She stopped thrashing instantly and twisted around so she could see him over her shoulder. "Dammit, what did you do that for? You scared me half to death!"

"To prove a point. It could just as easily been Bart Kelly or an Indian."

She slapped at his arm that still held her close to his body. "Why didn't you just tell me instead of scaring me like that?"

"Would you have believed me? No, of course not.

And the next thing I know you'd have done something stupid to prove a point and might well have gotten hurt. Now we don't have to go through any of that."

Brianna slumped against him in defeat. Though she didn't think much of his methods, she had to admit he was right. Her heart was still pounding in fright. "All right," she said sadly. "You win, I won't go swimming any more."

Something in his middle constricted as he felt the life go out of her and heard the defeated tone in her voice. "It's all or nothing with you isn't it? There is such a thing as compromise you know."

"Look who's talking, Mr. My-Way-Or-The-Highway himself."

Lucas grinned. "I'm not sure what that means but I assume you're saying you find me somewhat bull-headed."

"A bit."

"Well in this case I think we can come up with something that will make us both happy." Lucas released her reluctantly. She felt good in his arms, too good. His body was reacting in rather telling ways in spite of the cold water.

She swam a few feet away and turned to face him. "All right, Lucas. I'm listening."

"I understand you come down here almost every night."

"How did you know that?"

"Seth told me."

Brianna's eyes widened. "S-Seth."

"He and Billy have been following you and standing guard all summer."

"Oh, God." Brianna felt her face go hot.

"We could come down together. That way you'd get your swim but you wouldn't be alone."

"Together?"

"Sure why not? I like to swim, too."

"Hmm. That's not a bad idea. What would we wear?"

"Wear?"

"I can't very well get in the water with you every night if we're both naked."

"Why not? We're naked now."

Because there's only so much stimulation a girl can take, and I've about reached my limit, Brianna thought remembering the feel of that wonderful body pressed against her back. "There are special clothes people wear swimming."

"There are?" Lucas was skeptical. He'd never heard of such a thing.

"I can make you a pair of cutoffs easy enough if you have an old pair of pants," she said warming to her theme. "I think I have something that will work for me, too. That way we can even go swimming during the day if we have time."

"You really like it don't you?"

"I was on the swim team in school." Brianna could have bitten her tongue the minute the words were out of her mouth. When would she learn to think before she spoke?

Lucas grinned. "Right and you raced barrels, too. This school of yours must have been pretty amazing. Not only did you do the most unusual things, they taught you a completely different vocabulary than the rest of us."

"I-it was pretty innovative."

"Revolutionary I'd say. Since I'm in the water I think I'll go for a swim. Care to join me?"

Not unless you want the water to boil, she thought to herself. Just a few minutes of being held in his arms made her feel like she could go up in flames any minute. "I-I think I've had enough for tonight. Turn around so I can get out."

"All right." He obediently turned his back and listened to her splash out of the water.

"You know, Lucas, I never did pay you back for the other day," she said.

"What other day?"

"When Ian got here."

"Oh, you mean the bed? Are you still mad about that?" Lucas grinned to himself. "I really didn't think you'd take me seriously."

"Oh, no I'm not mad any more. Where I come from the saying is don't get mad, get even. That's what I'm about to do, Lucas."

"What?" he switched around in the water. Brianna had put on her nightgown and was standing on the bank holding his clothes in her arms.

"What's it going to be, Lucas? Are you going to apologize or do I take them with me?"

He looked shocked for a minute then relaxed with a smile. "You won't take my clothes, Brianna. The mosquitoes would eat me alive and you'd feel guilty. Besides, we both know I can't walk that far barefoot."

"I suppose that means you don't intend to apologize." She sighed dramatically. "There's no hope for it then. Have a nice walk home, Lucas." She turned and headed up the path.

"Very funny, Brianna," he called out. "I could almost believe you if I didn't know better."

No answer.

Lucas shrugged and began swimming. She'd come out when she saw he wasn't going to fall for her ploy. There was no way she'd pull something like that and not stay around to have a good laugh at his expense. After about fifteen minutes he stood up and called again. "All right, Brianna, I'm finished you can bring me my clothes now."

Silence.

He sighed. "You win, Brianna. I apologize for teasing you about sharing my bunk."

Nothing.

"And for scaring you tonight."

No answer.

"Brianna, that's enough. You've won."

"Brianna?"

"BRIANNA!"

17

"*Oh, come on, Seth.* It's not that tough to learn to swim," Brianna coaxed. "I can make you a pair of cutoffs just like Lucas's, and teach you before the weather gets cold."

"L-like Lucas's?"

"Sure. I owe it to you after the way you taught me how to throw a knife."

"Rider coming in, Seth," Ian said.

The look of relief that flashed across Seth's face was almost comical. Gotta go. See you Tuesday, Brianna."

"Have a good ride, Seth. You never know when you'll need to know how to swim," she called after him. "Give it some thought."

Ian grinned as he watched Seth hurry away. "You might have convinced him if you hadn't mentioned the . . . er . . . cutoffs you made Lucas."

"I just don't see what you men have against those cutoffs."

"You mean besides the fact that they're indecent?"

"They're not indecent. They cover everything that needs to be covered."

"Except his legs and chest and . . . "

"All right, all right so maybe they expose a little more skin than you're used to. Lucas adjusted quick enough."

"Really? He's never worn them in front of us you know. After you showed us at supper that night we've never seen them again."

"That's only because we go swimming at night."

"And you go at night because he's embarrassed."

"That's silly. He doesn't mind if I see him."

"You're his wife. It isn't quite the same thing."

"I never saw such prudes in my life!"

He chuckled. "Lucas was right you know. You are full of surprises."

"Why do you say that?"

"I've never been called a prude before and certainly not by a woman."

Brianna tossed her head. "Maybe I'm just a little less inhibited than the women you know."

Ian laughed outright. "That's true. In fact, you're less inhibited than most men I know."

They forgot all about Lucas and his cutoffs as Seth kicked his horse to a run and Billy galloped into the yard. Billy overtook them and passed the mochila to Seth without either of them slowing. It was the first time they'd ever done it that way. Brianna got goose bumps just watching.

"It looks like about fifty-eight seconds flat!" Lucas announced as soon as Billy came back to them and dismounted. "Good job!" He slapped the younger man on the back on the back.

"We did it?" Billy asked with a grin.

"You did it all right. Less than a minute!"

Ian pumped Billy's hand enthusiastically. "I

wouldn't have believed it if I hadn't seen it. Damn, you two can ride!"

"Oh, Billy I'm so proud of you and Seth!" Brianna hugged him tightly. "I'll never forget it as long as I live!"

"Blast it, Brianna, you're choking me!" Billy protested, his face turning bright red with embarrassment. But his grin widened, proving he didn't mind as much as he pretended to.

"It's just so exciting! Do you realize how few people actually saw what we just saw?"

Lucas chuckled. "Three. Or maybe we should count Seth and Billy, too, that would make five."

"Er . . . Right, and how many others will ever see it?" Brianna could have kicked herself for speaking in the past tense. These men weren't watching history unfold before their very eyes the way she was. They couldn't possibly imagine the romance and mystic that would surround what they were doing out here a hundred and thirty years from now. "It seems a shame somehow," she finished lamely.

"Uh, oh," Ian said as he began to walk the horse around to cool it down. "Better watch out, Billy. The next thing you know she'll be selling tickets and you'll have to fight your way through the crowd to find Seth."

"I've had enough of that already today."

Brianna raised her brows in surprise. "Crowds?"

"Close enough. There's a buffalo herd between here and Three Crossings. It took me almost an hour to get through it."

"An hour? It must be huge!"

"About the usual. Anyway a crowd would be easier to deal with. At least people get out of your way, and you don't have to worry about starting a stampede."

Lucas frowned. "Were they headed this way?"

"It's hard to tell. They might pass to the west of us."

"It could be trouble if they don't. Any idea when they might get here?"

"Probably not until late tomorrow. They're moving pretty slow."

"Any chance we could turn them?"

Billy shook his head. "I don't know. It's a pretty big herd. We could try, I guess, but I don't know that it would do any good. Not much that will convince a buffalo to change direction."

"I don't understand," Brianna said, thinking how much she'd like to see one of the legendary herds. "Why don't you want them coming this way?"

"After a really big herd moves through, there's no grass left. We have to depend entirely on the feed we ship in."

Brianna was puzzled. "Overgrazing? I thought cattle were responsible for that."

Lucas laughed. "I suppose they could be if there were ever enough, but the buffalo would crowd them right off the range just like they do all the other animals. If a herd the size of this one passes through, all the other game will leave because there won't be anything left to eat."

Billy grinned. "On the other hand, we'll have plenty of buffalo chips to burn this winter."

Somehow the thought of cooking over a fire fueled by dried buffalo dung didn't appeal to Brianna. That was one bit of the old West she'd just as soon not experience first hand. She reached up and wiped the sweat from her face with a grimace. It would probably be as much fun as living through a Wyoming summer without air-conditioning.

By the time supper was over that evening, Brianna was more than ready to head for the swimming hole. She was hot, tired, and felt like all the grime of the prairie had settled on her skin. Instead of changing clothes when

Brianna gave him the opportunity, Lucas took his pipe outside and settled down by the door to smoke.

"Aren't you going to get ready to go swimming with me?"

"Not tonight. I'm too tired," he said striking a match and lighting his pipe.

"Oh . . . all right." Brianna was surprisingly disappointed as she walked back into the cabin. Gradually over the last two weeks she'd come to enjoy his presence, which she had originally thought of as intrusive. Oh well, if he wasn't going there was no reason to wait until dark. She'd just go before she washed her dishes.

Changing into her very practical twentieth century underwear and covering it with her thigh length oversized T- shirt, Brianna grinned to herself. As scandalized as everyone was by Lucas's cutoffs they'd probably have heart failure if they saw her makeshift swimsuit.

Lucas had just stared at her the first time he'd seen it. In fact, the look he gave her had made her stomach do flip-flops and her temperature go up at least twenty degrees. Ever since, she'd wondered what he'd do if he ever saw her in the skimpy bikini she'd bought for herself and never had the courage to wear.

Brianna slipped Anna's loose-fitting granny gown over her head and dug her cornmeal bag of bathing supplies out of the trunk. At least she wouldn't have to hide her soap dish tonight. Soon it wouldn't matter because her soap would all be gone just like the shampoo and toothpaste. Brianna sighed as she headed for the door. She'd made them last as long as she could, but there hadn't been much to start with.

"Where do you think you're going?" Lucas asked as she walked out the door.

She looked down at him in surprise. "Where do you suppose?"

"I said I was too tired."

"So?"

"I thought we agreed you wouldn't go alone."

"We did? When?"

Lucas sighed in exasperation. "The night I proved to you how dangerous it was to go by yourself."

"No, Lucas, the only thing I agreed to that night was that you could come along if you wanted to." She smiled sweetly. "As I remember I proved my point, too, or have you forgotten your walk home?"

"Not likely. I'll have scars for the rest of my life."

Brianna laughed. "Only on your pride. Everything else was taken care of with baking powder and water."

"Your paste didn't stop all the itching," he grumbled. "I lost at least a pint of blood to those damn mosquitoes."

"It was your own fault, Lucas. Anyway, you don't need to worry about me going swimming alone. I'm a grown woman and perfectly able to take care of myself."

"I forbid you to go."

"You don't have the right to tell me what to do, Lucas."

"I can stop you."

"Maybe so, but you'll have a hard time explaining to Billy and Ian why I'm screaming my head off."

"You wouldn't."

"Wanna bet?" She smiled and patted his cheek. "Don't worry, Lucas, I'll be fine. It isn't even dark yet. Nobody could sneak up on me if they wanted to."

"Brianna . . . "

"Bye, Lucas" she called over her shoulder. "See you later." Her smile faded as she walked down the path. She really had to stop baiting him like that. His memories of that night were far from pleasant while hers . . . well . . . doctoring the bites on that glorious body of his hadn't exactly been punishment.

Suddenly, every thought of Lucas disappeared as

she saw a cloud of blue mist forming on the trail ahead of her. With a startled cry she stopped and stared for a full fifteen seconds before lifting her skirt and running toward it as fast as she could. Like an elusive rainbow, the shimmer of light seemed to move, staying exactly the same distance from her until it finally disappeared few seconds later.

Brianna stopped in the middle of the trail and stomped her foot. She felt like weeping with frustration. This time she was certain she had seen two people on the other side. Though the image was dim she was almost sure the taller of the two was Tom Shaffer.

He'd discovered the force that had brought her here and was trying to get her back. For the first time since she had arrived, Brianna really believed she was going to make it home. Frustration gave way to euphoria and then gradually foreboding. Surely if she went back Anna would be coming here. Until now Brianna really hadn't given any serious thought to what would happen if she did. No matter how much they looked alike, Lucas was going to know the difference. For that matter, so would Billy, Seth, and Ian.

Lucas would have to be prepared for the switch, that's all there was to it. A piece of cake she thought sardonically as she continued on down to the river. She could just imagine the conversation. "'I think you should know, Lucas, my great-great-grandmother who happens to look just like me will be dropping in any day now. Oh, and by the way, she's the one you're married to, not me. I won't be born for a hundred some odd years yet. I hope you like her because you two just have to get together so you can be my great-grandfather's parents.'" Right, and he'd commit her to the nearest insane asylum even if he had to go five hundred miles to do it.

Brianna kicked off her shoes, pulled her dress over

her head, and eased herself down into the cool water. Maybe she could tell him Anna was her identical twin. They had switched places because . . . hmm, now what plausible excuse would Lucas accept? The answer was nothing. To him it would be duplicity, exactly what he expected from women anyway.

The real fly in the ointment, of course, was that she wasn't precisely sure Lucas *was* her great-great-grandfather. Not only did Ian MacTavish fit the description, he was just the sort of man who would appeal to the gentle Anna. Though Brianna was attracted to a bit more muscle herself, Ian was a handsome man and far easier to deal with than Lucas. She smiled to herself as she paddled around the pool on her back. Anybody was easier to deal with than Lucas.

Her smiled faded. If Ian were the one Anna wound up with, why wasn't Brianna's last name MacTavish? The only possible explanation was that something had happened to Lucas and Ian had taken his name for some reason. Her heart clenched at the thought.

"I thought you said no one could sneak up on you." As if she had conjured him up, Lucas stood on the bank looking down at her with a forbidding frown on his face.

"I knew you were there," she lied.

"Uh huh," he said as he started to unbutton his shirt. That's why you looked as if your mind was a million miles away."

"Just pretending."

"Sure."

Brianna watched him strip down to the infamous cutoffs. In spite of everyone else's opinion she thought he looked fantastic. Lucas would probably have liked them better if she'd cut them longer, but she was glad she hadn't. With the mid-thigh length, she could almost forget where she was, for he looked just like someone from her time. Of course, if he walked around the edge of a swimming pool at home he'd turn every female head there. "How come you changed your mind?"

"One stubborn woman." He waded in waist deep then dove below the surface, and came up next to her. "Or should I say a spoiled one?"

She wrinkled her nose at him. "Determined is the word, Lucas."

"Is that what they called it in that school of yours? Maybe they should add a course in obedience."

"Oh, come on, Lucas, loosen up. You're down here now. Enjoy yourself." As she said the words she curled her leg around his knees and jerked his feet out from under him.

He yelped as he went down. When he came to the surface she was across the pool laughing at him. "You'll pay for that," he threatened wiping the water out of his eyes.

"Not unless you can catch me," she taunted. With that the chase was on. Lucas was a good swimmer but Brianna was faster and more agile. Every time he thought he had her she'd slip away like a water sprite. Before long they were both laughing as they cavorted around the pool. At last he dove under the water and swam around to attack from behind instead of from the front like she expected. She squealed in surprise as he burst through the surface and grabbed her.

"Now I've got you," he said with satisfaction as he wrapped his arms around her and pulled her close, but her attention was suddenly fixed on something else as she stared toward the north west.

"What's that sound, Lucas?"

"Hmm?" He lifted his head and listened. A rumble like distant thunder filled the air but, there wasn't a cloud in the sky. As he gazed northward he noticed a strange dark line across the horizon rolling toward them in a cloud of dust. His brow furrowed in confusion. "What the . . . ?"

Then suddenly he knew and panic clawed at his vitals. "Holy hell!" There was no way they'd ever make it to the station in time. Frantically, Lucas scanned the area around them. On the other side of the river he saw a small limestone outcropping about a hundred yards up a shallow gully. It wasn't much but it was the only chance they had. "Come on," he said urgently tugging Brianna toward the bank.

His terror communicated itself to her and she moved through the water as quickly as she could. "What is it Lucas?" she asked fearfully as they scrambled up the far bank.

"A buffalo stampede," he said swinging her up in his arms and heading toward the outcropping. "And they'll be here any minute."

18

"Lucas, put me down." Brianna had to shout over the sound of the approaching buffalo herd.

"This is no time to fight me, Brianna. We have to get under that outcropping."

"That's why I want down. We'll never make it if you carry me."

"No," he said stubbornly.

"Damn it, Lucas," she said squirming in his arms. "I can run as fast as you can." She managed to wiggle enough that he lost his grip. As her feet touched the ground she grabbed his hand and started running for all she was worth.

Having spent a good deal of her adult life walking around barefoot, Brianna's feet weren't nearly as sensitive to the rocks and gravel as Lucas's. Though his legs were longer and more powerful she was actually able to move faster. Lucas tried to pull his hand away when he realized it, but Brianna wouldn't let him. He hadn't considered going it alone, she didn't either.

The thunder of hooves became a roar that shook the earth as the buffalo herd bore down on them, a moving wave of death and destruction as far as the eye could see. The outcropping was still impossibly far away when Brianna tripped and landed on the side of her foot sending a wrenching pain shooting up her leg.

"My ankle!" she yelled.

Lucas threw his arm around her waist and lifted her injured foot off the ground. With him half carrying her, they moved nearly as fast as before, but the delay had cost precious time. They reached the outcropping only seconds before the buffalo.

Wrapping both arms around her, Lucas dove under its feeble protection just as the first animal went over the top. Dirt showered down on them, but the rock held. A few heart-stopping seconds later it became apparent very few of the animals were actually hitting the outcropping as they jumped the small gulch.

Brianna began to shake; moments later she started to cry. Lucas pulled her tightly into the safety of his embrace. "Shh," he said cupping the back of her head in his hand. "We're safe."

Brianna's response was to cry harder, great gulping sobs that shook her whole body and sent torrents of tears cascading down her cheeks onto his chest. Helplessly, Lucas held her as the buffalo thundered overhead and the earth rocked around them. Finally, after many minutes, the last hiccuping sobs died away and Brianna shifted slightly so she could wipe her eyes with one hand.

"Sorry Lucas," she said with a sniff. "It's a reaction I seem to have in life-threatening situations. I don't panic when it happens, I just fall to pieces when it's all over."

"You've done this before?"

"Once when I was in a c . . . er . . . in a wreck."

"Are you all right now?"

"I think so. I didn't mean to cry all over you," she said dabbing ineffectually at his chest for several seconds before giving up.

"It doesn't matter. We were both wet anyway."

The tiny space was so cramped neither of them could move more than an inch or two without risking exposure to the hooves that still pounded above them. "How long is this going to last?" she asked glancing nervously at the rock ceiling less than a foot over their heads.

"Hard to say. It could go on for an hour or more."

Brianna was aghast. "You're kidding!"

"It depends on the size of the herd. Anyway, we wouldn't be in this predicament if you hadn't insisted on going swimming."

"I just hate people who say I told you so," she grumbled.

"If you were right you'd refrain from pointing it out?"

"Of course!"

The shadow of a smile crossed Lucas's face. "I'll bet." At least he'd successfully distracted her from the buffalo pounding over their heads. "How's your ankle?"

"Hurts, but I don't suppose it's too serious. Probably just sprained. Thanks for giving me a hand."

"Up to that point you were dragging me along. I suppose you ran races in that school of yours, too."

Brianna grinned. "No, I never went out for track, though my older brother did, and I used to run from him a lot when we were kids." No sense mentioning her physical conditioning was largely due to aerobics classes three times a week.

"I didn't know you had a brother."

Brianna winced inwardly. "I-I don't any more," she said. "I . . . er . . . I lost him the same time I lost my parents." It was true, too. Bob hadn't been born yet.

Just then, a buffalo hit the rock above them with his

back feet. The sound was terrifying, as though the whole outcropping was going to crumble. Instinctively, Brianna squealed and threw her arms around Lucas. He ducked his head, and squeezed her tighter as the dirt and rocks fell around them in a shower.

The flow of debris gradually ceased but neither Lucas or Brianna raised their heads. After several minutes Lucas cautiously opened his eyes. The air was full of dust but breathable and the outcropping was still intact over their heads. "It's all right, Brianna."

She lifted her head. "It is?"

"I think s . . . " Lucas's words stuck in his throat when he looked down into her eyes. They widened slightly, and he felt like he was gazing into a fathomless lake. Her lips parted in unconscious invitation as his breath mingled with hers. Without an intentional move from either of them they came together in a kiss as natural as the rain in spring. Soft and warm like a ray of sunlight through a cloud, it enveloped them in a velvet haze blocking out everything else.

When it ended Brianna lifted her hand to his cheek in wonder. "Lucas?" she whispered.

His answer was a groan as his lips swooped down on hers once more. This time there as much passion as tenderness between them and a multitude of sensations crashed in on Brianna's senses. The length of his body pressed against her, the muscles of his back sleek and solid beneath her hands, the pounding of his heart against her chest as he explored the inside of her mouth. It was incredible, the kind of kiss she'd seen in movies but never expected to experience herself. She gave into the heady sensations overwhelming her.

Lucas couldn't get enough. She tasted of sunshine and laughter as her mouth accepted his gentle invasion. Her hands traced the contours of his back leaving a path of fire in their wake while her body molded itself to his. The more he asked the more she gave, sweetly and without restraint. Lucas had never had a woman respond to him the way she did. Desire, hot and lusty, rose within him like a tide.

He wanted her, needed her the way a starving man needed food or a flower needed rain. His ardor was intensified by the certain knowledge that she wanted him just as badly. As a widow, Brianna was no innocent; she knew what he offered and she welcomed it.

Of its own volition, his hand skimmed down her side to the swell of her hip, his fingers reaching for the bottom of her shirt. It wasn't wrong. In the eyes of the law they were man and wife.

Ironically, it was that thought that stopped him. Giving in to his baser instincts would legalize their marriage and tie them together for life. Lucas wasn't ready for that kind of commitment.

Reluctantly, he pulled away, feathering light kisses against her lips when he broke contact. Only the sound of their ragged breathing broke the silence as he rested his chin against the top of her head striving for control. Suddenly his head jerked up.

"It's over."

"Hmm?" Her expression was bemused, her eyes soft and luminous in the dim light of late afternoon as she gazed up at him.

Lucas was unable to resist running the pad of his thumb over her lips. "The stampede. It's over."

"Mmmhuh."

"We'd better get back to the station," he said gently.

"What? . . . Oh, right!" Brianna blushed as she disentangled herself and scooted out from under the ledge. "Ian and Billy will be worried."

Lucas crawled out and stood up. "I hope that's all. The stampede probably hit them, too."

"Oh, dear I hadn't thought of that."

"They should have been safe enough in the barn. Are you all right?"

"Fine." She reached up to brush dirt off his shoulders. He was covered with it from head to toe, except where her body had been pressed against him. "You're kind of dirty you know."

He grinned. "So are you. Guess we'll have to stop at the river on the way back."

It only took one step for Brianna to realize her ankle was twisted rather than sprained. Lucas put an arm around her for support as she limped along, but she was only too aware of the distance, physical and emotional, he put between them.

Logically, she should have been happy. For the first time in her life she had lacked the ability to say no. Not only wouldn't she have stopped him had he tried to make love to her, she'd have aided and abetted her own seduction. Rationally, she should be grateful that he hadn't, but logic had very little to do with the tiny piece of her heart that mourned the loss.

A glance at the muscles clenched in his jaw, and the frown on his face was enough to convince her he regretted the impulsive kiss. "It didn't mean anything," she said softly.

He looked startled. "What?"

"It's natural for people to react that way in life-threatening situations. I think it has something to do with the instinct for survival; you know like Mother Nature's way of perpetuating the species. That's why so many babies are born nine months after any natural disaster."

Lucas smiled reluctantly. She had the damnedest way of looking at things. "You're sure about that?"

"Positive. Notice we've never even been tempted before." Well maybe that wasn't completely true where Brianna was concerned, but she told herself it was just an overwhelming physical attraction to the man. Nothing more. "I doubt it will happen again."

"No, probably not."

"So we'll just forget it ever happened at all."

"Right."

Brianna resisted the urge to touch her lips where the imprint of his kiss still burned. *Forget it? Not in this lifetime, or her own either for that matter.*

The last colors of a spectacular sunset were fading as they made their way back down to the river. The stampede had lasted less than half an hour, but the devastation was complete. The prairie looked like a plowed field with the grass and sagebrush little more than a memory. The willows along the river had disappeared, stomped into the mud by the thousands of sharp hooves that had cut back the banks and transformed the pool into a muddy mess. The dirty water swirled and eddied around the bodies of three buffalo that had died where they'd fallen, trampled by their comrades.

Brianna made a face. "The environmentalists would have a fit if they could see this."

"Who?"

"They're people who get shook up about this kind of thing."

"Everybody gets 'shook up' as you call it when they're part of a stampede."

"Yeah, I guess so." Brianna knew they weren't talking about the same thing, but it would be useless to try to explain. Lucas wasn't even aware there was an environment.

"I don't know how clean we'll get," Lucas said eyeing the muddy water. "But it's better than nothing."

Brianna felt a surge of sadness as she stepped into the water. Her beautiful refuge was gone. The water would run clear again but the river would never be the same.

It took only a few minutes to wash away the worst

of the grime, but Lucas was already walking up and down the bank when she limped out. "What are you doing?" she asked.

"Looking for our clothes."

"Find anything?"

"Just this." He handed her was what left of her right sneaker. So much for her fifty dollar walking shoes.

"No sign of anything else, not even my boots."

"That's strange. Where do you suppose . . . "

The sudden sound of a rifle shot stopped her in mid-sentence. She and Lucas exchanged a startled glance.

"That came from the station," Brianna said.

With two strides Lucas was at her side. "Let's go," he said putting his arm around her waist and lifted her injured foot off the ground.

The trail had been obliterated, but they hardly noticed as they hurried toward the station. They were clear to the corral before they saw the light in the cabin. Billy came out of the barn carrying a rope. He stopped in surprise when he saw them, then gave out a whoop. "Ian, I found Lucas and Brianna! They're all right." Brianna pretended not to notice as he turned bright red and averted his eyes from her state of undress.

Ian stuck his head out the cabin door. "Where . . . Never mind, I can see." His face broke into a grin. "You two sure picked a good time to go swimming."

"Actually I was forced into it as I have already pointed out to Brianna."

"He couldn't wait to say I told you so."

Ian's grin broadened. "Looks like you may have to eat your words, Lucas."

"Why?"

"Take a look." He stepped aside so they could see inside the cabin. "We're not real certain how he got in or how the door got shut behind him, but he sure made a mess."

A buffalo carcass lay across the splintered remains of Lucas's bunk with its head hanging out the window. The condition of the cabin gave mute testimony to the animal's determination to leave the trap it had found itself in. The table was upended, two of the chairs smashed, and the side of Brianna's trunk crushed. Very little inside the cabin had escaped some sort of destruction.

"We heard the ruckus clear down at the barn," Billy said, his eyes twinkling merrily. "Thought you two were having a fight until he let out a beller."

"Yup," Ian agreed. "We knew even Lucas couldn't yell that loud so we came to investigate. He must have knocked the shutters open somehow and thought the window was a way out. We didn't have any choice but to shoot him. The wall was starting to give under the strain."

Brianna barely heard the conversation around her as she stared at what was left of Lucas's bunk. If she hadn't been here to tease him into going swimming, Lucas would most likely have been in it, crushed to death beneath the huge buffalo bull. Anna would be a widow. . . . all alone except for Ian . . . kind, gentle, red-haired Ian. Brianna thought she might be sick.

19

"*Do you think you can handle* it here for a few days, Ian?" Lucas said pushing back from the supper table.

"Sure, why?"

"I'm going to catch the stage and go on down to Platte River Bridge Station tomorrow. I need to buy some clothes."

"Good," Brianna said. "I'm going with you."

"No." Lucas didn't even have to think about it. A trip like this with Brianna was out of the question. Five days hadn't dimmed his memory of that kiss one bit.

"Why not? I've got to get some shoes. These boots of Billy's don't fit worth beans, not to mention how stupid they look with a dress."

"I'll be happy to pick up some shoes for you."

"Oh come on, Lucas, don't be such a party pooper. I haven't been anywhere since I got here."

"Party pooper, is that like a chauvinist?"

"Not usually, but in your case they probably mean the same thing." She gave him a shrewd look. "It's not going to work, Lucas. I won't be distracted. I'm going with you and that's that."

Ian glanced back and forth between them then scooted back his chair. "Er . . . I think it's time I turned in for the evening. How about you, Seth?"

"Sounds like a good idea," Seth said, hastily jumping to his feet. "I have to ride tomorrow anyway."

Lucas barely spared them a glance. "You're not going with me, Brianna."

"You can't stop me."

"Only employees of the company can ride the stage for free."

"Why am I not surprised?" Brianna shrugged and gathered the dishes. "No matter, I'll just buy a ticket."

"I won't sell you one."

"Whoever is driving the stage will."

"I'm riding back the next day on a company horse."

"I'll take my riding clothes."

"You can't ride company . . . "

". . . horses. I know. So what? I'll rent one from somebody else."

"It's a fort, and the army doesn't rent horses."

"Fine, I'll just stay there until the stage comes back through next week."

"You can't stay there." Lucas was clearly horrified by the idea. "It's completely full of men."

"So's this place in case you haven't noticed."

"That's different. You know us. The men at the Platte River Station are strangers."

"By the time you leave to come home, Seth will be there to protect me."

"He'll leave three days before you do."

Brianna shrugged. "So what? By that time I'll surely know somebody else."

Lucas slammed his hand down on the table. "You're not going with me and that's final."

"You can't intimidate me, Lucas, and you can't stop me. I'm going."

"I don't want you there."

That hurt but Brianna just turned away and finished clearing the table. "So what else is new, Lucas. You haven't wanted me around since the day I got here. I'm not going along to bug you. I just need a new pair of shoes."

She sounded so sad, so defeated, Lucas could have sworn he'd seen the sheen of tears in her eyes. As he watched her carry the dishes to the wash pan something twisted inside.

The day after the buffalo stampede Brianna appeared barefoot, accepting the loss of her shoes philosophically saying she really didn't like to wear shoes around the house anyway. It hadn't bothered her at all until she realized how scandalized they all were by her naked toes. She'd been wearing Billy's extra boots ever since. Even on the dirt floor they clomped noisily.

"I guess they don't go with a dress very well, do they," he said finally.

Brianna looked down at her feet. "No, not especially. They wouldn't be bad with pants, but mine don't fit any more. If they get any tighter I'm going to have to give up riding Ian's horse all together." She sighed. "I've got to stop putting on so much weight."

"It looks good."

"What does?"

"The weight. You've filled out."

"Gotten fat you mean."

Lucas blinked in surprise. "You're a long way from fat. In fact you could use another twenty pounds or so."

Brianna smiled in spite of herself. Talk about a fantasy come to life. Here was this gorgeous man telling her to put on weight. Bring on the hot fudge sundaes!

"All right, you can come with me," he said abruptly.

"I can? Oh, Lucas, thank you. I promise you won't regret it."

"I already do."

"Are we going swimming tonight?"

"Do I have a choice?"

"Always. I keep telling you I don't need a baby-sitter."

"Whatever that is." Lucas sighed and shook his head. "All right, we'll go. How is it you always seem to get your way?"

Brianna just smiled.

The next morning, Brianna was as excited as a schoolgirl when Lucas helped her onto the stage. She had made over a hundred dollars selling refreshments to stage passengers and she'd brought it all with her. One thing Brianna loved to do was shop. Of course, going to Suttler's Store at the fort wouldn't be quite the same as a trip to the mall, but she was looking forward to it all the same.

The other passengers consisted of a middle-aged woman and her husband. Lucas and Brianna had barely settled themselves when the stage started with a jerk and they were off. Brianna knew they couldn't be going more than thirty or forty miles an hour, but in the top-heavy stage it felt entirely too fast. It swayed and jolted over the road alarmingly. For the first time in her life Brianna had an inkling of what her cousin who was afraid to fly went through. Her nervousness must have communicated itself to Lucas, for he reached over and squeezed her hand comfortingly.

"Carriage sickness?" the lady asked sympathetically.

"Er . . . well I don't think so. I never have been before."

"I never was either unless I was in the family way. Could be that's your problem."

Brianna felt herself blush. "No . . . I . . . "

"Don't mind Martha," the woman's husband put in. "She has a habit of talking and then thinking."

"That's true. I'm sorry if I embarrassed you." She eyed the boots peeking out from under the hem of Brianna's blue dress but managed to refrain from asking about the odd footwear. "Where are you folks headed?"

"We're only going as far as the Platte River Bridge," Lucas said.

"Goodness, the middle of nowhere. What in heaven's name are you going there for?"

Brianna looked out the window, and listened with half an ear while Lucas fielded the woman's questions. Pregnant. If the kiss under the outcropping had ended differently she could very well be carrying Lucas's baby. Her own great-grandfather had been Lucas and Anna Daniels's first child. Had he been conceived under an outcropping during a buffalo stampede? Was *her* Lucas his father?

If Lucas had died that night, Ian would have undoubtedly comforted the widow. Had something started that they couldn't control? If they'd gotten carried away and created a child, would Ian have taken Lucas's name to protect it? It seemed unlikely yet the possibility was there. Had she completely changed history because she'd coaxed Lucas out of the house and saved his life? Lord, the more she thought about it the more complicated it became.

Brianna focused on the passing countryside instead. When her parents had come to visit she'd taken them from Riverton to Casper along the highway that followed the Oregon Trail. She had indulged her mother by stopping at all the historical markers and points of interest along the way. It was essentially the same trip they were taking today.

The land looked very different. It wasn't just the missing highway, fences and buildings; even the vegetation had changed. In her time the grass was sparse, and sagebrush reined supreme. Now the grass covered the land in a lush blanket with only an occasional sagebrush sticking above here and there.

Brianna was glad to see familiar landmarks in the foreign environment. The Sweetwater River still flowed through a huge cleft in the rock called Devil's Gate, and Independence Rock loomed above the prairie, the same gargantuan mound of weathered granite. The sameness of the landmarks only served to emphasize how much the land would change in the next one hundred and thirty-five years.

When they stopped to change horses at the Independence Rock station, Brianna hiked over to the historic landmark for a closer look. The names that had been so weathered they were nearly impossible to read the last time she'd been here were freshly scratched into the granite. They covered a vast amount of the rock's surface, a helter-skelter register of the people who had passed.

Brianna was reverently running her fingers over one of the names when Lucas joined her.

"Can't figure out why everybody wants to put their name on this hunk of rock."

She looked at him in surprise. "Why, to leave a record they were here, of course. A hundred years from now people will be thrilled to death to see Independence Rock."

"They'll probably wonder why their ancestors felt compelled to deface it. We'll be leaving shortly so don't wander too far."

Brianna stared after him in amazement. Graffiti? She looked back at the rock and realized he was right. How strange. In the future, tourists would come from all over the world to . . . Suddenly Brianna paused in mid-thought. If she ever made it home again she was going to want proof of her journey.

She glanced over her shoulder and saw they had just begun the process of changing the horses. Good, she still had a while. Grabbing a sharp chunk of rock, Brianna hurried around the far side scanning the surface looking for the right spot. Then she saw it, a small cave-like depression about halfway up the face of the rock. It only took a few moments to pull off her boots and scramble up to it. If she remembered correctly there were no fences here in the future to keep the curious away.

Carving the hard rock was more difficult than she had anticipated. She knew she'd never have time to finish her name. What could she leave here that would prove it had been written by someone from the future? Then she had it. With satisfied grin on her face, she quickly scratched a figure into the surface, shoved a protective rock into the opening, then headed back down. If it was ever found it would drive the archaeologists crazy. How would they explain a smiley face with 1860 carved on its forehead that carbon dating proved to be over a hundred years old?

As she arrived back at station, she was surprised to see everyone was standing around even though the stage was obviously ready to go. At first she thought they were waiting for her but realized that was not the case when the other woman grabbed Brianna's arm and pointed. "It's a Pony Express Rider," she said excitedly. "Look!"

Apparently oblivious to the crowd of onlookers, Seth galloped into the yard and hit the ground running before his horse had fully stopped. He dashed the short distance to his other mount, placed his hands on the rump of the horse, and vaulted over its back into the saddle. They were loping out of the yard before Brianna could blink an eye.

"My goodness," said her companion breathlessly. "I've never seen anything quite like that."

Brianna smiled proudly. "And you probably never will again. It's pretty amazing isn't it?"

"Congratulations," Lucas said in her ear. "You just got another name to add to your list of lucky people who get to see the Pony Express in action."

Brianna tried to think of a snappy comeback for his sarcastic remark but got distracted by his hand against the small of her back as he guided her toward the stage. The warmth of his touch burned through the material of her dress and branded her skin. Life would be much easier if she weren't so affected by him. Keeping her distance was like a piece of iron trying to keep away from a magnet.

The rest of the trip passed uneventfully and they reached the Platte River Bridge shortly after dark. Seth had already eaten and gone to bed but the station-master, a big Frenchman named Pierre Jeveraux, welcomed them with open arms. He seemed quite taken with Brianna, greeting her by kissing her hand and saying Seth talked about her so much he felt they were old friends. His bluff good humor instantly met with Brianna's approval and she thoroughly enjoyed his attentiveness at supper. It wasn't until they'd finished the hearty stew and corn bread that Brianna realized the men were waiting for her to leave to discuss what they considered the really important topics.

Trying not to be miffed, and failing, Brianna went to the bunk that had been assigned to her and Lucas. When Seth told him Lucas and his wife were on the way, Jeveraux had cordoned it off with a blanket. Brianna had worried how they were going to manage without giving away their secret, but suddenly it didn't matter if Lucas was embarrassed in front of his friend. He could sleep in the barn with Seth for all she cared!

She changed into her nightgown and crawled into bed. Even though the trip in the stagecoach had left her exhausted and feeling as if every inch of her body had been beaten, she fully intended to listen to what was being said on the other side of the curtain. They were discussing the transcontinental telegraph being completed as far as Fort Laramie. The company was having trouble keeping the line intact. If the Indians didn't cut the wires, buffalo knocked the poles down by rubbing against them to scratch their itchy hides.

Brianna smiled to herself as her eyes drifted closed. Her image of buffalo had certainly changed over the last week or so. . . .

It was well past midnight when Lucas bid Pierre good night and stepped around the curtain. Brianna was sound asleep just as he'd hoped she'd be. With any kind of luck, she'd stay that way. He grimaced as he blew out the lamp. It was going to be tough enough sharing a bunk with her.

Unbuttoning his shirt, Lucas sighed. He'd better get used to sleeping next to her, he was going to have to do it for three nights. There was no question of Brianna staying at the fort until the stage came back through. Jeveraux would have gladly kept her, but Lucas didn't trust him. Pushing Brianna into Ian MacTavish's arms was one thing; giving her to Pierre Jeveraux was something else. The man had the morals of a bull elk in rut.

To his credit, Jeveraux had been the perfect gentleman, even offering a solution to the problem of getting her back to Split Rock. Unfortunately, Pierre's idea was worse than leaving her here. In fact, Lucas had changed his mind and decided she could ride a company horse back with him. Too bad Pierre didn't have two horses to spare. As it was, Lucas didn't dare send her alone. It would mean getting back a day later than he'd planned, but he had no other choice.

Lucas stepped out of his pants and lay down next to her gingerly. Brianna shifted in her sleep, mumbling something unintelligible as she turned on her side and faced the wall. After several tense seconds Lucas let his breath out slowly. Closing his eyes he concentrated on going to sleep. He was going to need all his faculties in the morning. Brianna wasn't going to be any too pleased when she found out how they were getting home. Come to think of it, neither would Wild Bart Kelly.

20

"*Mmmm.*" *Brianna could* still feel Lucas's arms around her and the imprint of his kiss on her lips. Every nerve in her body tingled from his loving touch. She stretched languorously as the last vestiges of her dream drifted away. Her eyes jerked open a second later when she realized she was not alone.

"Good morning." Lucas was propped up on one elbow grinning down at her. "What were you dreaming about anyway?"

Brianna blushed. "Wh . . . why?"

"The way you were smiling, it must have been good. What I can't figure is why you kept muttering about your grandfather."

"What are you doing here?"

"Until you woke me up with all your moaning and groaning, I was sleeping."

"I know that, but why here?"

"I was tired and this is where Pierre told us to bed down."

"I thought you'd go bunk with Seth."

Lucas put his finger to his lips, then threw back the covers and got out of bed. He peered around the edge of the curtain for a moment before putting his pants on. "It's all right. Pierre's gone."

"Well?" Brianna said, trying to pretend she was glad he'd worn his long underwear to bed. "Why didn't you go sleep in the barn?"

"And leave you alone with Pierre Jeveraux? Not on your life."

"Why, what's wrong with Pierre?"

"Nothing unless you value your virtue. Pierre likes to brag that he's bedded more women than any other man this side of the Mississippi." Lucas finished buttoning his shirt and pulled his suspenders up over his shoulders. "I didn't think you'd want to become another of his conquests."

"But surely he wouldn't try to seduce a friend's wife!"

"He might not expect to succeed, but I think he'd try. It wouldn't be the first time. One jealous husband is pretty much the same as another to him." Lucas sat down on the edge of the bed and grimaced as he pulled on his boot. "I think that's part of why he does it."

"Talk about high risk behavior," Brianna murmured. "Lucky for him AIDS hasn't come along yet."

"Aids?"

"Er . . . it's a disease people get if they aren't careful who they sleep with."

"The clap?"

"Worse."

Lucas looked over his shoulder at her. "What could be worse than going insane before you die?"

Brianna blinked in surprise. She'd never really thought about how devastating gonorrhea and syphilis were before the days of penicillin. "It's kind of the same thing."

"Not a very pleasant death no matter what you call it." He pulled his watch out of his vest pocket and flipped it open. "It's after seven already. You'd better hurry and get dressed if you want to get any shopping done. We're leaving at nine."

"We are?"

"Unless Bart Kelly decides to leave earlier."

"Bart Kelly! Lucas, are you crazy? He wouldn't take me anywhere unless it was to a cliff so he could drop me over."

Lucas stood up and shrugged into his coat. "Let's hope you're wrong. Otherwise, you'll spend the next week trying to fight Pierre off by yourself. I have to head back today no matter what. I'll be back to get you in about forty-five minutes, and we'll go to the store."

"Forty-five minutes! That's half the time I have left before we leave. How about if I just meet you there?"

He regarded her consideringly for several long moments.

"All right," he said finally. "Just make sure you get Seth to go with you."

"For heaven's sake, Lucas. I came all the way West by myself."

"You were lucky. Promise me you'll get Seth."

"Oh, all right," she said grudgingly as Lucas headed out the door, "but only because I was planning on spending some time with him before I left anyway."

Brianna was somewhat disappointed by the suttler's store. Like the rest of the fort it was a rough log cabin, with gunpowder and uniforms filling an inordinate amount of shelf space. The main purpose of the facility was obviously as an army supply depot. She'd been expecting a general store stocked with everything from plows to coffee cups just like the ones that existed in every old West town on television. When would she ever learn?

At least the clerk behind the counter seemed genuinely glad to see her. "Can I get you something this morning?"

"I'm not sure," Brianna said looking over his merchandise skeptically. "Do you have any women's shoes?"

"Sure do." He reached under the counter and pulled out several pairs. "Not too much in the way of selection though."

Brianna ignored the several pairs stylishly pointed shoes. One glance was enough to tell they'd be horribly uncomfortable. The others resembled leather hiking shoes, not particularly attractive but very practical. "These look like what I need. Do you have them in an eight and a half double A?"

"Pardon?"

She resisted the urge to roll her eyes. He wasn't the first shoe salesman to show surprise at the size of her feet, but you'd think they'd be a little more polite. It wasn't like she could do anything about it. "Eight and a half double A. With these I might be able to make do with an A width."

The man looked confused. "You want eight and a half what?"

"Double . . . Oh . . . " Brianna felt like a fool as she suddenly realized he had no idea what she was talking about. Even Seth was looking at her funny. They probably didn't have shoe sizes in 1860 or something. "Maybe I'd better just try them on."

It didn't take long to see the sizing wasn't all that had changed. If the stock at the suttler store were any indication, women's feet were obviously much smaller in the past. Nothing was even close to Brianna's size. Of course it didn't appear there was much effort to make shoes that fit anyway. There wasn't even left or right in a pair, just two shoes more or less the same size.

After a frustrating fifteen minutes during which both Seth and the soldier-clerk seemed inordinately embarrassed by her stocking feet, Brianna gave up. Disappointed, she bought the only pair of footwear in the entire store that even came close to fitting, a pair of the black boots worn by cavalry soldiers. They were a little wide but with a thick pair of socks they were reasonably comfortable.

"What do you think, Seth?" she asked hiking her skirt a bit to show him. "Am I going to start a new fashion?"

"I doubt it, but at least you'll have a good pair of riding boots."

Brianna brightened. "I hadn't thought of that. You know, if I can't get the proper shoes to wear with a dress maybe I should buy clothes to go with the boots." She smiled at the clerk. "Let's see what you have in shirts and trousers."

"Don't forget a hat," Seth said with a grin.

"Right and a hat. Do you have any with one of those cute little rawhide strings to hold it on?"

"That I do."

Brianna had little trouble choosing her clothing from the limited selection and soon moved on to fresh potatoes and onions. "Don't you think your prices are a little high? It costs more for five pounds of potatoes than a shirt."

The clerk shrugged. "I know but shirts are a lot easier to freight in and they don't spoil if no one buys them."

"I don't suppose you have any eggs or milk," Brianna asked wistfully.

"No, ma'am."

"Chickens and cows are pretty scarce out here," Lucas said walking up beside her. "Kind of hard to get eggs and milk without them."

Brianna sighed. "I know but I had to ask just in case. Did you find Bart Kelly?"

"Yes, and even managed to persuade him you were reasonably harmless nowadays. I promised him you'd be on your best behavior."

"Did he promise to be on his?"

"No, but I think he's still scared of you."

"Good. Maybe he won't be so obnoxious."

Seth chuckled. "I'm afraid you're hoping for miracles, Brianna. Better wait for the next stage."

"Bart's wagon is out in front," Lucas said repressively. "Why don't you load these supplies for Brianna?"

Brianna plucked her new hat from the counter and plopped it on her head before picking up one of her packages. I need to go get the rest of my things, too. Don't leave without me, Lucas."

"Take Seth."

"Yes, sir." She snapped a salute. "I won't move an inch without him. Come along, Seth. If you're going to be my personal bodyguard, you'll have to step lively."

It didn't take Brianna long to gather her belongings and change into her new clothes. Lucas probably wouldn't be pleased, but that was just too bad. He wasn't the one who had to climb up to the high seat of the freight wagon in a long dress not to mention having to deal with the incessant wind. Seth raised his brows when he saw her outfit. "What's Lucas going to say?"

"Something rude I'm sure. Then I'll retaliate in kind, and the trip will be off to a good start. We'll probably fight all the way home."

Seth grinned. "I'm glad I'm not going along."

"Hmph, some bodyguard you are!"

Surprisingly, Lucas didn't say a word about her clothing. Other than a thinning of his lips and a muscle twitching in his jaw, he gave no indication that he even noticed.

Bart Kelly was not so reticent. Fresh from the saloon or wherever they sold liquor, he reeked of whiskey and false courage. "Who's this, Lucas, your wife or your little brother?" He laughed at his own joke. "Maybe she just decided she's gonna to be the man of the family."

"Jerk," Brianna muttered under her breath.

"Now, now, dear wife, you brought it on yourself," Lucas said in her ear as he started to help her up into the wagon. "You're the one who decided to dress like a man."

"No, I decided to dress practically for a change." She jerked her arm out of his hand and proceeded to climb into the wagon unassisted. "See? There's no way could I do that by myself in a dress."

Lucas climbed up beside her. "Is that what all this is about, independence?"

"I don't consider climbing into a wagon by myself independence. Holding down a job and living on my own is independence."

"Is that what you plan to do someday?"

"I've already done it."

"When?"

"Ever since I was twenty-two."

Lucas gave her an odd look. "A very long time I'm sure."

"Three years." She glanced up at him in exasperation. "I suppose you think I made that up."

"No," he said slowly. "What I think is that if any woman could take care of herself it's you. I just didn't realize you had."

Lucas's remark seemed like a compliment but she wasn't sure. She never quite knew what his opinion of her was. Conversation on the way back was desultory at best. Bart Kelly's crude comments had a tendency to put a damper on things anyway and the surreptitious swigs he took from his flask every so often didn't help matters. Still, Lucas seemed abnormally quiet and introspective.

By the time they stopped for the night, Brianna knew he was upset about something. The question was what? True he hadn't want to bring her along but he'd seemed reconciled to it. Surely the pants didn't bother him that much.

Whatever his problem, Brianna decided to ignore it. That turned out to be more difficult than she anticipated since she was aware of him every second. The glances he cast her way occasionally were so filled with suspicion that Brianna felt almost as though he'd slapped her.

Lucas's sudden hostility confused her so much she swallowed her irritation when she discovered both men just assumed she'd cook supper. It didn't seem worth the confrontation especially since Lucas sat smoking his pipe and staring at the campfire in brooding silence the whole time. The meal was eaten in silence and Bart wandered off as soon as it was over.

Lucas spread out their bedrolls while Brianna washed the dishes. She raised her brow at their close proximity but said nothing. Far be it for her to try and figure the man out. Maybe he was over his snit, whatever it was.

Lucas was in bed by the time she finished the dishes and appeared to be fast asleep when she finally crawled into her own bedroll. It was oddly comforting to be lying so close to him, even when he was less than happy with her. No matter how mad he was, she was safe at his side.

With a sigh, Brianna closed her eyes and tried to relax. Seconds later the sudden sound of the brush rustling a few feet away startled her. Almost before her eyes had time to open, Lucas had rolled over and was kissing her.

Everything was forgotten as passion exploded inside her and rose in a wave. With a groan of pure acquiescence, Brianna put her arms around him and opened her mouth beneath his. The slightly bitter taste of tobacco and the scratch of his whiskers only heightened her pleasure as something warm and wonderful uncurled in the pit of her stomach.

As suddenly as it began the kiss ended. Lucas pulled away and stared down at her in shock. "Jesus Christ, Brianna," he whispered raggedly. "What are you trying to do?"

She blinked up at him. "Me? You started it!"

"Shh." He put his lips next to her ear as though he were nuzzling her neck. "Bart Kelly is right over there watching us. I just wanted to convince him we're solidly married not give him a show."

"What difference does it make what he thinks?"

"He's not above trying something especially when he's been drinking. In case you haven't noticed, he's been drinking all day."

"Good lord, Lucas, he'd rather take poison than have anything to do with me. First Pierre Jeveraux and now Bart Kelly. You're paranoid."

"I wish you'd speak English when you insult me," he said irritably.

"It means . . . "

"Never mind." He pushed her head down on his shoulder before she had a chance to finish. "I don't want to know. Just go to sleep."

Brianna felt like an idiot the next morning when she thought about it all in retrospect. Lucas must have thought she'd lost her mind and maybe he wasn't so far wrong. There was no way she'd sleep with her great-great-grandfather, but somehow when he'd kissed her she'd forgotten that he was.

"Where do you think you're going?" Lucas's voice broke into her thoughts. From his tone it didn't sound like his mood had improved from yesterday.

"To get some water," she said in exasperation. "I don't think even I could get lost between here and the river!"

"Well, keep your eyes open. You never know who or what might be lurking in the brush."

"Don't worry, I'll be careful." Brianna shook her head as she walked the down to the water. This overprotective, controlling attitude of his was the pits.

All thought of Lucas fled as Brianna glanced up and saw the blue mist beginning to form on the bank in front of her. Determined to reach it, she was running before it even finished swirling. It didn't seem quite so elusive today. In fact as she ran toward it, she clearly saw Tom Shaffer holding something out to her on the other side.

Of course, he was going to reach through the blue mist and pull her through. If only she could get close enough . . .

Suddenly without warning, something burst out of the mist with a loud squawk. Brianna screamed and ducked as it flew over her head. She was so stunned she didn't even notice when the blue mist faded away behind her. All she could do was stare after the creature that had come through the mist and was running across the prairie in a panic.

Brianna rubbed her forehead in bewilderment. Was it a message of some kind? A warning perhaps? The more she thought about it the more confused she became. She could think of no logical reason why Tom Shaffer would send her a chicken.

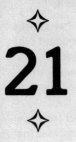

21

"Oh, hi." Scott stepped aside so Tom and Anna could enter the front door of his house.

"Sorry we're late. How's it going?"

"I have nearly all my data retrieved. I lost some when the fuses blew, but I think I can figure it out."

"Good." Tom handed him the hairbrush Anna had found. "This is Brianna's. Will it give you enough DNA?"

"Actually, it's better than I hoped for. Besides, it will be easy to get the same from Anna."

Anna's eyes widened in consternation.

"It's all right," Tom said comfortingly. "He only needs a lock of your hair."

"Oh."

They followed Scott into a large airy room off the living room. Every available space was covered with a variety of equipment.

Scott carefully put the brush down next to a microscope before making his way through the jumble to the two computers. "Dad made me promise I wouldn't take his computer out of the family room again so I decided to move everything in here," he explained tinkering with the back of one of the monitors. "Besides, it won't all fit in my bedroom. There, now all I have to do is turn it on, and . . ."

The screen flickered to life. Scott watched for a few moments before nodding with satisfaction and returning to Brianna's hairbrush.

"How long do you think it will be before we can transfer them?" Tom asked.

"Boy, I don't know, but I wouldn't think we'd even be ready to try it before tomorrow afternoon. Do you have any computer experience?"

"Not much, just some word processing and simple data entry."

Scott beamed. "Perfect. I only have about half of the ranch records back in Dad's computer. If you wouldn't mind typing them in for me, I could concentrate on putting the time warp together."

"Just show me what to do."

The job proved to be a simple one and sharing it with Anna kept it for being tedious. By nine o'clock that evening Scott had successfully isolated Brianna's DNA and Tom had processed about three quarters of the records.

Anna sighed and moved her neck to ease the strain of sitting so long.

"Tired?" Tom asked reaching over and massaging her shoulders.

"A little. Mmmm, that's feels wonderful."

"They don't call me Magic Fingers for nothing."

"Magic fingers?"

Tom grinned. "Never mind. Hey, Scott, what do you say we knock off for the night?

"Hmm?" Scott blinked a couple of times as though

he'd forgotten they were there, then gave a mighty stretch and scooted back from the computer. "Yeah, I'm getting kind of hungry. Mom said she'd leave some TV dinners in the freezer."

"TV dinners?" Anna glanced at the television on their way through the living room. "It cooks, too?"

Tom laughed. "No, TV dinners are ready-made meals. I think they were invented for people who like to eat in front of the TV."

"Why would they want to do that?"

"I have no idea. My mother never let us."

The first bite of her dinner convinced Anna that cooking had become a lost art in the twentieth century. Ice cream and fresh fruit aside, these people had no idea of what they'd given up for convenience. Tom and Scott were making huge sacrifices for her. Seeing they were decently fed was the least she could do. First thing tomorrow morning she'd have Scott explain how to use the stove.

"I still don't understand how you're going to make this work," Tom was saying as he finished his meal. "It seems impossible to me."

"Actually, it's not all that complicated. Here I'll show you." Scott picked up a pair of scissors and cut a half-inch wide strip off a piece of paper. He gave it a single twist then taped the ends together. "Have you ever played with a Möbius strip?"

"I vaguely remember something about it from high school math."

"It only has one side," he said laying it on the table. With a pen he began to draw a line down the middle of the strip. "See, I can draw a line clear around the thing without ever lifting my pen." When the line came back to the starting point, he put down the pen and untaped the strip of paper. Sure enough, the line was on both sides of the paper. "What's that got to do with time travel?"

"Time exists in a straight line. Events happen one after another and you can't ever go back." Scott gave the paper a deft twist and held the ends together with his thumb and forefinger. "Unless, of course, going back is actually going ahead and vise versa. Beautifully simple isn't it?"

Tom and Anna exchanged a bewildered look. "What happened to Brianna and me?" Anna wanted to know.

"I think you were on opposite ends of the strip when it twisted to form the time warp." Scott stared pensively at the Möbius strip in his hand. "I'm not sure why you traded places, if that really is what happened."

Tom's brows drew together. "What do you mean if?"

"Well, I assume Brianna is in 1860 but I can't be certain."

"In other words, there's a possibility we'll be sending Anna into oblivion instead of back where she belongs."

"W-well I . . ."

"Damn it, Scott, this isn't a game we're playing. We're talking about Anna's life here. You can't just . . ."

"Tom," Anna said laying her hand on his arm. "We're talking about two lives, not one. I'm willing to take the chance, and I'm sure Brianna would be, too. Scott did it once and I think he can do it again." She smiled at both men. "Why don't we go to bed and worry about all this in the morning?"

"That's a good idea." Scott jumped to his feet. "Anna, you can sleep in my sister's room, and you can have the guest room, Tom."

It wasn't long before they were all settled in their rooms and the house quieted for the night. Anna dutifully closed her eyes, but sleep eluded her. Memories of the night before were strong. A decent woman would have been scandalized when Tom came into her bedroom half naked and she certainly wouldn't have allowed herself to be drawn into his embrace.

Still, it wasn't shame that kept her awake, it was longing. The feel of his warmth surrounding her and her cheek pressed against his chest had been wonderful, like nothing she had ever experienced before. Tonight, all she could think of was how much she'd like to do it again. Was Aunt Grace right about her having no moral character or was Tom special? Anna didn't know which idea frightened her more.

Rising at first light the next morning, Scott gave Anna a quick lesson with the stove. His explanation about his father replacing the electric range with something called propane because of Scott's tendency to blow fuses at the most inconvenient times, made no sense to her, but she was pleased to see Tom found it humorous.

By the time the two men came in for breakfast all constraint from the night before had disappeared, and they seemed on the best of terms again.

"What's on the agenda for today, Scott?" Tom asked.

"First, a trip to Jeffery City."

Tom looked surprised. "Jeffery City? Isn't that the little town we drove by yesterday?"

"Yeah."

"It looked deserted."

"It is pretty much since the uranium mines closed down. I need a few things to make the time warp more stable and I'm pretty sure I can find them at one of the mines outside of town."

"You're going to steal them?"

"My dad is good friends with the owner."

Tom gave him a skeptical look. "And he gave you permission?"

"Well, not exactly, but he's always let me have what I needed before. Don't worry. Jim's the one who always tells my dad to let me do my experiments. This will make it safer for Anna and Brianna."

"I don't suppose we have a choice then, let's go."

It took a little over half an hour in Scott's beat-up pick up to reach the abandoned mine. A padlocked gate in the eight foot high chain-link fence hardly even slowed Scott down.

"I wonder if there's anything this kid can't do," Tom said as the fifteen year old easily picked the lock and waved them through the open gate. "Heaven help the world if he decides to turn to crime."

Scott pointed to a steel building across the yard. "The warehouse is over there. That's where he keeps all his electrical equipment."

Within a few minutes they were inside and Scott was digging through a large wooden storage box. "There must be a rheostat here somewhere."

When Scott finally reached the bottom of the box, an amazing amount of electrical equipment had found its way to the back of the pickup. "Think you have enough?" Tom asked facetiously.

"Actually, I was hoping to find another microwave antennae," Scott said with a sigh. "Oh, well, I do know where one is. This will get us by at least. Let's go."

Tom drove back to the ranch while Scott worked on one of the breaker boxes. "I hope this will handle that heavy cable I found. I need it to carry enough amps to run . . ."

Anna exchanged an amused glance with Tom as Scott rambled on and on about things she had no understanding of. His voice became an easily ignored background noise as she studied Tom's hands on the steering wheel. They were surprisingly attractive even with the light sprinkling of freckles that continued down his bare forearms. Her errant thoughts envisioned those long fingers winding through her hair and tracing the curve of her neck as he kissed her.

Embarrassed by her improper thoughts, Anna tried to concentrate on something else but she was vitally aware of the length of Tom's thigh pressed against her own on the crowded seat.

"Hey, a telephone repair truck," Scott said suddenly. "That gives me an idea. Pull in at that house down the road there, Tom."

"What's he doing now?" Anna asked as she and Tom watched Scott knock on the door then disappear inside with the lady who answered.

"I haven't got the slightest idea. There's no way I can follow the workings of his mind but then he's probably the next Thomas Edison or Albert Einstein."

"Who?"

"Two of the greatest scientists of the twentieth century. Here he comes."

"We've got half an hour or so before the telephone repair truck gets to my house." Scott said as he got back in.

Tom raised an eyebrow. "I didn't know the phone was out of order."

"It isn't yet. That's why we have to get there first."

"Scott, what are you doing?"

He gave Tom a speculative look. "It's probably better you don't know. You can carry out your part more convincingly if you don't know what's going on."

More than that he refused to say. When they arrived at the ranch, he disconnected a wire inside one of the wall jacks and another in one of the phones. "Now, when he gets here take him to the living room phone first."

"Me!" Tom said in surprise. "Where are you going to be?"

"Don't worry about it. Just make sure you keep him busy for a while."

By the time the repairman arrived Scott was nowhere

to be seen. Dutifully, Tom explained the phone was dead and led the man into the living room. It took less than fifteen minutes to find both wires, and fix the problem. Uncertain how much time Scott needed, Tom tried to stall but was only able to hold the repairman for a few more minutes.

"Boy, I didn't think he'd ever leave," Scott said coming to the front step and watching the repair truck disappear down the road.

"Well?" Tom asked curiously. "Were you successful?"

"Yup." Scott held up a long strand of white cable.

Tom frowned. "What's that?"

"Fiber optics. I was hoping he'd have some in his truck since the phone company is replacing a lot of their underground cable with it."

"Fiber optics! Good Lord, Scott what were you thinking of?"

"It'll help focus the time warp," he explained.

Tom rolled his eyes. So much for wondering what he would do after Anna returned to her own time. The way Scott was going, they'd both be in prison for grand larceny.

22

September 1860

"Whoa." The stage driver pulled back on the reins and brought his team to a halt. "Mornin' Miz Daniels. What've you got for us today?"

"Good morning, Jack. How does cake sound to you?"

"Cake? I ain't had cake in a coon's age. Made with real eggs, too, I'll wager."

"Of course." Brianna grinned. The hen and her eggs had become famous. Everyone was amazed a chicken that had obviously come from a wagon train earlier in the summer had survived so long on its own. Only Brianna was aware how much more amazing its presence was. "You have to have eggs to make cake."

"Miz Daniels, you just made my day. Be sure and save me a piece."

"I will."

Brianna chuckled to herself as she turned to her other customers. Jack would probably have the same response if she said she was serving buffalo chips and snake meat.

There were only three passengers on the stage today so Brianna was finished long before Ian and Lucas had the teams switched. She watched them wistfully. It had been almost a week and a half since their trip to Platte River Bridge and Lucas was still treating her like she had the plague. He barely even talked to her when they went swimming together.

There had been one evening last week when he seemed to thaw a bit, but they'd wound up having the weirdest conversation. For some odd reason he'd thought she'd been married before. When she denied it, Lucas and Seth both looked at her funny. Since then, Lucas had been even more distant.

"Reckon I'll just give this to you since Lucas is busy."

Startled, Brianna pulled her gaze away from Lucas and focused on Jack. He set a wooden crate on the ground, then wiped his forehead. "It's another order from Pennsylvania. Can't figure what a man like Lucas is getting from a glassworks."

"It's for his experiments." Not that she had any idea what those were or that he'd be inclined to tell her if she asked. "I'll get Billy to take it down to him later. Would you like some coffee with your cake?"

"Don't mind if I do." He smiled. "Lucas is a lucky man."

I doubt that he'd agree. A sudden lump formed in her throat. Lord but she missed the friendship she and Lucas had. If only she knew what she'd done. She glanced down at the blue dress. Maybe she should go back to wearing dresses all the time instead of just when she had to serve the stage passengers. They really didn't go with her boots but maybe Lucas really hated the pants. It was so hard to know.

When the stage finally pulled out five minutes later,

Lucas disappeared into the barn without even glancing her way. That clinched it. She was going to find out what was going on even if she had to force him to talk to her.

He didn't much like to be disturbed when he was working in his lab, but he couldn't be any madder at her than he was right now. Telling herself to stop being such a coward, she carried her dishes back into the station, then picked up the heavy crate and set out for the barn.

Brianna hadn't been in Lucas's workshop since the first time she'd met Billy. At first glance she thought it was deserted for the stool in front of the workbench was empty. "What do you want?"

Startled Brianna turned toward the window where Lucas was leaning against the sill and watching her with a distinctly unfriendly expression.

"J-Jack left this for you," she said setting the crate on the floor. "It's from a glassworks so I thought I'd better bring it down before something got broken."

Lucas brightened immediately. "From Pittsburgh?"

"I think so."

"Talk about perfect timing!" His whole attitude changed as he crossed the small room and knelt by the crate. "Hand me that crowbar, would you please, Brianna?"

She did as he asked and watched in amazement as he pried the slats off the top. Like a small boy at Christmas he dug down into the packing, excitement radiating from him. His eyes fairly shone as he pulled out what looked like a small round flask. "Perfect," he murmured.

Curious, Brianna followed him over to his workbench where he carefully lay the flask on a piece of flannel next to an odd looking tube.

"I think this style will work better," he said using a small brush to whisk a pile of burnt material into the trash.

"Heating was too rapid when the tube was open at both ends. This way I should be able to prevent combustion. Are you busy right now?"

"I . . . no. I'm not busy at all."

"Good. Do you suppose you could give me a hand here?"

Brianna could hardly believe her ears. He actually wanted her to stay. "Sure. What do you want me to do?"

He picked up a length of copper wire. "Just hand me things when I ask for them. Here, hold this."

For the next three quarters of an hour Brianna saw a side of Lucas she had seen before. His eyes seemed to glow while his nimble fingers twisted wires and snippets of metal together into a complicated gadget. This was his passion.

At first Brianna was fascinated, then incredulous as his experiment began to take shape. "You're trying to build an electric light!" she blurted out when he finally inserted the contraption into the upside down flask to see if it would fit.

Lucas looked up in surprise. "How did you know that?"

"Oh . . . ah . . . it was just a guess." Brianna didn't know exactly when the electric light had been invented but it sure wasn't before the Civil War. Thomas Edison was probably still in grade school.

"Pretty amazing guess," he said going back to his work. "Actually it isn't the same as the arc lamps they're using in France."

"I-it isn't?" They had lights in France already?

"I'm trying to improve on Robert Grove's incandescent lamp. It's a completely different principal. Arc lamps produce light by forming an arc between two carbon rods. Grove ran a current of electricity through a coil of platinum wire in a glass tube . . . "

Brianna listened with growing astonishment as he

expounded on the virtues of incandescent lighting. Gone was the autocratic stationmaster who irritated the devil out of her. In his place was a scientist with an awesome intellect who envisioned a world lighted by affordable incandescent bulbs. She was captivated.

As the morning wore on Brianna realized how intensely curious Lucas about anything to do with electricity. He had obviously studied extensively before he ever started experimenting. He knew far more than she who had grown up in a world powered by it. Gratified by her genuine interest, he explained why the incandescent lamp was superior, how he'd built his generator, and even what made magnetoes work.

"You really love this don't you?" Brianna asked as he finished connecting all the wires together.

"Mmm. I suppose you could call it that."

"Then why are you clear out here in the middle of nowhere? Surely your experiments would be easier to perform closer to civilization."

"Maybe, but then coming out here had nothing to do with my experiments."

"Oh," Brianna said. Suddenly it all made sense, his self-imposed isolation, his surly attitude, even his distrust of her. "You came because of Marie didn't you?"

He gave her a sharp glance then turned his attention back to the workbench in front of him. "It's time to test this and see if it works. Better step back. You never know what'll happen."

He rose from the stool and began cranking the handle on his generator. For several long moments nothing happened then, slowly the wire inside the flask began to glow.

Brianna clapped her hands together in excitement. "Oh, Lucas, look it's working!" But even as she said the words there was a flash of light and then the bulb went dark. "What happened?"

"The filament burned out just like it always does. It lasted a lot longer this time, though. I think I'm on the right track at last. Maybe it's just a matter of finding the best material to use for a filament, something that won't burn up as quickly."

"That must be why it has to be a vacuum," Brianna murmured as she contemplated the inverted flask.

"What did you say?"

Startled Brianna looked up and encountered Lucas's intense stare. She hadn't even realized she'd spoken aloud.

"Oh, nothing important."

"Yes it was, you said something about a vacuum."

Brianna's eyes widened into what she hoped passed for an innocent look. "A what?"

He gazed at her suspiciously for a long moment before shaking his head and turning back to his experiment. "No, of course you wouldn't know what that is. Still, it's worth looking into."

Oh lord, what had she done? As little as Brianna knew about light bulbs she could tell Lucas was fairly close to inventing a workable one. What if she had just given him the last little piece of information he needed? Whatever else had happened in the past she knew Lucas Daniels hadn't invented the light bulb.

"Is this the only thing you're working on?" she asked hoping to distract him long enough that he'd forget all about vacuums.

"No. I have a couple of other ideas."

"Like what?"

"Well, the talking telegraph for one."

"The talking telegraph?"

Lucas smiled. "I have a theory that it's possible to change voices into electrical impulses, send them across a telegraph wire, and change them back at the other end. Sounds crazy doesn't it?"

Crazy? Lord, he ought to see her phone bill every month. "You think you could really do that?"

"I've run into a problem, but I'm pretty sure I can work it out. Actually I'm closer on the talking telegraph than I am on the incandescent light."

"You're incredible, Lucas. I had no idea."

"Most people just think I'm touched in the upper works."

"That's what they say about all great inventors."

He rubbed the side of his nose self-consciously. "Well, one thing's sure. You're bound to like my other invention."

"Oh, what's that?"

"Come on, I'll show you."

As he took her hand and pulled her across the room, Brianna was once again reminded of an excited child. Whatever it was he couldn't wait to show her. If her half-dressed swimming partner was attractive and the highly intelligent scientist fascinating, this tousle-haired little boy was completely irresistible. Her heart turned over in her chest. *I'm in love with him!*

The thought hit her with the suddenness of a lightning strike. Oh God, how could she be so stupid? Of all the men in her life, why did he have to be the one? Her own great-great-grandfather for heaven's sake, and a man who didn't particularly like her to boot. Ian would have been a much safer choice. Even Seth or Billy would have made more sense. At least they liked to have her around.

"Are you all right?"

"Wh . . . what?"

"You look . . . strange." Lucas was watching her with real concern.

"I'm fine."

He reached over and brushed the backs of his fingers against her forehead to check for fever. "Are you sure? Your face is a little peaked."

"Just a little dizzy. I think I moved too fast." Her hand tingled where his fingers still clasped hers, and she pulled away. "What was it you wanted to show me?"

Lucas gazed at her intently for a moment. Then, apparently satisfied that she was all right, he relaxed and nodded toward the corner. "After the stampede, I realized going swimming every day was more than just for fun for you. You have a real penchant for being clean. The river's going to be too cold soon so I rigged this up for you."

Brianna looked at the apparatus in confusion. By no stretch of the imagination could it be a bathtub. A pipe with a strange flat metal piece attached to the end of it extended out and downward from half a barrel. A thin chain was hooked to a metal piece behind the pipe. "What is it?"

"First you heat your water and pour it in here," he said indicating the top of the barrel. "When you pull the chain the water comes down the pipe and spreads out across this plate. I've drilled holes in the bottom so it comes out in a spray. I'll hang it on the wall in the cabin and build a stall around it for privacy. You may not be able to bathe every day, but it won't use as much water as a tub."

"You made me a shower?" Brianna was incredulous.

Lucas shrugged. "I guess that's as good a name as any."

As she stared at the primitive shower, Brianna felt tears form in her eyes. He must have spent hours working on it. "Thank you, Lucas. It's wonderful."

He looked at her oddly. "Then why are you crying?"

"It's just such a surprise," she said wiping her eyes. "You built this before we went to Platte River Bridge didn't you?"

"As a matter of fact I did. Why?"

"Because something happened on that trip that

changed our whole relationship. I came down here today find out what."

It was like watching a door slam. The beautiful gray eyes became distant and a muscle jumped in his jaw as he gritted his teeth.

"What is it, Lucas?" she asked softly, fear of his answer squeezing her heart. "I've gone over it a hundred times and can't think of anything except maybe wearing clothes you don't like."

"You didn't do anything on the trip."

"Then it was something I said?"

"You might say that." He walked to window and leaned his arm against the frame as he stared out unseeingly. "The only thing I detest more than lies are the people who tell them."

Brianna's brows came together in surprise. "I didn't lie to you, Lucas."

"You've been living a lie since the day you got here."

A shock of apprehension ran through her as goose bumps rose on her skin. "Wh-what do you mean?"

He turned to stare at her, his eyes as cold as polished steel. "I don't know who the hell you are, but you're not Anna Daniels."

23

"I never said I was Anna Daniels," Brianna said cautiously as she faced Lucas across his workshop. "My name is Brianna."

"I suppose you're going to try and tell me it was you that wrote all those letters to Billy and Seth."

"You obviously don't think so."

He snorted and leaned back against the window frame with his arms folded across his chest. "I know you didn't. The woman who wrote those letters was a nineteen year old orphan who had spent her entire life living with her spinster aunt. She didn't have a father or a brother, couldn't remember her mother, and as far as I can tell never set foot inside that school of yours. The one thing she did have was a husband even if it was for a short time. If you wrote those letters, then everything you've told me since you got here was a lie."

Brianna sighed. This was going to take very careful handling. "No, I didn't write them and I didn't realize Anna had either. It's only because I've been telling you the truth that you figured it out."

"So you admit you're not Anna Daniels then?"

"No, I'm not Anna."

"Who are you?"

"I didn't lie about that either. My name really is Brianna. Anna and I are . . . closely related."

"Where is she?"

"I-I'm not really sure, but I know she's trying to get here. It's just a matter of time." Brianna swallowed a hysterical giggle at her choice of words.

"I don't suppose you'd consider telling me what the hell is going on?"

Oh lord she was tempted. All she had to do was show him the contents of Tom's backpack and Lucas would believe she was a time traveler. If this conversation had come up yesterday she'd probably have done just that, but now she knew she couldn't. It would take him about thirty seconds to figure out the flashlight or camera strobe. That knowledge would throw the world ahead at least twenty years; it could conceivably change the outcome of the Civil War. Even the batteries or calculator were dangerous. There was no way she could let that technology fall into his far too capable hands.

"Well?" He was waiting for an answer, and none too patiently at that.

"I won't lie to you, Lucas, but I can't explain. It's not my secret alone."

"Anna's involved in something illegal isn't she?"

"No, it's nothing like that. I'm not sure where she is or when she'll be back, but neither of us is a danger to anyone. Come on, Lucas, two helpless women who can't even communicate with each other, what could we do?"

"I don't know about Anna, but I wouldn't exactly describe you as a helpless woman."

"What? Did I just imagine it, or did you actually admit I can take care of myself?"

Lucas gave a ghost of a smile. "Don't try to change the subject."

"Somehow I didn't think you'd concede that point." Then her smile faded. "I know this is hard, Lucas. If you can't trust me, at least believe I mean you no harm."

He stared at her thoughtfully. "What about Anna?" he asked finally.

"You'll find her much easier to get along with," Brianna said without hesitation. "And she won't be as out of place here as I am. In fact I think the two of you will really hit it off."

"Hit what off?"

Brianna smiled. "That means you'll really like each other. She even speaks the same language as you do."

"Which one of you am I supposedly married to?"

"Anna."

"Then why have you insisted on staying here?"

"Because I have to be here when she comes back."

"Why?"

"I can't explain, Lucas." Brianna sighed. "Look, nothing's changed except your perception. I'm the same person that's been here for the last three months. There's no reason to act any differently until Anna arrives."

"And what the hell am I supposed to do when she shows up, welcome her with open arms?"

"That would be nice." Brianna tried to ignore the stab of jealousy his words evoked. After all he was going to have to do more than hug Anna if the Daniels family was going to exist in her time. "At least try to stay open minded toward her."

"That's asking a lot isn't it?"

"Maybe, but don't worry, you won't find Anna nearly as aggravating as you do me."

"I'm kind of getting used to being aggravated."

She grinned slightly. "I like you, too."

He turned back to the window with a sigh. "I don't have much choice in this do I?"

"None of us do, Lucas. Anna and I don't like it any better than you."

Brianna had always heard that confession was good for the soul, but she felt guilty instead of purged. Though Lucas had said little else, she was conscious of his speculative glances all day. It was obvious he still didn't trust her, and she really couldn't blame him. At least now she understood the distance he put between them.

By supper time the next day, she almost had herself convinced it was for the best. She certainly didn't have to worry about giving in to her baser instincts; he'd never again get close enough to be a temptation.

Brianna was determined to act normal and thought she'd been fairly successful until the men came in for supper. It was obvious Ian and Billy thought she and Lucas had argued. Their overly cheerful banter was meant to boost her spirits, but it only served to emphasize Lucas's unusual silence.

"You looked mighty pretty this morning when the stage came in, Brianna." Billy said toward the end of the meal.

Brianna was startled. "Why, thank you, Billy."

"Reckon I've missed seein' you in a dress."

She bit back a smile. Was he trying to give her a subtle hint about what he thought would please Lucas? "I don't have any shoes to wear with a dress. My boots look kind of funny."

"You know," Ian said suddenly. "I just might have something that will work."

Lucas raised his brows. "You have a pair of women's shoes?"

"No, but . . . heck, I'll just go get them." The other three exchanged a surprised glance as he left.

When Ian returned he was grinning from ear to ear. "Don't know why I didn't think of these before."

Brianna looked down at the shoes he put in her hands. "Moccasins!" She measured one against the bottom of her boot. "Looks like they'll fit perfectly. Where did you get these, Ian? They're beautiful."

"My . . . friend made them for me."

Something in his voice made Brianna glance up in surprise. She thought caught a fleeting glimpse of pain in his eyes, but it was gone so quickly she wasn't positive. "Are you sure you want me to wear these?"

"I outgrew them a long time ago." There was a touch of sadness to his smile. "Besides, I think my friend would approve."

"Thank you," Brianna said softly. "I'll take very good care of them."

She jumped slightly as Lucas abruptly scooted his chair back and stomped outside to smoke his pipe.

When he didn't return by the time the dishes were done, Brianna decided she didn't feel like swimming and went to bed early. She was fast asleep when Lucas finally came back in and stood by her bunk staring down at her.

His eyes were sad as his gaze followed the line of her body under the blanket and then returned to her face. After a moment, he reached down and gently touched her cheek. With a sigh, she turned her face into his hand. Her lips brushed against his palm and Lucas jerked his hand away as though it had been burned. With a sound like a growl he retreated to his own side of the cabin, where he undressed and threw himself down on his bunk in disgust.

*   *   *

It was dawn when the sound of high-pitched screams and whinnies brought them both straight up in bed.

"What's going on?" Brianna asked fearfully.

"Something's bothering the horses." Lucas pulled on his pants, grabbed his rifle, and strode to the door with Brianna right behind him.

Outside pandemonium reigned supreme. Horses milled both inside and outside the corral while a huge stallion reared up on his hind feet above the wild herd. His were the screams that split the air as he called to the mares behind the pole fence.

Brianna stared at the stallion in awestruck silence. His palomino coat shone golden in the first rays of the sun as his hooves pawed the air with lethal intent. He was magnificent.

The click of a rifle hammer being cocked near-by drew her attention. Her eyes widened in horror as she saw Lucas take careful aim. He was going to shoot the stallion!

"No!" She threw herself at Lucas just as the charge went off knocking them both back against the side of the cabin.

"Jesus, Brianna, what do you think you're doing?" he yelled struggling back to his feet.

"You don't have any reason to kill him."

"The hell I don't." Lucas reached inside the door, grabbed his powder horn and upended it into his barrel. "He's stealing the horses!"

Even as he said the words the fence gave way with a loud crack and the horses surged out. With one last defiant cry, the stallion wheeled and headed toward the open prairie with all the other horses, wild and tame running behind him. Belatedly, Brianna realized the enormity of what she'd done. Without the horses, they were stranded in the middle of nowhere with no way of even letting anyone know they were in trouble. She hadn't even stopped the senseless killing of an innocent animal. A young buckskin lay on its side bleeding from the crease Lucas's misfired bullet had put in its skull.

"Christ, Billy, it isn't worth getting killed over," Lucas muttered.

Brianna looked toward the barn and froze in horror. As the last of the horses streamed out of the corral, Billy ran along side them. With a sudden leap he was on DaVinci's back leaning low over the gelding's neck. For one heart-stopping moment it looked as though his attempt would prove futile and he'd be killed for his efforts. Then he straightened and the horse began to slow. With the pressure from his knees and a fistful of mane in his hand, Billy brought DaVinci under control.

A sudden familiar whistle split the air. Ian was calling his horse Taffy and Brianna watched in amazement as the big sorrel turned away from the herd. She hadn't realized the bond between the man and his horse was so strong.

"Damn it to hell," Lucas swore as the last of the horses disappeared in a cloud of dust. Brianna nearly had to run to keep up with him as he strode across the yard to the corral.

Billy rode DaVinci into what was left of the enclosure and slid from his back. "Could be worse. At least we can go after them. With three men on horseback we have a chance."

Three? Brianna followed the line of his gaze and was startled to see one horse was still in the corral. Franklin.

"Of all the horses to stay behind," Ian said. "Wonder why he didn't go with the others?"

"I don't think he wanted to tangle with that stallion," Lucas said.

"Neither do I." Billy shook his head. "Too bad you missed him, Lucas. I couldn't ever get a clear shot."

"I probably wouldn't have missed if Brianna had

kept her nose out of it. She hit my arm and knocked my aim off."

Brianna's bare toes curled into the soft dirt in guilty dismay as three pairs of accusing eyes suddenly turned her way. She gave them an apologetic smile. "Oops."

24

"*Oops?*" *Lucas's tone* was sarcastic as he echoed Brianna. "Is that an explanation or an apology?"

"I-I didn't understand what was happening," she said. "I'm sorry."

"Well that helps a lot. It should bring the horses right back."

"Er . . . don't you think we'd better get the corral fixed and go after the horses?" asked Billy.

Brianna turned to go. "I'll get breakfast."

"We won't have time to cat," Lucas said. "That herd is getting farther away by the minute."

"Then I'll throw together something you can take with you."

The dead horse lay between her and the station. With a grimace, she stepped around it. What a fiasco. As if Lucas weren't mad enough at her already.

Brianna dressed hurriedly before fixing their lunch. She hadn't missed the consternation on Ian's and Billy's faces when they saw her dressed only in her nightgown and realized they were both bare-chested. Honestly, the men in this century were so hung up on modesty it was a wonder there were any babies born at all.

It took only a few minutes to slice an entire loaf of bread and add thick slices of meat left over from supper the night before. "Hold the mayo," she muttered thinking how dry the sandwiches were going to be. She wrapped them in a clean dish towel, stuck them in an empty flour sack and added a generous supply of buffalo jerky. Without potato chips or dessert it wasn't a very exciting lunch, but maybe they wouldn't care. After all, the days of high calorie snack foods were still in the distant future. The men couldn't miss what they'd never had.

Brianna was just starting to fill Lucas's canteen when he came in to finish getting dressed. One look at his face was enough to convince her that keeping silent was a good idea. She pretended to ignore him as he put on his shirt and suspenders.

Lucas gave her a sidelong glance as he sat down on the edge of the bed and put on a sock. "We may be gone all day."

"I know, that's why I fixed enough for two meals." She put the lid on the canteen and laid it down next to the food sack. "What if you can't find the wild herd?"

"Then we'll have to ride to Devil's Gate and Three Crossings to get more stock. In that case, we could be gone all night. We can't move horses after dark."

"Oh."

"Will you be all right here by yourself?"

Brianna looked at him in surprise. "Well, of course I will be. What is there to be afraid of?"

"I've told you at least a dozen times," Lucas said in exasperation as he pulled on a boot. "Not that you ever paid any attention."

"If I ever encounter a bad guy, I might start listening

to you. So far Bart Kelly is the closest I've seen and I can handle him."

"I don't suppose it will do me any good to remind you, it was a pretty close call with him?"

"No."

"Somehow I didn't think so." Lucas put on his other sock and boot. "I'll leave my rifle."

"It wouldn't help. Not only couldn't I hit the broad side of a barn, I wouldn't have the faintest idea how to reload a black powder rifle once I fired it."

"I'll teach you."

Brianna smiled. "If you don't have time for breakfast, you don't have time for that either. Don't worry, Lucas, nobody will bother me. Besides I've got my knife, and Seth taught me how to use it. I'm perfectly safe."

"Last I knew it was in your trunk," he pointed out as he buttoned his vest put on his coat. "Not exactly accessible is it?"

Brianna went to her trunk, got the knife out, held it up to show him, then walked over and put it on the mantle. "Satisfied?"

"I guess I'll have to be." His jaw looked hard as a piece of granite as he picked up the canteen and lunch sack. "You'll do what you want just like you always do."

"Don't be mad, Lucas."

"Why should I be mad?" he asked sarcastically. "You obviously think I'm a fool and refuse to listen to anything I say."

"No, that's not what . . . " But Lucas slammed out of the cabin before she could finish. By the time Brianna got to the door, the three men were mounted and riding out of the yard. "Damn!" Brianna said fighting tears. She hadn't meant to make him mad, it just seemed to be something she did naturally, kind of like breathing. It shouldn't come as any surprise. He'd never made any secret of his feelings about having her around, but it hurt.

"That's what you get for falling in love with him. It's not like you didn't know better," she told herself. It made no sense to stand there staring after the three men, but she didn't move until they rode out of sight.

Brianna was turning to go inside when she caught a movement out of the corner of her eye and took good look. The "dead" horse was moving!

Oh lord, the bullet had only wounded it. The poor thing would be have to be put out of its misery and Lucas had taken his rifle. Her heart sank as she realized what she was going to have to do. Her knife was equal to the task, Seth had always insisted she keep it razor sharp. The question was whether she could bring herself to slit the animal's throat.

Sickened by the thought but determined not to let an animal suffer unduly, she went to get her knife. When she returned, she was astonished to see the horse had lifted its head off the ground and was attempting to rise. Maybe his injuries weren't so bad after all.

"Come on, you can do it," Brianna whispered as the animal tried to struggle to its feet. Relief flooded through her when he finally succeeded. There was no question of killing him now. Though he was obviously shaken and disoriented, the bullet must have merely glanced across his skull knocking him unconscious.

As she stood there watching him, Brianna wondered if she could get him into the corral. He appeared to be a two or three year old, just right to begin breaking to ride. The idea of having her own horse was tempting. "I won't hurt you, boy," she said soothingly. "You and I are going to be great friends. Just a few steps forward. That's all we need."

He turned his head and eyed her warily as she slowly approached from the rear. Her steady advance and the sound of her voice made him nervous. With a snort, he moved several steps away, straight toward the open gate of the corral.

It took several minutes and a great deal of effort to work him into the corral but Brianna smiled in satisfaction as she closed the gate behind him. She couldn't wait to see the men's faces when they returned.

Then she sobered. Billy and Ian would be pleased, but Lucas might be another matter entirely. Given the mood he was in, he'd probably tell her they couldn't give company feed to a noncompany horse. She could just hear him.

It wasn't as if she'd be mooching. Heaven knew she did enough work around here for "company" employees and wasn't paid a penny for any of it. Maybe it was time to point that out. If she went on strike and refused to cook, clean or do laundry unless he let her keep the horse he'd be forced to see things her way wouldn't he?

"No, he'd probably tell us both and hit the road," she told the buckskin as she threw a generous portion of hay over the fence for him. "Don't worry, I'll come up with something."

She returned to the cabin deep in thought. This would take careful planning. If she could somehow get Lucas in a receptive mood. . . . The memory of cleaning the entire house without being asked so her mother would let her keep a stray dog flashed through her mind and she smiled. It had worked once.

What would impress Lucas? The answer hit her almost immediately. Sweet rolls! The man loved bread in any form and had a sweet tooth that wouldn't quit. One taste and he'd be putty in her hands. Brianna grinned at the ridiculous notion that Lucas could be ruled by his stomach. Still, he was easier to deal with full and happy than hungry and grouchy.

She was about to lay her knife on the trunk then

remembered Lucas's warning. He did have a point. The mantle was a far better place for the knife to be in the unlikely event that she had to defend herself. She set it next to the lantern and promptly forgot all about it as she set to work.

There was a nip of fall in the air, and the fire in the fireplace felt good for a change. Brianna puttered around the cabin while she waited for the bread to rise. She had her chores done in record time. Without breakfast dishes to wash or lunch to fix she found herself with time on her hands.

The luxury of a full day without interruptions stretched before her like an unexpected gift. She couldn't even manage to feel guilty about it as she checked on the horse in the corral and found him contentedly munching on the hay she'd left him. Brianna briefly considered beginning his training but knew he needed a few days to adjust to his new surroundings.

When she returned to the station, she realized this would be the perfect day to catch up on her journal. In her odd moments of privacy the last couple of days, she'd managed to keep up with day to day happenings, but hadn't had time to tell Anna about her confrontation with Lucas.

It was imperative that Anna understand for it would be up to her to explain it all to Lucas and in such a way that he would trust her. It seemed an impossible task, especially for someone who didn't know the volatile stationmaster. Maybe she should tell Anna to let Lucas read the journal. That way Brianna herself could explain why she'd been so reluctant to tell him everything. Surely he'd understand why she'd felt she couldn't let him see the flashlight or . . .

Brianna's musings came to a sudden halt. Oh Lord, she couldn't leave Tom's backpack and its contents here! Nor was it likely she'd have it with her if she and

Anna ever traded places again. She hadn't even thought of it before. Her gaze flew to the trunk. With sick certainly she knew she was going to have to destroy everything she'd brought along. With no idea of when Tom would succeed and take her back to her own time, she couldn't put it off.

As she set the journal down on the bunk and took the backpack out of the trunk, she felt a peculiar wrench. What if this was how Tom was locating her? But there could be no connection; the blue mist always appeared where she was even when the backpack was miles away. She knew it was just an excuse because she was reluctant to part with the only contact she had with her own world.

She dumped the contents out on the bunk. Perhaps there were some things that could be salvaged. But she soon realized it would all have to go. Even the nylon of the bag itself was a dangerous anachronism.

With a pang, she ran her fingers over Tom's camera. It was an expensive piece of equipment, and she was going to have to dismantle it clear down to nuts and bolts. Even the lenses would have to be destroyed beyond recognition. Who knew what Lucas could do with advanced optics like these. She flipped the button on the back of the strobe and listened to the familiar whine as it charged.

With a sigh, she lay the camera aside and picked up the flashlight. She clicked the switch and grimaced at the bright light. Darn Tom Shaffer and his conscientiousness. Dead batteries would be a whole lot easier to dispose of than good ones. Now she had to worry about making sure they were unusable before she got rid of them.

The unexpected whinny of a horse brought her head up in alarm. They were back! She started to stuff everything back into the bag but was less than halfway done when someone outside lifted the door latch. Grabbing the first thing that came to her hand, Brianna jerked Anna's crinoline out of the trunk and threw it over the pile on her bed. Hopefully the men would be too embarrassed to look closely. Standing there by her bunk trying to look innocent, Brianna felt like a naughty child caught red-handed as the door swung open.

In the next instant every vestige of her guilt disappeared as an Indian brave stepped inside. Brianna could have sworn he looked surprised when he saw her. He said a few unintelligible words over his shoulder and was immediately joined by three others who stared at her as if she was some kind of circus freak.

In spite of the slight chill in the air, they were dressed only in buckskin leggings and breechcloths, with their long black hair hanging loose around their shoulders. Two carried rifles, and all four watched her with unnerving stares. But most frightening of all was the fact that they were between her and the knife on the mantle.

25

"D-do you speak English?" Brianna asked
nervously. The Indians obviously hadn't expected to
find her here. If she'd played it cool, they might leave
her alone.

The four braves looked at each other then one walked
across the room and grabbed her chin. He turned her
face this way and that, staring at her the whole time.
After several minutes of intense scrutiny, he apparently
lost interest in her face and dropped his hand to the
collar of her dress. With a quick jerk, he tore it open
and ran his fingers down the middle of her chest.

Brianna held back a scream of pure terror as he
reached inside her dress and felt her breast. Instead of
continuing his lecherous advance, he pulled out his
hand and looked at his fingertips as though he expected
to see her white coloration on his own skin.

Before she had a chance to figure that out, the brave
pushed her backward onto her bunk and flipped her
skirt up. Knowing rape was imminent, Brianna decided

it was time to fight even though she didn't stand a chance against four of them. She might get herself killed, but that was probably better than lying there passively while they took turns with her.

She waited for her chance, biting back sobs as he ran his hand up her leg, squeezing occasionally as though checking the shape of her thigh beneath the pantalets. Gathering herself for the attack, Brianna tensed her muscles. A well-placed kick at the proper moment would put this one out of commission for a while. Then she'd only have three to contend with.

But instead of proceeding as she expected him to, he turned away and said something to his companions. They all laughed. With his curiosity apparently satisfied, he rejoined his friends.

Brianna sat up and straightened her skirt, grateful beyond words that he hadn't been impressed with her. Though they all ignored her as they explored the contents of the cabin she knew she wasn't out of danger yet.

One moved to the table and stuck his hand into her bread dough. A look of astonishment crossed his face as his fingers sank in the spongy mass. He called the others to come and look. As they stood around the table cautiously smelling and tasting the dough, Brianna wondered suddenly if they were merely hungry. That would certainly explain their disinterest in her. Maybe if she gave them food . . .

Before the thought had a chance to gel, Seth's story of the stationmaster and stock tender at Egan's station in Utah came forcibly to mind. It hadn't done them any good to feed the Indians. She glanced surreptitiously toward the mantle. If there were only some way to get to her knife.

Brianna moved a few inches toward the far end of the bunk experimentally. No reaction. She waited a few seconds then tried it again. This time one of the braves pinned her with a piercing stare. He said a few terse words and pointed to where she'd been before.

She didn't understand his language, but there was no mistaking his meaning or the threat in his voice. Brianna scooted back to her original position. As she sat and watched them ransack the trunk at the foot of Lucas's bed, she became aware of the crinoline her hand rested against and remembered what was under it. Of course!

Slowly easing her hand underneath the stiff garment, she searched the contents of the backpack with stealthy movements. Just as her fingers landed on the hard surface she was looking for, one of the Indians glanced up. His eyes narrowed suspiciously as his gaze traveled down to where her hand was hidden beneath the crinoline.

He spoke sharply and his companions all ceased their activities to stare at her. When he started toward her, Brianna knew the moment had arrived.

Praying for success, she tighten her grip on the camera and whipped it out from under the crinoline as she jumped to her feet.

"Smile guys," Brianna said pushing the shutter release. The bright flash of light stopped the Indians in their tracks, and Brianna sprinted over to the mantle. She could hear the whine of the strobe recharging as she grabbed her knife.

When she whirled around, the braves had recovered from their surprise and started menacingly toward her. Brianna took aim and sent her knife whistling through the air just the way Seth had taught her. One of the braves cried out and went down.

Brianna didn't even have time to wonder if she'd killed him or not. The other three had barely slowed. She raised the camera again and flashed the strobe. They covered their eyes and fell back. Looking around, she saw the knife she used to cut bread still lying next to the pots and pans at the end of the fireplace.

Within seconds it was in her hand, then singing through the air toward another human target. This knife was lighter than the one she was used to and her aim was less accurate. Instead of hitting the man mid-chest, it buried itself in his shoulder. It didn't matter. With a howl of agony he went to his knees.

Brianna raised the camera and flashed again. A meat fork found its mark this time but lacked the force to knock the man down. She searched desperately for another sharp weapon but there was nothing else to throw except pots and pans. Brianna set her jaw. So be it. If her attempt was going to prove futile at least she'd know she gave it her best shot. Besides, a barrage of cooking utensils was bound to cause a bruise or two.

When she lifted the camera a fourth time, the two who were left on their feet ducked. At first Brianna thought they had figured out how to keep the bright light from blinding them, but she soon realized they were afraid of it. She waited until they peeked over the edge of the table before flashing the strobe.

This time three of them scrambled for the door dragging their fallen comrade with them. Brianna flashed them one more time and crashed two pans together for good measure. The minute they hit the outside air they were on their feet running, carrying Brianna's first victim between them. Brianna ran across the room and slammed the door behind them. She jerked the latchstring in through the hole and dropped the bar into place. Then she rushed to Lucas's bunk to close and bar the shutters.

What if they went for reinforcements? The bar on the door wouldn't hold them very long. The bread knife and the meat fork were her only weapons. The Indians had taken her knife with them, obviously not wanting to take the time to pull it out of their friend.

Brianna glanced around frantically. The table. If she shoved it up against the door nothing would budge it. Moving the table proved to be far more difficult than she had anticipated. Made of solid oak, it was incredibly heavy and very cumbersome.

"Where's my adrenaline when I need it?" she muttered as she tried to shove it across the room. By the time she had it maneuvered into place, she was out of breath and sweating.

Brianna sank to the floor and leaned her back against the table. With a sigh she closed her eyes. God help her if the Indians came back, but for the moment at least, she was safe. Thank heavens the strobe was handy and charged. Without it . . . Brianna shuddered.

The Indians probably figured they'd encountered a witch or something. Laughter bubbled from deep inside and erupted in a wild fit of giggles. Then suddenly her hysteria changed to sobs. With a flood of tears running down her cheeks, she lowered her face to her bent knees and cried.

"The days are sure getting shorter fast," Ian observed as he squinted at the sun. "It'll be dark in a couple of hours. We're lucky we were able to get the horses into that box canyon or we'd never have made it back today."

"I can't believe that stallion was smart enough to know what we were up to," Billy marveled.

"He'd been in the canyon before and knew there was no way out," Lucas said. "He was smart enough to stay clear of it, that's all."

"Still pretty amazing for a horse."

Ian shook his head. "Not for a stallion. Only the intelligent ones are able to hang onto their herd. We were lucky we only lost four mares to him."

"He'll be back," Lucas said with certainty. "Too bad

I didn't get him this morning. It would have solved a lot of problems."

"Brianna didn't realize what was at stake."

"Only a fool would knock a man's aim off when he's shooting."

Ian frowned. "She apologized, Lucas. What more do you want?"

"He wants her gone," Billy said belligerently. "This is just another excuse to be mad at her."

"There's more to it than you know, Billy . . ."

"I know she deserves to be treated better than she is!" Billy wheeled his horse away angrily. "I think I'll go ride the flank."

"Young hot head!" Lucas muttered. Then he sighed. "I know she doesn't do these things on purpose. It's just a matter of not knowing any better. Brianna told me herself she doesn't belong out here and she's right. Billy would see it too if he weren't half in love with her."

Ian smiled ruefully. "I think we all are. Your wife is a very special lady, Lucas. You're a lucky man."

There it was. The opening Lucas had been waiting for. All he had to do was explain the situation to Ian and step out of the picture. Yet, for some reason, the words stuck in his throat.

Images of Brianna kept tumbling through his thoughts just as they had for the last month. It was far too easy to remember the way she felt in his arms and her honeyed kisses. Even more devastating to his peace of mind was the memory of her in his lab. Not only had she understood the difficult concept he was working with, she was genuinely interested. As they worked side-by-side Lucas suddenly realized he'd found a woman who could share his dreams.

Brianna had shattered that vision moments later when she freely admitted she'd lied to him from the beginning. Her vague explanation had only muddied the waters and convinced him it would be foolhardy to trust her.

Oddly enough her duplicity didn't him hurt nearly as bad as her assurances that Anna would suit him better. It was as though Brianna thought he didn't like her. Lucas's mouth twisted into a grimace. Truth was if he liked her any better he'd go up in smoke.

"Lucas, come take a look at this."

The alarm in Billy's voice brought Lucas out of his musings with a jerk. He glanced at the herd. Ian could handle them alone with no difficulty. It took less than a minute to reach Billy where he squatted near a granite boulder.

"What is it?" Lucas asked swinging out of the saddle.

Billy pointed to the ground. "Blood."

"Good lord."

"From the tracks, I'd say there were four horses." Billy gave Lucas a worried look. "They were unshod."

"Indians."

"It might just be a hunting party."

"True, but they're a little too close to the station for comfort." Lucas followed the trail of blood around the boulder. "I'd say one of them was hurt pretty bad." He eyed a dark stain on a large flat rock protected by the boulder. "They must have carried him back here to doctor him. I wonder what they thought they needed to hide from."

"Jesus, Lucas, look at this!"

Lucas's heart lurched when he saw what Billy had picked up from the ground nearby. Blood covered the familiar knife from the point to the end of the handle. "Oh, God, it's Brianna's!"

He was around the boulder and back on his horse in the blink of an eye. "Tell Ian what's going on, then get to the station as fast as you can," he yelled over his shoulder. "Better have him bring the herd on in. We'll need them if we have to go after her."

Lucas tried not to think about whose blood it was or what they must have done to her. How could he have let her goad him into taking his rifle when he knew she was virtually defenseless without it? *Please, God let her be all right.* Recriminating thoughts kept running through his mind as he raced toward Split Rock station. The mile-long trip seemed to take forever, but at last he was there.

The sight of an unfamiliar horse in the corral brought him up short. It had blood all over its face. What in the hell was going on?

Lucas kept his horse between himself and the cabin as he dismounted and pulled his rifle out of the scabbard. Ducking low, he ran across the open space and slammed his back up against the outside wall of the station. The silence was unnerving.

With a feeling of dread, he crept along the side of the building until he got to the door. Clutching his rifle tightly, he took a deep breath and kicked the door with the heel of his boot. Nothing happened. He tried again, this time putting the full weight of his body behind his kick. One of the boards cracked and the hinges squeaked in protest, but the door didn't budge.

As he stood there contemplating his next move, he heard something on the other side of the door. It sounded suspiciously like a whimper. For the first time hope flared.

"Brianna, are you in there?"

"L-Lucas?"

The sound of her voice brought an overwhelming wave of relief. Thank God she was alive! "Yes, it's me. Open the door."

There was a scraping noise like something heavy being dragged across the floor. The minutes passed and

Lucas's nervousness grew. Was she too badly injured to get the door open? At last he heard the sound of the bar being lifted and the door swung open. The next instant, Brianna was in his arms sobbing against his neck.

Brianna's words came tumbling out, her terror still obvious in slightly hysterical tone of her voice. Lucas's suspicions and distrust of the last few weeks suddenly didn't matter as much as his overwhelming need to make her feel safe again.

He set his rifle aside, swept her up in his arms, and carried her inside. The world around them disappeared as he sat down on his bunk and hugged her tightly, rocking back and forth murmuring small words of comfort against her head.

Billy arrived moments later. Though the two men tried, it was impossible to piece the story together from her disjointed account. But by the time Ian drove the herd into the corral, Brianna was calming down and becoming coherent. She told them everything except for the all important role of the camera strobe. Neither she nor Lucas was inclined to move, and she remained there, sitting on his lap within the circle of his arms as the four of them discussed the Indians' odd behavior.

"You were probably the first white woman they'd ever seen close up," Ian told her. "And they were curious."

Brianna nodded in sudden understanding. "That's why they looked at my legs. They must have thought white women were shaped like a bell from the waist down. At least they decided I wasn't worth messing with."

The three men exchanged glances. Better not to upset her again by telling her the truth. Lucas tightened his arms around her as he thought of what the Indians probably would have done if Brianna hadn't scared them away. It was all he could do not to yell at her for being so damned naive

As she sat there in the shelter of Lucas's embrace

Brianna slowly regained her composure. After spending most of the day terrified that the Indians were coming back, it was reassuring to listen to the men analyze the situation and decide they'd probably seen the last of them.

Of course, without knowing about the camera, which was again safely hidden away in her trunk, they couldn't understand the Indians reasons for leaving. "It's odd they didn't press their advantage," Ian said. "Surely they could see you'd run out of weapons and realized you'd done about all the damage you could."

Lucas looked pensive for a moment. "It's possible they heard something and thought we were coming back. They probably didn't want to tangle with our guns."

Brianna bit back a bubble of hysterical laughter. More like they didn't want to tangle with the white witch and her bloodthirsty camera.

26

July 19, 1995

Tom stopped in the doorway and surveyed the family room with a sense of unreality. It looked like a mad scientist's lab in an old horror movie. Since their trip to the mine two days ago, Scott had worked almost continuously, wiring, splicing, cutting, taping. "Is that the microwave from the kitchen?" Tom asked.

Scott's voice came from behind the dismantled machine. "Uhhuh. I need a second microwave antennae. "

"Don't you think your father might be a little unhappy about you taking it apart?"

"Not as much as my mom will be. She made me promise I wouldn't mess with her appliances after I turned her food processor into a centrifuge. With any kind of luck we'll be done here today, and I can put it back together before she gets home. Did you find the wire cutters?"

"They were in the shop right where you said they'd be." Tom glanced around. "Where's Anna?"

"In the kitchen fixing lunch. I tried to tell her sandwiches would be enough."

"I take it she had other ideas?"

"She said to leave the woman's work to the women."

"Anything you want me to do?"

"Just the ranch records."

"All done and saved onto a disk like you told me to."

"Good. Then I can clear everything off the hard drive and network the two computers together. We should be ready to try the transfer this afternoon."

A knot formed in Tom's throat. Suddenly everything was happening too fast. "Do you think it will work?"

"I don't know. The system is a lot more refined this time, but I'm not sure the microwave antennas will be powerful enough."

"Why, what did you use before?"

"The TV satellite dish, and I think that's where the big ugly cloud came from. I'm hoping the smaller antennae will create less of a disturbance."

Tom glanced outside. The big white dish looked just like all the others that had replaced TV antennas across rural America. He had a sudden image of a killer ray emanating from the center. "If size has anything to do with it they should. Well, I'll be in the kitchen if you want me."

The sight that met his eyes when he entered the kitchen brought Tom to a halt. He crossed his arms and leaned against the door jamb to watch. Anna stood on her tiptoes balancing on a step stool as she stretched to reach the cupboard over her head. The soft clinging material of Brianna's sarong outlined Anna's figure in the most appealing way.

Tom smiled as he remembered how delighted Anna had been when she'd found it in the back of the closet. Unfamiliar with synthetics, all she saw was the floor-length skirt and high collar. With a judiciously applied needle she'd sewn up the thigh high slits in the sides and pronounced it decent enough to wear. If she could see herself, she'd probably revise her opinion quick enough. Personally, he thought it looked fantastic.

"Need some help?" he asked stepping into the room.

"What? Oh . . . " As Anna turned toward him, the tight sheath of the skirt caught around her legs and she teetered precariously on the edge of the stool.

In two strides, Tom was across the kitchen. He reached the stool just as Anna toppled forward into his arms. The momentum of her fall threw him off balance, and they staggered against the counter. Tom tightened his hold and somehow managed to keep them both upright.

"Are you all right?" he asked setting her feet on the floor and bracing one hand behind her on the edge of the sink.

"I-I think so." Actually, standing so close to him, she was finding it a little difficult to breathe. The air had suddenly become too thin.

He reached up to brush a wayward strand of hair back from her face. "I shouldn't have distracted you like that."

"It was the dress," she whispered. "The skirt's too tight."

"That dress is a distraction all right but not because it's too tight. It's perfect, and so are you."

His voice was a soft, sexy rumble that seemed to vibrate through her entire body. Anna placed her hands on his chest to push him away, but the muscles in her arms had no strength. His warmth beneath her fingers seemed to sap her resistance.

"Anna?"

The husky whisper was filled with longing. Powerless to resist the appeal in his voice, Anna raised her head and caught her breath in surprise. No one had ever looked at her that way before. He was going to kiss her, she could see it in his expression, and her heart pounded in anticipation. Closing her eyes, she leaned against him with a soft sigh of surrender.

His mouth was gently persuasive and her lips parted beneath his with warm welcome. The tender invasion of his tongue was a bit shocking at first, but she soon decided she liked it very much. Tom pulled her closer, and Anna's insides melted. A moan rose unbidden to her lips.

He ended it then, and she sagged against him, unable to stand on her wobbly legs.

"Oh Lord, Anna," he said stroking the back of her head with his hand. "I didn't mean to do that."

"P-please don't apologize," she whispered against his chest. "It wasn't your fault.

"Of course it was, and I don't regret it a bit. I've been wanting to do that since I met you." He smiled and dropped a kiss on top of her head. "Unfortunately, it was just as fantastic as I thought it would be."

"Oh, Tom you're such a wonderful liar."

"It's the honest truth," he said in surprise. "You're a beautiful, desirable woman, and I find you completely irresistible. I never thought I'd say that, never expected to meet someone like you."

"I-I feel the same about you," Anna whispered. "I didn't want to b-but I couldn't help myself."

He hugged her tighter. "You don't know how good that makes me feel. It does complicate matters a bit, though."

"No, Tom, it doesn't change a thing. It can't. Brianna's depending on us."

Tom closed his eyes and dropped his chin to the top of her head. "I suppose you're right. What did I do to deserve such pain?"

"Maybe it's a reward, not a punishment."

"How do you figure that?"

"I was born a hundred and fifty years ago and probably died before your grandfather was out of shortcoats."

"So?"

Anna smiled softly and raised her hand to his face. "Don't you see, Tom? We never even should have met. Every minute we have together is a gift, an impossible quirk. You asked what you did to be punished, but I wonder how I got so lucky."

"Then we'd better make every second count enough to last us a lifetime," he said softly, lifting her chin with his finger and staring deeply into her eyes.

Their breaths mingled for a moment before his lips captured hers and her arms swept up around his neck. Where their first kiss had been tentative and sweet, this was hot and demanding. Tenderness gave way to wanting, gentleness to desire.

"Tom?" Scott's voice coming from the other room broke over them like a wave of cold water. They jerked apart and stood gazing at each other, shocked by the power of the emotions that had just passed between them.

"Tom," Scott repeated stepping around the half-closed door. "Will you help me wire the cable into the breaker box? I think we'll need the extra weight to . . . Hey, what's wrong?" He stopped and stared at them in surprise.

"Wrong?" Tom's voice held a convincing note of surprise. "Yeah, you both look kind of . . . I don't know, scared I guess."

"I-I fell off the stool, and Tom caught me," Anna murmured. "It was a close call."

"Geeze, are you all right?"

Anna looked away, afraid of what her face would reveal if her eyes met Tom's. "Oh, yes, never better."

"What was it you needed help with, Scott?" Tom asked steering him back into the family room.

"I'm pretty sure the wire was too light last time,"
Scott said as they disappeared from sight. "You can
send megavolts through a small wire with no problem
but I think the amperage was way too much for . . . "

Shaken, Anna leaned against the counter. In spite
of her words to the contrary, Tom was right, it wasn't
fair. Fate had finally given her the love she had craved
all her life, but with the wrong man. God help her, but
she wanted him. Wanted him in ways that didn't even
bear thinking of. There was no future for her with
Tom Shaffer. She covered her face with her hands. No
future and no past.

By the time they sat down to lunch an hour later,
Tom and Anna had themselves well in hand. Though
neither of them spoke much, Scott didn't seem to notice
as he explained all the innovations he'd come up with.

Anna glanced at Tom only once. He was watching
her, his gaze warmly caressing and possessive. A hot
thrill ran through her, and she looked away in confusion. The way he made her feel was immoral, depraved,
and completely wonderful. Forbidden images tumbled
through her mind in helpless abandon, tempting
visions of what would never be. Scott's words suddenly
brought her back with a jerk.

"We'll be able to try it in about half an hour."

"You mean it's ready?" she squeaked.

Scott looked at her in surprise. "What do you think
I've been talking about?"

Embarrassed to admit she hadn't been listening, she
murmured something noncommittal.

"Are you sure it's safe?" Tom demanded.

"I think so, but there's no real way of testing it."

"Why not?"

"If we send an inanimate object back in time, we
might be able to tell whether it had arrived but not the
condition it was in."

"What about some kind of small animal?"

"We could send a mouse or something but there'd be no way of tracking it on the other side."

"What if the changes you've made haven't been improvements? Maybe the transfer will be worse instead of better."

"If I'm right, the time warp will be far more stable. Besides, last time it all happened by chance. Now everything is built specifically to accommodate Anna and Brianna. By focusing on them, the process should be much safer."

"Should be. But if you're wrong, you could kill them. Seems to me you have a bad habit of going off half cocked without testing your theories out. That's how we got into this mess in the first place and now you're going to use the same kind of logic to get us out?" Tom jumped to his feet and paced around the room in agitation. "Christ, Scott, you're talking about sending people through time, not just one but two. There's not a reputable scientist in the world that wouldn't call you crazy."

Scott stared at him for a moment, then dropped his gaze to the bowl of stew in front of him. "Yeah, I guess you're right." His voice was so filled with hurt it trembled. He suddenly seemed very young to Anna.

"Don't mind Tom. He's just nervous."

"He's got a point," Scott mumbled. "I don't know what I'm doing."

"Of course you do. You just spent the last half hour explaining it all to us."

"But it's just a theory. None of it's ever been proven."

"Scott, look at me," Anna demanded. "I was born in 1841. Do I look a hundred and fifty-four years old to you?"

He smiled slightly. "No."

"There, you see? That's proof your theories are correct. So what if no one else has your vision? Maybe you're just smarter. As for Tom, he told me he thinks you're next Thomas Einstein."

"Albert Einstein," Tom corrected gruffly, dropping a hand on Scott's shoulder. "Anna's right. I had no business talking to you like that, and I'm sorry. No one else would be capable of what you've accomplished. I trust you and your time machine, I'm just worried something will go wrong."

"A time machine," Scott murmured momentarily distracted by the thought. "It is, isn't it? I hadn't thought of it that way."

"That's exactly what it is," Anna said with conviction, "and it's going to work perfectly. So let's finish eating and get on with it."

In the end it was nearly an hour before Scott was ready. Though he was a bit reserved with Tom at first, his reticence soon disappeared in his mounting excitement. "I'm glad you gave me the idea of making the Möbius strip out of fiber optics. It will focus the laser perfectly."

Tom blinked in surprise. "I gave you the idea . . . Wait a minute, did you say laser?"

"Yeah, I built it for my science project last year. I got a blue ribbon at State."

"This year you'll probably win a trophy at Nationals," Tom said with a wry smile.

At last everything was in place, even Anna had changed back into her own clothes. Tom watched intently as Scott started to feed data into the computer. After a few moments, Scott spoke back over his shoulder. "Are you ready, Anna?"

Anna picked up Tom's hand and pressed it to her cheek. "Yes, I'm ready," she said returning Tom's hand to his leg, and folding her own in her lap.

"All right, then. Here goes."

A multicolored Möbius strip appeared on the computer screen and a low whine filled the room. It was reminiscent of the horrible screeching they had heard the first time but without volume or the nerve-wrenching pitch.

"Look at that," Tom said, pointing to a spot near the window where a small cloud of blue mist suddenly appeared. Before their eyes it grew until it stretched nearly to the ceiling. Slowly the mist began revolving, gathering near the center. With a tiny pop it became opaque and an image of a woman formed in the middle.

"Oh my, God," Tom whispered as she seemed to stare at them from several yards away in wide-eyed shock. The picture wavered for a moment then disappeared in a puff of blue mist.

"What happened, Scott?"

"I don't know. I'm not even sure we were in the right time or place. I couldn't hold on to it long enough to make an identification."

Tom reached over and grasped Anna's hand in a tight grip. "Oh we were in the right place all right. Unless these two have a third look alike somewhere, we just made contact with Brianna Daniels."

27

September 26, 1860

"Lucas, could I have a minute of your time?" Brianna asked as the men rose from the supper table.

"As a matter-of-fact I wanted to talk to you, too." He glanced toward the apparatus he'd rigged up in the corner. "How did the bathing machine work?"

"Like a charm. You can't imagine how nice it was to take a hot shower again."

"Again?"

"Er . . . I meant a hot bath." Brianna cursed her slip as she finished clearing the table. Would she ever learn? "Anyway it's great. You'll have to try it."

"Maybe I will." He smiled. "We might even manage to get Billy and Seth into it before the winter's over. Now then what was the problem you wanted to discuss?"

"I'm not exactly sure it is a problem." She gripped the plates in her hands tighter. He'd been so much more reasonable since the Indian attack. Maybe . . . "I want to keep the buckskin."

"The buckskin? What for?"

"I want to break him to ride. He's just the right age."

After Brianna's close call with Indians, Lucas wanted to wrap her in cotton wool to protect her, and never let her out of his sight. The image of her body, broken and trampled by the wild horse, popped into his mind. His stomach knotted at the thought. "No."

"Give me one good reason."

"Neither Ian or I have time to help you break a horse."

"I don't need your help."

"Oh? And just how do you plan to do it? You don't have the faintest idea how to go about it."

"As a matter of fact, I can break a horse fully as well as you can."

"I might have known," Lucas said sarcastically. "Something more from your unorthodox education no doubt."

"My grandfather taught me."

"It wouldn't matter if you'd spent your life breaking horses," Lucas said trying another tack. "The hay and grain is intended for company horses. It's against regulations to feed others."

Brianna gave a slight smile. "God, Lucas, you are so predictable. That's hogwash and you know it. No one has ever said a word about Ian's horse and Taffy eats just as much as any of the others."

"That's different. Ian works for the company."

"All the work I do around here is for company personnel. I don't get paid a dime for it except for room and board."

"That's all any stationmaster's wife would get."

"But we both know I'm not your wife, Lucas."

"So what's your point?"

"I more than earn Oz's food."

"Oz?"

Brianna shrugged. "It seems appropriate."

"What does it mean?"

"It's just a name. Don't try to change the subject, Lucas. Are you going to let me keep him or not?"

"That's not my decision."

"Whose is it?"

"James Bromley. He's the superintendent for this stretch of the trail."

"And if he agreed you'd go along with it?"

Lucas shrugged. "Of course." He knew Bromley wasn't due to come through for another three months.

"Then I'll start working with Oz in the meantime."

"No you won't."

"Why not?"

"Because company regulations say . . . "

"We can't feed noncompany horses," she finished for him. "I still say I more than earn the hay he'll eat. Anyway he's already here and you're feeding him."

"The wild herd will be back."

"Not to get Oz. In case you missed it, he's a male. The stallion would have run him off soon anyway. Face it, Lucas he's here to stay."

"Then he belongs to the company."

"I don't think so. If you'll remember I caught him. That makes him mine. Which brings us back to the question of whether or not I earn his feed. You have a choice. Either you see it my way or I go out on strike."

"You'll do what?"

"Go on strike. That means I quit working until you change your attitude."

Lucas laughed. "Go right ahead. In case you've forgotten we got along just fine before you got here, we can again."

"Fine." She dumped the last of the dishes into the

dish pan. "I could use a vacation anyway. I'll be in the barn visiting with Ian and Seth if you change your mind."

Lucas watched her with reluctant admiration as she swept out of the cabin. Too bad her little show of independence was doomed to failure. It had never been his idea to bring a woman out here to do the cooking and cleaning, and he didn't mind taking the duties back. On the other hand, Brianna would be bored to tears with nothing to do and she wasn't the type to sit idle. She was bound to give in before he did.

The dishes were done and Lucas in his bunk pretending to be sound asleep when Brianna returned. He smiled to himself as he heard her walk over to the cupboard where the dishes were before she undressed and went to bed. It wouldn't take much to win this stand off.

Brianna was still sound asleep when Seth came in for breakfast the next morning.

"Are you sick, Brianna?" he asked with concern.

"No."

"Then why aren't you up?"

She rolled over and looked up at him with sleepy eyes. "Because I intend to sleep in. Don't worry, Lucas is fixing your breakfast. He'll probably be in soon."

"Lucas is cooking?"

"That's right."

"Oh." Seth's voice sounded distinctly unhappy.

Brianna swallowed a smile as she turned back over and snuggled down into her pillow. "I just decided to indulge myself since Lucas gave me the day off."

"I'm sorry I bothered you."

"No need to apologize. You're supposed to be sitting down to breakfast right now. It might not be a bad idea to remind Lucas. You know how forgetful he is sometimes."

Brianna was jerked out of a sound sleep when the men came in to eat twenty minutes later. Though Ian and Seth kept their voices low and tried to be quiet, Lucas made a big show of clanging pans together as he cooked breakfast. She pretended to sleep right through it.

"Put the plates on, Billy," Lucas said finally. "It's ready."

It was all Brianna could do to keep from giggling out loud as the men sat down to eat. "What is this?" Ian asked in surprise.

"Cornmeal mush."

"It has a crust."

"That's the way Lucas cooks it," Seth said with a deep sigh. "Don't ask what the black chunks are. We've never figured it out and he won't tell."

"Shut up and eat," Lucas growled.

Unlike most meals, that breakfast passed in near silence. It wasn't long before Brianna heard the chairs scoot back as Ian and Seth made excuses to leave. When the door swung shut behind them she rolled over and stretched.

Lucas looked up from clearing the table. "I wondered if you were going to stay in bed all day."

"I like to sleep in on my vacation." She sat up and rubbed her eyes. "What time is it?"

"Eight-thirty."

She swung her legs over the edge of the bed. "Goodness. I didn't realize it was so late. I'd better get busy if I'm going to have anything for the stage passengers."

"I thought you were on strike."

"Only against the company. This is my own little business."

"You want breakfast?"

She eyed what was left of the mush. "No thanks I'll fix myself something later."

"Suit yourself." He busied himself with the dishes as she stepped behind the curtain where the shower was to get dressed.

"Your strike isn't going to work, you know," he said after a moment. "I really don't mind doing any of this."

She grinned. "We'll see."

Lucas pretended not to notice that Seth and Ian were two of Brianna's best customers both Wednesday and Thursday when the stage came in. He ignored his own hunger and the mess that began to develop on his side of the cabin. Even the other men's complaints didn't phase him. What finally began to wear on him was the amount of time he spent cooking and washing dishes. Certain that he was on the verge of a breakthrough with his electric light, he resented every second he was away from his workbench.

Surreptitiously, he watched Brianna for signs of weakening but there were none. In fact, she seemed to be thoroughly enjoying herself. She was perfectly content to lay on her bunk all day reading his collection of novels, and writing in her journal. He began to wonder which of them was the most stubborn.

Late on the third day of Brianna's strike a traveling peddler named Simon Francois showed up and Lucas knew his cause was lost. Amid the wagon full of wares there enough trinkets and gadgets to keep even the most energetic entertained for days. Brianna could easily buy enough to keep her busy for months. He might as well admit to defeat immediately.

Predictably she was fascinated and spent over an hour shopping. "This was almost as much fun as going to the mall," she said as she paid for her purchases.

Francois raised his eyebrows. "The mall?"

"It's a big store not far from where I used to live."

Lucas glanced at the sun where it hung low in the sky. "It'll be dark soon. Better set up camp here for tonight. We've had some trouble with the Indians."

"Don't mind if I do. It'll be nice to have some companionship for a change."

"We'd be pleased if you joined us for supper, too," Brianna added.

"I'd be delighted. It's been a while since I had a home-cooked meal."

"Good. We'll expect you as soon as you've looked after your horse."

"I dunno if you want to eat with us," Seth said in a low voice when Lucas and Brianna were out of earshot. "Lucas has been doing the cooking and to tell the truth he's not much good at it."

Ian nodded woefully. "The worst of it is that he doesn't seem to realize how really awful it is. Sure wish Brianna would take it up again."

"Why did she quit?" the peddler asked curiously.

Ian shrugged. "Don't know for sure. They had words about something and now she says she's on strike, whatever that is."

"Says she won't lift a finger around here until her pig-headed husband sees reason," Seth added.

"And there's no chance of that. Lucas is the most stubborn man alive," Ian said mournfully. "At least Seth and Billy are only here three days at a stretch. I'll starve to death if it goes on much longer."

Francois rubbed his nose thoughtfully. "Could be a simple matter of getting them back into charity with each other." His eyes twinkled mischievously. "This may turn out to be a very entertaining evening indeed."

Seth and Ian exchanged an uncertain glances. "What do you mean?"

"Nothing for you to worry about," Francois assured them. "I promise your Mr. and Mrs. Daniels won't be hurt in the least. In fact they may well thank me in the morning."

"What do you get out of this," Seth asked suspiciously.

"Ah, 'tis the French blood in my veins I fear. I'm an incurable romantic." The peddler grinned. "Besides, it isn't at all unusual for a husband to give his wife an extravagant gift at such times. I'm often well rewarded for my time."

Beyond that Simon Francois would say nothing. He proved to be an entertaining dinner companion, regaling them all with humorous tales of his travels. After dinner when they all went outside to enjoy one of the last warm evenings of Indian summer he produced his fiddle and began to play.

It wasn't long before everyone's toes were tapping in time to the sprightly tunes. Suddenly Ian jumped to his feet and grabbed Brianna's hands.

"This music was meant for dancing," he said swinging her around.

"Oh, Ian I don't know . . . "

"Just let your feet follow the music."

There appeared to be no specific steps, just uninhibited movement. Before long Brianna caught Ian's enthusiasm and was dancing with the same abandon he was. She laughed joyously. When the next song started Seth claimed her hand, and Brianna was again swept away in a energetic dance. As they kept trading her back and forth between songs Brianna became aware of Lucas standing outside the door with a scowl on his face.

Too bad. She was having too much fun to let him ruin it for her. Gradually the music began to slow and Brianna found herself having to stand closer and closer to her partner in order to follow their movements. She was busily watching her feet when Seth let her go right in the middle of the dance.

Brianna looked up in surprise as Lucas's arm went around her waist. "I'm cutting in," he said simply. She glanced over his shoulder at Seth who just shrugged.

"Why?"

"I wanted to dance with you." He smiled down at her as the music changed subtly. "I don't suppose they taught you how to waltz in that school of yours?"

"As a matter of fact I'm rather good at it."

His smile deepened. "So am I."

It took about thirty seconds for Brianna to realize he wasn't bragging even a little. He was better than good. The world around them seemed to disappear as they twirled and swayed in time to the music. In his arms, the waltz became more than a dance. It was wordless communication, a form of artistic expression and a mating ritual all rolled into one.

Brianna was mesmerized by the glow she saw in his eyes for she knew it was a reflection of her own. She wondered vaguely if her heart would burst with love before she went up in flames, then decided it didn't matter. Either way she would die happy.

The music went on far longer than even several renditions of the song but neither noticed. When it finally ended they were out of breath but could barely tear their eyes away from each other.

"Well," Ian said with an exaggerated stretch. "I'm heading to bed. How about you Seth?"

"Sounds good to me. Come on Simon, we'll walk you to your wagon."

Still wrapped in a magical haze, Brianna was only vaguely aware of the other three men bidding them good night and leaving for the barn.

"Where did you learn to dance like that?" she asked in a slightly unsteady voice.

"My mother hired a dance instructor for my sister and made me take lessons with her."

"He must have been some teacher."

"It's never been like that before." Lucas brushed her temple with his lips. "But then you're not my sister," he whispered against her mouth.

A bucket of ice cold water wouldn't have doused the fire within Brianna any more effectively than Lucas's words. There was no doubt in her mind where they would wind up if she let nature take its course and she couldn't allow that to happen. She stepped back before he could go any further. It would only take one of those devastating kisses of his to completely befuddle her mind. "I think I'd better go inside."

"That sounds like a great idea." His voice was like a silken caress as he reached for her again. "This is a little too public for my tastes."

"No, Lucas. I mean by myself."

"Brianna . . . "

"No." She put her hand on his chest and nearly snatched it back again as she felt the warmth of his body and the heavy beating of his heart. "What we're feeling isn't real. It's an illusion brought on by music and moonlight. Think how we'd feel tomorrow morning if we follow our instincts."

Satiated at the very least or maybe ready for more, Lucas thought to himself. There were far worse ways to wake up in the morning. "How do *you* think we'd feel?"

How about fantastic? "Guilty. Have you forgotten Anna?"

He had but then he felt no loyalty to a woman he'd never met, one who had put them in this impossible mess for some obscure reason of her own. Still, Brianna was right. Sleeping with her would complicate matters even more. He dropped his arms. "If that's what you want, I won't try to change your mind."

God no it wasn't what she wanted, but she had no choice.

She felt like weeping as he sat down by the door and pulled out his pipe. "G . . . Good night, Lucas."

"Night," he said without even looking at her.

Brianna thought her heart would break as she fled to the safety of the cabin.

Brianna was up and out of the cabin by breakfast time the next morning. Her feelings were still too raw for her to face Lucas and his anger. She stayed away until she heard Ian yell "Rider coming in!" Then she went to tell Seth good-bye and greet Billy as he came in.

Though she'd seen it dozens of times, the thrill of watching them pass the mochila never faded. Today was no different and she was practically bouncing up and down when Billy swung down off his horse with a grin.

"I brought an answer to your letter," he said pulling a folded piece of paper out of his pocket.

"Already?"

"He was in Green River. I . . . ah . . . I bought you something else, too."

Brianna raised her eyebrows in surprise. "A present?"

"Sort of." He took a shiny new pistol out of his holster and handed it to her. "I rode over to Fort Bridger to get it.

"You got me a gun?"

"It's a five-shot pocket pistol," he said, "a thirty-one caliber Colt. After last week I realized you need more than that knife to protect yourself with. I figured this would be light enough for you to handle. I'll train you to be a crack shot inside of a month."

"Oh, Billy." Tears filled her eyes at his thoughtfulness. She gave him a big hug. "How can I thank you?"

Billy turned fiery red. "Aw, heck, Brianna. It ain't that big a deal. Reckon I'd better help Ian see to my horse."

"All right. Thank you, Billy."

He was clear to the corral before Brianna remembered the letter. Tucking her new pistol into the waistband of her skirt, she unfolded the single sheet and read.

It was the chance Lucas had been waiting for. He'd been trying to get a minute alone with her all day but she been avoiding him as if he had the plague. Brianna was obviously still upset about last night. Too bad she didn't know what he wanted to say to her. If she had realized he'd changed his mind about the buckskin she'd probably have fixed breakfast for them.

"Brianna?"

"Ah, Lucas. Just the man I want to see. Remember you said you'd leave the decision about the horse to Mr. Bromley?"

"Well, yes but. . . . "

"I sent a letter with Billy last time. Mr. Bromley was kind enough to answer it already."

"So quickly?"

"He was in Green River." She grinned and handed him the letter. "You lose, Lucas. Now if you'll excuse me I have to go see about fixing lunch before everybody around here succumbs to malnutrition."

Lucas didn't have to read the letter to know what it said. He'd clearly been out-maneuvered. A reluctant smile tugged at the corners of his mouth as he stuck the letter in his pocket and headed toward the barn. He wondered if he dared ask what the devil malnutrition was.

28

October 1860

"Lucas, what is it?" Brianna said sitting up in bed as Lucas jumped out of bed and grabbed his rifle.

"The wild horses are back. Stay where you are," he barked over his shoulder as he jerked the door open and strode out into the night.

Ignoring Lucas's orders, Brianna slipped out of bed, pulled her pistol out from under her pillow, and followed him outside. It was pitch dark with no moon and clouds obscuring the stars. The horses were a confused mass of black shapes in the darkness. Even the stallion was indistinguishable though his defiant screams proved he was there.

"Damn, I can't see a thing," Lucas muttered raising his rifle into the air and firing a shot. Two shots sounded from the other side of the herd as Lucas upended his powder horn into the barrel of his rifle. Behind Lucas, Brianna raised her pistol and pulled the trigger just as another shot sounded from the barn.

Lucas jumped slightly and glanced over his shoulder as he took a patch out of his mouth slapped it around a lead ball and shoved it down the barrel with his thumb. "I thought I told you to stay inside," he said tamping down his load with the ramrod.

"I don't have time to argue right now. I still have four more shots before I have to reload." She waited until a shot came from the other side of the herd before firing again. Lucas's rifle barked a second later, then another from the other side.

Brianna's five chambers were empty when the stallion finally turned his herd away from the corral and led them off across the prairie.

"Did we lose any?" Lucas called as he ran toward the corral in their wake.

"Nope," Billy's voice came out of the darkness. "We scared them off before they managed to break down the fence."

Ian suddenly appeared next to them by the gate. "If it hadn't been for Billy's personal arsenal we'd never have succeeded. How did you get your shots off so fast?"

"Most of them were Brianna's," Lucas admitted.

"Think we better post a guard?"

"We don't have enough men to do it effectively." Lucas sighed. "At least we always know when the herd's here; they aren't exactly quiet."

"Maybe they'll leave us alone," Brianna said hopefully.

All three men just looked at her. "Obviously not."

"Well," Ian said. "I think we've managed to scare them off for tonight, anyway. May as well go back to bed."

"I suppose so. See you in the morning."

"Can't you invent something that will scare the horses away?" Brianna asked as they walked back to the cabin.

"I hadn't really thought about it." His voice was cold.

"If you put that creative mind of yours to work on it, I'm sure . . . "

"You disobeyed me."

"What?"

"I told you to stay in the cabin."

"Oh, for pity sake . . . "

"When I give an order I expect it to be followed."

"Who died and made you king?"

"That flippant attitude of yours is completely out of place in this discussion. You recklessly endangered yourself . . . "

"So what?" Brianna spun around to face him. "I have as much right to endanger myself as any of the rest of you. You're not my father, Lucas. You're not even my husband. I will do *what* I want, *when* I want without asking your permission to do so." She whirled and stomped into the house.

"Brianna . . . "

"The subject is closed. I'm going to bed." Brianna set the empty pistol on her trunk and climbed into bed. "And if you have any sense at all, you won't bring this up again tomorrow." She turned on her side and faced the wall. "Good night!"

There was a lengthy silence then a resigned sigh, and the sound of him crawling into bed. Brianna smiled slightly. He really wasn't so difficult to deal with if you simply never let him get a word in edgewise.

The next morning, Brianna had a difficult time keeping a straight face during breakfast. Lucas was obviously not speaking to her. Pretending not to notice, she ate her breakfast and wondered how long she was to be punished.

The stage had come and gone and it was nearly lunch time before he showed any sign of relenting. When he came to watch her work with Oz in the small corral, Brianna wasn't sure whether he wanted to resume their fight, apologize, or pretend it never happened. She decided to follow his lead.

"Well, well, well," he said, leaning his arms on the top rail of the fence. "It took almost a month but you finally got up the courage to buck him out." Brianna had worked with the horse every day since he'd been here but this was the first time she'd ever taken anything other than a hackamore into the corral with her.

She didn't even look up as she threw the saddle blanket over her horse's back. "I've never bucked a horse out in my life."

"I seem to remember you being quite adamant that you knew how to break a horse as well as I did."

"I do. I also know better than to jump on a three year old that's scared anyway and let him buck until he wears himself out. You're as likely to break their spirit as anything else."

"Is that right? I suppose they taught you a different way to break a horse at that school of yours."

"For your information, I don't break horses, I gentle them."

"How does that work?"

She flashed him a saucy grin. "Pretty well, thank you."

Lucas returned her grin in spite of himself. "You could have fooled me," he observed as the horse succeeded in shaking the saddle blanket off. "Looks like Oz has other ideas."

Brianna scooped the blanket up and put it back on.

"Of course he does. That's the whole point. By the time I'm done with him he won't mind the blanket a bit."

"And after that?"

"Then we start on the saddle."

"How long before you ride him then?"

"Oh, probably another couple of weeks or so." Oz dislodged the blanket again.

"This method of yours seems to take quite a bit of time."

"I suppose so, but it's well worth the wait." Brianna leaned over, picked up the blanket and put it back in place. "When I finally get around to riding him, he probably won't buck at all."

"Are you sure about that?"

"No, but I *am* sure he won't be as scared as if I'd thrown my saddle on him a month ago a tried to ride him. That's why I spend so much time getting him used to me."

"Ah, so that's what you're doing." Lucas nodded wisely. "Ian and I were beginning to wonder if you'd decided to make him a pet instead of a saddle horse."

"Very funny. Did you want something or did you just come out here to bug me?"

"Bug?" One black eyebrow arched questioningly. "I swear Brianna, you've got the damnedest vocabulary."

"It means to irritate me. Is that why you're here?"

Lucas grinned again. "No, though I'll have to admit the temptation is strong. I've come up with something to keep the wild horses away. I was wondering if you'd have time to help me set it up after lunch?"

Brianna glanced up in surprise. "I'd be glad to. What are you going to do?"

"It's very simple really. I'll put some black powder on a flat piece of metal and stick two wires into it.

Then when the horses come . . . " He stopped suddenly and smiled a bit sheepishly. "Sorry. I get carried away when I'm talking about my experiments."

Brianna blinked in surprise. He'd obviously misunderstood the expression on her face. What he perceived as bafflement was in reality fascination. The transformation in him was astounding. When he talked of his inventions he became animated, boyish, and completely irresistible. "No, I want to know."

"Then I'll show you after lunch." He pulled out his watch and gave her a questioning look. "It's eleven-thirty already."

"I know. There's a stew on the fire and I plan on being done here in about ten minutes."

"Oz will be trained by then?"

"Close to it. If you'll notice he hasn't knocked the blanket off for several minutes."

Lucas grinned as he pushed away from the fence. "What an optimist you are."

"And you're a doubting Thomas." Oz chose that moment to rid himself of the blanket and Lucas laughed. Brianna made a face at him before stooping to pick up the blanket. "Oh, I nearly forgot. A package came for you on the stage today."

"Oh?"

"I left it on your bunk."

"That will give me something to do while I wait hours for lunch."

Brianna stuck her tongue out at him. "I'll be there before you know it."

Honestly, that man was the worst tease she'd ever met in her life she thought as he left. Just one more lovable facet of his sterling personality. She smiled to herself. The truth was she enjoyed the sparring back and forth as much as he did.

When she entered the cabin slightly less than ten minutes later, the last thing she expected was to see Lucas sitting on his bunk, his face lined with anguish.

"Lucas?"

He didn't even seemed to realize she was there.

Brianna crossed the floor, knelt in front of him, and covered his clenched hands with hers. "Lucas, what is it?"

"The package was from my cousin Charles." Lucas looked bewildered as he focused on her face. "Th-there was a carriage accident. My mother and sister . . . " His voice faltered and his eyes closed against the pain.

"Oh, Lucas!" Brianna cried sitting on the edge of the bunk and pulling him into her embrace. His arms went around her, hugging her tightly, desperately. She wondered for a moment if her ribs would break, but then the muffled sobs began against her shoulder and she thought her heart would.

She comforted him as though he were a small child, murmuring soothing words, rubbing his back, stroking his hair, rocking him back and forth in her arms. Lucas didn't cry in the traditional sense; the only tears were Brianna's. But the deep gut-wrenching sounds of sorrow and grief were the most heartbreaking she had ever heard.

Eventually it ran its course but he didn't loosen his hold. It was as though he were afraid to let her go.

"Mother didn't want me to come here," he said at last. "She had a premonition we'd never see each other again, but I wouldn't listen."

"All mothers feel that way when their sons leave. Mine cried for two days when my brother joined the navy."

"What did she do when you left?"

Brianna smiled. "Bought me new luggage and loaded my car with cookies."

"Must have baked for days to get enough cookies to fill a train car," he murmured.

"My mother always thought I was in danger of starving to death." Brianna made a face. "Mom ought to see me now. She'd be ecstatic."

Lucas sighed as he released her. "Mine was afraid I'd never come out of my lab long enough to fall in love. I was a great disappointment to her. She wanted grandchildren."

"I'm sure she was very proud of her brilliant son. She only wanted you to fall in love because she wanted you to be happy." Brianna rubbed the hand that was still balled into a fist. "It'll happen, Lucas." *Just as soon as Anna gets here.* Her heart clenched at the thought.

"My mother obviously agreed with you," he said opening his hand.

Brianna gasped at the ring that lay in his palm. It was an oval sapphire nearly the size of a dime surrounded by an intricate filigree setting of white gold. "How beautiful!"

"The Daniels are an odd bunch," he said staring at the ring. "They marry for love. This is the ring the oldest son traditionally gives his wife. My mother never took it off until the day I left to come West. I wouldn't take it." He smiled sadly. "I thought she was overwrought. She never even thought of giving it to me when I was betrothed to Marie."

Privately, Brianna thought Lucas's mother had probably seen Marie a little more clearly than her son had.

"Her dying words were to send it to me." His voice cracked. "God, I'm going to miss them."

"I know, Lucas," Brianna murmured laying her cheek against his shoulder and rubbing his back comfortingly. She stared down at the ring in his hand. If it were passed down through the oldest son it should have come down her line. With a sick feeling, Brianna wondered why she'd never seen it before.

29

November 1860

"You're really going to ride him today?" Billy
asked as he leaned against the fence.

Brianna finished tightening the cinch. "Sure am. Just
as soon as the stage leaves. In the meantime Oz will
wear the saddle until he forgets it's on his back."

"I hope Seth comes in late today," Billy said with a
grin. "This is one ride I want to see."

"And who do you think is going to win the bet?"

"Bet, what bet?"

"You don't lie worth spit, Billy," she said sardonically as she took the stirrup off the horn and let it fall
into place over the cinch. "I know all about the bet
Lucas has with Ian. So who do you think is going to
win?"

"Which one is right?"

Brianna's eyes danced. "Ian, of course. Oz won't
even think of bucking."

"Are you sure of that?"

"Absolutely." She gave him a sidelong glance as she blew on her fingers to warm them before putting her gloves back on.

"You don't lie worth spit either," he said softly.

"All right, I'm not positive, but I do know he won't buck me off. Put your money with Ian."

"I already have."

Brianna climbed over the fence carefully avoiding the wire that ran along the top pole and jumped down. "I don't know, I think the wild stallion has forgotten all about us," Brianna said eyeing Lucas's intricate system of defense as they headed toward the yard where Ian was untying Billy's horse. "It's been almost a month since they were here last."

"Maybe we scared him bad enough last time he decided it wasn't worth the danger."

"Rider coming in!"

"Oh, blast," Billy said. "Why did Seth have to be early this morning?"

"If anybody comes through in the next three days I'll send word of how it went."

"No matter who wins?"

She grinned as Billy took the reins and swung up into the saddle. "No matter who."

Lucas wasn't even listening to them. His full attention was focused on the rider coming in. "What's that Seth is yelling?"

"Abraham Lincoln was elected president!" Seth called thundering into the yard.

"Abe Lincoln's our next president?" Billy yelled as Seth passed him the mochila. A nod from the other rider and he was on his way to spread the news.

"Did you hear anything else, Seth?" Ian asked anxiously. "Like whether the South seceded?"

"No. Charlie just told me what I passed on to Billy."

"If anybody can hold the Union together it's

Lincoln," Lucas said. "He isn't anti-South at all. Maybe he'll convince them to stay."

"Not if he doesn't change his stand on slavery not moving West. He's right, too. Nobody has the right to own another person," Ian said hotly.

"Slavery is a dying institution, anyway," Lucas said walking the horse back and forth to cool him down. "If we leave well enough alone it will crumble on its own."

"Maybe so but that'll take years. I'm not willing to wait that long."

"Will you fight for the Union, Ian?" Brianna asked quietly.

"If it comes to war I will. I'll do whatever I can for my country."

"Suppose they asked you to fly a hot air balloon over enemy lines as a spy?"

He gave her a startled look. "A balloon?"

"Brianna likes balloons," Seth said. "You'd better say yes if you don't want to lose standing with her."

Ian grinned. "In that case I'll suggest a balloon brigade myself if I ever get the chance."

Would he be the one to pilot Dream Chaser over enemy lines? Brianna wondered. It was easy to imagine him doing it. He was always game for a new adventure.

When the stage came in forty minutes later the passengers already knew the news. Seth had yelled it to the driver as he rode past.

Brianna had moved her concessions inside with the coming of the colder weather and the passengers all clustered around the table drinking coffee and discussing the possibilities. Like the men at the station, they were full of speculation about what effect Lincoln's election would have. All had an opinion, many agreed it would mean war but unlike Lucas none seemed to have any real concept of what that would mean to the country.

To Brianna, the Civil War had always been a dull collections of names and dates that her history teachers droned on and on about every a year between the Revolution and World War I. Suddenly, it was all too real. Seth and Ian were sure to fight for the Union, while Billy with his Virginian origins would probably join the South. Any of them could die, all of them might. She didn't even know when the stupid war was going to start. Maybe it already had.

Brianna was so lost in thought she hardly noticed when her customers left and the stage lumbered out of the yard.

Ian stuck his head in the door. "Well, when's the big show?"

"What?"

"When are you going to ride Oz?"

"Oh. Just as soon as I get this cleared away and get my clothes changed. About fifteen minutes I think."

The threat of war had driven all thought of her first ride on Oz from her mind. By the time she had cleaned up and changed clothes some of her enthusiasm had returned. She'd spent months preparing for this.

It was always exciting to ride a horse for the first time but this was going to be even better than usual. Ian, Seth, and Billy might pretend they were on her side but they had no more confidence in her ability to ride that horse than Lucas did.

Brianna smiled as she walked out of the cabin. She was going to set three nineteenth century males right on their chauvinist attitude. One in particular.

They were all gathered at the corral waiting for her. All three had big grins on their faces. She smiled back as she climbed into the corral and walked over to Oz. "Hello, sweetheart," she said rubbing his neck. "Shall we go for a ride today?"

He nuzzled her palm in greeting. Brianna untied the

reins, put them on either side of his neck, and waited. Oz bumped her shoulder with his nose and nibbled at the braid hanging over her shoulder. It was now or never.

Brianna put her foot in the stirrup and swung up into the saddle with one smooth motion. Oz tossed his head and pranced a little, startled by the unfamiliar weight on his back. "It's just me, boy," she said patting his neck. "You're all right."

He settled at the sound of her familiar voice though he was still clearly nervous. "All right let's take a little walk," she said nudging him slightly with the heels of her boots. With a snort he started forward. The trip around the corral wasn't without its tense moments. Oz was clearly skittish and even shied at the gate as they went by it. What he didn't do was buck, not even a little.

Brianna rode him around the corral several times then turned him and rode the other direction. After about twenty minutes she stopped in front of the men and smiled down at them.

"I hate to say I told you so, Lucas, but I did you know." With that she rode Oz to the opposite side of the corral dismounted and tied him to the fence.

"I never would have believed it if I hadn't seen it. Here's your money, Lucas."

"Mine, too."

Brianna turned in astonishment. They were paying Lucas?

"What's going on?"

Lucas shrugged. "I'm collecting on my bet."

"But Oz never bucked."

"I didn't expect him to."

"You didn't?"

"Congratulations, Brianna," Ian said. "You did a fine job of breaking him. It won't be long before you've turned him into a top quality saddle horse."

"Never seen one quite so tame the first time out," Seth agreed. "You've got a real touch with horses."

She watched in total bewilderment as the three men walked away. Lucas hadn't expected Oz to buck? But then it didn't really sound like the others had either. What was going on?

The conversation during lunch and supper centered on politics and the possibility of war. It wasn't until Ian and Seth headed for the barn and Lucas settle down to smoke his pipe that he brought up the subject of her ride. "How long before you take Oz out of the corral?" he asked tamping the tobacco into his pipe with his thumb.

"Not for a while yet. He has to learn the turns."

Lucas gave a satisfied nod then stuck a splint into the fireplace and lit his pipe.

Brianna watched him draw contentedly for a moment. "How come you knew Oz wouldn't buck today?"

"You have him so tame you could probably take a nap and use him for a shade tree."

"But I thought you didn't think my method of training would work."

"I knew it would, I use it myself when I have time. I just didn't think you'd be able to carry it out. You proved me wrong."

"So you bet he wouldn't buck?"

"Nope."

"No? But I saw you take money from both Ian and Seth."

"Sure did, and I'll get some from Billy, too."

Brianna had a sudden feeling she had missed something. "What exactly was the bet about?"

"That if you were successful you wouldn't be able to resist rubbing my nose in it." He took the pipe out of his mouth. "The others don't know you as well as I do."

She tried to remember exactly what was said during the conversation she'd overheard the night before. "You set me up!"

"Yup." He grinned. "At least I guess that's what you call it. It took me almost a week to get you to eavesdrop. After that I knew I couldn't lose. Easiest money I've earned in a long time."

"You rat. I'll think of some way to get even. Just you wait."

"You won't get me so easily this time. I know better than to leave my clothes on the bank of the river."

"We'll see."

The wild horses returned late that night just as the full moon rose in the east. This time the rifle shots didn't seem to bother them much. They milled around but showed no sign of leaving.

"Guess it's time to try out my invention," Lucas said leaning his rifle against the side of the cabin. He squatted down next to the step and revved the crank on the generator he'd set there every night for the last month.

"Better hurry, Lucas," Brianna said nervously as she shot her pistol in the air. "The horses in the corral are pushing against the fence pretty hard."

"I have to get a charge built up . . . there that should do it . . . all right . . . now!" He threw the switch. There was a spark then a bright flash and a loud boom as the electricity ignited the black powder at the other end.

The wild horses whinnied in fear and wheeled away from the unknown menace. The stallion's cry rang out above the panicked herd and seemed to rally them.

"Damn. I guess I need to set one off in his face. Do you see him, Brianna?"

"No, but it sounds like he's in the center somewhere."

She fired into the air again as another volley erupted from Ian and Seth.

"Good, that's where the big one is." Lucas picked up another set of wires. "See how you like this one, my friend," he said hooking them to the generator. But when he revved up the machine and threw the switch nothing happened. "The wire must have come unhooked," he muttered. In the next breath he was on his feet running toward the flash pan.

Suddenly the stallion reared up above the herd less than a dozen yards away from him. "Lucas!" Brianna called in alarm as the stallion screamed defiantly at the intruder.

Brianna fired her pistol three times in rapid succession but the stallion paid no heed. Neither did Lucas who was crouched on the ground trying to fix whatever was wrong with his invention. Her pistol clicked on an empty chamber just as the stallion headed for Lucas with bared teeth.

"*LUCAS!*" Brianna screamed. With no thought of the danger she was putting herself in, she grabbed his rifle and ran toward him. If she could get to him in time . . .

She'd run less than halfway when the stallion reached Lucas and reared above him, the deadly hooves flashing in the moonlight. The horrifying tableau in front of her seemed to move in slow motion.

Belatedly, Lucas made a half turn and stared up at the menace above him. Finally realizing his danger, he turned back covering his face with his arm just as the stallion started to come down.

"*NO!*" Brianna screamed. With one smooth motion she swung Lucas's rifle to her shoulder and fired. The explosion sounded incredibly loud and the unexpected recoil knocked her off balance causing her stumble and fall. When she scrambled to her feet the wild herd was surging past her in a solid wall of flying feet and horse flesh.

She ran parallel to the herd toward the fence terrified of what she'd find. It seemed to take forever but in reality it was less than a minute before she got to the corral and another second to reach Lucas who was struggling to stand up.

"Lucas!" she cried rushing to him and helping him get to his feet. "You're all right," she said closing her eyes and hugging him tightly.

"My right arm hurts but other than that I'm fine." He put his left arm around her and pulled her close. "Here now don't cry. It's all over."

For the first time she realized her face was wet with tears. "Oh, Lucas, I was so scared."

"Damn, Lucas, that was cutting it kind of close wasn't it?" Ian said coming up from the other side.

Seth let go with a low whistle of admiration. "Nice shot."

"It was Brianna's," Lucas admitted giving her a little squeeze. "Seems I underestimated her marksmanship."

Brianna open her eyes in surprise and stared down at the dead stallion that lay less than a yard from her feet. There was a single bullet hole slightly behind his eye. "I . . . I killed him?"

"He dropped like a poleaxed steer."

Brianna swallowed. "Oh," she said in a small voice.

Lucas smiled down at her. "Is this going to become a habit with you?"

"What?"

"First it was the buffalo stampede and now this. Seems to me this is the second time you've saved my life."

30

December 1860

"Here use these." *Lucas* handed Brianna a hand-made tool that looked a great deal like a pair of needle nosed pliers. "Now just hold the wire tight while I twist it . . ."

"Like that?"

"Perfect."

She tried to concentrate on holding the wire in place. In the month since the stallion had broken Lucas's right arm, Brianna had become adept as a lab assistant but it was difficult to pay attention with the wind whistling outside. With the cold winter weather, Lucas had abandoned the unheated lab, but today even the cabin felt chilly.

As though he read her mind, Lucas glanced at the shuttered window. "I'd better finish up here then go find Ian and Seth. Sounds like we're in for a storm."

"A blizzard do you think?"

"Could be." He straightened with a sigh. "If it is we're going to have a problem."

She shivered. "The stock?"

"No. We'll string ropes out to the barn so we can get out there to feed no matter how bad it gets. Water could be something of a problem if we can't take them down to the river but we'll fill all the barrels. Of course we'll have to thaw it out but . . . "

"Lucas?" Brianna put her hand on his good arm. "What is it?"

"What do you mean?"

"I've never known you to rattle before."

"Rattle?"

"Go on and on about nothing. Is it your arm?"

"No. It hurts a little but that elixir of yours will take care of it."

Brianna nodded and made a mental note to grind up a couple more of Tom's painkillers for him. Mixed in water they passed for medicine she'd bought from the peddler and had kept the pain from Lucas's broken arm at bay.

"It's the sleeping arrangements," Lucas said.

"What?"

"If a blizzard hits everybody will have to stay in the cabin."

"Oh." She glanced at her feet. "Lucas it's way too cold for anybody to sleep on the floor."

"I know. Ian and Seth can both fit in your bunk if they spoon."

Brianna was appalled. The image it brought to mind was very odd to say the least. "What in the world does that mean?"

He gave her strange look. "Where have you been all your life? When two people spoon they sleep head to foot with each other."

"Oh, I get it. That way they can share body heat without getting too close."

"Right." Lucas suddenly became very busy gathering his tools. "I'm sorry, Brianna, but there's no other solution."

"Well, for heaven's sake, Lucas, as though I begrudge them the use of my bed. It really should be Ian's anyw . . ." With a flash of clarity, Brianna understood. If Ian and Seth were in her bed, she and Lucas would have to share the other. "Oh, my."

"Yes. It could be a bit difficult."

"Well. . . . can't we just . . . spoon, too?"

"We can if you want to, but married couples don't spoon. Ian will know the truth immediately. It will please him I'm sure." Lucas paused. "But it could complicate things."

Boy could it. Though Ian had never tried to be anything but a good friend to Brianna, a blind man could see he was smitten. If he knew her marriage to Lucas wasn't real . . . "You and I have shared a bed before, Lucas," she said with a nonchalance she didn't feel. "If we have to, we can do it again."

"And maybe it won't blizzard at all."

"Right. Would you like some help with your coat?" With the splint and sling on his right arm there were some things he couldn't do. He'd solved the problem of shaving easily enough by growing a beard. Getting dressed was another matter. Over the month he and Brianna had worked out a system, but he hated being dependent on her.

"I suppose," he said with ill-concealed disgust. "I'll be glad when I get this thing off my arm. You have better things to do that wait on me," he grumbled as she buttoned his coat. "Makes me feel like a child."

Brianna smiled. It was an old refrain, one she heard several times a day. "It's only temporary, and I don't mind in the least."

Mind, heck she enjoyed it. Not only had she missed

their shared swimming trips, the coming of winter had forced him to start wearing long underwear to bed. Helping him button his shirt might not be as satisfying as watching the thick muscles of his back as he swam, or seeing that gorgeous torso outlined in moonlight, but it was better than nothing. "With the three of us it shouldn't take much more than an hour," Lucas said wiggling his fingers into the glove she held.

"Do you need my help, too?"

"No, just have plenty of hot coffee ready."

"All right then. See you at supper." Brianna sighed as she closed the door behind him. The forced intimacy caused by his broken arm had been wonderful. She loved helping him with his experiments almost as much as she loved touching him without worrying about what he'd think.

Sharing a narrow bunk with him was another matter entirely. Surely she'd be able to control herself . . . wouldn't she? Maybe she should wear a suit of armor she thought with a wry grin as she knelt by her trunk to get the painkillers.

She almost giggled when she lifted the lid for the crinoline lay on top. It was about as close to armor as a person could get. No only was it a rather formidable piece of clothing, if she wore it there wouldn't be room for Lucas in the bed.

Then she sobered. If only she could figure out what to do. Maybe she should be encouraging Ian. For all she knew Lucas would be dead by now, crushed by a buffalo or savaged by a wild horse. Surely if Anna were here she'd have made her choice.

War loomed in the near future for the Southern states had seceded. The nation held its breath waiting to see what would happen. Brianna knew the four men would soon go their separate ways and she didn't have a clue what her great-great-grandmother had done when the time came. *Oh, Anna how I wish you were here to straighten out your own life.*

Brianna out pulled Tom's medicine pouch. She hadn't destroyed the backpack and its incriminating contents after the Indian attack. Every time she thought of doing it she remembered how the strobe had saved her life and decided to wait a few more days. After Lucas broke his arm she knew she wouldn't ever do it.

Brianna would never forget the horrible sound he'd made when Ian set the break. Half-way between a groan and a scream it had raised the hairs on the back of her neck and twisted her insides into knots. She'd practically run to the trunk to dig out Tom's medicine pouch. There had been no less than three different types of painkillers. She'd picked the one marked extra-strength and dissolved four tablets in a glass of water. For a while she'd been afraid she'd given him too much; he'd slept for hours. Since then she'd been very careful with the dosage, grinding up two pills at a time. The first bottle was gone and the other two wouldn't last forever. As she emptied the aspirin into a small wooden box and rehid the bottle, she wondered if the time would come when she wished she'd saved some for herself. She hadn't seen the blue mist for a long time. Had Tom given up trying to reach her? The possibility of being stuck here forever didn't bear thinking of. She hated everything about this century except Lucas; the one man she could never have.

By the time the men came in the wind had intensified until it shrieked around the cabin like a banshee and Brianna had wrapped herself in Anna's shawl to ward off the cold air that came in through the walls.

"I brought you a visitor," Seth said cheerfully as he crossed the room and deposited a crate near the fireplace. "Hate to have Gertrude freeze her pinfeathers.

It's not like you could go out and find another chicken to replace her."

"Oh heavens, I forgot all about her. Thank you, Seth."

Ian chuckled. "It's a good thing you found a chicken instead of a milk cow, Brianna. Might be a trifle crowded in here with a cow."

"Could be a little tight anyway if this storm lasts any length of time," Lucas put in as he dumped a load of wood in the wood box.

"It could be worse," Seth said. "Bart Kelly could be here you know. He's due in next week."

"Is it a blizzard then?" Brianna asked as she set the table for supper.

Lucas nodded. "Looks like it. I hear they're pretty bad in this part of the country."

"Haven't you ever seen one?"

"Not here. I came out when the Pony Express started in April."

Brianna was startled. It hadn't occurred to her that none of the men had ever spent a winter in Wyoming. Her stomach clenched as she thought of the subzero weather that was bound to follow the storm. There was no way the cabin was built for it. Thank heavens Ian wasn't completely ignorant of what to expect. He'd gone to Green Mountain several times to get wood. For the first time she wondered if it was enough.

As bedtime approached, Brianna became more and more nervous. Lucas watched her with a kind of irritated amusement. What did she think he was going to do to her with Seth and Ian right in the same room with them? He started to pull out his pipe then thought better of it. No sense filling the air with smoke. They might be breathing it for quite awhile.

All too soon it was time to call it an evening. Brianna

pulled off Lucas's boots and unbuttoned his shirt before stepping behind the curtain to change into her nightgown. She stayed there until Seth and Ian were covered by their blankets, then Lucas blew out the lantern and she came to bed.

"Inside or outside?" she whispered in Lucas's ear.

"You take the inside. It will be warmer."

She nodded and lay down facing the wall. As Lucas slipped in behind her, she pulled the blanket over them both.

"Good night," she said to the room at large.

"Good night," Ian and Seth chimed in unison.

Lucas just grunted as he settled himself more comfortably and shut his eyes. Suddenly he was surrounded by the essence of Brianna. He'd never in his life met anyone who bathed as much as she did. Maybe that was why she always smelled so good. The urge to sink his face into her hair was almost irresistible.

She shifted slightly and his hand accidentally brushed her hip. He started to pull it away, then stopped and ran his hand lightly down her leg. "What are you wearing," he whispered.

"My nightgown."

"No, I mean underneath."

"Two pairs of long underwear, my socks, and a flannel shirt."

He stiffened. "Are you that afraid of me?"

"No, I'm that cold." She lifted his splinted arm from her hip and carefully placed it around her waist in a more natural position for him. "If I were afraid of you I'd have worn my gun."

"Cold, huh."

"Frozen. I don't do winter well. Now start kicking out that body heat."

He smiled in the darkness. "Anything to please the lady."

"Do you have enough room?"

"I'm fine." He was better than fine, at least for the moment. He might not feel that way by morning but for right now he was content.

Lucas lips traced a path of fire down her neck as he caressed her naked body with sure masterful strokes. Desire ran through her like a molten river of sheer pleasure. It was heaven. She arched against him wanting more . . . much more. Suddenly a soft feminine voice intruded. "You mustn't, Brianna. He's mine."

Brianna jerked awake with Anna's accusing words still ringing in her ears. Sometime during the night she had rolled over and now lay in Lucas's arms with her head pillowed against his left shoulder. What a dream! Her heart was still pounding, as much from arousal as her sudden awakening.

She glanced up at his face and sighed in relief. He was still asleep. As far as she could tell, so were Ian and Seth. Carefully extricating herself she crawled to the end of the bunk and got up. Lord, but it was cold!

Brianna got her clothes out of her trunk then hurried behind the curtain to use the chamber pot and to get dressed. She put her trousers on over the long underwear, exchanged her nightgown for a dress and wore her flannel shirt over the top of everything. It was a good thing Anna's clothes were still slightly loose on her otherwise she wouldn't be able to move.

The fire was going and the coffee brewing when the men began to stir. Beyond a brief good morning, Brianna ignored them, keeping her back turned while they dressed. With her dream still fresh in her mind, she was a little nervous about facing Lucas, but when the time came he was very matter of fact.

"Did you sleep well?" she asked buttoning his shirt.

"Like a baby. How about you?"

"Fine."

"Are you warm enough this morning?"

"Lucas, you can see your breath in here!"

"There must be something more you can put on."

"Nope." Brianna pulled up her skirt slightly to show him her trousers. "I'm wearing it all."

His laughter and the subsequent explanation to Seth and Ian went a long way toward reestablishing her equilibrium. All three gave her a gentle ribbing all through breakfast to which she responded with good humor. Her complacency disappeared in a flash when they all began to get ready to go outside.

"That blizzard is still howling out there," she said fearfully.

"Don't worry, Ian knew what it was going to be like. We strung ropes from here to the corral."

"Can't you wait awhile? It could blow itself out in an hour or two."

"We have to be ready when Billy gets here."

"Billy! Surely he's not coming in this."

"Of course he is," Seth said. "This is the day the mail comes through."

"But you're not going on . . . are you? . . . Seth, it's too dangerous. You can't."

"It's my job, Brianna. The mail moves no matter what. That's why they pay us so much." Seth drew himself up to his full height. "I'll get the mail to Platte River Bridge or die trying!"

"Billy feels the same way. They won't thank you for trying to protect them," Lucas said gently as Ian and Seth went outside into the storm. "The company's very picky about who they hire."

As a rebuke it was pretty mild, but Brianna got the message loud and clear. "All right Lucas I won't make it any harder for them."

"I knew we could count on you." With a smile he was gone and Brianna pushed the door shut behind him.

Did they have any idea what they were asking Seth to do?

Probably not. A Wyoming blizzard had to be experienced to be understood. She'd never forget the first time she'd been caught in one by herself. It had taken her six hours to make the ninety mile drive from Shoshoni to Casper, a trip that usually took an hour and a half. She had prayed she wouldn't slide off the road or get stuck as she drove from one reflector pole to the next because she couldn't see any farther. Seth and Billy wouldn't even have the reflectors to mark the trail.

In her time, smart winter travelers always had sleeping bags in the trunk for warmth and high energy food in the glove box to . . . Tom's trail mix! Of course. She couldn't keep Seth here but she could improve his chances of surviving.

As she pulled the plastic sack out of Tom's backpack, she considered how she was going to disguise the mixture of sunflower nuts, chocolate chips, raisins, and bite-sized candies. It looked so twentieth century. That's why she'd never used any of it in her baking.

Then it hit her. The coffee grinder! It only took a moment to empty out the beans and refill it with the trail mix. The grinder worked like a charm. For the first time all winter, she was thankful for the cold weather. Without it the chocolate would have gummed up the works.

By the time the men returned she had fashioned small nuggets held together by a mixture of flour and molasses. The result wasn't exactly an epicurean delight but the burst of energy they could provide might mean the difference between survival and not.

Seth was surprised by the "trail snacks," but tucked them into the pocket of his coat.

The morning passed in endless checker games as Ian and Lucas took turns waiting in the barn for Billy. Brianna refused to consider the possibility that he wouldn't make it; that he lay frozen to death on the trail somewhere.

A little after noon, Ian stuck his head in the door. "Rider coming in, Seth."

"Be right there." He wrapped his scarf around his head, put on his hat, and grabbed his coat.

Though Brianna knew she might never see him again she resisted the urge to throw her arms around him and bid him a tearful farewell. "Good luck, Seth."

He gave her a jaunty grin. "See you Thursday. Thanks for the trail snacks."

"Save them in case you get into trouble out there, Seth," she called after him as he went out the door. Peering out into the storm she gasped in horror. Billy sat on his horse wavering, unable to dismount. Ian pulled him off while Lucas jerked the mochila from Billy's saddle and threw it over Seth's. The other rider was up and away, disappearing into the gloom almost immediately.

Lucas and Ian carried Billy to the cabin, his frozen legs dangling uselessly between them. They lay him on Brianna's bunk, then Ian hurried back outside to take care of the horse who wasn't in much better shape than his rider.

"Get some water heating," Lucas said pulling his glove off with his teeth. "We've got to get him warmed up."

Brianna set the kettle and three pans full of water on the fire.

"Damn it, hang on, Billy," Lucas said sharply. "Don't go to sleep on me."

Brianna fought tears as she hurried over to help. "We have to get your coat and gloves off, Billy. I'm going to need your help."

Billy lifted his hand still curled into a fist. "Fr-roze around the reins." His teeth chattered. "C-can't str-straighten my fin-g-gers."

"Let's do the other one first," Brianna said easing off the right glove instead. "Now for the coat."

It took Lucas and Brianna several minutes to get Billy out of his coat and boots. They were finally able to loosen his left hand enough to take off the glove. Lucas studied him closely while Brianna rubbed life back into the frozen limbs. "Doesn't look like any frostbite," he said at last.

"I got lost and couldn't tell where I was going." A spasm of pain crossed his face as the feeling began to come back to his fingers and toes. "Finally found the river."

"And you followed it in?" Brianna asked.

"Not at first. I was so turned around I didn't know which way to go. Then I found a place where the water flows too fast for ice to form. How the devil did you get your hands so hot, Brianna?"

Brianna moved from one foot to the other. "They're not hot at all. It just seems that way because you're cold. So you followed the river upstream then?"

"Blasted snow was so thick I couldn't tell which way it was running. Finally thought of my lariat. I tossed the end in the river and watched which way it went then rode the opposite direction."

Lucas glanced Brianna's way as he poured hot coffee into a cup. "See what I mean about the company being picky about their riders. They only hired the best."

"Or the dumbest," Billy said curling his hands around the cup. "Only an idiot would ride in weather like this."

By supper time Billy was almost back to normal and the storm had blown itself out. Unfortunately Brianna had been right about the cold that would follow. Without a thermometer, it was impossible to tell how cold it was but temperatures as low as twenty below were common after a blizzard. Brianna knew she should be grateful she didn't have to use the chamber pot in a roomful of men any more, but the bitterly cold trip to the outhouse was almost worse.

Even though the storm was over there was no question of Ian and Billy sleeping in the barn. As Brianna prepared to crawl into bed with Lucas again she suddenly realized tomorrow was Christmas eve. It wasn't right somehow. They should have spent the day popping popcorn, decorating a tree, and drinking eggnog. Instead they'd fought to save the life of a boy who would still be in high school in her time.

Worst of all, this was only December. The coldest weather was yet to come. That meant she'd probably be sharing Lucas's bed far more than just one night.

Oh the joy she had to look forward to in the next few months; living with a chicken, worrying constantly about Seth and Billy, having erotic dreams of Lucas, and trying to stay warm in a cabin that was approximately the same temperature as a refrigerator.

It was going to be a long winter.

31

February 1861

"Again!" Billy threw down his cards in disgust. "Blast it, Brianna, that's the third time in a row!"

Lucas chuckled. "You're the one who didn't want to play Spades or checkers any more and suggested Five Card Stud."

"I thought we'd play for money."

Ian grinned. "Do you want to change the stakes again?"

"Are you crazy? Playing for buffalo chips is bad enough. God only knows what she'll switch to next time."

"You didn't want to play for buckets of water anymore," Brianna reminded him. "Besides there's all kinds of buffalo chips outside and most of the snow is blown off so they're easy to find."

"Most of them are frozen down," he muttered.

Brianna nonchalantly studied her nails as Ian shuffled the cards. "That's why I suggested it. I'm tired of gathering them all myself. You only owe me fifty. What time is it, Lucas?"

He looked at his watch. "Eleven-fifteen."

"Already? I'd better finish getting lunch."

"You're not going to give us a chance to win our chips back," Billy demanded indignantly.

"Do you want lunch?"

"We could always play for who cooks," Lucas suggested.

"No!" the other three said in unison. Lucas had lost even more consistently than Billy.

"I guess I'd better get started paying off my debt," Billy grumbled. "Seven buckets of water and fifty buffalo chips, I'll be busy all afternoon."

"You ought to know better than to bet on a pair of twos," Ian said with a grin as he stood and stretched. "Brianna taught you a valuable lesson, and it didn't cost you a dime."

Lucas put on his coat. "May as well bring the water barrel Billy. Ian and I have to take the sled down to the river anyway." He glanced at Brianna. "Have we got time to bring another load of water up for the horses?"

"You should. Lunch won't be ready for an hour or so." Brianna frowned. Lucas was rubbing his arm again. The splint was gone but it still bothered him. She was worried about it but there was nothing she could do. There wouldn't be an X-ray around for a hundred years or so. Just like everything else that was worthwhile.

Brianna sighed as the door shut behind the men. She knew what her problem was. Cabin fever. The winter had been even worse than she had imagined. The intense cold had continued almost unabated for a full month before it rose above zero. Even then it wasn't exactly warm. Little things she'd never even thought of before were a constant irritant like having to break the ice on the water bucket every morning or never being able to ride Oz for more than a few minutes at a time. By far the worst was going to the bathroom. She either had to use the far too public chamber pot behind the curtain or freeze her posterior in the outhouse.

She hated it all, the boredom, the constant worry about four men who seemed determined to put themselves in danger at every opportunity, a coat and mittens that were completely inadequate, wind that whistled through the cracks in the walls, the smell of burning buffalo chips, the list was endless.

But most of all she hated sleeping with Lucas. Every second was sheer torture. There was only so much arousal a person could stand before it became unpleasant. She was far beyond that point. Thank heavens Lucas seemed unaffected. If he so much as nibbled her neck she'd probably rip his clothes off and make a total fool of herself.

The one night Ian and Billy had tried to sleep in the barn Brianna had been ecstatic. Her own bed at last, a good night's sleep, no erotic dreams, no lustful longings. But it hadn't been wonderful at all. She'd been so cold she had almost crawled back in with Lucas on her own. The only reason she hadn't was she was afraid of what might happen without a chaperone in the cabin with them. Nobody had been happier than Brianna when Ian and Billy froze out and came back to the cabin. At least when she shared Lucas's bed she got warm once a day.

She didn't even look forward to the riders changing or the stagecoach coming any more for she knew one day the news would be that war had broken out. And underneath it all was the fear that Tom had given up trying to reach her. The blue mist hadn't appeared since the first part of November. It was beginning to look as if she might be stuck in this century for the rest of her life.

"Here's your water," Billy said as he and Ian came in carrying the water barrel. "It's my seven buckets and Ian's five, plus a whole lot more. Does that get me a reduced sentence?"

Brianna felt a sharp stab of guilt. He had carried water for her since the beginning. She knew he disliked the unpleasant task of collecting buffalo chips to supplement the wood supply even more than she did. Like many cowboys, he hated to walk. "All right, I'll tell you what. If you'll go cut me a deer roast, and fill the wood box, I'll let you off the hook for only ten buffalo chips."

"What about the rest?"

"Lucas and Ian still owe me some."

"It's a deal. How big a roast do you want?"

"Oh, about like this," she said indicating the size with her hands. "I'll fix it for supper."

Ian cocked an eyebrow. "Seems to me I deserve some special consideration, too. Billy didn't get that water by himself."

"Hmm, that's true. Maybe . . . "

"Hello in the house."

The three inside exchanged a startled glance. There hadn't been any visitors other than the stage for three months. Brianna reached over and opened the door.

"Mr. Bromley! This is a surprise."

"Good morning, Mrs. Daniels. Didn't know I'd be coming so soon or I'd have sent word."

"You're always welcome," she said with a smile as she stepped aside. "Come on in. You must be half frozen."

"Close to it. Good morning, MacTavish, Fry." Mr. Bromley glanced back at Brianna. "Is your husband around?"

"He took the sled to the barn," Billy said. "We were just headed out to help him unload the water for the horses."

"Do you need him right now?"

"Actually I need to talk to all three of you, but there's no real hurry."

Brianna took his hat. "They'll be in for lunch in about twenty minutes. Would you like to sit by the fire and warm yourself until then?"

"If I wouldn't be in your way."

"Heaven's no. I'd be glad of the company."

"Just don't play poker with her," Billy muttered walking out the door.

Ian grinned as Bromley raised his eyebrows in surprise.

"Sore loser."

"What does that mean?"

"Billy doesn't like to lose at cards."

As Ian put on his hat and followed Billy outside Brianna wondered uneasily how many of her twentieth century idioms were now firmly entrenched in the speech patterns of the men she lived with. "Would you like some coffee?"

"Yes, thank you." Bromley settled back in the chair she set by the fireplace for him. "Been fleecing my men at cards have you?"

Brianna blushed slightly. "Not intentionally. Billy just has a hard time backing down. He bet fifty chips this morning on a pair of twos when I had a full house. He hasn't forgiven me yet."

"Can't say as I blame him. You won half a month's pay."

"Oh no, we don't play for money."

"Then what did he lose?"

"Fifty buffalo chips." Brianna admitted reluctantly. It sounded so stupid. The man was looking at her as though she'd gone crazy. "We use them to supplement our wood supply, only I got tired of gathering them . . . so I thought . . . "

She didn't get a chance to finish. Bromley's laughter cut her off mid-sentence.

"So he has to go out and find fifty buffalo chips?"

"No, only ten. There's a frozen deer carcass hanging in Lucas's lab. Billy's going to cut me off a roast for supper. That and the barrel of water over there will make us even."

Bromley chuckled again. "You are a most resourceful woman, Mrs. Daniels. Now then, tell me about this wild horse you wanted to keep."

James Bromley seemed content to drink coffee and chat with her about Oz, the weather, even Gertrude. After twenty minutes Brianna still didn't have a clue what the purpose of this surprise visit was, but she had the feeling it was important.

It wasn't until halfway through the meal that he broached the subject that had brought him to Split Rock.

"Gentlemen, the Pony Express in is trouble," he said. "We're on the verge of bankruptcy and the telegraph is advancing across the country from the East and West both. Once that line is completed, our speed will no longer be needed."

Billy frowned. "Does that mean we don't have jobs any more?"

"Not yet. Even with the telegraph, there will still be a need for mail to go back and forth across the country."

"The government mail contract belongs to the Butterfield Express," Lucas said.

"There is a bill in Congress right now to give that contract to our company. It passed the House but looks like it may die in the Senate. We don't have President Buchanan's support."

"But the choice is obvious," Ian protested. "The Butterfield Express takes twenty days to get mail to California. We do it in half that."

"Our route is also much shorter and less susceptible to attack from the South if it does come to war. We need to prove that the Central Overland and Pikes Peak Express can carry the mail safer and faster than any other."

"But we already do," Billy pointed out.

"True, but we need to remind everyone of that."

Lucas sat back a crossed his arms. "Something tells me the company has come up with a dramatic way to do just that."

"As a matter of fact they have. On March fourth, Abraham Lincoln will take office. The entire country will be watching and waiting to see what he intends to do about the states that have seceded. What he says in his inaugural address may well decide whether we go to war or not. It will take three weeks to get the news to California on the Butterfield line. We intend to get it there in one."

"One!" All three men were stunned.

"That's eighteen hundred miles in seven days," Bromley said. "A full three days less than we've ever done it before."

"And the world will never forget," Brianna murmured in awe.

"Exactly. Even though Buchanan isn't supporting us, Lincoln may, especially if we can get his message to California quickly."

Lucas nodded. "It makes sense, but how are you going to speed it up. We're already going as fast as we can."

"We're going to add more riders for one thing."

Billy set his jaw. "Are you going to cut my route?"

"No." Bromley smiled. "The stretch from Platte River Bridge to Green River is one of the fastest on the trail anyway. Putting another rider between you and Seth would only slow us down. But it won't be easy.

We're going to try to average fifteen miles an hour. There will be some places we get up to twenty."

"That's asking an awful lot," Ian said warningly. "You're going to lose horses if you push them that hard."

Bromley sighed. "I know but it can't be helped. If we don't get that mail contract the whole line is doomed."

Fingers of apprehension ran down Brianna's spine. If the Pony Express failed there would be no reason for anyone to live at the Split Rock station and Bart Kelly wouldn't come through with supplies. For all she knew the stage might not even stop there anymore. If she left she would lose any chance of getting home again, but if she stayed, she'd be all alone in the middle of nowhere.

In short, nobody sitting at that table had more to lose if the Pony Express failed than Brianna Daniels.

32

July 20, 1995

"Tom, are you sure it was Brianna we just saw?" Scott asked watching the last of the blue mist from his first attempt to switch the two women disappear.

"Well, pretty sure. It looked like her."

"It was Brianna," Anna said positively. "She was wearing my clothes."

"It works!" Scott jumped out of his chair in his excitement. "Did you see how it zeroed right in on her? It actually works."

"Of course it does," Anna said calmly. "I never had any doubt. "

"It was absolutely incredible, Scott!" Tom shook his head in amazement. "She looked like she was standing right outside."

"That's the fiber optics. It's kind of like looking through a window to the past. "Hey," he said glancing out the window at the yard. "That gives me an idea. I'll be right back."

Tom hardly noticed when Scott left the room. "A window in time," he whispered in awe. For the first time he began to think they might succeed, that Scott might actually accomplish the impossible. A surge of emotion, an odd mixture of euphoria and grief, shot through him. Everything would be the way it should be, but Anna would be gone forever.

"Tom?" Anna said softly.

He suddenly became aware that he was crushing her fingers in his grip and relaxed his hold. "I'm sorry," he murmured.

"It's all right," she said rubbing his knuckles with her free hand. "I feel the same way. We just have to remember it's a gift, a stolen moment that shouldn't have happened."

"And we have to return everyone where they should be or risk changing the present. I know all that, but it doesn't make losing you any easier."

She gave him a sad little smile. "I'm glad. I wouldn't want it to be easy."

"You don't have to worry about . . . What the hell?"

A loud squawking could be heard outside. "He's got one of the chickens!" Tom said looking through the big picture window. "What do you suppose he's up to now?"

They didn't have long to wait. Scott came in with the chicken in a cage and a triumphant grin on his face.

"We'll use a hen!" Scott said beaming at them.

"For dinner?" Anna asked uncertainly. "It's getting kind of late to get it plucked, dressed, and cooled out in time but if you have a hatchet I can . . . "

"No, we're not going to eat it. We're going to use it to test the time machine."

Anna and Tom exchanged a bewildered look.

"I've been thinking about what you said, Tom, and you're right. We really should make sure it's safe, only I couldn't figure out how to do it."

"Oh, I get it," Tom said suddenly. "You'll send the chicken."

Scott nodded eagerly. "Right. It's big enough to track once it goes through the time warp. Even if I can only keep the portal open a few seconds we'll be able to see what happens."

It took fifteen minutes to get set up again. The hen complained loudly the whole time but no one took the time to set the cage back outside. When the blue mist began to form, Tom pushed Anna away with sudden urgency. "Stay clear until we're ready. You were pulled in once. I don't want to take the chance of it happening again."

"He's right," Scott agreed. "The computer is programmed to transfer you. I don't know how powerful the magnetic field is, but it's better to be safe than sorry."

Anna nodded and moved to the other side of the room. Once she was far enough away, Tom removed the chicken and held it ready.

"OK, Tom," Scott said as the blue mist began to swirl. "Get ready . . . and . . . now!"

Tom thrust the hen into the mist. His hands started to tingle uncomfortably as he dropped the chicken through the portal. The sight that met his eyes when he looked up was not what he expected.

Brianna was running toward them as fast as she could with a look of steely determination on her face. Though no sound came through the time warp, all three watchers saw the silent scream as the chicken burst through the blue mist, flew over her head, and ran across the prairie flapping its wings. The last image they saw before the picture faded was Brianna Daniels standing in the middle of nowhere staring after the hen in total bewilderment.

"Oh, poor Brianna," Anna said trying to keep a

straight face. "Can you imagine what she must be thinking?"

"That somebody on this side of the blue mist is crazy."

"Or that we're sending her fast food."

Tom and Scott exchanged a grin. Suddenly all three were laughing and a great deal of the tension they were under eased.

"You two can laugh," Tom said with mock severity. "I'm the only one Brianna knows and she's probably cursing my name."

"Or thanking you for supper," Scott added. "That is if she can catch it."

"Oh my, I wish I could be here when you try to explain it to her," Anna said wiping her eyes.

Tom sobered instantly. "Yeah, me, too." Their eyes met.

"And that should be soon," Scott said with satisfaction, scooting his chair up to his computer. "Let's try again." With typical teenage preoccupation, he was oblivious to the emotions of the other two.

And try they did. Time after time, the blue mist appeared, swirled into an opaque window and disappeared in less time than it took to make a long distance phone call. Scott programmed and reprogrammed but nothing made a difference. They worked until they fell into bed exhausted. The next morning they were up again at first light. More times than they could count, Brianna appeared in the blue window only to evaporate into a wisp of mist a few moments later. Her life was an open book to them though she was not usually aware they were watching her. They saw her hauling buckets of water, washing clothes, going for walks, riding horseback, and even feeding the chicken.

Some of it made no sense. Several times they saw her standing behind some sort of lunch counter and once crouched down on a huge rock carving something into its surface. There was one at night where she seemed to be outside dressed in her nightgown. She had a big grin on her face as she hurried along a path with a bundle of something in her arms. They were still trying to puzzle that out when they caught her swimming in the nude. Anna made Scott and Tom close their eyes.

It was Anna who finally noticed something they had all missed. Brianna was riding a horse hell-bent for leather down a well-traveled road. Tom and Scott were wondering if Brianna was in some sort of danger when Anna suddenly sat up straighter and pointed to a corner of the picture.

"What's that?"

"It looks like . . . snow," Tom said in surprise. "Snow in July?"

Anna shook her head as the mist faded. "I don't think it is July. In fact, when you think about it, the seasons have been changing back and forth all along. We've seen wildflowers and green grass, then yellow dry prairie the next time. Half an hour ago she was swimming, obviously during the summertime, and now there's snow on the ground. If you think about it the length of her hair keeps changing back and forth, too, and so does her weight."

"By gosh, you're right. That's the key somehow. It's got to be . . . Scott stroked his upper lip thoughtfully. Suddenly he closed his eyes and dropped his head on the back of his chair. "Oh, God I can't believe I'm so stupid!"

"What?" Tom and Anna said in unison.

"Anna," Scott said sitting up and leaning forward intently. "What day was it when you came forward?"

"July fifteenth."

"And what time?"

"I don't know, around ten o'clock."

"What about you Tom?"

"About the same I guess."

"I'll bet it was precisely the same. That's why Brianna and Anna switched in the first place. They were in exactly the same place at exactly the same time when the time warp came together," Scott said. "And that's what we've been doing wrong. The Möbius strip won't stay together because I haven't been gluing the ends together in the same place. It won't work unless the time is the same. Let's see . . ." He moved to the other computer and made some quick calculations.

"The DNA will take care of the place so all we need is to get the time right. I'm not sure how much time has passed for Brianna, but I don't think more than a year. I'll program it for July 1861 to be sure. Let's see, the optimum time for a transfer should be . . . hmmm . . . twelve forty-five tomorrow afternoon. That's when we'll try again."

"Good," Tom said standing up and stretching. "I don't know about you, but I've stared at that darn blue window about as much as I care to for one day."

Scott grinned. "Me, too . . . " He broke off as the phone rang. "I wonder who that is. Everybody thinks we're on the mountain."

"Do you think he's right about tomorrow?" Anna asked watching Scott cross the room to answer the phone.

"I'd say there's a good chance of it."

"Then this is probably our last night together."

Tom reached over and gave her hand a squeeze. "Yeah, I guess it is."

"Tom," Anna said hesitantly. "Can we go back to Brianna's house tonight?"

"Do you think that's a good idea?"

"I know it is."

"What about Scott?"

"From the look of that silly grin on his face, I'd say he's got some plans of his own."

"And Sam's going along, too?" Scott was saying. "All right, I'll ask." He put his hand over the receiver. "Some of my friends are headed to a dance in Lander tonight. Do you care if I go?"

Tom was startled. He wasn't used to being cast in the role of parent. "I'm not sure . . . "

"Personally, I think Scott ought to go have some fun," Ann put in. "He's worked very hard these last few days."

"That's certainly true. Well, I guess it would be all right . . . "

"Yeah, I can go," Scott said into the phone. "I can get a ride to your place if you can bring me home. . . . Okay, see you then." He sighed happily as hung up the phone. "Ryan's been my best buddy since we were kids. We've both been so busy this summer we haven't got to do much. If you can give me a ride over they'll bring me home afterwards. He and Sam only live a couple of miles away."

"Why not take your pickup?"

"No headlights."

"Oh." Tom stood up and stretched. "Anna and I were thinking of going to town anyway so we'll just drop you off on the way."

"Great. It'll only take me a minute to get ready."

"One thing, Scott," Tom said as the teen turned to go. "Absolutely no partying, and I'll be calling you later to make sure."

"You sound just like my dad!"

"From what I hear of the man, I'll take that as a compliment."

Scott looked surprised for a moment then grinned. "Yeah, I guess it is. Anyway, I promise I'll be good. Tomorrow is a pretty important day."

"For all of us." Anna wondered if she would have the courage to follow her heart tonight or if she would spend the rest of her life regretting her cowardice.

It was still early afternoon when they pulled up to the rambling old ranch house. "Now who's this?" Tom asked watching a pretty girl come running down the steps, her long dark hair flying out behind her.

Scott shrugged nonchalantly. "Oh, that's just Ryan's little sister, Sam."

"I thought you'd never get here, Scott," Sam said as she reached the car. "I've been waiting for you ever since Ryan called."

"You have?" All semblance of indifference disappeared as he got out of the car wearing a grin that seemed to stretch clear across his face. "What for?"

"You promised to hook up my dad's modem so we could talk to each other on the computers, remember?"

"That won't take long. First let me introduce you to my friends. Tom, Anna, this is Samantha . . . "

"Well, well," Anna murmured in satisfaction as she and Tom drove back down the lane a few minutes later. "I do believe our Scott is in love. Did you see him blush?"

"Yes, and I was glad of it. I was beginning to think he spent his whole life cooped up with his computers. Sam seemed pretty impressed with him, too. Now then, on to us. How does a candlelight dinner for two sound to you?"

"Why? Are Brianna's touchlights broken?"

Tom laughed. "No, we use candlelight when we want to be romantic."

"How strange. Touchlights are brighter. You can see so much better."

"That's the whole point. Dim lights tend to improve

one's looks, you see." Tom grinned. " Tell you what, we'll skip the candles and get a bottle of wine."

Anna was appalled by the huge variety of alcoholic beverages in the liquor store they stopped at when they finally reached Riverton. But it was soon forgotten when they entered the grocery store. She stared in amazement at women hurrying by with overflowing grocery carts. Never in her wildest dreams had she imagined such a cornucopia. Fresh fruits and vegetables, meats, milk, already baked bread, and aisles and aisles of things she'd never even seen before.

"You have all of this and people eat TV dinners?"

"Only when they don't have time to cook."

"But there should plenty of time with all the machines you have to clean house and do the laundry. Women don't even have to make soap or candles anymore."

"No, but most of them have jobs."

Anna was aghast. "You mean they work like their husbands? Who takes care of the children."

"They hire people to do it." He smiled at her horrified expression. "Not everything has been a change for the better, I guess. Come on, let's find something decadent for dessert."

They finished their shopping and returned to Brianna's trailer. Tom was tempted to use the barbecue in the back yard but decided against it. The last thing they needed was a curious neighbor dropping by for a visit.

Ignoring Anna's protests, Tom did most of the cooking, though she insisted on helping him with the fresh fruit salad. The steaks were done to perfection and smothered with sautéed mushrooms and onions. Baked potatoes oozing with sour cream and melted butter, fresh green beans, salad and a delicious light wine completed the main course. Topped off with a generous slice of cheesecake, the meal left them both feeling well-fed and satisfied.

"Brianna's going to have a fit when she sees what we left in her refrigerator," Tom commented as they finished loading the dishwater and turned it on. "Shall we have some more wine?"

"If you like. What's wrong with what we left?"

"Nothing really," he said handing her a glass of wine and switching off the kitchen light. "But from the looks of her, I'd say Brianna's more into health food than fat and cholesterol."

"Is that why she's so pitifully thin?"

Tom smiled as he sat down on the big overstuffed sofa in the living room and put his feet up on the coffee table. "Exactly, but she does it on purpose. What's the matter?" he asked with concern when she lifted her hand to rub her forehead.

I have a slight headache. It happens sometimes when I have my hair braided tight like this."

"Staring at that blue mist all day probably didn't help either." He set his wine on the end table. "Come here. I'll see what I can do." He unpinned the long thick braid from her head and unplaited it. The honey gold hair felt like spun silk in his hands.

"Mmmm," Anna sighed as he began massaging her neck and shoulders. "That feels wonderful. You really do have magic fingers."

Tom smiled as he felt the muscles under his hands relax. At last when her head was lolling like a rag doll, he put his arms around her and pulled her back against his chest. "Better?"

"My headache's completely gone." She leaned her head against his shoulder and hugged his arms to her. "Do you have any idea what a special man you are?"

"Of course," he said with a chuckle as closed his eyes and rested his chin on top of her head. "People come from miles around just to have their necks massaged."

She turned in his arms and looked up at him.

"That's not what I meant," she said running her fingers down the strong line of his jaw.

Tom couldn't resist the invitation of those luminous blue eyes and the slightly parted lips. He didn't even try.

At first his kiss was tentative, but intensified rapidly with her eager response. Anna's fingers wandered through the crisp hairs on his neck as he explored the inside of her mouth. Desire escalated quickly like a forest fire raging out of control in tinder dry underbrush.

Tom pulled away before he lost what little restraint he had left. "I knew coming here was a mistake," he said huskily.

"And I think not coming would have been." She lay her head on his chest. "I love you, Tom."

"Oh, God." He pulled her tight against him. "I don't know if I can let you go tomorrow."

"You don't have a choice."

"I know."

Anna pulled his head down and kissed him lightly. "I want you to make love to me," she whispered against his lips.

"No!" With an almost superhuman effort he pushed her away and jumped up from the couch. "Damn, it Anna, we can't."

"Why not?"

"Lucas is expecting a virgin. How could you hide the fact that you aren't?"

"Tom, I'm a widow and Lucas knows it."

"What?"

"I was married for a few weeks. H-he was an old man, but he consummated the union. I guess he thought it was his duty because after the first time he never bothered me that way again."

"Oh, my poor Anna," he cried in anguish dropping down beside her and gripping her hands.

"It wasn't so bad really. He was kind to me and got me away from my aunt for a little while. I was sorry when he died, but I didn't love him. I didn't think I'd ever love anyone, until I met you." Anna returned the pressure of his fingers and smiled mistily. "I know it's wrong but I may never have another chance at happiness."

"Lucas . . ."

" . . . has been with Brianna for a year. Hasn't it occurred to you that his feelings for me might not be the same as they would have been?" She cupped Tom's face in her hands. "Lucas and I have a lifetime together, but you and I have only tonight. Please, Tom."

His resistance disappeared in an uncontrollable flood of longing and desire. Wordlessly, he stood and brought her to her feet. With one fluid motion he swept her up in his arms and headed down the hall to Brianna's bedroom.

"I love you, Anna Daniels," he whispered laying her down on the bed. "I've loved you as long as I can remember. No one will ever take your place in my heart."

Their bodies molded together in perfect symmetry as they shared the joy of discovery. Buttons moved unhindered through buttonholes, and cloth slid across deliciously sensitive flesh. Soft feminine curves conformed to hard male muscles, similarities and contrasts to be explored and savored. Finally, the last piece of clothing fell to the floor, and a combined sigh of pure pleasure greeted its departure.

The sensation of their totally naked bodies shifting together, skin against skin sent them both reeling into a haze of sudden uncontrollable need as they caressed each other with glorious abandon. Though they would have liked to prolong the moment, it was impossible to quell the tides of passion that rocked them both.

There was no guilt, no inhibitions when they came

together at last, only soul-searing intensity as their ecstasy mounted to undreamed of heights. The end, when it came, was like shattering into a million pieces, the fragments mixing together until the two entities became one. Reality returned slowly and with it the conviction that there could be no wrong in something that felt so very very right.

33

March, 1861

"Oh, for heaven's sake, Seth, sit still," Brianna said with irritation. "If you keep wiggling around like that your hair will be a disaster. I'm not much of a barber anyway."

"It itches!"

"Of course it does. Every time you move more goes down your neck."

"You sound like my big sister."

"And you act just like my brother."

"Children, children, stop your bickering," Ian said with a grin.

"Wait till she starts on you," Seth warned. "You won't think it's so funny then. I don't see why we had to do this anyway."

"Because spring is finally here and I'm tired of living with a bunch of grizzly bears." Brianna stood in front of him and eyed the hair cut critically. "Hmm, I think a little more off here . . . and . . . there, that should do it.

Now into the shower with you. Lucas just finished pouring the water so it's all ready."

"Why can't you just scrub the walls and beat the rugs like most women do when they start spring cleaning?"

"We don't have any rugs. Besides, you all *smell* like grizzlies, too."

"Remind me never to get married," Seth grumbled getting up from the chair and unbuttoning his shirt as he walked to the shower.

Brianna frowned. If it had been Billy she wouldn't have given it a second thought, but it wasn't like Seth to be so grouchy.

"Which one of us is next?" Ian asked.

"It doesn't matter to me."

Lucas didn't even look up from the wires he was splicing together at the table. "Go ahead."

Ian plopped down in the chair. "Are you going to trim my beard, too?"

"Do you want me to?"

"I don't know. I may just shave it off. What do you think?"

Brianna shrugged. "I'm not a good person to ask. Beards have never really impressed me, though I am rather partial to mustaches."

"That clinches it then. The beard goes."

"Don't do it on my account. You might even want to wait until you're sure winter's over. Now then, any preferences as to how I cut your hair?"

Unlike Seth, Ian submitted to the haircut with cheerful surrender. Though he was still somewhat skeptical about Lucas's shower, he even said he was looking forward to his bath. Brianna was about half done when Seth emerged from the shower dressed in the clean clothes she had left on her trunk for him. By the time he'd dumped the dirty water outside and carried the tub back in, he was extremely pale.

"Do you feel all right?" Brianna asked with concern.

"Not really. I think I'll go sleep for awhile. Didn't get much chance when I came in off my ride today."

"I'll wake you for supper."

He just nodded and walked out the door rubbing his forehead.

Brianna bit her lip. "Do you suppose he's sick?"

Lucas looked up. "Could be. Did you hear about his last ride?"

"No, what happened?"

"Charlie was sick when Seth got to Platte River Bridge," Ian said, "so sick he couldn't even get out of bed. There wasn't anybody else to ride so Seth wound up going all the way to Fort Laramie."

"That's over a hundred miles! He must have been exhausted." Brianna looked upset. "Worn out like that, Seth probably caught whatever Charlie had. What was wrong with him?"

"Hard to say. He seemed to be over it by the time Seth got back to Platte River Bridge the next day."

Brianna breathed a sigh of relief. "Just a twenty-four hour bug, then."

"Maybe you ought to give him some of that elixir of yours," Lucas said.

"It might not be a bad idea. We'll see what he feels like when he wakes up."

Lucas finished his project and sat back to watch Brianna cut Ian's hair. He was envious of the easy camaraderie that existed between the two. Their friendship seemed comfortable and satisfying for both of them. As they bantered back and forth Lucas found himself wishing his relationship with Brianna was as uncomplicated. He wondered if it was as confusing to her as it was to him.

"There, you look almost human, Ian," she said with satisfaction. "Your water's ready, and there are clean clothes for you on my bed."

"My head does feel lighter." Ian stood up and shook the loose hair from his shirt.

"It will be even better after your shower. All right, Lucas, it's your turn."

"You don't give any quarter do you?"

"Nope." She pointed to the chair and he ambled over pretending to be dismayed by the prospect.

"I swear you'd think this was an electric chair the way you men act."

Lucas raised an eyebrow. "Now that's an intriguing thought. What exactly would an electric chair do?"

"Something unpleasant I'm sure." She ran the comb through his hair experimentally. "Good grief, Lucas when was the last time you had a haircut?"

"Just before I came out here last April."

"April! No wonder it's almost to your shoulders."

He shrugged. "I haven't been anywhere near a barber except the few times I've gone to Platte River Bridge and I didn't have time then."

"I've never tackled a job quite this big before." Brianna tisked as she combed the long black hair. "This may take a while."

It wasn't long before Lucas decided she could take as long as she wanted. Never had a haircut felt so good. The rhythmic movement of the comb was more relaxing than sensual until she started to run her fingers through his hair. He swallowed the sigh of pure pleasure that rose in his throat, closed his eyes and just enjoyed. The snip of the scissors and the splash of Ian's shower were the only sounds in the room.

With Brianna's good clean scent in his nose and her fingers in his hair, Lucas let his mind drift in a pleasant haze of bliss. It was much like sharing his bunk with her. For the most part it had been a delightful combination of sensations that he enjoyed to the fullest.

Of course, there were nights that weren't quite so

agreeable when she turned in her sleep and cuddled up to his warmth. Lucas would wake up with their bodies intertwined and Brianna making incredibly sexy little noises against his chest. The effect on him was always immediate and not particularly pleasant since there was nothing he could do about it.

"You know, Lucas, you might just have something with this shower," Ian said stepping out from behind the curtain. "Not only does it take less water, it makes a lot more sense than sitting in a tub and letting the dirt float around you. I haven't felt this clean in a long time."

"You haven't *been* clean in a long time," Brianna reminded him. "Don't forget to dump your water outside."

As Ian went outside, Lucas closed his eyes again.

"Do you want me to refill the barrel for Lucas, Brianna?" Ian said a few minutes later when he came back in.

"No, not yet. The water will be cold by the time I'm done with him."

"Looks like he's about to go sleep."

"He is?" Brianna put her hands on Lucas's shoulders and leaned forward to look. "Am I boring you?"

"I didn't sleep well last night," he lied, opening his eyes.

"I wondered why you were being so quiet. It's not like you to pass up a chance to be obnoxious." She straightened and went back to work. "Don't worry. I should be finished before too long."

"Take your time. I'm in no hurry."

Brianna snorted. "If you think you're going to get out of taking a bath by going to sleep, you've got another thing coming."

"I wouldn't dream of it."

"It's a good thing," Ian grinned. "She'll probably throw water on you."

"That's not a bad idea," Brianna said thoughtfully.

"Don't you have important business in the barn, Ian," Lucas asked.

Ian chuckled. "I suppose I do at that. You sure I can't get you a dipper of water before I go, Brianna?"

"You do and you'll be the one wearing it," Lucas said with a growl.

Ian laughed outright at that and left.

Within seconds Lucas was under Brianna's spell again. It was enough to make a man wish he could have a haircut every day of the week he thought with a satisfied smile.

"How do you wear the front when it's short?" Brianna asked a few minutes later as she brushed his forelock off his forehead with her hand.

Lucas opened his eyes once more and found Brianna's face less than six inches from his while she focused on making the stubborn lock cooperate.

Several tendrils of hair had escaped the ever present braid she wore and framed her face in a most appealing way. Even with her lips pursed and her brows knit in concentration she was beautiful. Almost without conscious thought, Lucas lifted his hand to the back of her neck and pulled her head down.

Astonished, Brianna sucked in her breath then let it go in a soft sigh when his lips captured hers. Her mouth opened in glad response to the pressure of his and her arms swept around his neck as he pulled her down onto his lap.

It was like taking the first sip of a potent summer wine, wonderfully sweet and incredibly intoxicating. Lucas was vaguely surprised by the sudden wave of longing that rose within him. There was desire and passion aplenty but it was more than that. From deep inside came a primitive urge, almost a hunger, that had nothing to do with lust. He wanted to keep her there in his arms forever, to lay claim to her the way a wolf claims his mate, fiercely, permanently. The feeling was nearly irresistible and completely unexpected.

"Brianna, Lucas!" Ian's voice came from outside, loud and panicky.

Lucas and Brianna broke apart and stared at each other in shocked dismay.

"Oh, God." Brianna sprang up from his lap, her eyes wide and horrified.

"Brianna . . ." Lucas began but never got the chance to finish when Ian came through the door at a dead run.

"It's Seth, Brianna. He's really sick. I think you'd better come."

The three of them hurried out to the barn and found Seth on his bunk in the tack room. His eyes were closed and a thin film of perspiration covered his forehead.

"Seth what is it?" Brianna asked.

As if to answer her, he rolled over and threw up in the chamber pot that sat on the floor next to the bed. "I think it may be what Charlie had," he said when he was finally able to.

Brianna felt his forehead worriedly. "You're burning up. I have something that will help if you can keep it down. I hope it's just a twenty-four hour flu."

"If it isn't, I'll be dead by morning anyway," Seth said fatalistically.

Brianna traded beds with Ian so she could stay with Seth most of the night. By noon the worst of it seemed to have passed and he fell into a deep restful sleep. Even most of the weakness was gone by morning of the second day. Though Brianna was skeptical, Seth assured her he would be perfectly able to carry the mail when Billy came in the next day. His next trip back he'd be caring Lincoln's inaugural address and there was no way he was going to miss that.

Ian and Brianna both came down with the malady that night. Seth stayed with Ian while Lucas nursed Brianna through it.

"This can't be much fun for you," she mumbled after a particularly violent attack. "Why don't you go to bed and leave me to my misery?"

Because I love you. The realization came with startling clarity. This was the woman he wanted to spend the rest of his life with though it wasn't exactly the moment to tell her. Lucas smoothed her hair back from her face. "You should only have a few more hours of it."

She groaned. "That's supposed to make me feel better? Why don't you just let me die and get it over with?"

"You can't die. I fully expect you to take care of me when I have it, that's why."

"If it's tomorrow, you can forget it."

He smiled slightly. "I promise I won't get sick until you're better."

"I'll hold you to that."

But Lucas didn't succumb, not the next day or the next. By Thursday Brianna and Ian were fully recovered. It looked as though the scourge was over. And none too soon, for Seth would be back the next night, a full day and a half early and this time he'd be carrying Lincoln's inaugural message.

Brianna was filled with apprehension. Though she didn't know what Lincoln said in his speech, she did know what the end result was, war. She wondered if the news would come tomorrow as Seth passed the mochila on to Billy. Of Lucas's kiss she tried not to think at all. He appeared to have forgotten all about it and Brianna decided to do the same. Everyone went to bed early for Seth was expected to come about three in the morning. The moon was just coming up over the horizon when Brianna woke to Lucas stirring on the other side of the cabin. "What time is it?"

"It's a little after midnight. You don't need to get up."

"I wouldn't miss it for the world," Brianna said swinging her legs out of bed." The air seemed filled with a heady sense of anticipation. But Brianna hadn't even finished dressing when Ian came in with bad news.

"We're in trouble, Lucas," he said. "Billy's down at the barn puking his guts out."

"Oh, Lord. Any chance he'll be over it by the time Seth gets here?"

"No. It's the same thing the rest of us had."

"Oh, dear." Brianna went to her trunk to get her bottles of aspirin water and diarrhea medication. Both supplies were seriously depleted.

"Damn." Lucas slapped the table with the flat of his hand. "Why didn't Bromley put an extra man on this run like he did the others?"

"Can't someone else make the ride?" Brianna asked.

Ian shook his head. "Lucas and I are both too big. Even on the regular run our weight would slow the horses down. With the extra speed we could kill them."

"Seth will never be able to keep going for the full hundred and fifty miles." Lucas ran his fingers through his hair worriedly. "There's got to be solution."

"There is," Brianna said calmly. "All we need is another rider."

Lucas gave a short laugh. "Another rider with the stamina to ride seventy miles at a dead run, change horses eight times and who weighs less than one hundred and twenty-five pounds. Where are we going to find someone like that?"

Brianna smiled. "Me."

34

"No!" *Lucas's tone brooked* no argument.

Brianna ignored it. "Oh, come on, Lucas. Billy can't even get out of bed. What other choice do we have?"

"*We* doesn't come into this. Ian and I will figure out something."

"There's no other way to figure it out. Somebody has got to be ready to ride when Seth gets here."

"It won't be you."

"Who else is going to do it? You said yourself neither Ian or you can."

"Seth will just have to go on."

"He can't, not with the extra speed they're asking for. That's why Bromley didn't put an extra man on here. He didn't figure he could improve the time. If Seth goes on he's sure to slow down."

"Then we'll just have to lose time."

"That's dumb. I'm perfectly capable of making the ride and you know it."

"For God's sake, woman, what will it take to get it though your head? You're not going."

Brianna put her hands on her hips. He could be the most exasperating man. "Lucas, the whole future of the Pony Express rests on this ride. Are you going to let it go down because your male ego can't stand the thought of a woman having a part in it?"

Lucas glanced at Ian. "You talk to her. Maybe she'll listen to you."

Ian shook his head. "To tell the truth, Lucas, I'm afraid I agree with Brianna. She's the only hope we've got."

"You can't be serious!" Lucas was incredulous. "What's Billy going to say? He didn't even want another Pony Express rider taking his place. He'll never stand for a woman doing it."

"Actually, Billy suggested it," Ian said. "Look, Lucas, I don't like it any better than you do, but as the lady said we really don't have much choice."

Lucas looked back and forth between Ian's apologetic expression and Brianna's determined one. Finally he threw his hands up in defeat. "All right, what can I say? I'm obviously outnumbered. Come on, Ian we've got work to do."

Ian cleared his throat. "Aren't you forgetting something?"

"What?"

"Billy pointed out she'll have to take the oath to be an official rider."

"She's *not* going to be an official rider! This is her one and only ride."

"But she'll be carrying important government documents."

"Oh for . . . all right." He stalked over to his trunk and rummaged around inside it for a moment before pulling out a small book. It took a moment to find the page he wanted then he turned back to Brianna. "Raise your right hand and repeat after me. While I am an employee of Russell Majors & Wadell, I will . . . "

Brianna repeated the hundred and fifty year old oath with a prickly feeling. As far a she knew no woman had ever ridden for the Pony Express. Was she changing history? " . . . I will drink no intoxicating liquors, I will not quarrel or fight with any employee of the firm . . . So help me God."

Ian grinned. "Maybe this isn't all bad, Lucas. In case you missed it, Brianna just took an oath not to argue with you any more."

"Ian, what are you thinking of? The poor man has just given up his favorite pastime. He can't argue with me either."

"Usually, the rider is presented with a bible at this point, but I don't have one to give you," Lucas said ignoring them both. "If you're going, you'd better get in there and let Billy brief you on the trail."

Brianna didn't need any further urging. She spent the next hour alternately holding Billy's head as he threw up, dosing him with medicine, and pumping him for information. At one-thirty she went in to change clothes and get ready. She'd borrowed a vest and coat from Billy and he insisted she take his holster for her gun. It was specially made to fit right over the mochila so it could be switched with ease. After stowing several pieces of jerky in her pocket, and her knife in her boot, she was back out to the barn with Billy.

By the time she heard the familiar call, "Rider coming in," Brianna knew every landmark, every twist or turn in the trail and the quirks of coming into each station. "Wish me luck, Billy."

"You'll be fine. I just wish I could do it."

She smiled ruefully. "Yeah, me, too."

Lucas was waiting with DaVinci as she hurried up

to them. Ian and Lucas had decided not to chance passing the mochila on the run so Ian had gone up the trail a way to warn Seth. Brianna hadn't anticipated the reduced visibility; she'd never seen the switch at night. Seth was nearly there already.

She had barely reached Lucas when she heard Ian yell his message to the other rider as he thundered past. Before she even had time to wonder if Seth had understood, Lucas stuffed something into the watch pocket of her vest.

"For luck," he said. Then he kissed her. It was hard, and fast; she felt branded by the heat. The next second he grabbed the mochila from Seth, threw it on DaVinci, and boosted her into the saddle. "For God's sake, be careful," he yelled as he slapped the horse on the rump.

Brianna was off down the trail in the blink of an eye. The unfamiliar saddle felt strange but DaVinci ran like a dream. She leaned forward as he lengthened his stride, and they fairly flew over the ground.

Lucas's kiss had thrown Brianna for a loop. It was the last thing she'd expected especially since he wasn't exactly happy about what she was doing. Unsettling as it was, she didn't have time to puzzle his motives out right now. There would be plenty of time for that when she got to Green River. The sky was just beginning to lighten when she arrived at Three Crossing's station. The stationmaster and stock tender, gave her startled looks as she dismounted, pulled the mochila off and raced to the other horse. She didn't know if they realized she was a woman or if they were merely surprised she wasn't Billy.

Brianna didn't even attempt the rear mount she knew Billy and Seth used when they changed horses. In spite of that she was rather proud of the way she stuck her foot in the stirrup and vaulted into the saddle. It couldn't have taken much more than a minute before she was on her way once more.

The piebald roan was bigger than DaVinci but fully as fast. Brianna was instantly in love as the prairie passed beneath them in a blur. She instinctively knew this was one of the animals that would allow his rider to run him to death; he put his whole heart into it.

Brianna was breathing nearly as hard as the horse by the time she reached St. Mary's Station and exchanged the roan for a black and white pinto mare that was much stockier and slower than the other two. Brianna was puzzled by the choice until they started up the Wind River mountains. The horse had clearly been selected for her endurance.

It was the first time Brianna had gone over South Pass along the Oregon Trail. In her time the highway took a much different route. The difference was immediately obvious for this was a much gentler slope. Even so, the mare was lathered and her sides heaving by the time they reached the top.

The sun was well up in the sky when she arrived at Rock Creek and jumped off the exhausted horse. Brianna's hat fell off and dangled from the string around her neck as she sprinted across the ground between the two horses. This time there was no doubt that the men realized they were dealing with a woman. Their mouths fell open. So much for masquerading as a boy. Billy was obviously right when he said she'd never be able to pull it off.

Brianna was breathing as though she were doing the running herself as she covered the distance to the South Pass station. The exertion was beginning to take its toll on her. It wasn't unexpected but she was vaguely surprised it was happening so soon. She wasn't quite halfway to the Green River station.

A stitch developed in her side between the South Pass and the Pacific Springs stations. She had reached the other side of the mountain and once again found herself riding fast, smooth runners rather than the slower, stockier mountain horses, but her legs were starting to cramp by Dry Sandy.

Her growing fatigue was apparently obvious to the stationmasters and stock tenders along the way for she received more and more help at each stop. Brianna didn't know if they were aware she was a woman or not, but she was grateful for the strong hands that boosted her into the saddle.

Big Sandy and Big Bend blurred together in a haze of pain and exhaustion. The only part that stood out in her tired mind was a man's voice saying, "Hang on. You're on your last stretch."

Almost there, almost there, almost there, it was a litany that played over and over in her mind. At long last, Green River station came into sight.

Billy had warned her that the rider at Green River would be expecting her to pass the mochila on the run. There was no way to let him know about a change of plans. Any deviation would cause a loss of time and time was of the essence. Though Brianna had done her best she knew she'd been far slower than Billy's would have.

With a last surge of adrenaline, Brianna stood in the stirrups, pulled the mochila out from underneath her and stretched her arm out toward the other rider. Just when she didn't think she could hold the heavy mochila a second longer, he grabbed it and the weight was gone with a sudden jerk.

Brianna didn't even remember bringing her horse to a stop. One minute she was in the stripped down saddle, the next she was on the ground with her arm around a stranger's shoulders as he supported her sagging body.

"Now who do we have here?"

"Br-Brianna Daniels," she gasped, as she tried to catch her breath.

"Lucas's wife?"

She nodded. "Billy . . . was sick."

"You can tell us all about it later. We'd best get you inside. Looks like you're about done in."

Brianna nodded again and let them half carry her into the cabin. She was vaguely aware of the smell of leather and coffee and the rough texture of a wool blanket as they lay her on a bunk. "Thanks," she murmured gratefully as her eyes drifted closed.

She woke some time later to the sound of distant male laughter. She opened her eyes and was momentarily confused by the unfamiliar room. Then she remembered. With a groan she sat up. "Boy, am I out of shape," she muttered, as she became aware of stiff muscles in every part of her body.

Brianna glanced around the cabin curiously. It was much bigger than the one at Split Rock but no more luxurious. Russell, Majors, and Wadell might pay their employees extremely well but they weren't overly worried about the living conditions.

From the half light that came in through the window, Brianna knew it was either sun-up or sun-down but she had no idea which. Ah well, she'd know when the men came in. Billy had assured her she'd like the six men who inhabited the station.

As she shifted slightly, the side of her hand brushed the good luck talisman Lucas had tucked into the watch pocket of her vest. Curious, Brianna pulled out the small leather pouch, loosened the strings, and emptied the contents into her hand.

Her eyes widened in shock. His parting kiss loomed large in her mind as she stared down at the blue fire in her palm. Lucas had given her his mother's ring!

35

✦

"Rider coming in."

Brianna peered through the darkness searching for the other rider. It had never occurred to her that Billy always left in the wee hours of the morning. Nor had she ever considered that many riders along the eighteen hundred mile journey rode through the night. The Pony Express didn't stop for anything. "Neither sleet nor hail nor gloom of night," she said softly.

"What?" The stationmaster leaned closer to hear what she said.

She smiled. "I just wanted to say thanks. You've all been so nice."

"It was our pleasure, Mrs. Daniels. It's not often we have a woman around. Doesn't seem right sending you out by yourself like this."

"St. Jo to San Francisco in seven days and seventeen hours!" the other rider called as he handed the mochila off to Brianna.

"Seven days and seventeen hours," she yelled back.

He nodded as she threw the mochila over the horn. It wasn't without a sense of relief that she vaulted into the saddle and headed down the trail. The men at the Green River station had practically waited on her hand and foot. She'd loved it at first, but it wasn't long before being treated like a fairy princess began to pall on her.

Within the first day she was bored to tears. By the end of the second she was close to screaming. They wouldn't let her do anything even remotely energetic, though she suspected they'd have handed over the housework quickly enough.

Truth was, Brianna missed the four men she regarded as her family, one extremely irritating one in particular. She even missed the hassles and inconveniences she'd come to accept as a daily routine. In short, she was homesick. The irony of the situation didn't escape her. It also left her with far too much time think.

Not surprisingly, her mind was constantly on Lucas and his ring. Over and over she replayed the scene when he'd mourned his mother. "We Daniels marry for love. This is the ring the oldest son traditionally gives his wife."

Was he saying he loved her and wanted her to marry him? The thought was frightening. Even worse was the realization of how bad she wanted it to be so. What about Anna? What about the future generations of the Daniels family? Then again what if she never made it back to her own time? Should she throw away her chance at happiness? Lord, was she really contemplating marrying her own great-great-grandfather?

Then again, maybe he'd just given it to her for a good luck charm and meant nothing else by it. Three days of mulling it over and over in her mind with no resolution had about driven her crazy. It was a relief to concentrate on the trail instead.

The switch at Big Bend went without a hitch. The stationmaster and stock tender cheered when she yelled the message the other rider had given her. Big Sandy was much the same, but by Little Sandy she knew she was in trouble. The Wind Rivers were still miles away and she was already feeling the strain. Though she had exercised her sore muscles some since the first ride, it obviously hadn't been enough. The stitch in her side showed up about halfway to Pacific Springs. By the time she'd got to the station, her breath was already coming in hard painful gasps.

As she started up the mountain, she wondered if she'd make it back to Split Rock. Lucas and the others had talked about horses that had been ridden to death on the trail. Was she to become the first rider to meet a similar fate? The trail seemed endless. Where was the South Pass station?

At last it came into sight. Halfway. Thank God, the worst of the trail was behind her. As she drew closer she saw four men standing by her horse instead of the usual two. Suddenly one of them waved to her and jumped on the horse. What in the world?

Then she realized who it was. Billy! He'd come to meet her. With a surge of relief, she stood up in the stirrups and pulled the mochila free. "St. Jo to San Francisco in seven days and seventeen hours."

He repeated the message as he took the mochila. Then he gave her a big grin and a wink. She slowed her horse and stared after him as he headed off down the trail.

"Seven days and seventeen hours. I guess you didn't slow them down much, after all."

At the sound of the deep, familiar voice, Brianna looked over her shoulder in astonishment. "Lucas! What are you doing here?"

"When Billy realized he was going to have stay in

the same place for a full nine days he got so fidgety we decided to send him out to meet you. I came along for the ride," he said as she slid off her horse. "So how was it?"

"Exhausting."

"I'll resist the temptation to say I told you so."

Brianna was too out of breath to give him the response he deserved so she settled for making a face at him.

The stationmaster and stock tender were as solicitous as the men at Green River had been and Brianna soon found herself seated at the table with a huge breakfast set in front of her. Luckily the stationmaster of South Pass was a much better cook than Lucas. By the time they had finished eating, she had recovered enough to face the ride home with equanimity. Spending the whole day alone with Lucas was another matter.

"I can't wait for spring," she said as they skirted a snow drift and headed off across the mountain.

"It'll be a month or two before it really comes to stay up here. Shouldn't be long where we are, though. If Bromley was right, the telegraph will be getting to us within a month or two."

Brianna's stomach tightened. "Does that mean they'll be closing the Pony Express stations?"

"The ones that aren't used as stage stops they will. Stages stop at every other one."

"What happens to the people that work there?"

Lucas shrugged. "Some will be reassigned others won't have a job."

"Billy and Seth?"

"Are two of the best riders on the line. Bromley will keep them if there's any way to do it. Of course if the transcontinental telegraph actually works when it's finished I suppose none of them will have a job. It's hard to say where any of us will wind up." He paused. "What about you?"

She carefully avoided looking at him. "I'll stay at Split Rock."

"Even if everyone you know is gone?"

"Yes."

"Why?"

"It's the only place Anna will know to look for me."

Lucas frowned. "She's that important to you?"

Suddenly Brianna wasn't as sure as she had been. What if Tom couldn't switch them back? "I-it's more important than you can possibly know, Lucas."

He studied her silently for a moment. "What about us?" he asked softly.

"There is no us."

"What do you mean there's no us? Don't you realize I love you?"

Brianna thought her heart would break. "I was afraid that's what you meant with the ring," she said thickly, "and that's why I can't accept it. Anna . . . "

"I don't give a damn about Anna. She isn't here, and even if she were I wouldn't want her."

"You can't be sure about that, Lucas."

"The hell I can't. I'm in love with you not her."

"We look almost exactly alike except she's shorter and built more the way you like your women built. You'll p-probably come to love her far more than you do me." Brianna's lip quivered slightly as she tried to smile. "She won't be near as hard to get along with."

He stared at her. "You think I fell in love with your looks? What kind of a man would do a stupid thing like that?"

"One that's been away from civilization for a long time. Hasn't it occurred to you I'm the only woman you've been around for over a year?"

"Hell yes I know that. I came out here to get away from women. Falling in love with you was the last thing I wanted to do. That's why I'm sure it's real."

"Y-you're only looking at it from your own point of view," she said desperately. "You haven't even asked how I feel."

His eyes narrowed. "Do you expect me to believe you don't care? Your kisses tell me differently. Don't try to deny it," he said angrily as she started to shake her head. "It wouldn't take much to prove you were lying. Shall I pull you off that horse and show you? How many kisses do you think it would take before you were moaning in my arms and begging for more? I could make love to you right here and never hear a whimper of protest."

Oh God, it was true. His words and the picture they painted in her mind were almost enough to bring a moan to her lips without him ever laying a hand on her. If he carried out his threat, he'd hear whimpers a plenty, but they wouldn't be of protest. "Please try to understand, Lucas."

"How can I understand when I don't know what the hell is going on?" he snapped.

Brianna could think of nothing to say. Silence fell between them heavy and oppressive all the way to Rock Creek and beyond. The mood brightened when they reached St. Mary's Station and Brianna discovered Lucas had left Oz there for her. By the time they had lunch at the station, changed horses, and headed out again, the restraint between them lifted somewhat. Lucas even unbent enough to tell the tale of Billy's and Seth's first meeting.

"It hadn't occurred to any of us that they'd never actually met each other face to face. Seth didn't know Billy had a southern accent."

"Oh, no. Did they get into an argument about secession?"

Lucas chuckled. "No, to be honest with you, I don't think it even occurred to Seth, but Ian and I both figured that's what was going through his mind. He just stood and looked at Billy for the longest time. You know Billy, the longer Seth stared at him the more belligerent he got. Ian and I thought we were going to have a fight on our hands."

"What happened?"

"Finally Seth gave Billy that grin of his and said, 'Heck, Billy, you sound a lot different on paper!'"

Brianna giggled. "Oh, if that isn't just like him. Did they get along after that?"

"If you call trying to out do each other at everything getting along. Once Billy got well that's about all they did. Of course Ian did say they spent quite a bit of time down at the corral working horses yesterday so it's hard to say . . . what the hell?"

"Hmm?" Brianna turned to look at what had caught his eye. A line of riders was coming at them from the south.

Lucas shaded his eyes to look. "Indians!"

"Are they friendly?"

"We aren't going to stick around and find out." Lucas reached over and grabbed the pistol holster off her saddle before smacking his horse on the rump with his reins and digging his heels in. "Go!"

It only took a few minutes to tell that horse Lucas was riding could easily outdistance the smaller, younger Oz, and probably the Indians. He didn't consider leaving Brianna behind and she knew better than to suggest it. Even if the Three Crossings station were in sight and he knew there was a troop of horse soldiers there, he wouldn't have left her.

They raced across the prairie side by side but the Indians began to gain on them immediately. Brianna's heart hammered in terror. Would they make it to Three Crossings before the Indians got them or was this where it all ended?

Three Crossings Station was just a dot on the horizon when the Indians caught up with them. Expecting to feel an arrow in her back at any moment, Brianna was surprised when an Indian appeared at her side and leaned over to grab Oz's bridle. The Indians were trying to capture them alive. Lucas's rifle gave a loud boom and a red flower bloomed in the middle of the brave's forehead. He fell to the ground without a sound though his horse continued to run along side Brianna for several minutes.

Lucas shot two more with Brianna's pistol, then another and another. The station still seemed impossibly far away and they only had one more shot. Only a miracle could save them now.

Brianna turned regretful eyes toward Lucas and encountered a look of intense suffering and grief. With a sudden jolt of horror, Brianna realized why Lucas hadn't used the last bullet. He was saving it for her. It was then she understood how very much he loved her. They would torture him horribly if they took him alive.

A sudden blast of anger burned through her fear and she reached down into her boot. What a wimp she was. Lucas wasn't going to die in agony because of her. She gritted her teeth as her hand closed over the smooth handle of her knife. There was no way she could fight them all off, but maybe she could distract them enough so Lucas could get away. Without her holding him back he might even be able to make the station. At the very least she could make them kill her so Lucas wouldn't have to.

Brianna saw a a pair of buckskin leggings out of the corner of her eye and felt a hand on her shoulder. It was now or never. "REMEMBER THE ALAMO!" she yelled and came up slashing.

The startled brave knocked her hat off as he pulled back. Brianna saw his eyes widen when the sharp blade narrowly missed his arm. For an instant she thought she saw a flash of startled recognition in the dark eyes, then he was yelling something at the top of his lungs as he wheeled his horse way from her. Brianna pulled back on Oz's reins. Lucas and his horse continued on just as she had planned.

"BRIANNA!"

She ignored his anguished yell as she fell behind and the Indians turned back to get her. "YEEHA!" Brandishing the knife with wicked intent, Brianna headed Oz toward the biggest concentration of Indians, her lips pulled back from her teeth in a snarl. To her surprise they seemed to melt away in front of her. No matter which way she turned they fled. Within minutes she was alone, watching the Indians riding away from her as though the devil were on their heels.

"For God's sake, Brianna, come on!"

Dumbfounded, she wheeled Oz around and loped ahead to join Lucas. Afraid their reprieve was a temporary one, they raced on to the station. The men there pulled them inside to safety, barred the door, and went back to their rifle positions.

White-lipped, Lucas held an equally shaken Brianna in his arms as he related what had happened.

"Are you sure that's what they yelled?" one of the men asked.

"Positive. What does it mean?"

The man gave Brianna an odd look. "Roughly translated it means fire demon. The Snakes have been talking about an evil spirit with hair of fire and eyes of ice all winter. They say it can produce a knife from a bolt of lightning and strike a man dead with it. They must have thought it was disguised as your wife, but that doesn't make sense unless they thought only a spirit would be crazy enough attack in such a situation."

But it made perfect sense to Brianna. The brave

she'd slashed at *had* recognized her. He was one who had visited the station in the fall and was afraid she'd attack with her killer camera again. Hysterical laughter bubbled up in her throat.

Lucas must have sensed how her control was slipping for he hugged her even tighter. "One thing I'm curious about," he said resting his chin on top of her head. "Why did you yell at them like that?"

"I thought a battle cry might scare them."

"Remember the Alamo?"

"So I wasn't real creative."

He smiled. "You mean they didn't teach you any battle cries in that school of yours?"

"One but somehow 'Go, Indians' didn't seem appropriate."

36

April 1861

"*Lucas? . . . Lucas, where* are you?" Brianna peered around the empty workshop then stalked into the tack room. "Ian, have you seen Lucas?"

Ian grabbed his shirt and held it up in front of his naked chest. His face was bright red and dotted with patches of soap lather. "Er . . . ah . . . I think he went to the house. We . . . we both decided it was time to shave."

"Thanks. Sorry I bothered you." Brianna ignored the strangled, "You're welcome" in her wake as she left. She was mad . . . no . . . furious and Lucas Daniels wasn't going to wiggle his way out of this one.

"Just who do you think you are?" she asked slamming the door open.

Lucas looked up. "Good morning Brianna," he said, calmly stropping his razor.

"Don't good morning me you . . . you . . . Judas."

"Something on your mind?"

"I've just been down to the telegraph camp to deliver the sweet rolls I promised them."

He took the first swipe of his razor down his jaw. "And?"

"How could you Lucas?"

"I thought you *wanted* me to tell their cook you'd sell him fresh rolls. If you'll remember I warned you they'd have to be delivered by six."

"That's not what I'm talking about."

He rinsed his razor and took another swipe. "Then you'll have to enlighten me. I can't recall anything else I might have said."

"You don't recall telling them there wasn't any reason to build a separate relay station for the telegraph since you could wire everything into this cabin?"

"Is there something wrong with that?"

"Something wrong? . . . Dammit, Lucas, I live here!"

"So?"

"So I don't want to share my home with a stranger."

"Nobody's asking you to."

"Oh, no, just the telegrapher who will start his job sometime this week and any Tom, Dick or Harry who decides to send a telegram."

"I doubt there will be much in the way of outgoing messages. Split Rock isn't exactly in the middle of town."

"What about the telegrapher? You're forcing me to live with a man I don't even know! If you think you can change my mind about leaving with you by making my living conditions here . . . "

"I'm the new telegrapher," he said in the middle of her tirade.

" . . . intolerable you've got . . . What?"

"I'm the new telegrapher. Bromley said we wouldn't need a full-time stationmaster *and* a stock tender after the telegraph came through, so I applied for the job of telegrapher."

"You know Morse code?"

He grinned. "Of course."

"Of course," she echoed faintly. It was probably a stupid question. For all she knew, Samuel Morse had gotten the idea from Lucas. "Won't working for The Pony Express and Western Union be conflict of interest?"

"If you mean what I think you do the answer is no. James Bromley is the one who suggested I take on the job, probably trying to save Russell, Majors, and Waddell money without cutting back on personnel."

"I still think it's unfair that Congress gave the mail contract to Butterfield when we're faster."

"I know. Frankly I don't see any way to save the company. It's just a matter of time until bankruptcy forces us to close down. That's why I took the job with the telegraph." He locked gazes with her. "I want to make very sure I have a reason to stay here as long as I need to."

"Oh." Brianna returned his look for a long moment then carefully shut the door and went to fix breakfast. He was doing it again, damn him. It was pretty hard to resist a man who made you feel as if he thought the world revolved around you. The Indian attack had ended any pretense of her indifference to him and there had been a steady assault on her emotions ever since.

She'd laid the ring on his trunk and it had never been mentioned again. But it was obvious he hadn't given up.

Brianna glanced at him out of the corner of her eye. There was something incredibly sensual about watching a man shave, especially a man who looked like Lucas. If he was appealing in his cutoffs, he was devastating dressed only in britches and suspenders. There he stood, calmly shaving as if he had no idea what his half-naked body did to her. He did of course. Over the last month she'd seen more of that gorgeous body than she had in the first nine. He was doing it on purpose, the rat.

Determined to ignore him, Brianna turned her

shoulder and went back to work. Yet over and over again she found herself watching him. She began to suspect he was deliberately taking his time. Ian had been nearly finished when she came by and they'd supposedly started at the same time. Admittedly, Lucas had a much heavier beard and he'd had to do some trimming before he started, but still . . .

"Will you watch the bacon for me, Lucas? I need to run get a bucket of water and see if Gertrude laid an egg yet this morning."

"Sure."

His grin told her he knew exactly why she was leaving, and Brianna gritted her teeth. Oooo! That man was irritating.

She took her own sweet time, going so far as to walk clear to the river for her water instead of taking it from the barrel bedside the house. When she returned, the table was already set. She started to thank Lucas for his thoughtfulness but the words lodged in her throat.

The beard was gone but not the mustache. It was just the surprise, she told herself. If it had happened gradually it wouldn't have had such a devastating effect on her. But this was not a pathetic, bristly darkening of his upper lip; it was a thick, luxurious, full-grown mustache and it looked fantastic. Had she told him she liked mustaches? Obviously she had, for the smile on his face couldn't be described as anything but a self-satisfied smirk.

"Well, were there any?"

"Any what?"

His grin widened. "Eggs. Isn't that what you went out for?"

The urge to wipe that look off his face was irresistible. "There was one," she said carrying to bucket of water to its place by the fireplace, "but I gave it to Richard Kincade."

"Who?"

"Richard Kincade. He's one of the men building the telegraph. I felt sorry for him. They haven't had eggs since they left Fort Laramie in February." She sighed as she bent over to take the mush off the fire. "He has the prettiest green eyes."

"Where the hell did you meet him?"

Lucas's smirk was gone when she stood and turned back toward the table. Brianna wished she could allow herself the luxury of giving him one of her own. "I met him down by the river yesterday when I went down to check out the swimming hole."

"You what?" His frown was so intense, his brows nearly met in the middle. "Have you no modesty? Good Lord, woman! Those men are total strangers. Don't you realize . . . "

"Relax, Lucas," she said relenting a bit. "I didn't go down to swim. I figured the water would still be too cold and it was. We'll probably be able to go next month sometime."

"Don't try to change the subject."

Brianna raised her brows questioningly. "I thought we were talking about swimming."

"We're discussing this Kincade person and how friendly you are with him. It seems pretty convenient he was at the river the same time you were for two days in a row."

"Yes, it was wasn't it. He's really quite fascinating to talk to," she said with an innocent smile. There was no need to tell Lucas Richard Kincade was all of thirteen years old and the cook's son. "Do you know how they convinced the Indians to stay away from the telegraph wires."

"No, and I don't really . . . "

"You mean they've actually come up with a way?" Ian asked from the doorway as he and Billy came in for breakfast. "That was one of the reasons people didn't think a transcontinental telegraph was feasible."

"From what Richard said they get two groups to stand at either end of a line about a mile apart. The telegraphers send messages back and forth between for a few minutes. The Indians think the words are actually going through their hands."

Billy looked skeptical. "And it scares them?"

"No, but they always want to try it themselves. The crew hands an Indian on each end a wire and send a jolt of electricity through it the first time they say a word."

"I imagine that would convince them to stay away, all right," Ian said with a grin.

Brianna frowned. "It seems kind of cruel to me."

"You're a good one to talk about being mean to the Indians," Ian put in with a chuckle. "Lucas said you chased a whole hunting party off at knife point."

Brianna stuck her tongue out at him and finished putting breakfast on the table. Lucas didn't say anything during the meal. Whenever she glanced at him from under lowered lashes she saw that he was watching her. Good, maybe that would make him mad enough to back off for a while and let her breathe.

That morning the news Brianna had been dreading for months finally came. Seth rode into the yard with a grim expression on his usually sunny face. "The Confederate States have taken Fort Sumter. The War of Secession has begun."

The Civil War. Brianna had almost begun to think it wasn't going to happen, that history had been changed somehow. Now she realized it was just the slow communication that had delayed the inevitable.

Over the next week, everyone talked of little else. They all seemed to think it would be over quickly. Lucas said little on the subject and Billy nothing at all, but every other man who came through had an opinion.

There was a steady stream of male passengers from the far West who had dropped what they were doing and headed back East to join one army or the other. Lucas and the stage drivers had to stop men who had differing viewpoints from killing each other more than once.

As the men talked of glory and fighting for the cause, Brianna remembered names like Gettysburg, Appomattox, Bull Run, and Vicksburg and wondered how many of them would die in the bloody years to come. She recalled her history teacher referring to it as the Uncivil War. For the first time she understood what he meant.

There was, of course, no one Brianna could talk to about it all so she wrote page after page in her journal. She tried not to put anything in that would give Anna too much knowledge if she returned, but she aired all her fears about the men she had come to care about. It was only a matter of time until she lost one of them to the War and she dreaded it with almost maternal agony.

Even so she had no premonition of danger when James Bromley stopped on his home from a trip to the East.

"Mr. Bromley, what a pleasant surprise," she said when she answered his knock. "What brings you to Split Rock?"

"I wish I could say it was on my way so I thought I'd stop for a visit, but I'm afraid it's more serious that."

"Oh dear. I think the men are all down at the barn. Do you want me to run get them?"

"No, I'll go down myself. You might want to come along though because it will affect you, too."

It wasn't difficult to find them. All three men were in the corral doctoring a mare with a split hoof. Bromley came directly to the point.

"The company is in serious difficulty, gentlemen. The money originally promised to Russell, Majors, and

Wadell has been appropriated to fund the War instead. To make matters worse Congress is talking of giving the Butterfield Express our northern route since it's faster."

"They can't do that!" Brianna said indignantly. "There are laws against that kind of thing."

All four men looked at her as if she'd suddenly sprouted horns.

"Well, if there aren't there should be." She finished lamely. Surely governmental checks and balances weren't a modern invention. Of course without instant press coverage, the government probably tended to get away with more, as did everybody else.

"At any rate Wells Fargo has bought out Butterfield and may well do the same with the Central Overland and Pikes Peak Express," Bromley continued as though she hadn't spoken. "In the meantime we need to cut costs wherever we can."

"What are you suggesting?" Lucas asked.

"We've lost several of our men to the War. Rather than hiring replacements, William Russell decided to reassign the men we have. Since the telegraph is this far, one of the riders will move farther down the line and we need a new stationmaster at Simpson's Springs."

All three men looked at each other. "Who goes and who stays?" Ian asked finally.

"That's up to you. Seth has already volunteered to move since his route is gone anyway so unless you really want a change, Billy, that's taken care of. MacTavish, you and Lucas can decide which of you will go to Simpson's Springs and which stays here."

"I wouldn't mind going to Simpson's Springs," Ian said after a moment of consideration. "It's closer to my mother. I might get to see her a little more often."

"Well that was easy enough," Bromley said with a smile.

"Do you have time for a roll and coffee? "Brianna asked him.

"As a matter of fact I do. I was hoping you'd ask. Oh there is one more thing, gentlemen. Because of the War, Mr. Majors wants all the Overland employees to take an oath of allegiance to the United States."

"What if we refuse?" Billy demanded.

"Then you'd no longer have a job with Central Overland and Pike's Peak Express."

Billy stared at him for a long moment. "Well then," he said, "looks like Seth won't have to be leaving this station after all. I reckon it's time I went to join the War."

"Oh, Billy, no!" Brianna cried as a wave of dread ran through her.

Lucas gave her shoulder a warning squeeze. "Don't, Brianna," he said quietly. "Sometimes a man has to follow his conscience."

Billy flashed her a crooked grin. "I've been thinking of leaving anyway. This just gives me a reason."

A week later Brianna stood outside the Split Rock Pony Express station trying hard not to cry. All four men were down at the barn getting the horses ready. Billy and Ian were leaving today, one to the West the other to the East. Seth would be leaving within the month to a different home station as the telegraph continued to push west.

Good-byes had always been tough for Brianna but this one was going to be especially difficult for she knew she'd never see either of them again. For the first time she had an inkling of what it must have taken for people to leave their families and everything they knew to go West. Communication was nearly nonexistent.

Ian was the first out of the barn. "I thought I'd come

say good-bye now and avoid the rush later," he said as he approached her.

"I'll miss you, Ian."

But when she went to hug him, he pulled her into his arms and kissed her full on the mouth. "I'd have never forgiven myself if I hadn't done that at least once," he said softly. "You're one special lady, Brianna Daniels."

His words made her feel horribly guilty. If Anna had been here she'd probably be going with him. "Ian . . . "

He put his fingers against her lips. "Shh, I know. You don't feel it. Lucas is the only man in the world for you. But if anything ever happens to him. . . . "

"Oh, Ian."

He gave her one more hug then went to get his horse. By the time he returned Billy, Seth, and Lucas were with him. All five of them stood there for several uncomfortable minutes making small talk trying to put off the inevitable. At last they could delay no longer and the round of handshakes and well-wishing began. In spite of her best efforts tears were streaming down Brianna's face.

"Don't worry, Brianna," Billy said with a jaunty smile. "If I can outrun Snake and Sioux arrows, I can dodge Yankee bullets."

"Just make sure you dodge," she said as she hugged him. Five minutes later Ian and Billy rode away in opposite directions, and Brianna grasped Lucas's hand for comfort. There was nothing she could do to protect them. The Civil War had begun.

37

May 1861

"Letter for you, Mrs. Daniels." The driver of the eastbound stage handed it to her.

"For me? Are you sure?"

"Has your name on it and it's addressed to Split Rock Station."

"How strange." Brianna looked at the letter curiously. "We'll see you next week," the driver said tipping his hat."

Brianna smiled and waved. "Have a good trip," she called as he gave his team the signal to start. Then she turned her full attention to the mysterious letter. As she began to read the single page a smile lit her face.

"What are grinning about?" Lucas asked.

"We got a letter from Seth. Listen to this. 'Dear Brianna and Lucas. I thought I'd write to let you know where I am. I have been reassigned three times since I left Split Rock. It seemed like I would just get to know the trail and they'd move me again. This is supposed to be my last station. Believe it or not, they sent me to the same one as Ian MacTavish. We're both happy about that but it isn't the same without the two of you. Ian's cooking isn't quite as bad as yours, Lucas, but it isn't very good either. Do you think I should send for a wife for him?'"

Lucas snorted at that. Brianna just grinned and kept reading.

"'Ian's family came for a visit just after I got here. You wouldn't believe how pretty his sisters are, especially the one that's the same age as me. Her name is Melissa. Do you ever hear from Billy? I wonder about him sometimes. The other rider here isn't near as friendly.'"

"Good Lord," Lucas said. "He's less friendly than Billy? I almost feel sorry for Ian."

"Billy just acts tough to hide the fact that he's a marshmallow inside."

"A what?"

"It just means he's like a bowl of mush."

"Ah. And that means?"

"That he's actually a softie at heart."

Lucas shook his head. "The more you explain the less I understand. Maybe you better just read the rest of the letter."

"There isn't much else. It just says Ian sends his love and says he misses us both."

Brianna sighed as she folded the letter. "I sure miss them. It seems so quiet."

"I know but you won't have to worry about quiet for a day or two."

"Oh? Why not?"

"That's why," he said pointing to the south.

In the far distance Brianna could see a huge cloud of dust. "What is it?"

"Unless I miss my guess it's a wagon train. Kind of

early but about the only other thing that will raise a cloud of dust like that is a buffalo stampede. I've been watching it move this way all morning. Buffalo would either have stopped or they'd have been here by now."

"Then it'll be here this afternoon?"

"More like tomorrow sometime. They only make about eight or ten miles a day. If they don't stop when they go by, we can ride out to their camp tomorrow night."

"I'd like that."

"You might want to come up with some barter."

"Why?"

"They almost always have cows."

Brianna's eyes widened. "Milk?"

"There's a good chance of it. Some of them even have butter. The motion of the wagon churns the cream as they travel."

"Oooh!" she said with a kind of breathless wonder. "I'd better get busy. Do you think I might even be able to buy a cow?"

"Who knows? If not, there'll be others along soon enough. They keep coming all of June and sometimes into July. You just missed the last one last year."

"I'll take my money just in case."

"Sure is hot today," Lucas observed casually as she turned to go. "Could be a real scorcher by this afternoon. Don't you think it's about time to start swimming again?"

Brianna repressed a smile. He probably thought he'd have better luck wearing down her resistance if he got her out of her clothes. Honestly, he was so transparent sometimes. "It kind of depends on whether the wagon train gets here by tonight doesn't it?"

"I suppose so, but it sure is hot for this time of year."

"Maybe what you need is a nice cold shower," she said and ran into the cabin before he could answer. It wasn't until later that it occurred to her he wouldn't have had any idea what she was talking about.

The wagon train didn't arrive that night, but Lucas and Brianna didn't go swimming either. Huge threatening black thunderclouds filled the sky like a silent ominous presence. The air was still nearly stifling as though the very earth lay in wait for the storm. Lucas kept rubbing his arm where it had been broken and Brianna knew it was bothering him. She gave him a light dose of aspirin just before bed. He was asleep almost immediately.

Brianna wasn't so lucky. She lay in bed for the longest time, miserably hot and sweltering. She'd left the window open hoping to catch any breeze that might come along but there was none. She was still horribly uncomfortable when she finally fell asleep only to have disturbing dreams. Once again she was in a balloon high over the Wyoming prairie, only this time Lucas was the pilot and he wasn't particularly interested in flying the balloon. They stood silhouetted against the sky, their naked bodies pressed together as they explored each other with eager hands and hot kisses.

Suddenly there was an earsplitting crack of thunder and a bolt of lightning snaked out of the heavens with a white-hot intensity that seared and blinded. Lucas exploded into a shower of sparks and slumped to the floor of the gondola, a charred skeleton where living flesh had been a moment before.

Brianna started screaming and couldn't quit. On and on, louder and louder until the entire world became an echo of her horror. Then suddenly Lucas was there holding her in his arms rocking her as he stroked the back of her head.

"Shh, it's all right. You're safe."

"Oh, Lucas," she cried throwing her arms around his neck. "I thought you were dead."

"It was only a dream. I'm fine."

A flash of lightning lit up the prairie just beyond the window followed almost immediately by crack of thunder. The sound was an instant replay of her dream and Brianna pressed herself tighter into his warm, comforting embrace with a shudder. She ran her hands frantically over his body to assure herself he was alive, desperately trying to break the link between dream and reality. "The . . . lightning st . . . struck you, and . . . and oh, God, Lucas, it was awful."

"Don't even think about it, love," he whispered kissing her forehead. "It's over." As his lips traced a gentle path across her face, the horror of the nightmare faded and the erotic fantasy returned. Brianna closed her eyes and gave herself over to the sensations. When his mustache touched her cheek she turned her head and met his lips with her own. At first it was soft and gentle; a delicate exchange of kisses so light they might have been created by butterfly wings. Yet the feelings they aroused were so intense that Brianna and Lucas weren't even aware of the thunder moving away and the storm finally breaking outside. Torrents of rain fell from the heavens, but the two inside were conscious only of each other as their kisses deepened and they drifted down into the welcoming comfort of the bunk.

Brianna gloried in the body that was so familiar yet so foreign as her fingers explored smooth hard muscles beneath warm supple skin. It was as though all the months of lust-filled dreams had come to life and she indulged herself to the fullest, touching, caressing, worshiping. There was no part of him that didn't receive her homage, but there was no shame or embarrassment, only love and adoration.

The instinct to protect had been the only thing on Lucas's mind when the thunder and Brianna's screams awakened him from a sound sleep. He hadn't even stopped to put on trousers in his rush to get to her. Now his original intentions were forgotten as his entire being was focused on the woman in his arms, his other half, his love, his mate. His only thought was to consummate the magic that flowed between them, to become one with her.

As Brianna enjoyed his body, Lucas did the same with hers. His hands slowly explored her from shoulders down to hips, thighs, knees even her toes received his undivided attention. Then he started back up again, his passage all the more stimulating because she was still dressed in her nightgown. The soft material against her fevered skin added to the stimulation as his hand moved across her ribs to the swell of her breast. He swallowed the moan that came from deep within her when he caressed the sensitive tip with his palm.

The sensation was like nothing Lucas had ever experienced before. Hot, lustful, prurient, an overwhelming need rose in him. He wanted to take her right then, joining their bodies and riding the wave of passion until they exploded together in glorious harmony. Instinctively he knew it was too soon for her, he needed to feed the fire within her, to stoke it until it raged out of control.

His fingers undid the buttons of her nightgown and pushed the material aside as his lips began an even more sensual journey down her throat and body. If his hands had given her pleasure, his mouth drove her wild. The sounds that came from her throat were very familiar. He'd heard them all winter long, night after night as she cuddled into his solid warmth. Only this time she was awake, and they were alone. Lucas's iron control began to slip.

Brianna was in heaven. Lucas was creating the most incredible inferno within her. At first she wanted it to go on forever, then she thought she might die if it didn't end soon. Her already sensitized skin reacted to the soft, seductive caress of his lips by sending tremors of hot delight through her whole body. A molten pool of desire seemed to gather near the center of her being. Brianna wondered if it were truly possible for a person to go up in smoke.

She sought his mouth, bringing his body back into full contact with hers. It was too much. The wanton mating of their tongues and silken heat of skin against skin was more than she could stand. With a sound halfway between a whimper and a groan she pulled her mouth away and arched up to him, wanting, seeking, needing.

Lucas's restraint was at an end. When her legs parted to receive him, he lost his control completely. No longer able resist the urge, he buried himself within her in a single powerful thrust. He felt the delicate membrane tear and heard her cry of pain in the same instant. The significance of it slammed into him with the subtly of a cannon shell.

The tableau seemed frozen in time as Lucas and Brianna stared at each other, his eyes reflecting shocked surprise hers full of horror.

"Oh my God, what have I done?" Brianna whispered.

"It's all right, love," he said soothingly as she started to struggle underneath him. "It will only last a minute."

"No, you don't understand. I . . . oh hell! Let me go, Lucas."

"No, I . . . "

"For God sake, Lucas!"

"Don't worry, sweetheart, I can make it better."

"No, you can't. It has nothing to do with my virginity or loss of it." Her squirming did little to dislodge him from her body, but obviously caused her a great deal of pain. "Jesus Christ, Lucas, can't you figure it out? I don't want you to make love to me," she cried. "Just let me go."

The anguish in her voice and the tears in her eyes hurt nearly as badly as her words. He withdrew and rolled to the side, fully intending to hold her in his arms and somehow fix whatever was wrong. But she was too fast for him. In the blink of an eye she was off the bed and running for the door. He started after her and got clear outside before he realized he was stark naked. The rain hit his fevered skin like tiny bullets as he watched her white nightgown disappear into the darkness. What the hell was the matter with her?

Shaking with emotion, he turned back into the cabin and lit a lantern. The sight of her blood on his body hit him like a hammer blow, and he swore under his breath. Damn it to hell anyway. Why hadn't she told him she was a virgin? He'd been too rough. No wonder she ran away from him.

Lucas dressed hurriedly, his fingers fumbling with buttons in his haste. She'd be soaked to the skin and freezing by the time he found her, *if* he found her. He started to pull the blanket from his bed to wrap her in then realized it was wet. He hadn't even noticed the rain coming in through the open window. Reluctant to take the blood-stained blanket from the other bunk, he turned to Brianna's trunk. He could take the heavy flannel nightgown she wore in the winter and grab one of the blankets Seth and Billy had used on his way out.

He found the nightgown immediately; it was right on top. The minute Lucas lifted it, he realized the garment had been used to hide something underneath. Frowning, he picked up the oddly heavy bag. He'd never seen anything even remotely like the substance it was made of, nor the strange metal closing across the top. The intensely curious scientist in him couldn't resist the urge to look inside.

*   *   *

Brianna sat huddled beneath the granite boulder and shivered in abject misery. Nobody had ever been a bigger fool. That she was cold and wet were minor irritations compared to the turmoil within her. How could she have let herself get so carried away? The very worst of it was the look on Lucas's face when she said she didn't want him to make love to her. It made her want to die. She wished she could go back and do it over, to replay the scene and stop herself at the very beginning.

She sank her head to her bent knees. Who was she kidding? What she wanted to do was go back and finish what she and Lucas had started. In all her years of dating, Brianna had kissed many boys and men, she'd even considered sleeping with a few. But never in her wildest dreams had she ever imagined it could be so wonderful with a man she truly loved, and they hadn't even gotten to the good part yet. Brianna wasn't aware of Lucas's presence until a heavy blanket dropped around her shoulders. She looked up in surprise. The first thing she saw was the frown on his face and Tom's backpack in his hand.

She winced as it dropped at her feet with a heavy thud. Some much for Tom's expensive camera. "I guess you want an explanation," she mumbled.

"I think," Lucas said with heavy sarcasm, "that one is long overdue."

38

Brianna swallowed hard. The moment of truth had arrived. "I know it's hard to believe, Lucas, but I . . . I'm from the future. 1995 to be exact."

"1995. No wonder." Lucas closed his eyes and rubbed the bridge of his nose for a moment. Then he sighed deeply and handed her the heavy flannel nightgown. "Here, you'd better change before you catch a chill."

"You mean you believe me?"

He nudged the backpack with his toe. "There's some pretty damn convincing evidence in this . . . whatever it is. You can change behind the rock. Keep the blanket. I brought another."

When Brianna returned Lucas had built a fire, though she had no idea where he found the dry wood. Everything outside the overhang was soaking wet. The other blanket lay on the ground with the contents of the backpack spread out upon it.

Lucas said nothing when she sat down next to the

fire and pulled blanket closer around her shoulders. Silence filled only with the crackling of the fire surrounded them as he picked up the flashlight and studied it. "You must have seen some pretty amazing things in your life," he said at last.

"I . . . I suppose I have, but I never really thought about it." Brianna wanted to cry. She hadn't known how he'd take it, but she certainly hadn't expected this brittle quality about him as though she had somehow betrayed him. She hadn't even told him the worst of it yet. "Lucas I'm sorry . . . "

"What purpose were you sent here for?" He interrupted as he flipped the switch on the flashlight and played the beam across the surface of the glacier scarred rock that loomed above them. "Are you supposed to be studying this time period in general or me specifically?"

She frowned in confusion. "Wh . . . what do you mean?"

He glared at her. "Did you come back to watch me struggle through my feeble attempts at invention? Lord how you must have been laughing at me all this time."

"Oh, Lucas, no, never. You're the most brilliant man I've ever known. I lived my whole life around electricity, but I never even began to understand it until you taught me. Your feeble attempts as you call them are years ahead of your time. I don't know exactly when Thomas Edison invented the light bulb but I know it wasn't before the Civil War and . . . " She trailed off when saw the look on his face. She might just as well have struck him.

"Thomas Edison?"

"Y . . . yes."

"I see. And the talking telegraph?"

"It . . . it's called the telephone."

"Edison again?"

She shook her head miserably. "Alexander Graham Bell."

"Ah." He turned off the flashlight before carefully setting it back on the blanket and picking up the camera. "So much for my importance. You'd obviously never even heard of me before."

"A . . . actually I had. Lucas Daniels was a famous balloonist who spied for the Union army during the Civil War." She didn't have the courage to tell him the rest.

He gave a humorless laugh. "Well, sweetheart, somebody didn't do their research. They plunked you down with the wrong Lucas Daniels."

"No, Lucas, you don't understand," she said desperately. "I wasn't sent by anybody. At least not intentionally."

"What do you mean you weren't sent? How did you get here?"

"I haven't got a clue. Time travel isn't any more possible in 1995 than it is now. The only thing I know is that I've apparently traded places with my great-great-grandmother somehow."

"Anna?"

"Right. The last thing I remember was a horrible black cloud and a bolt of lightning. I came to in the middle of Bart Kelly's wagon wreck."

"Tell me everything from the very beginning."

Brianna described it all starting with the errant breeze that blew them off course, right up through the last time she'd seen the blue mist. For the first time she had hope. Lucas was listening with rapt attention; he *wanted* to believe her. The more she talked the more like himself Lucas became and she gradually began to relax. He paid strict attention, interrupting only occasionally to ask questions. He seemed to have forgotten everything else. He'd even stopped investigating the contents of the backpack.

"It sounds like some kind of electrical field," he said thoughtfully when she finished, "except that it's visible and somehow can connect two different times. It moves when you try to reach it so light has to be involved somehow. Any idea what we're dealing with here?"

She gave a short laugh. "You're asking me? Come on, Lucas. What little I know about electricity you taught me and I don't understand all of that."

"Damn, if I could see it once . . ."

"Small chance of that." She stared bleakly into the fire. "I haven't caught a glimpse of it since November."

"You really want to go back don't you?" he asked softly. Brianna looked at him in surprise. "Of course I do. As you've pointed out since the day I arrived, I don't exactly belong here."

"Do you realize there may be no way home, that you're stuck here forever?"

Brianna hunched her shoulders under the blanket. "The thought has occurred to me, but I refuse to consider it."

"Why?"

"Because I don't want to be here forever."

"Isn't there anything you like about it?"

The corner of her mouth quirked a little. "Mmm, well there are a couple of things. The horses are absolutely fantastic. Of course, somebody has to practically die before I'm allowed to ride them."

"And?"

"And watching the Pony Express in action was exciting."

"Nothing else?"

She knew exactly what he wanted to hear but she couldn't very well tell him the truth. Or could she? He loved her fully as much as she loved him. Maybe he had the right to know.

"You haven't thought it all through, Lucas. Anna was on the way here when we switched."

"So?"

She sighed. This was going to be harder than she had anticipated. "I'm not just *her* great-great-granddaughter. She was married to my great-great-grandfather."

"That is the way it usually works."

"His name was Lucas Daniels."

"Lucas Dan . . . " Suddenly he began to grin. "That's why you've kept me at arm's length all this time. You think we're related."

"Given the facts, it's a pretty logical assumption."

"And do you believe it?"

"No," she said truthfully. "I haven't for a long time but, there are some things I can't ignore. My uncle has your watch for one thing." She gave him a little smile. "You can't believe how many stories we made up about Marie. We thought she must have died."

"That still doesn't explain why you've kept me away."

"Oh, come on, Lucas, be serious."

"I am. Even if you were my great-great-granddaughter we wouldn't be any more closely related than third cousins. Marriages between third cousins happen all the time; my parents for example. So it wouldn't matter even if we were related, which we're not."

"We're not? How do you know?"

"I've seen your feet." His grin widened. "More importantly you've seen mine."

She gave him a bewildered look. "What are you talking about?"

"Haven't you ever noticed my toe?"

Brianna thought about it for a moment. He did have a rather oddly twisted little toe. "You mean the one you broke?"

"It isn't broken, I was born that way. Have you ever seen another like it?"

"No."

"Ha," he said triumphantly. "I knew it. This toe is fondly known as the Daniel's curse. Almost everybody in my family, including some very distant relatives, have it. If you were truly my descendant you would have recognized it immediately, even if you were one of the few who didn't have it."

"The Daniel's curse," she said in amazement. "In my time it's red hair."

"I don't think anybody in my family has red hair."

The stared at each other for a long moment. "Ian?" Lucas said at last.

"I don't know. It's possible I guess."

"I'd say it's more than possible," Lucas said. "The man was half in love with you. If you'd given him the least encouragement . . . anyway he'd have been there for Anna. I'm sure of it. On the other hand, Anna and I wouldn't have suited at all."

"You don't know that."

"Don't I? You forget I read her letters. She'd have never stood up to me the way you do."

Brianna smiled. "Gee, and I could have sworn you didn't like that."

"Very perceptive of you," he said sardonically. "Anyway I'd have probably sent her on her way the first day."

"Except you obviously didn't," she pointed out. "Which brings us back to Ian. I've thought this out a hundred times but I keep coming up with the same question. If he and Anna did wind up together why isn't my name MacTavish?"

They looked at each other again. Finally Lucas shrugged. "I guess we'll never know. Maybe it doesn't matter. The question is what do we do now?"

"Wait."

"For how long? Are you willing to spend the rest of

your life here waiting for something that may never happen?"

"I . . . I don't know."

Lucas watched her stare into the fire. He wouldn't soon forget the horrible burning anger that had ripped through him when he thought she had come to study him like some kind of scientific specimen. The truth was much more palatable, but what if knowing he wasn't related to her didn't change anything? What if she still didn't want him? Brianna had said she hadn't believed it anyway. In that moment he knew himself for a coward. He couldn't face the possibility of another rejection. "What is this thing anyway?" he asked picking up the contraption on his lap.

Brianna glanced up. Unbelievably she grinned. "An evil spirit."

"What?"

She scooted over and flipped a switch on the back to produce a high pitched whine. "I was lucky enough to have this out when the Indians came that day. It saved my life."

He raised his brows. "They were scared of a mad mosquito? It's not a particularly pleasant sound but . . ."

"Just wait." Brianna smiled mysteriously. The whine stopped and a small light came on. She pointed to a button. "All right it's ready. Push that."

Lucas did as he was told. "Jesus Christ!" he yelped as a brilliant white light shot out of the box in his hand. He dropped it as though he'd been burned.

Brianna laughed as she caught it. "That's exactly what the Indians thought, too. Especially since I hit one of them with my knife right after it flashed."

"What is it?"

"A camera. The strobe makes it possible to take pictures at night."

"Well I'll be damned." He took it back and examined

it more closely. Now that he knew what it was, he could see a vague resemblance to the cameras of his day. "And I thought the ones we have were wonderful inventions."

"Oh, Lucas, I wish I could show you my world," she said wistfully. "It would be such fun."

"I think I'd like to see it." He put the camera aside and picked up a small flat object. "Now what's this?"

"That's a solar calculator. We use it to do math problems. I'll have to show you tomorrow. It runs on light."

They went through the contents of the backpack item by item. Lucas was fascinated by all he saw. His fingers fairly itched to take things apart and find out what made them work, but Brianna wouldn't let him. He was more than a little irritated but her explanation went a long way toward soothing his wounded pride. It was pretty hard to feel abused when he realized how brilliant she thought he was. He didn't bother telling her she'd overestimated his abilities.

"What do you have there?" he asked when he saw her stuff something back in the bag.

"It's . . . ah . . . just a magazine."

Lucas might have left it at that if she hadn't blushed. His curiosity thoroughly aroused he held out his hand. "Let's see it." He wiggled his fingers. "Come on."

"Oh, all right," she said handing it over reluctantly. "But I want you to know I don't buy this sort of stuff myself."

It took about half a second to see why. It was full of women wearing very little more than smiles. "Good Lord!"

Lucas hardly even noticed the sleek machines they were standing by as he flipped through the glossy pages. "Is this the way women dress in your time?"

"Only when they go swimming."

His eyes widened in astonishment. "Swimming?

Good God are you telling me you've actually let people see you like this?"

"My suit isn't quite so revealing, though I don't suppose you'd approve."

He turned the magazine sideways to better view a picture that covered two pages. "It depends on where you wore it. If I was the only one to see it I wouldn't mind. You'd look lot better than these women. They're all so blasted thin! Isn't there enough to eat in the future?"

"It's in style," Brianna said absurdly pleased by the compliment. "Lucas, about tonight . . . "

"Brianna . . . "

"No, let me finish. I'm sorry I ran. I . . . I was scared."

"I hurt you."

"No you didn't. Well, maybe a little," she admitted when he gave her a disbelieving look. "But it wasn't nearly as bad as I thought it would be."

"You were a virgin."

"I never found a man I loved enough to take a chance with," she paused, "until now."

Lucas hardly dared breathe. "You love me?"

"Almost since the beginning. Can you imagine what it's like thinking you've fallen for your own great-great-grandfather?"

"You said you didn't believe it."

"I didn't want to but I was afraid it was wishful thinking. I wish you'd told me about your stupid toe earlier. Do you realize how much time we've wasted?"

"Too damn much. We're going to start making up for that right now." Lucas pulled out his watch and handed it to her.

She looked at him blankly. "What's this for?"

"I don't need it any more," he said unfolding the space blanket and spreading it out. "I found a woman I can trust."

Her smile was like the sun coming out from behind the clouds. "In spite of everything I've told you?"

"You told me the truth even when you didn't think I'd like it." He pulled her into his arms and kissed her. "Do these space blankets really keep you warm?" He whispered when they finally came up for air.

"Yes, why?"

"Because," he said laying down and pulling it up over them both. "You and I have some very important business to finish, and I don't want to go clear back to the cabin first."

Brianna snuggled down next to him happily. "You know I sort of forgot the first part. Can we just start over again from the beginning?"

He gave a low chuckle. "I'll be happy to refresh your memory."

39

July 21, 1861

"Brianna, I have to get up." Lucas said. "There's a telegraph message."

"Don't they know it's the middle of the night?" she grumbled as he disentangle himself and got out of bed.

"It's almost dawn." He gave her a quick kiss. "Don't worry, I'll be back before you know it."

Brianna smiled with anticipation. He'd be back all right. For two months they had started and ended every day by making love, sometimes more than once. Today would be no different.

She was aware of the intermittent tap of the telegraph key as she drifted in and out of sleep. The door opened and closed twice as he went to the outhouse and returned. There was the soft rustle of clothing dropping to the floor, the mattress dipped behind her and a naked male body pressed against her back. Brianna smiled as large hand closed over her breast. "Took you long enough," she muttered.

"Sorry," he whispered trailing hot kisses down her neck. "I didn't think he'd ever leave."

"Mmmm, I like that," she said as his fingers wandered down her body enticingly. "Who wouldn't leave?"

"Lucas."

"What?" Her eyes flew open and she jerked around to find Lucas grinning down at her.

"You rat!" she cried smacking his shoulder. "You almost gave me a heart attack."

"I couldn't resist. You're such a sleepy head this morning."

She rolled to her back and put her arms around his neck. "How much time do we have before the wagon train gets here?"

"Probably an hour."

Brianna smiled seductively. "Just right. How about some exercise before breakfast?"

"My God, woman," he said in mock horror, "you're insatiable."

She wiggled her hips. "I know. So are you. Do you think we'll ever get tired of it?"

"Maybe in thirty years or so. Have I told you lately how much I love you?"

"Why don't you show me?"

"I thought you'd never ask."

The wagon train was already long gone when they finally emerged from the cabin two hours later.

"I don't suppose you'd consider letting this one pass by?" Lucas said as they walked down to the corral.

"Nope. You said yourself it may be the last one this year." She patted the pouch she carried her money in. "Besides this might be the one with an extra cow to sell."

"You never give up do you?"

She grinned. "Not when we're talking about fresh milk."

"Just be careful. Damn, I wish I didn't have to stay

by the telegraph. I don't like the idea of you riding out alone."

"I have my gun and my knife. Besides, they aren't even out of sight yet. I'll be back before you know it." She chuckled when Oz came up the fence and nuzzled her shoulder. "See even Oz is anxious to go."

"He's anxious for the grain you give him."

Brianna slipped the bit into Oz's mouth and the bridle straps up over his ears. "You know, Lucas maybe we should consider going West to Oregon or California. Between the two of us we have enough money to buy a nice little place. We could be packed and out of here before winter hits."

"Are you serious?"

"Yes."

"It will end any chance you have of getting home."

Brianna looked up at him. "I think that chance is gone anyway. I haven't seen the blue mist since last fall." She reached up and caressed his cheek with her hand. "Funny thing is I really don't mind. My home is wherever you are."

He covered her hand with his own and kissed her palm. "We'll talk about it when you get back."

"I love you, Lucas," she whispered putting her arms around his neck and pulling his head down for a kiss. It was several more minutes before she got around to setting off after the wagon train.

It was nearly eleven o'clock before Lucas began to worry about her. Even with her late start she should be home by now. Maybe she'd managed to talk one of the settlers out of a cow.

At eleven-thirty he sat down at the telegraph key and tapped out a message to the relay stations on either side of him. They both expressed their concern for his missing wife and wished him luck in his search.

He found her less than three miles from the station.

Oz lay on his side, his eyes glazed in death. Lucas hardly spared a glance for the unfortunate animal. He only had eyes for the still form that lay so close to the dead horse. A few more inches to the left and . . . With his heart in his throat, he knelt at Brianna's side and searched for a pulse. He sighed in relief when he felt the strong thump under his fingers.

It only took a moment to figure out what had happened. Apparently something had startled Oz into rearing. He'd gone over backwards and broken his neck. Brianna had thrown herself clear but had hit her head when she landed. A lump the size of a goose egg was the only injury he could find. Worry curled around the edge of his relief. Head injuries were so unpredictable. She could still die.

Brianna was as limp as a rag doll in his arms all the way back to the cabin. He put her on the bed and covered her with a blanket, wondering desperately if any of the pills in the backpack would help.

He was reading the information on the back of the pill bottles when he heard a strange high-pitched whine behind him. Lucas whirled around and found a cloud of blue mist revolving slowly at the foot of the bunk. He could see a strangely different image of Brianna on the other side. Even as he watched, both women began to glow with a weird blue light and started to waver before his horrified eyes.

"NO!" His anguished cry bounced back from the walls, mocking him and his helplessness.

40

July 21, 1995

Waking up next to Anna was bittersweet. Tom propped himself up on one elbow and stared down into her sleeping face. She was so beautiful, his heart turned over in his chest. Their long night of loving showed in the dark shadows under her eyes, but she slept with a smile on her face.

Tom reached out to touch the golden mane of hair that lay across his arm. He'd never known how erotic a woman's long hair could be. Just thinking of the way it had caressed his body during the night brought instant reaction to a portion of his anatomy he'd thought too tired to stir.

As though sensing his mood Anna open her eyes. "Mmmm, good morning." She yawned and smiled up at him. "If you keep looking at me that way, you'll make me blush."

"I'd like to do more than look."

"So what's stopping you."

"Aren't you stiff and sore?"

"A little, but I'm not complaining."

He fingered the locket at her throat. "You really don't ever take this off do you?"

"Not since the day my aunt gave it to me. It's the only thing I have that belonged to my mother." She stretched sensuously then ran her hand across the plane of his chest. "Your freckles are sexy."

He raised his brows. "Where did you get that word?"

"From watching TV at Scott's. Anyway I like your freckles. They make your chest much more interesting to look at than other men's."

"Is that right? And just how many naked male chests have you seen?"

"You mean counting yours?"

"Yes."

"One."

Tom laughed and leaned down for a long leisurely kiss. "Ah, Anna," he said regretfully when it ended. "We should have years and years of waking up together this way. It just isn't fair . . . "

"Shh." Anna put her finger against his lips. "Don't spoil it, Tom. We still have a few hours left."

"That's true," he said getting out of bed.

"Where are you going?"

"Not me, us." Tom held out his hand to her. "We have a wonderful invention called the shower. I'm going to show you a very entertaining way to use it."

Tom had almost finished fixing breakfast when the doorbell rang. "Just what we need," he muttered when he unobtrusively lifted the corner of the curtain. It was his brother Chuck.

Three strides and he was across the room opening the door. "What the hell are you doing back?"

"If you didn't want me here you should have

answered the messages I left on Brianna's answering machine. I got worried." The two brothers glared at each for a long moment, then Chuck smiled crookedly. "Can I come in?"

"Don't suppose I have much choice," Tom said grudgingly as he stepped aside.

"So are you going to tell me why you didn't answer my messages?" Chuck asked sitting down at the table.

"It's a long story."

"I have lots of time."

"You won't believe it."

"Try me."

"It's kind of hard to expla . . . "

"You were right about the shower, Tom. It was very entertaining," Anna said coming into the kitchen. "But I don't like hair blowers at all."

"Good grief, Anna, what happened?" Tom asked staring at the waist length hair hanging around her in a tousled golden cloud. "You look like you got caught in a tornado."

"No, just this stupid hair blower," she said in disgust. "It's all wound up in my hair. Can you get the blasted thing loose?"

"I can try. Hold still."

"It made a horrible mess of . . . Oh my . . . " For the first time she saw Chuck through the curtain of hair. "I-I didn't know any one else was here."

"Chuck came to check on me. I don't suppose he'll be happy until we tell him the whole story."

Chuck nodded. "That's right so you might as well start talking."

"All right, but don't say I didn't warn you. Let's see, it started about five miles beyond Split Rock. I was starting to look for a place to land when this nightmare cloud showed up . . . "

Chuck's expression ranged from skeptical to frankly

disbelieving. "Do you expect me to believe a fifteen-year-old kid invented a time machine?" Chuck asked when Tom finally finished.

"Nope. In fact, I knew you wouldn't. There you go, Anna. Do you want me to help you brush the snarls out?"

She glanced uneasily at Chuck. "No, I can get it."

"All right." He leaned down and kissed her.

"Tom!" she whispered warningly.

"Look, Anna, Chuck being here doesn't change the fact our time is limited. I'm not going to waste a minute of it."

She smiled up at him. "Fine by me."

"Your breakfast is ready when you are," Tom called after her as she went back down the hall.

"You're in love aren't you?" Chuck said in wonder.

"That's a pretty mild description for what we feel. Unfortunately, in about four hours she's going back to 1861." Tom sat down at the table and ran his fingers roughly through his hair. "Christ, Chuck, she died half a century before I was born! Can you imagine how you'd feel if you knew you were never going to see Sandy again?"

Chuck was silent for a long moment. "If she feels the same way, there must be something you can do."

"We've thought it through a dozen times and there is no other way, Chuck. Anything we do will change the past." Tom closed his eyes and leaned his forehead against his clasped hands. "I've never felt so helpless in my life."

There seemed nothing more to say.

Chuck volunteered to drive out to the ranch and Tom let him. Even if Chuck was only going along to keep an eye on things, it was that much more time Tom and

Anna could spend together. They held hands all the way, their fingers interlaced in silent testimony to the heartbreak that was coming.

Tom knew the minute Chuck began to give credence to the story. His older brother took one astonished look around Scott's family room and his mouth fell open.

"I'll be damned."

"Wait until he turns it on," Tom said. "Believe me, Chuck, this is not your average fifteen year old playing around."

Of course at that moment he seemed pretty typical as Anna grilled him about his previous night's activities. "Did you have a good time?"

"It was ok." Scott tried to shrug nonchalantly but his goofy grin gave him away.

Anna's eyes widened. "Scott, you stole a kiss didn't you?"

He turned bright red. "Well I didn't steal it exactly."

"Uh, oh," Tom said in mock seriousness. "Mamas better lock up your daughters."

"Aw come on guys. It wasn't that big a deal."

"I'll bet Sam thought it was," Anna said with a twinkle in her eye.

"Yeah, I guess she did." Scott ducked his head in embarrassment, then glanced at his watch. "Holy cow. It's twelve-fifteen. If you want to wear your own clothes you better go change."

"Oh . . . " Anna's gaze flew to Tom's. The stricken look in her eyes went straight to his heart.

"Chuck, you help Scott set up. Come on, Anna, we'll do this together."

The minute the bedroom door closed behind them they were in each other's arms. They kissed deeply, hungrily, as though they could make up for all the years they wouldn't have together. When it ended, they clung to each other in an almost painful embrace.

"We better get you dressed," he said at last.

"A-all right. It w-will be nice to have someone pull my corset strings tight," she said trying to sound normal. "I've had to wear it loose since I left home."

"I don't know how much use I'll be." Tom swallowed hard as he watched her shed the trappings of the twentieth century and don her own. "I won't have the slightest idea what do to."

In spite of his reservations he was able to tighten the corset enough to suit her. He watching in growing amazement as she put on a corset cover, an oddly stiff petticoat-like garment she called a crinoline and no less than three petticoats.

"Good lord, how many layers do you wear?"

"Usually more than this. I stopped wearing my crinolines and most of my petticoats on the trail because of the wind." She knew she was rattling on as she slipped her dress over her head, but she couldn't help herself. "That's why my skirt's too long though it's better than it has been. I wore my small crinoline that day because I knew I'd be meeting Lucas and I w-wanted to make a g-good impression." Her lip quivered suddenly. "Oh, Tom, I don't even want to meet him anymore."

He folded his arms around her. "Don't, Anna. I happen to know you and Lucas will have a long happy life together."

"I only want you."

"You said yourself our time together shouldn't have happened, that it was a quirk, a gift of fate. It's been wonderful, but now you have to forget it ever happened."

She pulled back and stared up at him in shock. "Forget it? Are you insane? You're the most wonderful thing that ever happened to me."

"But you haven't met Lucas yet. He'll be even more

wonderful, and I'll be an old memory that makes you smile once in awhile." Tom's heart cried out at his words. He couldn't help hoping it wasn't true but knew he was being incredibly selfish. "Let's not spend our last few minutes arguing," he said gruffly.

She put her arms around his neck and pulled his head down. "I'll never forget you, Tom Shaffer," she whispered against his lips, "my first and only love."

His protest died stillborn as her kiss wiped everything from his mind. The world ceased to exist for them until Scott finally came to see what was keeping Anna.

"Hurry up. It's almost time," he called from the kitchen doorway.

"We'll be right there," Anna called. "I'm not so unselfish as you," she said putting something in Tom's hand. "I love you, Tom. I *want* you to remember me."

She turned and hurried from the room leaving Tom alone to stare at the locket she'd given him. With a groan, he closed his hand and leaned against the door. The rest of his life stretched ahead of him in empty loneliness.

By the time he entered the family room, the blue mist was already beginning to form. Unlike the others who had grown accustomed to it, Chuck stared at it in disbelief.

"You haven't seen anything yet," Tom said.

At that moment the spinning mist solidified and a picture formed. The difference between this and the previous windows was immediately obvious. The picture was much sharper. Brianna Daniels appeared to be sleeping and was so close she looked as though she was in the room with them.

The moment Brianna became visible, Anna began to glow with a weird blue light, and Tom took an involuntary step toward her. "Anna!"

Chuck grabbed his arm. "No!"

Anna's and Tom's gazes locked across the room. Their pain was clearly visible to anyone who cared to look as she began to waver. Suddenly, the blue light disappeared and Anna returned to normal.

"What the hell?" Scott said staring at the time portal. A man had thrown himself across Brianna's body and was hanging on to her for all he was worth.

"I can't make the transfer," Scott yelled. "The mass isn't even. Who is that guy?"

Tom shook his head. "I don't know, but it's not Lucas Daniels. He isn't a redhead."

"Lucas doesn't have red hair," Anna said in surprise. "It's coal black. Seth told me."

"But that's impossible. In his journal he talked about it all the time. He seemed to think it was import . . . Oh, my God," Tom said as the full impact of his words hit him. "Of course it was important. It was the only way to let me know . . . Scott, if the mass is equal on both sides of the window, will the transfer take place?"

"I don't know. It should, but I can't be sure."

"Tom, no, you can't do this." Chuck held his brother's arm in a frantic grip.

"I already have, Chuck. That's why I always felt like Lucas Daniels was writing directly to me. He was, or rather I was. We've made this switch before. Don't you see *I* was the balloon pilot during the Civil War and I wrote the journals so I'd know to what to do when the time came. Anna and I are meant to be together but in her time not mine."

"You're crazy," Chuck said desperately. "Time travel is impossible. If you go into that thing you could die. For God sake, Tom, use your head!"

"I am, Chuck. I've spent my whole life preparing for this. I just didn't realize it. I'm going with or without your approval. I'd rather you backed me but it won't stop me if you don't."

Chuck looked at Anna and back at his brother. In his mind's eye he saw Tom sitting at the table so anguished it hurt to see him. "Damn it anyway. You always did have a way of getting me to do what you want," Chuck said giving Tom a big bear hug. "I'll miss you, baby brother, God, how I'll miss you." He dropped his arms and tried to ignore the strange burning behind his eyes that felt suspiciously like tears.

"They'll need my Social Security card and birth certificate. You have all the numbers to my bank accounts." Tom pulled out his wallet and handed it to him. "Chuck, I . . . "

Chuck clapped him on the shoulder. "Yeah, I know. I love you, too. Now get going before it's too late."

Tom was across the room in two swift stride. "Our stolen moment is forever, Anna," he said folding her into his arms. As the blue haze formed around them, their shapes began to blur together into an indistinct mass.

Suddenly there was a brilliant flash of light and loud sizzling pop. When the smoke cleared, Tom and Anna were gone. Scott sat staring a the misshapen lump of melted plastic, burnt wiring and broken glass that had once been his father's computer. "Boy, it's a good thing Tom saved the ranch records to a floppy disk!"

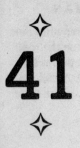

41

July 24, 1995

Brianna opened her eyes and tried to focus through the fuzz in front of her. She blinked. Her vision cleared but not her confusion. The plastic tube in her arm, the white sheet covering her, and the antiseptic smell seemed to indicate she was in a twentieth century hospital. A small sound called her attention and she carefully turned her head.

A woman with graying hair sat next to the bed reading a book with the title *Meadowlark* splashed across the cover in bright blue letters. She seemed totally engrossed in the novel.

"Mom?" Brianna croaked, her voice sounding like a rusty hinge.

Startled, the woman looked up. "Oh, honey you're awake!" She reached over and pushed the button for the nurse.

"Where am I?"

"In the hospital. You had an accident and hit your head."

"I think I remember," Brianna said furrowing her brow in concentration. "There was a snake on the trail. My horse reared and . . . " She faltered as a dozen confusing images suddenly crowded her mind. A balloon, Oz, wagon trains, and . . . Lucas. "Mom, what's the date?" she said urgently.

"The date?"

"Yes, what day is it?"

"It's Monday." Mrs. Daniels looked at her watch, "July the twenty-fourth."

"What year?"

"The year? Why 1995 . . . Honey what's wrong?" She touched Brianna's forehead worriedly. "The nurse should be here any minute"

"I-I'm just tired." Brianna squeezed her eyes shut. 1995. How could that be when she'd gone been over a year? If her mother was right the balloon rally had only been last week. Was it all a dream then and Lucas only a figment of her imagination? Oh, God it couldn't be. Lucas was real . . . as real as her mother. Wasn't he?

Brianna opened her eyes to find her mother watching her with a worried expression her face. "It's all right, Mom," she said forcing a smile. "I'm just a little confused."

"The doctor said you might be at first. That was a pretty hard bump on the head. Oh, good here's the nurse." Mrs. Daniels smiled at the woman in relief. "I called you as soon as she woke up."

By the time the nurse had peered into her eyes, checked her vital signs, and raised her bed, Brianna's mind had cleared a little, but she still couldn't make sense of what had happened.

"Who called you, Mom?"

"It was either Tom Shaffer or his brother. I was so upset I forget which." She was quiet for a moment. "I know it's none of my business, Brianna, but is this thing between you and Tom serious?"

Brianna looked at her in surprise. "Tom Shaffer?"

"Who else? He hasn't left this room for more than a few minutes since they brought you in. The only reason he isn't here now is because your father dragged him out to get something to eat."

"We're just friends, Mom. So tell me about your trip out."

"That's a nice way of saying mind your own business isn't it? All right if that's the way you want it. The trip out was just like it always is. You know what your father's like . . . "

Brianna let her mother talk. The sound was calming and kept the black grief at bay. It was so much easier to lay there listening than to think about Lucas and wonder if she'd made him up. Her mind drifted along until she suddenly was riveted by something her mother was saying.

"Oh, that reminds me, you got a package from a distant relative of your father's. She sent you an old picture and a ring. I forget now which grandparents the picture is of but . . . "

"Lucas and Anna Daniels?" Brianna asked, her voice taut with emotion.

"Why yes, I believe it is."

"What does he look like?"

"Like a typical Daniels. Tall, and thin, probably red haired though it's kind of hard to tell in an old picture like that. The amazing thing is how much you look like his wife. You could be twins."

But Brianna no longer cared about the picture. None of it was true. She closed her eyes against the pain. Lucas . . . her Lucas . . . was nothing more than a delusion caused by her concussion.

"Honey?" Mrs. Daniels was hesitant, and Brianna

opened her eyes in surprise. Her mother was rarely hesitant about anything. "You know your father and I will love you no matter what, don't you?"

Uh oh, what had she done now? Her mother only said that when they were disappointed in her. "Of course, Mom, and I love you, too."

"You can tell us anything, no matter how bad it seems. We'll understand. Everybody makes mistakes."

"Helen!" A deep voice came from the open door. "You promised."

"I just wanted her to know we're on her side," Helen Daniels said defensively.

"Uh huh."

"Hello, Daddy." Brianna smiled as he crossed the room and gave her a big bear hug. "Maybe you'd better tell me what I've done so I can be properly contrite."

"She's just worried about you," he said gruffly. "We both are."

Brianna pulled back and looked at him in surprise. Her father never let her mother's anxieties affect him. What in the world had she done?

"What did you do with Tom?" Helen asked.

"The nurse told us Brianna was awake so he went back to the car to get that package from my cousin Betsy." John Daniels shook his head. "He said she'd want to see it right away. I like this young man of yours, Brianna, but I can't figure out this obsession he has with Lucas Daniels."

Brianna smiled. "He's not my young man, Daddy. And his interest in Lucas Daniels is purely professional. He's a balloon pilot."

"I've always been a great admirer of Lucas Daniels," said an achingly familiar voice. "You might say he brought your daughter and me together."

For an instant Brianna thought she was hallucinating, seeing the man she wished were there instead of the one that was. Then she was in his arms, and he was kissing her. Oh, God, it *was* Lucas! Really, truly Lucas. Desperately, she ran her hands over his back trying to convince herself he wasn't an illusion. He wasn't. Somehow Lucas had found a way to come back with her.

Brianna heard her parents' voices as if from a great distance. "Hmph, just friends my eye!"

"Come on, Helen, we're in the way here."

"Don't go too far," Lucas said pulling back slightly but never taking his eyes off Brianna. "We'll have something important to tell you in a little while."

"Take your time, son. We'll be in the waiting room. Just don't forget what I told you."

"I won't, Mr. Daniels."

"What did Daddy tell you?"

"That you're just like your mother." Lucas kissed her again. "You scared the hell out of me, and all because you wouldn't listen. I'm lucky I found you when I did or you'd be here by yourself and up to your neck in trouble."

Brianna hugged him tightly. "How did you get here?"

"The same way you did." He picked up a manila envelope he'd dropped on the bed and pulled out an old photograph. "I think you'd best look at this first."

Brianna gasped in surprise. It was a wedding picture of Tom Shaffer and an oddly different version of herself.

"In case you haven't figured it out, that's your great-great-grandparents, Lucas and Anna Daniels."

"It was Tom not Ian," she murmured. "I never even thought of that."

"As far as we can tell, Ian MacTavish never even met Anna."

"No, I suppose they went out of their way to avoid him and everybody else that knew us." She was silent for a moment considering. "My journal must have helped them. I'm glad I wrote everything down. They even knew what to do with your watch so my uncle would find it." Brianna ran her fingers over the picture lightly. "It's all so confusing."

"I know, but the more you think about it, the more it makes sense. Scott can explain it to you when you meet him."

"Who?"

"A young man I fully intend to know better. He's responsible for all this and a fascinating person to talk to. I don't precisely understand how but right now he and Chuck Shaffer are accessing all of Tom's vital information on the computer and changing it to fit me. I'm going to assume his identity for awhile, though Chuck says we can legally change my name to Lucas Daniels later if we decide to. In the meantime Scott's going to teach me all there is to know about computers."

"Oh, Lord I can just see you turning into a computer nerd. I guess I'll just have to drag you away occasionally and have my way with you to keep you human."

Lucas chuckled. "I don't understand exactly what you're worried about, but the cure sounds fine to me. I suppose I should tell you we're buying Scott a new computer to replace the one that was destroyed when we came forward. I figured it was the least we could do.

"Oh dear. We may owe him one, Lucas but I can't afford a computer. They're very expensive."

"Cheaper than a cow it seems," Lucas said with a chuckle. "Remember your money pouch?"

"Yes?"

"It was full of very old, very valuable coins. You brought a fortune back with you. Anyway, Scott says we've done this all before. He's convinced time is a loop rather than a straight line."

"What does that mean?"

"That you didn't change history because you were

supposed to be there. It wasn't until we opened the picture that I finally understood."

"You mean Anna and I were meant to trade places?"

"Exactly, and so were Tom and I."

"Then what did you mean if you hadn't found me I'd be up to my neck in trouble?"

Lucas grinned. "We didn't come alone."

"What?"

"You have a little stowaway." He put his hand on her abdomen. "Everyone was a bit shocked when the doctor discovered him."

Brianna frowned in confusion then gasped as his meaning hit her. "I'm pregnant?"

"It looks that way."

She threw her arms around his neck. "Oh, Lucas, I'm going to have your baby!"

"I'm glad you're pleased. Your father was none too happy to find out he was going to be a grandpa."

"Oops."

"My thoughts exactly. Luckily he was reasonable about it."

"He was?"

"I have exactly three and a half minutes to convince you to stop being so stubborn and marry me."

"That's reasonable?"

"It is compared to what your mother wanted to do to me."

"You're pulling my leg."

Lucas raised his eyebrows. "I suppose I'll eventually learn to understand what you're saying to me."

"My parents didn't threaten you at all."

He sighed. "Your father told me you wouldn't believe it."

"You discussed it with him?"

"Actually, we had a long talk about the best way to approach you with the idea of marriage right after I formally asked him for your hand. You should have seen the look on his face."

Brianna giggled. "I'll bet. People don't do that any more."

"So I gathered. Anyway your father did give me some valuable advice on handling this bull-headed streak you get from your mother."

"What's that?"

"Sorry I can't tell you," he said with a grin. "You might reveal his secret strategy to your mother."

"Daddy's strategy is to drag my mother off to the bedroom. It's taken her years to train him that way."

"Your mother told you that?" He was clearly startled.

"Of course not, but I'm neither blind nor stupid. I figured it out years ago.

Lucas chuckled. "So much for your father's approach."

"Oh, I don't know. I never heard either of them complain. In case you haven't noticed, my parents are very much in love."

He smiled. "That's one Daniels tradition that hasn't changed at least." With that he reached into his pocket for something. Brianna's eyes widened in astonishment as he opened his hand and blue fire flashed in the sunlight.

"Your mother's ring," she whispered. "You brought it with you?"

"No, it was with the picture. Anna sent it."

"Anna! How . . . ?"

"It's a long story. The important thing is that it's here. I'm warning you, I won't take no for an answer this time." He slipped the ring on her finger. "I love you, Brianna Daniels, and want to spend the rest of my life with you. Will you marry me?"

"It took you long enough," she said holding her hand up to the light. "I've been waiting a hundred and thirty-five years for you to ask me."

"Well, are you going to say yes or do I have to use your father's tactics?"

She put her arms around his neck. "I don't know, stubbornness does have it's compensations. Maybe you'd better convince me."

"It could be a little embarrassing." Lucas glanced over his shoulder at the open door. "There are people in and out of this room all the time."

Brianna grinned. "I won't need *that* much convincing. Ten minutes of concentrated huggy-bear, kissy-face ought to do it."

"And you aren't worried about your father coming back in here demanding I make an honest woman of you?"

"Nope. I heard what Daddy told you."

"He did say to take my time didn't he?"

"Yes, but he won't wait forever so you'd better get started."

And Lucas did just that.

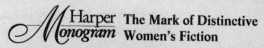

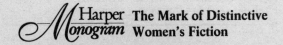

Time Travel Romance from ℳ Harper Monogram

ONCE UPON A PIRATE *by Nancy Block*
It's love on the high seas when Zoe Dunham plunges into the past and lands on the deck of Black Jack Alexander's pirate ship. Her sexy captor's virile charm unlocks her passion and allows her to overcome past heartbreak. (April 1995)

♥

PRAIRIE KNIGHT *by Donna Valentino*
A 13th-century knight in shining armor suddenly appears on the Kansas prairie in 1859, but the last thing the practical, young widow Juliette Walburn needs is a romance with an iron-clad stranger. (May 1995)

♥

BRIDGE TO YESTERDAY *by Stephanie Mittman*
Mary Grace O'Reilly, a crusader for lost children in the 1990s, finds herself in love and on the run with a kidnapper in the year 1894. (June 1995)

♥

YESTERDAY'S TOMORROWS *by Margaret Lane*
On a mission to save her family's Montana homestead, Abby De Coux somehow lands in the year 1875, along with rugged Elan Le Taureau, a French-Canadian trapper from the early 19th century. (October 1995)

♥

TILL THE END OF TIME *by Suzanne Elizabeth*
Scott Ramsey has a taste for adventure and a way with the ladies. When his time-travel experiment transports him back to Civil War Georgia, he meets his match in Rachel Ann Warren, a beautiful Union spy who embroils him in a dangerous scheme and steals his heart in the process. (November 1995)

♥

WHEN MIDNIGHT COMES *by Robin Burcell*
Kendra Browning longs for romance, but little does she expect that to find it she must go back to the year 1830. When her boat capsizes off the Atlantic, she is rescued by a dashing duke. *A Golden Heart finalist.* (December 1995)

♥

GLORY IN THE SPLENDOR OF SUMMER WITH

HarperMonogram's

101 Days of Romance

BUY 3 BOOKS, GET 1 FREE!

Take a book to the beach, relax by the pool, or read in the most quiet and romantic spot in your home. You can live through love all summer long when you redeem this exciting offer from HarperMonogram. Buy any three HarperMonogram romances in June, July, or August, and get a fourth book sent to you for FREE. See next page for the list of top-selling novels and romances by your favorite authors that you can choose from for your premium!